12

ENGLISH
DETECTIVE
STORIES

MICHAEL COX is a senior commissioning editor with Oxford University Press. He has edited *The Oxford Book of English Ghost Stories* (1986), *Victorian Ghost Stories* (1991) (both with R. A. Gilbert), *Victorian Detective Stories* (1992), *The Oxford Book of Historical Stories* (with Jack Adrian, 1994), *The Oxford Book of Spy Stories* (1996), and *The Oxford Book of Twentieth-Century Ghost Stories* (1996).

Oxford Twelves

Twelve Mystery Stories
JACK ADRIAN

Twelve Tales of Murder
JACK ADRIAN

Twelve English Detective Stories
MICHAEL COX

Twelve Tales of the Supernatural
MICHAEL COX

Twelve Victorian Ghost Stories
MICHAEL COX

Twelve Irish Ghost Stories
PATRICIA CRAIG

Twelve Gothic Tales
RICHARD DALBY

Twelve American Crime Stories
ROSEMARY HERBERT

Twelve American Detective Stories
EDWARD D. HOCH

Twelve Women Detective Stories
LAURA MARCUS

12

ENGLISH DETECTIVE STORIES

Selected and introduced by

MICHAEL COX

Oxford   New York

OXFORD UNIVERSITY PRESS

1998

Oxford University Press, Great Clarendon Street, Oxford OX2 6DP

Oxford New York

Athens Auckland Bangkok Bogota Buenos Aires
Calcutta Cape Town Chennai Dar es Salaam Delhi Florence Hong Kong Istanbul
Karachi Kuala Lumpur Madrid Melbourne Mexico City Mumbai
Nairobi Paris Singapore Taipei Tokyo Toronto Warsaw

and associated companies
in Berlin Ibadan

Oxford is a trade mark of Oxford University Press

British Library Cataloguing in Publication Data

Data available

Library of Congress Cataloging in Publication Data
12 English detective stories / selected and introduced by Michael Cox.
Contents: The adventure of the stockbroker's clerk / A. Conan Doyle—The Lenton Croft robberies /
Arthur Morrison—The greenstone god and the stockbroker / Fergus Hume—The blue sequin /
R. Austin Freeman—The strange crime of John Boulnois / G. K. Chesterton—Who killed Charlie Winpole? /
Ernest Bramah—The poetical policeman / Edgar Wallace—The man with no face /
Dorothy L. Sayers—The yellow slugs / H. C. Bailey—The unknown peer /
E. C. Bentley—Lessons in anatomy / Michael Innes—The flaw / Julian Symons.
1. Detective and mystery stories, English.   I. Cox, Michael, 1948–
PR1309.D4A138 1998   823'.087208–dc21   98-30773

ISBN 0-19-288096-9

1 3 5 7 9 10 8 6 4 2

Typeset by Jayvee, Trivandrum, India
Printed in Great Britain by
Cox & Wyman
Reading, Berkshire

CONTENTS

Contents

INTRODUCTION

Poe said: Let there be a detective story; and it was so; and when Poe created the detective story in his own image, and saw everything that he had made, behold, it was very good; and he cast the detective story originally in the short form, and that form was, and is, and forever will be the true form. Amen.[1]

From 1841, when Edgar Allen Poe wrote 'The Murders in the Rue Morgue', to the early 1920s, the short story—or the long short story—dominated detective fiction. In only five stories Poe laid down many of the basic principles of the detective story, as well as creating what can now be seen as a related genre—the tale of mystery, in which the processes of criminal detection are fused with elements from the tale of terror. It was Poe who first presented readers with the locked-room puzzle; with the device of throwing suspicion on the wrong person; with the solution that turns upon the most obvious, and therefore the most easily overlooked, point, or, conversely, on the agency of the most unlikely person; above all, in C. Auguste Dupin, Poe created the figure of the brilliant freelance detective possessed of abilities far superior to those of the official agents of investigation. For several decades, the fictional detective went about his business within the compass of the short story, often episodically in monthly magazines, rather than pursuing his quarry through the leisurely convolutions of the full-length novel. The most famous of them all, Sherlock Holmes, burst upon a mass public through a series of short stories published in the *Strand* magazine in 1892. It was not until the 1920s that the short story began to lose some of its popularity and the ascendancy of the detective novel began in earnest. The short story was not completely overwhelmed; it continued to flourish in specialist magazines and anthologies; and in the age of television the episodic form has re-emerged with the series detective—be it Morse, Wexford, or Dalziell and Pascoe. But its great days were over.

---

[1] Ellery Queen, introduction to *The Queen's Awards, 1946* (1946, 1948).

The period from 1892 to 1930 thus puts a chronological frame round the detective short story, defining a Golden Age that precedes, and partly overlaps with, the golden age of the classic English detective novel. For generations of readers, the detective short story established an enduring fictional stereotype. In the wake of Sherlock Holmes appeared a variety of sleuths—omniscient supermen in the mould of Holmes himself, as well as more workaday detectives who relied less on eccentric brilliance than on simple plodding deduction. In the pages of turn-of-the-century magazines such as *Pearson's*, the *Windsor Magazine*, and the *Ludgate Monthly* they solved murders, retrieved stolen jewels, and unmasked dastardly foreign spies: amongst them Dorcas Dene, Loveday Brooke, Martin Hewitt, Sebastian Zambra, Paul Beck, Eugene Valmont, and Dr Thorndyke—largely forgotten names now, except to aficionados, but in their day serious rivals to the great detective of Baker Street.

But after the end of the First World War things began to change. The all-knowing, volatile super-detective in the Holmes mould increasingly seemed something of a period piece and was gradually replaced by sleuths of quieter dispositions, who nevertheless often retained some mark of peculiarity that set them apart—such as Ernest Bramah's blind detective Max Carrados (represented here), or Baroness Orczy's Old Man in the Corner, who sits in an ABC teashop drinking milk and eating cheesecake and solves the most baffling crimes without moving from his seat. Despite the continuing appearance of such figures it began to be apparent that an era was passing. Ronald Knox, a supreme connoisseur of detective fiction in all its forms, observed in 1929 that 'The short story must always take an honourable place in detective fiction'; but he then went on to confess 'an uneasy suspicion that the day of the old straight detective episode is done; that there can be no more murders in the Rue Morgue which can baffle the *Sûreté*, because it has all been done before and there is nothing new under the sun.' Here was the crux. The writers of detective stories had been too successful and had, in effect, exhausted the possibilities of the short form. Dorothy Sayers, both a short-story writer and a novelist, likened the situation to a city built between the sea and a precipice: on one side the short story was being gradually but inexorably undermined by the increasing popularity of the detective novel; on the other, it was being prevented by its physical limitations from expanding and developing:

A short story has all its eggs in one basket; it can turn one trick and one trick only; its detective-interest cannot involve a long investigation—it must be summed up in a single surprise. And so hard have detective-writers worked in the last half-century, that there are now remarkably few tricks the reader does not know . . . In the course of telling a long story it is possible to camouflage them by a multitude of complicating circumstances. But in the short story they have to stand unsupported, and their eyelids are a little weary. Thus the detective short story, prevented from following the natural line of development of its companion, the detective-novel, is growing rarer and rarer.[2]

There were also more pragmatic reasons for the decline of the detective short story than the lack of good ideas, as Sayers also pointed out:

The very great labour involved in getting a bright, novel and agreeable murder, inventing a suitable detective, dragging in the human interest and then compressing the thing into 6,000 words is scarcely worth while. After an amount of brain exhaustion which would almost suffice to produce a full-length novel, the net result usually is that the writer feels himself to have merely wasted a perfectly good plot . . . The writer feels, very properly, that he has sold his birthright for a mess of pottage, since the price paid, even by a high-class magazine, for a short detective-story is seldom comparable with the advance payment on a full-length novel.[3]

In the 1930s and 1940s there were comparatively few British writers of detective fiction who turned naturally to the short-story form in the way earlier writers such as Conan Doyle or G. K. Chesterton had done. Those that did included H. C. Bailey (1878–1961), who achieved considerable contemporary popularity with his Reggie Fortune stories, the first collection of which was published in 1920. The story included here, from 1935, is one of the best: it is perhaps not coincidental that it is also one of the longest. In America, the detective short story enjoyed a renaissance with the foundation in 1941 of *Ellery Queen's Mystery Magazine*, a hugely influential magazine devoted entirely to short crime fiction, whilst in Britain anthology series such as the John Creasey *Crime Collections* or the *Winter's Crimes* series (first

---

[2] Introduction to *Great Short Stories of Detection, Mystery and Horror*, first series (1931).
[3] Ibid.

published in 1969) showed at least that there was a residual market for short detective stories.

This collection brings together twelve examples of the detective short story published between 1893 and 1986. Six of them cover the period up to the First World War, beginning with Sherlock Holmes and ending with G. K. Chesterton's priest-detective Father Brown and also including two other notable creations—R. Austin Freeman's Dr Thorndyke, in the classic story of 'The Blue Sequin' (first published in the Christmas Number of *Pearson's Magazine* in 1908), and E. C. Bentley's Philip Trent, who first appeared in the *Trent's Last Case* (1913), one of the most celebrated detective novels of its time, written, as Bentley himself said, 'not so much [as] a detective story as an exposure of detective stories'. Together these four stories—along with those of Arthur Morrison (whose anti-Holmesian detective, Martin Hewitt, also began life in the *Strand* magazine) and Fergus Hume (author of one of the biggest-selling crime and detection novels of the nineteenth century)—encapsulate the essential qualities of short detective fiction during its heyday. We find ourselves in a world that is completely English—in its settings, characters, language, and social landscape. Here for instance is Mr Hall Pycroft, in Conan Doyle's 'The Adventure of the Stockbroker's Clerk': 'He wore a very shiny top-hat and a neat suit of sober black, which made him look what he was—a smart young City man, of the class who have been labelled Cockneys, but who give us our crack Volunteer regiments, and who turn out more fine athletes and sportsmen than any body of men in these islands.' The Englishness embodied in this description—the unworried acceptance of class distinctions in tandem with an ingrained sense of fair play—is matched by the disbelief verging on outrage expressed by Mr Bradshaw in E. C. Bentley's 'The Unknown Peer' at the idea of a man taking claret with fish.

The other six stories in this selection are no less English in tone and ambience—from the suburban villas in Firling Street in Edgar Wallace's 'The Poetical Policeman' to the West End theatre background in Julian Symons' 'The Flaw'. All twelve stories are representative of the rich tradition of short detective fiction that was given irresistible momentum by the advent of Sherlock Holmes in 1892 and bear testimony to the English fascination with fictional puzzle-making. But their appeal lies not just in cleverness and contrivance. The problem and its resolution is central to them all and provides each story's basic and inescapable dynamic; but the best of them are *stories*, not simply detective stories: they maintain a human focus—whether it is the powerful depiction of spiritual cruelty in H. C. Bailey's 'The Yellow Slugs' or the complex moral tensions set up by Chesterton in 'The Strange Crime of John Boulnois'.

The Golden Age of the detective short story may have passed into history, and the unflinching eye of modernity now produces crime fiction of a very different sort; but these stories still retain their original capacity to entertain and surprise. It is, of course, a two-way transaction, for we as readers must also play the game; indeed it is imperative that we do so in full complicity and with a complete acceptance of the rules. Though times have changed—for the detective story as well as for its readers—we only need to come to these little entertainments with what Dorothy Sayers called 'an alert and amiable mind' to share in the thrill and pleasure enjoyed by their original readers. For those who are unfamiliar with the detective story genre, I hope these twelve stories will encourage further exploration of this entertaining corner of English popular fiction. There is plenty more where these came from.

MICHAEL COX
December 1997

1

A. CONAN DOYLE

The Stockbroker's Clerk

Shortly after my marriage I had bought a connection in the Paddington district. Old Mr Farquhar, from whom I purchased it, had at one time an excellent general practice, but his age, and an affliction of the nature of St Vitus' dance from which he suffered, had very much thinned it. The public, not unnaturally, goes upon the principle that he who would heal others must himself be whole, and looks askance at the curative powers of the man whose own case is beyond the reach of his drugs. Thus, as my predecessor weakened his practice declined, until when I purchased it from him it had sunk from twelve hundred to little more than three hundred a year. I had confidence, however, in my own youth and energy, and was convinced that in a very few years the concern would be as flourishing as ever.

For three months after taking over the practice I was kept very closely at work, and saw little of my friend Sherlock Holmes, for I was too busy to visit Baker Street, and he seldom went anywhere himself save upon professional business. I was surprised, therefore, when one morning in June, as I sat reading the *British Medical Journal* after breakfast, I heard a ring at the bell followed by the high, somewhat strident, tones of my old companion's voice.

'Ah, my dear Watson,' said he, striding into the room, 'I am very delighted to see you. I trust that Mrs Watson has entirely recovered from all the little excitements connected with our adventure of the "Sign of Four"?'

'Thank you, we are both very well,' said I, shaking him warmly by the hand.

'And I hope also,' he continued, sitting down in the rocking-chair, 'that the cares of medical practice have not entirely obliterated the interest which you used to take in our little deductive problems.'

'On the contrary,' I answered; 'it was only last night that I was looking over my old notes and classifying some of our past results.'

'I trust that you don't consider your collection closed?'

'Not at all. I should wish nothing better than to have some more of such experiences.'

'Today, for example?'

'Yes; today, if you like.'

'And as far off as Birmingham?'

'Certainly, if you wish it.'

'And the practice?'

'I do my neighbour's when he goes. He is always ready to work off the debt.'

'Ha! Nothing could be better!' said Holmes, leaning back in his chair and looking keenly at me from under his half-closed lids. 'I perceive that you have been unwell lately. Summer colds are always a little trying.'

'I was confined to the house by a severe chill for three days last week. I thought, however, that I had cast off every trace of it.'

'So you have. You look remarkably robust.'

'How, then, did you know of it?'

'My dear fellow, you know my methods.'

'You deduced it, then?'

'Certainly.'

'And from what?'

'From your slippers.'

I glanced down at the new patent leathers which I was wearing. 'How on earth——?' I began, but Holmes answered my question before it was asked.

'Your slippers are new,' he said. 'You could not have had them more than a few weeks. The soles which you are at this moment presenting to me are slightly scorched. For a moment I thought they might have got wet and been burned in the drying. But near the instep there is a small circular wafer of paper with the shopman's hieroglyphics upon it. Damp would of course have removed this. You had then been sitting with your feet outstretched to the fire, which a man would hardly do even in so wet a June as this if he were in his full health.'

Like all Holmes' reasoning, the thing seemed simplicity itself when it was once explained. He read the thought upon my features, and his smile had a tinge of bitterness.

'I am afraid that I rather give myself away when I explain,' said he. 'Results without causes are much more impressive. You are ready to come to Birmingham, then?'

'Certainly. What is the case?'

'You shall hear it all in the train. My client is outside in a four-wheeler. Can you come at once?'

'In an instant.' I scribbled a note to my neighbour, rushed upstairs to explain the matter to my wife, and joined Holmes upon the doorstep.

'Your neighbour is a doctor?' said he, nodding at the brass plate.

'Yes. He bought a practice, as I did.'

'An old-established one?'

'Just the same as mine. Both have been ever since the houses were built.'

'Ah, then you got hold of the better of the two.'

'I think I did. But how do you know?'

'By the steps, my boy. Yours are worn three inches deeper than his. But this gentleman in the cab is my client, Mr Hall Pycroft. Allow me to introduce you to him. Whip your horse up, cabby, for we have only just time to catch our train.'

The man whom I found myself facing was a well-built, fresh-complexioned young fellow with a frank, honest face and a slight, crisp, yellow moustache. He wore a very shiny top-hat and a neat suit of sober black, which made him look what he was—a smart young City man, of the class who have been labelled Cockneys, but who give us our crack Volunteer regiments, and who turn out more fine athletes and sportsmen than any body of men in these islands. His round, ruddy face was naturally full of cheeriness, but the corners of his mouth seemed to me to be pulled down in a half-comical distress. It was not, however, until we were all in a first-class carriage and well started upon our journey to Birmingham, that I was able to learn what the trouble was which had driven him to Sherlock Holmes.

'We have a clear run here of seventy minutes,' Holmes remarked. 'I want you, Mr Hall Pycroft, to tell my friend your very interesting experience exactly as you have told it to me, or with more detail if possible. It will be of use to me to hear the succession of events again. It is a case, Watson, which may prove to have something in it, or may prove to have nothing, but which at least presents those unusual and *outré* features which are as dear to you as they are to me. Now, Mr Pycroft, I shall not interrupt you again.'

Our young companion looked at me with a twinkle in his eye.

'The worst of the story is,' said he, 'that I show myself up as such a confounded fool. Of course, it may work out all right, and I don't see that I could have done otherwise; but if I have lost my crib and get nothing in exchange, I shall feel what a soft Johnny I have been. I'm not very good at telling a story, Dr Watson, but it is like this with me.

'I used to have a billet at Coxon & Woodhouse, of Drapers' Gardens, but they were let in early in the spring through the Venezuelan loan, as no doubt you remember, and came a nasty cropper. I had been with them five years, and old Coxon gave me a ripping good testimonial when the smash came; but, of course, we clerks were all turned adrift, the twenty-seven of us. I tried here and tried there, but there were lots of other chaps on the same lay as myself, and it was a perfect frost for a long time. I had been taking three pounds a week at Coxon's, and I had saved about seventy of them, but I soon worked my way through that and out at the other end. I was fairly at the end of my tether at last, and could hardly find the stamps to answer the advertisements or the envelopes to stick them to. I had worn out my boots padding up office stairs, and I seemed just as far from getting a billet as ever.

'At last I saw a vacancy at Mawson & Williams', the great stock-broking firm in Lombard Street. I dare say E.C. is not much in your line, but I can tell you that this is about the richest house in London. The advertisement was to be answered by letter only. I sent in my testimonial and application, but without the least hope of getting it. Back came as answer by return saying that if I would appear next Monday I might take over my new duties at once, provided that my appearance was satisfactory. No one knows how these things are worked. Some people say the manager just plunges his hand into the heap and takes the first that comes. Anyhow, it was my innings that time, and I don't ever wish to feel better pleased. The screw was a pound a week rise, and the duties just about the same as at Coxon's.

'And now I come to the queer part of the business. I was in diggings out Hampstead way—17 Potter's Terrace, was the address. Well, I was sitting doing a smoke that very evening after I had been promised the appointment, when up came my landlady with a card which had "Arthur Pinner, financial agent," printed upon it. I had never heard the name before, and could not imagine what he wanted with me, but of course I asked her to show him up. In he walked—a middle-sized, dark-haired, dark-eyed, black-bearded man, with a touch of the sheeny about his nose. He had a brisk kind of way with him and spoke sharply, like a man that knew the value of time.

' "Mr Hall Pycroft, I believe?" said he.

' "Yes, sir," I answered, and pushed a chair towards him.

' "Lately engaged at Coxon & Woodhouse's?"

' "Yes, sir."

' "And now on the staff of Mawson's?"

' "Quite, so."

' "Well," said he. "The fact is that I have heard some really extraordinary stories about your financial ability. You remember Parker who used to be Coxon's manager? He can never say enough about it."

'Of course I was pleased to hear this. I had always been pretty smart in the office, but I had never dreamed that I was talked about in the City in this fashion.

' "You have a good memory?" said he.

' "Pretty fair," I answered, modestly.

' "Have you kept in touch with the market while you have been out of work?" he asked.

' "Yes; I read the Stock Exchange List every morning."

' "Now, that shows real application!" he cried. "That is the way to prosper! You won't mind my testing you, will you? Let me see! How are Ayrshires?"

' "One hundred and five, to one hundred and five and a quarter."

' "And New Zealand Consolidated?"

' "A hundred and four."

' "And British Broken Hills?"

' "Seven to seven and six."

' "Wonderful!" he cried, with his hands up, "This quite fits in with all that I had heard. My boy, my boy, you are very much too good to be a clerk at Mawson's!"

'This outburst rather astonished me, as you can think. "Well," said I, "other people don't think quite so much of me as you seem to do, Mr Pinner. I had a hard enough fight to get this berth, and I am very glad to have it."

' "Pooh, man, you should soar above it. You are not in your true sphere. Now I'll tell you how it stands with me. What I have to offer is little enough when measured by your ability, but when compared with Mawson's it is light to dark. Let me see! When do you go to Mawson's?"

' "On Monday."

' "Ha! ha! I think I would risk a little sporting flutter that you don't go there at all."

' "Not go to Mawson's?"

' "No, sir. By that day you will be business manager of the Franco-Midland Hardware Company, Limited, with one hundred and thirty-four branches in the towns and villages of France, not counting one in Brussels and one in San Remo."

'This took my breath away. "I never heard of it," said I.

' "Very likely not. It has been kept very quiet, for the capital was all privately subscribed, and it is too good a thing to let the public into. My brother, Harry Pinner, is promoter, and joins the board after allotment as managing director. He knew that I was in the swim down here, and he asked me to pick up a good man cheap—a young, pushing man with plenty of snap about him. Parker spoke of you, and that brought me here tonight. We can only offer you a beggarly five hundred to start with——"

' "Five hundred a year!" I shouted.

' "Only that at the beginning, but you are to have an overriding commission of 1 per cent on all business done by your agents, and you may take my word for it that this will come to more than your salary."

' "But I know nothing about hardware."

' "Tut, my boy, you know about figures."

'My head buzzed, and I could hardly sit still in the chair. But suddenly a little chill of doubt came over me.

' "I must be frank with you," said I. "Mawson only gives me two hundred, but Mawson is safe. Now, really, I know so little about your company that——"

' "Ah, smart, smart!" he cried, in a kind of ecstasy of delight. "You are the very man for us! You are not to be talked over, and quite right too. Now here's a note for a hundred pounds; and if you think that we can do business you may just slip it into your pocket as an advance upon your salary."

' "That is very handsome," said I. "When shall I take over my new duties?"

' "Be in Birmingham tomorrow at one," said he. "I have a note in my pocket here which you will take to my brother. You will find him at 126B Corporation Street, where the temporary offices of the company are situated. Of course he must confirm your engagement, but between ourselves it will be all right."

' "Really, I hardly know how to express my gratitude, Mr Pinner," said I.

' "Not at all, my boy. You have only got your deserts. There are one or two small things—mere formalities—which I must arrange with you. You have a bit of paper beside you there. Kindly write upon it, 'I am perfectly willing to act as business manager to the Franco-Midland Hardware Company, Limited, at a minimum salary of £500.' "

'I did as he asked, and he put the paper in his pocket.

' "There is one other detail," said he. "What do you intend to do about Mawson's?"

'I had forgotten all about Mawson's in my joy.

' "I'll write and resign," said I.

' "Precisely what I don't want you to do. I had a row over you with Mawson's manager. I had gone up to ask him about you, and he was very offensive—accused me of coaxing you away from the service of the firm, and that sort of thing. At last I fairly lost my temper. 'If you want good men you should pay them a good price,' said I. 'He would rather have our small price than your big one,' said he. 'I'll lay you a fiver,' said I, 'that when he has my offer you will never so much as hear from him again.' 'Done!' said he. 'We picked him out of the gutter, and he won't leave us so easily.' Those were his very words."

' "The impudent scoundrel!" I cried. "I've never so much as seen him in my life. Why should I consider him in any way? I shall certainly not write if you would rather that I didn't."

' "Good! That's a promise!" said he, rising from his chair. "Well,

I am delighted to have got so good a man for my brother. Here is your advance of a hundred pounds, and here is the letter. Make a note of the address, 126B Corporation Street, and remember that one o'clock tomorrow is your appointment. Good night, and may you have all the fortune that you deserve."

'That's just about all that passed between us as near as I can remember it. You can imagine, Dr Watson, how pleased I was at such an extraordinary piece of good fortune. I sat up half the night hugging myself over it, and next day I was off to Birmingham in a train that would take me in plenty of time for my appointment. I took my things to an hotel in New Street, and then I made my way to the address which had been given me.

'It was a quarter of an hour before my time, but I thought that would make no difference. 126B was a passage between two large shops which led to a winding stone stair, from which there were many flats, let as offices to companies or professional men. The names of the occupants were painted up at the bottom on the wall, but there was no such name as the Franco-Midland Hardware Company, Limited. I stood for a few minutes with my heart in my boots, wondering whether the whole thing was an elaborate hoax or not, when up came a man and addressed me. He was very like the chap that I had seen the night before, the same figure and voice, but he was clean shaven and his hair was lighter.

' "Are you Mr Hall Pycroft?" he asked.

' "Yes," said I.

' "Ah! I was expecting you, but you are a trifle before your time. I had a note from my brother this morning, in which he sang your praises very loudly."

' "I was just looking for the offices when you came."

' "We have not got our name up yet, for we only secured these temporary premises last week. Come up with me and we will talk the matter over."

'I followed him to the top of a very lofty stair, and there right under the slates were a couple of empty and dusty little rooms, uncarpeted and uncurtained, into which he led me. I had thought of a great office with shining tables and rows of clerks such as I was used to, and I dare say I stared rather straight at the two deal chairs and one little table, which, with a ledger and a waste-paper basket, made up the whole furniture.

' "Don't be disheartened, Mr Pycroft," said my new acquaintance, seeing the length of my face. "Rome was not built in a day, and we have lots of money at our backs, though we don't cut much dash yet in offices. Pray sit down and let me have your letter."

'I gave it to him, and he read it over very carefully.

' "You seem to have made a vast impression upon my brother Arthur," said he, "and I know that he is a pretty shrewd judge. He swears by London, you know, and I by Birmingham, but this time I shall follow his advice. Pray consider yourself definitely engaged."

' "What are my duties?" I asked.

' "You will eventually manage the great depot in Paris, which will pour a flood of English crockery into the shops of one hundred and thirty-four agents in France. The purchase will be completed in a week, and meanwhile you will remain in Birmingham and make yourself useful."

' "How?"

'For answer he took a big red book out of a drawer. "This is a directory of Paris," said he, "with the trades after the names of the people. I want you to take it home with you, and to mark off all the hardware sellers with their addresses. It would be of the greatest use to me to have them."

' "Surely, there are classified lists?" I suggested.

' "Not reliable ones. Their system is different to ours. Stick at it and let me have the lists by Monday, at twelve. Good day, Mr Pycroft; if you continue to show zeal and intelligence, you will find the company a good master."

'I went back to the hotel with the big book under my arm, and with very conflicting feelings in my breast. On the one hand I was definitely engaged, and had a hundred pounds in my pocket. On the other, the look of the offices, the absence of name on the wall, and other of the points which would strike a business man, had left a bad impression as to the position of my employers. However, come what might, I had my money, so I settled down to my task. All Sunday I was kept hard at work, and yet by Monday I had only got as far as H. I went round to my employer, found him in the same dismantled kind of room, and was told to keep at it until Wednesday, and then come again. On Wednesday it was still unfinished, so I hammered away until Friday— that is, yesterday. Then I brought it round to Mr Harry Pinner.

' "Thank you very much," said he. "I fear that I underrated the difficulty of the task. This list will be of very material assistance to me."

' "It took some time," said I.

' "And now," said he, "I want you to make a list of the furniture shops, for they all sell crockery."

' "Very good."

' "And you can come up tomorrow evening at seven, and let me know how you are getting on. Don't overwork yourself. A couple of hours at Day's Music-Hall in the evening would do you no harm after your labours." He laughed as he spoke, and I saw with a thrill that his second tooth upon the left-hand side had been very badly stuffed with gold.'

Sherlock Holmes rubbed his hands with delight, and I stared in astonishment at our client.

'You may well look surprised, Dr Watson, but it is this way,' said he. 'When I was speaking to the other chap in London at the time that he laughed at my not going to Mawson's, I happened to notice that his tooth was stuffed in this very identical fashion. The glint of the gold in each case caught my eye, you see. When I put that with the voice and figure being the same, and only those things altered which might be changed by a razor or a wig, I could not doubt that it was the same man. Of course, you expect two brothers to be alike, but not that they should have the same tooth stuffed in the same way. He bowed me out and I found myself in the street, hardly knowing whether I was on my head or my heels. Back I went to my hotel, put my head in a basin of cold water, and tried to think it out. Why had he sent me from London to Birmingham; why had he got there before me; and why had he written a letter from himself to himself? It was altogether too much for me, and I could make no sense of it. And then suddenly it struck me that what was dark to me might be very light to Mr Sherlock Holmes. I had just time to get up to town by the night train, to see him this morning, and to bring you both back with me to Birmingham.'

There was a pause after the stockbroker's clerk had concluded his surprising experience. Then Sherlock Holmes cocked his eye at me, leaning back on the cushions with a pleased and yet critical face, like a connoisseur who had just taken his first sip of a comet vintage.

'Rather fine, Watson, is it not?' said he. 'There are points in it which please me. I think you will agree with me that an interview with Mr Arthur Harry Pinner in the temporary offices of the Franco-Midland Hardware Company, Limited, would be a rather interesting experience for both of us.'

'But how can we do it?' I asked.

'Oh, easily enough,' said Hall Pycroft, cheerily. 'You are two friends of mine who are in want of a billet, and what could be more natural than that I should bring you both round to the managing director?'

'Quite so! Of course!' said Holmes. 'I should like to have a look at the gentleman and see if I can make anything of his little game. What qualities have you, my friend, which would make your services so valuable? or is it possible that——' He began biting his nails and staring blankly out of the window, and we hardly drew another word from him until we were in New Street.

At seven o'clock that evening we were walking, the three of us, down Corporation Street to the company's offices.

'It is of no use our being at all before our time,' said our client. 'He only comes there to see me apparently, for the place is deserted up to the very hour he names.'

'That is suggestive,' remarked Holmes.

'By Jove, I told you so!' cried the clerk. 'That's he walking ahead of us there.'

He pointed to a smallish, blond, well-dressed man, who was bustling along the other side of the road. As we watched him he looked across at a boy who was bawling out the latest edition of the evening paper, and, running over among the cabs and 'buses, he bought one from him. Then clutching it in his hand he vanished through a doorway.

'There he goes!' cried Hall Pycroft. 'Those are the company's offices into which he has gone. Come with me and I'll fix it up as easily as possible.'

Following his lead we ascended five storeys, until we found our-selves outside a half-opened door, at which our client tapped. A voice within bade us 'Come in,' and we entered a bare, unfurnished room, such as Hall Pycroft had described. At the single table sat the man whom we had seen in the street, with his evening paper spread out in front of him, and as he looked up at us it seemed to me that I had never looked upon a face which bore such marks of grief, and of something beyond grief—of a horror such as comes to few men in a lifetime. His brow glistened with perspiration, his cheeks were of the dull dead white of a fish's belly, and his eyes were wild and staring. He looked at his clerk as though he failed to recognize him, and I could see, by the astonishment depicted upon our conductor's face, that this was by no means the usual appearance of his employer.

'You look ill, Mr Pinner,' he exclaimed.

'Yes, I am not very well,' answered the other, making obvious efforts to pull himself together, and licking his dry lips before he spoke. 'Who are these gentlemen whom you have brought with you?'

'One is Mr Harris, of Bermondsey, and the other is Mr Price, of this town,' said our clerk, glibly. 'They are friends of mine, and gentlemen of experience, but they have been out of a place for some little time, and they hoped that perhaps you might find an opening for them in the company's employment.'

'Very possibly! Very possibly!' cried Mr Pinner, with a ghastly smile. 'Yes, I have no doubt that we shall be able to do something for you. What is your particular line, Mr Harris?'

'I am an accountant,' said Holmes.

'Ah, yes, we shall want something of the sort. And you, Mr Price?'

'A clerk,' said I.

'I have every hope that the company may accommodate you. I will let you know about it as soon as we come to any conclusion. And now I beg that you will go. For God's sake, leave me to myself!'

These last words were shot out of him, as though the constraint which he was evidently setting upon himself had suddenly and utterly burst asunder. Holmes and I glanced at each other, and Hall Pycroft took a step towards the table.

'You forget, Mr Pinner, that I am here by appointment to receive some directions from you,' said he.

'Certainly, Mr Pycroft, certainly,' the other answered in a calmer tone. 'You may wait here a moment, and there is no reason why your friends should not wait with you. I will be entirely at your service in three minutes, if I might trespass upon your patience so far.' He rose with a very courteous air, and bowing to us he passed out through a door at the farther end of the room, which he closed behind him.

'What now?' whispered Holmes. 'Is he giving us the slip?'

'Impossible,' answered Pycroft.

'Why so?'

'That door leads into an inner room.'

'There is no exit?'

'None.'

'Is it furnished?'

'It was empty yesterday.'

'Then what on earth can he be doing? There is something which I don't understand in this matter. If ever a man was three parts mad with terror, that man's name is Pinner. What can have put the shivers on him?'

'He suspects that we are detectives,' I suggested.

'That's it,' said Pycroft.

Holmes shook his head. 'He did not turn pale. He *was* pale when we entered the room,' said he. 'It is just possible that——'

His words were interrupted by a sharp rat-tat from the direction of the inner door.

'What the deuce is he knocking at his own door for?' cried the clerk.

Again and much louder came the rat-tat-tat. We all gazed expectantly at the closed door. Glancing at Holmes I saw his face turn rigid, and he leaned forward in intense excitement. Then suddenly came a low gurgling, gargling sound and a brisk drumming upon woodwork. Holmes sprang frantically across the room and pushed at the door. It was fastened on the inner side. Following his example, we threw ourselves upon it with all our weight. One hinge snapped, then the other, and down came the door with a crash. Rushing over it, we found ourselves in the inner room.

It was empty.

But it was only for a moment that we were at fault. At one corner, the corner nearest the room which we had left, there was a second door. Holmes sprang to it and pulled it open. A coat and waistcoat were lying on the floor, and from a hook behind the door, with his own braces round his neck, was hanging the managing director of the Franco-Midland Hardware Company. His knees were drawn up, his head hung at a dreadful angle to his body, and the clatter of his heels against the door made the noise which had broken in upon our conversation. In an instant I had caught him round the waist and held him up, while Holmes and Pycroft untied the elastic bands which had disappeared between the livid creases of skin. Then we carried him into the other room, where he lay with a slate-coloured face, puffing his purple lips in and out with every breath—a dreadful wreck of all that he had been but five minutes before.

'What do you think of him, Watson?' asked Holmes.

I stooped over him and examined him. His pulse was feeble and intermittent, but his breathing grew longer, and there was a little shivering of his eyelids which showed a thin white slit of ball beneath.

'It has been touch and go with him,' said I, 'but he'll live now. Just open that window and hand me the water carafe.' I undid his collar, poured the cold water over his face, and raised and sank his arms until he drew a long natural breath.

'It's only a question of time now,' said I, as I turned away from him.

Holmes stood by the table with his hands deep in his trousers pockets and his chin upon his breast.

'I suppose we ought to call the police in now,' said he; 'and yet I confess that I like to give them a complete case when they come.'

'It's a blessed mystery to me,' cried Pycroft, scratching his head. 'Whatever they wanted to bring me all the way up here for, and then——'

'Pooh! All that is clear enough,' said Holmes impatiently. 'It is this last sudden move.'

'You understand the rest, then?'

'I think that is fairly obvious. What do you say, Watson?'

I shrugged my shoulders.

'I must confess that I am out of my depths,' said I.

'Oh, surely, if you consider the events at first they can only point to one conclusion.'

'What do you make of them?'

'Well, the whole thing hinges upon two points. The first is the making of Pycroft write a declaration by which he entered the service of this preposterous company. Do you not see how very suggestive that is?'

'I am afraid I miss the point.'

'Well, why did they want him to do it? Not as a business matter, for these arrangements are usually verbal, and there was no earthly business reason why this should be an exception. Don't you see, my young friend, that they were very anxious to obtain a specimen of your handwriting, and had no other way of doing it?'

'And why?'

'Quite so. Why? When we answer that, we have made some progress with our little problem. Why? There can be only one adequate reason. Someone wanted to learn to imitate your writing, and had to procure a specimen of it first. And now if we pass on to the second point, we find that each throws light upon the other. That point is the request made by Pinner that you should not resign your place, but should leave the manager of this important business in the full expectation that a Mr Hall Pycroft, whom he had never seen, was about to enter the office upon the Monday morning.'

'My God!' cried our client, 'what a blind beetle I have been!'

'Now you see the point about the handwriting. Suppose that someone turned up in your place who wrote a completely different hand from that in which you had applied for the vacancy, of course the game would have been up. But in the interval the rogue learnt to imitate you, and his position was therefore secure, as I presume that nobody in the office had ever set eyes upon you?'

'Not a soul,' groaned Hall Pycroft.

'Very good. Of course, it was of the utmost importance to prevent you from thinking better of it, and also to keep you from coming into contact with anyone who might tell you that your double was at work in Mawson's office. Therefore they gave you a handsome advance on your salary, and ran you off to the Midlands, where they gave you enough work to do to prevent your going to London, where you might have burst their little game up. That is all plain enough.'

'But why should this man pretend to be his own brother?'

'Well, that is pretty clear also. There are evidently only two of them in it. The other is personating you at the office. This one acted as your engager, and then found that he could not find you an employer without admitting a third person into his plot. That he was most unwilling to do. He changed his appearance as far as he could, and trusted that the likeness, which you could not fail to observe, would be put down to a family resemblance. But for the happy chance of the gold stuffing your suspicions would probably have never been aroused.'

Hall Pycroft shook his clenched hands in the air. 'Good Lord!' he cried. 'While I have been fooled in this way, what has this other Hall Pycroft been doing at Mawson's? What should we do, Mr Holmes? Tell me what to do!'

'We must wire to Mawson's.'

'They shut at twelve on Saturdays.'

'Never mind; there may be some door-keeper or attendant——'

'Ah, yes; they keep a permanent guard there on account of the value of the securities that they hold. I remember hearing it talked of in the City.'

'Very good, we shall wire to him, and see if all is well, and if a clerk of your name is working there. That is clear enough, but what is not so clear is why at sight of us one of the rogues should instantly walk out of the room and hang himself.'

'The paper!' croaked a voice behind us. The man was sitting up, blanched and ghastly, with returning reason in his eyes, and hands which rubbed nervously at the broad red band which still encircled his throat.

'The paper! Of course!' yelled Holmes, in a paroxysm of excitement. 'Idiot that I was! I thought so much of our visit that the paper never entered my head for an instant. To be sure, the secret must lie there.' He flattened it out on the table, and a cry of triumph burst from his lips.

'Look at this, Watson!' he cried. 'It is a London paper, an early edition of the *Evening Standard*. Here is what we want. Look at the headlines—"Crime in the City. Murder at Mawson & Williams'. Gigantic Attempted Robbery; Capture of the Criminal." Here, Watson, we are all equally anxious to hear it, so kindly read it aloud to us.'

It appeared from its position in the paper to have been the one event of importance in town, and the account of it ran in this way:

'A desperate attempt at robbery, culminating in the death of one man and the capture of the criminal, occurred this afternoon in the City. For some time back Mawson & Williams, the famous financial house, have been the guardians of securities which amount in the aggregate to a sum of considerably over a million sterling. So conscious was the manager of the responsibility which devolved upon him in consequence of the great interests at stake, that safes of the very latest construction have been employed, and an armed watchman has been left day and night in the building. It appears that last week a new clerk, named Hall Pycroft, was engaged by the firm. This person appears to have been none other than Beddington, the famous forger and cracksman, who, with his brother, has only recently emerged from a five years' spell of penal servitude. By some means, which are not yet clear, he succeeded in winning, under a false name, this official position in the office, which he utilized in order to obtain mouldings of various locks and a thorough knowledge of the position of the strong-room and the safes.

'It is customary at Mawson's for the clerks to leave at midday on Saturday. Sergeant Tuson, of the City Police, was somewhat surprised therefore to see a gentleman with a carpet bag come down the steps at twenty minutes past one. His suspicions being aroused, the sergeant followed the man, and with the aid of Constable Pollock succeeded, after a most desperate resistance, in arresting him. It was at once clear that a daring and gigantic robbery had been committed. Nearly a hundred thousand pounds' worth of American railway bonds, with a large amount of scrip in other mines and companies, were discovered in the bag. On examining the premises the body of the unfortunate watchman was found doubled up and thrust into the largest of the safes, where it would not have been discovered until Monday morning had it not been for the prompt action of Sergeant Tuson. The man's skull had been shattered by a blow from a poker, delivered from behind. There could be no doubt that Beddington had obtained entrance by pretending that he had left something behind him, and having murdered the watchman, rapidly rifled the large safe, and then made off with his booty. His brother, who usually works with him, has not appeared in this job, as far as can at present be ascertained, although the police are making energetic inquiries as to his whereabouts.'

'Well, we may save the police some little trouble in that direction,' said Holmes, glancing at the haggard figure huddled up by the window. 'Human nature is a strange mixture, Watson. You see that even a villain and a murderer can inspire such affection that this brother turns to suicide when he learns that his neck is forfeited. However, we have no choice as to our action. The doctor and I will remain on guard, Mr Pycroft, if you will have the kindness to step out for the police.'

2

ARTHUR MORRISON

The Lenton Croft Robberies

Those who retain any memory of the great law cases of fifteen or twenty years back will remember the title at least of that extra-ordinary will case, 'Bartley *v*. Bartley and others', which occupied the Probate Court for some weeks on end, and caused an amount of public interest rarely accorded to any but the cases considered in the other division of the same court. The case itself was noted for the large quantity of remarkable and unusual evidence presented by the plaintiff's side—evidence that took the other party completely by surprise, and overthrew their case like a house of cards. The affair will, perhaps, be more readily recalled as the occasion of the sudden rise to eminence in their profession of Messrs Crellan, Hunt, and Crellan, solicitors for the plaintiff—a result due entirely to the wonderful ability shown in this case of building up, apparently out of nothing, a smashing weight of irresistible evidence. That the firm has since maintained—indeed, enhanced—the position it then won for itself, need scarcely be said here; its name is familiar to everybody. But there are not many of the outside public who know that the credit of the whole performance was primarily due to a young clerk in the employ of Messrs Crellan, who had been given charge of the seemingly des-perate task of collecting evidence in the case.

This Mr Martin Hewitt had, however, full credit and reward for his exploit from his firm and from their client, and more than one other firm of lawyers engaged in contentious work made good offers to induce Hewitt to change his employers. Instead of this, however, he determined to work independently for the future, having conceived the idea of making a regular business of doing, on behalf of such

19

clients as might retain him, similar work to that he had just done, with such conspicuous success, for Messrs Crellan, Hunt, and Crellan. This was the beginning of the private detective business of Martin Hewitt, and his action at that time has been completely justified by the brilliant professional successes he has since achieved.

His business has always been conducted in the most private manner, and he has always declined the help of professional assistants, preferring to carry out himself such of the many investigations offered him as he could manage. He has always maintained that he has never lost by this policy, since the chance of his refusing a case begets competition for his services, and his fees rise by a natural process. At the same time, no man could know better how to employ casual assistance at the right time.

Some curiosity has been expressed as to Mr Martin Hewitt's system, and as he himself always consistently maintains that he has no system beyond a judicious use of ordinary faculties, I intend setting forth in detail a few of the more interesting of his cases, in order that the public may judge for itself if I am right in estimating Mr Hewitt's 'ordinary faculties' as faculties very extraordinary indeed. He is not a man who has made many friendships (this, probably, for professional reasons), notwithstanding his genial and companionable manners. I myself first made his acquaintance as a result of an accident involving a fire at the old house in which Hewitt's office was situated, and in an upper floor of which I occupied bachelor chambers. I was able to help in saving a quantity of extremely important papers relating to his business, and, while repairs were being made, allowed him to lock them in an old wall-safe in one of my rooms, which the fire had scarcely damaged.

The acquaintance thus begun has lasted many years, and has become a rather close friendship. I have even accompanied Hewitt on some of his expeditions, and, in a humble way, helped him. Such of the cases, however, as I personally saw nothing of I have put into narrative form from the particulars given me.

'I consider you, Brett,' he said, addressing me, 'the most remarkable journalist alive. Not because you're particularly clever, you know—because, between ourselves, I hope you'll admit you're not—but because you have known something of me and my doings for some years, and have never yet been guilty of giving away any of my little business secrets you may have become acquainted with. I'm afraid you're not so enterprising a journalist as some, Brett. But now, since you ask, you shall write something—if you think it worth while.'

This he said, as he said most things, with a cheery, chaffing good-nature that would have been, perhaps, surprising to a stranger who thought of him only as a grim and mysterious discoverer of secrets and crimes. Indeed, the man had always as little of the aspect of the conventional detective as may be imagined. Nobody could appear more cordial or less observant in manner, although there was to be seen a certain sharpness of the eye—which might, after all, only be the twinkle of good-humour.

I *did* think it worth while to write something of Martin Hewitt's investigations, and a description of one of his adventures follows.

*

At the head of the first flight of a dingy staircase leading up from an ever-open portal in a street by the Strand, stood a door, the dusty ground-glass upper panel of which carried in its centre the single word 'Hewitt', while at its right-hand lower corner, in smaller letters, 'Clerk's Office' appeared. On a morning when the clerks in the ground-floor offices had barely hung up their hats, a short, well-dressed young man, wearing spectacles, hastening to open the dusty door, ran into the arms of another man who suddenly issued from it.

'I beg pardon,' the first said. 'Is this Hewitt's Detective Agency Office?'

'Yes, I believe you will find it so,' the other replied. He was a stoutish, clean-shaven man, of middle height, and of a cheerful, round countenance. 'You'd better speak to the clerk.'

In the little outer office the visitor was met by a sharp lad with inky fingers, who presented him with a pen and a printed slip. The printed slip having been filled with the visitor's name and present business, and conveyed through an inner door, the lad reappeared with an invitation to the private office. There, behind a writing-table, sat the stoutish man himself, who had only just advised an appeal to the clerk.

'Good morning, Mr Lloyd—Mr Vernon Lloyd,' he said affably, looking again at the slip. 'You'll excuse my care to start even with my visitors—I must, you know. You come from Sir James Norris, I see.'

'Yes; I am his secretary. I have only to ask you to go straight to Lenton Croft at once, if you can, on very important business. Sir James would have wired, but had not your precise address. Can you go by the next train? Eleven-thirty is the first available from Paddington.'

'Quite possibly. Do you know anything of the business?'

'It is a case of a robbery in the house, or rather, I fancy, of several robberies. Jewellery has been stolen from rooms occupied by visitors to the Croft. The first case occurred some months ago—nearly a year ago, in fact. Last night there was another. But I think you had better get the details on the spot; Sir James has told me to telegraph if you are coming, so that he may meet you himself at the station; and I must hurry, as his drive to the station will be rather a long one. Then I take it you will go, Mr Hewitt? Twyford is the station.'

'Yes, I shall come, and by the eleven-thirty. Are you going by that train yourself?'

'No; I have several things to attend to now I am in town. Good-morning; I shall wire at once.'

Mr Martin Hewitt locked the drawer of his table and sent his clerk for a cab.

At Twyford Station Sir James Norris was waiting with a dog-cart. Sir James was a tall, florid man of fifty or thereabout, known away from home as something of a county historian, and nearer his own parts as a great supporter of the hunt, and a gentleman much troubled with poachers. As soon as he and Hewitt had found one another, the baronet hurried the detective into his dog-cart. 'We've something over seven miles to drive,' he said, 'and I can tell you all about this wretched business as we go. That is why I came for you myself, and alone.'

Hewitt nodded.

'I have sent for you, as Lloyd probably told you, because of a robbery at my place last evening. It appears, as far as I can guess, to be one of three by the same hand, or by the same gang. Late yesterday afternoon——'

'Pardon me, Sir James,' Hewitt interrupted, 'but I think I must ask you to begin at the first robbery and tell me the whole tale in proper order. It makes things clearer, and sets them in their proper shape.'

'Very well. Eleven months ago, or thereabout, I had rather a large

22

party of visitors, and among them Colonel Heath and Mrs Heath—the lady being a relative of my own late wife. Colonel Heath has not been long retired, you know—used to be political resident in an Indian native State. Mrs Heath had rather a good stock of jewellery of one sort and another, about the most valuable piece being a bracelet set with a particularly fine pearl—quite an exceptional pearl, in fact—that had been one of a heap of presents from the Maharajah of his State when Heath left India.

'It was a very noticeable bracelet, the gold setting being a mere featherweight piece of native filigree work—almost too fragile to trust on the wrist—and the pearl being, as I have said, of a size and quality not often seen. Well, Heath and his wife arrived late one evening, and after lunch the following day, most of the men being off by themselves—shooting, I think—my daughter, my sister (who is very often down here), and Mrs Heath took it into their heads to go walking—fern-hunting, and so on. My sister was rather long dressing, and while they waited, my daughter went into Mrs Heath's room, where Mrs Heath turned over all her treasures to show her—as women do, you know. When my sister was at last ready they came straight away, leaving the things littering about the room rather than stay longer to pack them up. The bracelet, with other things, was on the dressing-table then.'

'One moment. As to the door?'

'They locked it. As they came away my daughter suggested turning the key, as we had one or two new servants about.'

'And the window?'

'That they left open, as I was going to tell you. Well, they went on their walk and came back, with Lloyd (whom they had met somewhere) carrying their ferns for them. It was dusk and almost dinner time. Mrs Heath went straight to her room, and—the bracelet was gone.'

'Was the room disturbed?'

'Not a bit. Everything was precisely where it had been left, except the bracelet. The door hadn't been tampered with, but of course the window was open, as I have told you.'

'You called the police, of course?'

'Yes, and had a man from Scotland Yard down in the morning. He seemed a pretty smart fellow, and the first thing he noticed on the dressing-table, within an inch or two of where the bracelet had been, was a match, which had been lit and thrown down. Now, nobody about the house had had occasion to use a match in that room that day, and, if they had, certainly wouldn't have thrown it on the cover of the dressing-table. So that, presuming the thief to have used that match, the robbery must have been committed when the room was getting dark—immediately before Mrs Heath returned, in fact. The thief had evidently struck the match, passed it hurriedly over the various trinkets lying about, and taken the most valuable.'

'Nothing else was even moved?'

'Nothing at all. Then the thief must have escaped by the window, although it was not quite clear how. The walking party approached the house with a full view of the window, but saw nothing, although the robbery must have been actually taking place a moment or two before they turned up.

'There was no water-pipe within any practicable distance of the window. But a ladder usually kept in the stable-yard was found lying along the edge of the lawn. The gardener explained, however, that he had put the ladder there after using it himself early in the afternoon.'

'Of course, it might easily have been used again after that and put back.'

'Just what the Scotland Yard man said. He was pretty sharp, too, on the gardener, but very soon decided that he knew nothing of it. No stranger had been seen in the neighbourhood, nor had passed the lodge gates. Besides, as the detective said, it scarcely seemed the work of a stranger. A stranger could scarcely have known enough to go straight to the room where a lady—only arrived the day before—had left a valuable jewel, and away again without being seen. So all the people about the house were suspected in turn. The servants offered, in a body, to have their boxes searched, and this was done; everything was turned over, from the butler's to the new kitchenmaid's. I don't know that I should have had this carried quite so far if I had been the loser myself, but it was my guest, and I was in such a horrible position. Well, there's little more to be said about that, unfortunately. Nothing came of it all, and the thing's as great a mystery now as ever. I believe the Scotland Yard man got as far as suspecting *me* before he gave it up altogether, but give it up he did in the end. I think that's all I know about the first robbery. Is it clear?'

'Oh, yes; I shall probably want to ask a few questions when I have seen the place, but they can wait. What next?'

'Well,' Sir James pursued, 'the next was a very trumpery affair, that I should have forgotten all about, probably, if it hadn't been for one circumstance. Even now I hardly think it could have been the work of the same hand. Four months or thereabout after Mrs Heath's disaster—in February of this year, in fact—Mrs Armitage, a young widow, who had been a schoolfellow of my daughter's, stayed with us for a week or so. The girls don't trouble about the London season, you know, and I have no town house, so they were glad to have their old friend here for a little in the dull time. Mrs Armitage is a very active young lady, and was scarcely in the house half an hour before she arranged a drive in a pony-cart with Eva—my daughter—to look up old people in the village that she used to know before she was married. So they set off in the afternoon, and made such a round of it that they were late for dinner. Mrs Armitage had a small plain gold brooch—not at all valuable, you know; two or three pounds, I suppose—which she used to pin up a cloak or anything of that sort. Before she went out she stuck this in the pin-cushion on her dressing-table, and left a ring—rather a good one, I believe—lying close by.'

'This,' asked Hewitt, 'was not in the room that Mrs Heath had occupied, I take it?'

'No; this was in another part of the building. Well, the brooch went—taken, evidently, by some one in a deuce of a hurry, for when Mrs Armitage got back to her room, there was the pin-cushion with a little tear in it, where the brooch had been simply snatched off. But the curious thing was that the ring—worth a dozen of the brooch—was left where it had been put. Mrs Armitage didn't remember whether or not she had locked the door herself, although she found it locked when she returned; but my niece, who was indoors all the time, went and tried it once—because she remembered that a gasfitter was at work on the landing near by—and found it safely locked. The gasfitter, whom we didn't know at the time, but who since seems to be quite an honest fellow, was ready to swear that nobody but my niece had been to the door while he was in sight of it—which was almost all the time. As to the window, the sash-line had broken that very morning, and Mrs Armitage had propped open the bottom half about eight or ten inches with a brush; and when she returned, that brush, sash and all, were exactly as she had left them. Now, I scarcely need tell *you* what an awkward job it must have been for anybody to get noiselessly in at that unsupported window; and how unlikely he would have been to replace it, with the brush, exactly as he found it.'

'Just so. I suppose the brooch was really gone? I mean, there was no chance of Mrs Armitage having mislaid it?'

'Oh, none at all. There was a most careful search.'

'Then, as to getting in at the window, would it have been easy?'

'Well, yes,' Sir James replied; 'yes, perhaps it would. It is a first-floor window, and it looks over the roof and skylight of the billiard-room. I built the billiard-room myself—built it out from a smoking-room just at this corner. It would be easy enough to get at the window from the billiard-room roof. But then,' he added, 'that couldn't have been the way. Somebody or other was in the billiard-room the whole time, and nobody could have got over the roof (which is nearly all skylight) without being seen and heard. I was there myself for an hour or two, taking a little practice.'

'Well, was anything done?'

'Strict inquiry was made among the servants, of course, but nothing came of it. It was such a small matter that Mrs Armitage wouldn't hear of my calling in the police or anything of that sort, although I felt pretty certain that there must be a dishonest servant about somewhere. A servant might take a plain brooch, you know, who would feel afraid of a valuable ring, the loss of which would be made a greater matter of.'

'Well, yes—perhaps so, in the case of an inexperienced thief, who also would be likely to snatch up whatever she took in a hurry. But I'm doubtful. What made you connect these two robberies together?'

'Nothing whatever—for some months. They seemed quite of a different sort. But scarcely more than a month ago I met Mrs Armitage at Brighton, and we talked, among other things, of the previous robbery—that of Mrs Heath's bracelet. I described the circumstances pretty minutely, and when I mentioned the match found on the table she said, "How strange! Why, *my* thief left a match on the dressing-table when he took my poor little brooch!" '

Hewitt nodded. 'Yes,' he said. 'A spent match, of course?'

'Yes, of course, a spent match. She noticed it lying close by the pin-cushion, but threw it away without mentioning the circumstance. Still, it seemed rather curious to me that a match should be lit and dropped, in each case, on the dressing-cover an inch from where the article was taken. I mentioned it to Lloyd when I got back, and he agreed that it seemed significant.'

'Scarcely,' said Hewitt, shaking his head. 'Scarcely, so far, to be called significant, although worth following up. Everybody uses matches in the dark, you know.'

'Well, at any rate, the coincidence appealed to me so far that it struck me it might be worth while to describe the brooch to the police in order that they could trace it if it had been pawned. They had tried that, of course, over the bracelet, without any result, but I fancied the shot might be worth making, and might possibly lead us on the track of the more serious robbery.'

'Quite so. It was the right thing to do. Well?'

'Well, they found it. A woman had pawned it in London—at a shop in Chelsea. But that was some time before, and the pawnbroker had clean forgotten all about the woman's appearance. The name and address she gave were false. So that was the end of that business.'

'Had any of your servants left you between the time the brooch was lost and the date of the pawn-ticket?'

'No.'

'Were all your servants at home on the day the brooch was pawned?'

'Oh, yes. I made that inquiry myself.'

'Very good. What next?'

'Yesterday—and this is what made me send for you. My late wife's sister came here last Tuesday, and we gave her the room from which Mrs Heath lost her bracelet. She had with her a very old-fashioned brooch, containing a miniature of her father, and set, in front, with three very fine brilliants and a few smaller stones. Here we are, though, at the Croft; I'll tell you the rest indoors.'

Hewitt laid his hand on the baronet's arm. 'Don't pull up,

Sir James,' he said. 'Drive a little further. I should like to have a general idea of the whole case before we go in.'

'Very good.' Sir James Norris straightened the horse's head again and went on. 'Late yesterday afternoon, as my sister-in-law was changing her dress, she left her room for a moment to speak to my daughter in her room, almost adjoining. She was gone no more than three minutes, or five at most; but on her return the brooch, which had been left on the table, had gone. Now, the window was shut fast, and had not been tampered with. Of course the door was open, but so was my daughter's, and anybody walking near must have been heard. But the strangest circumstance, and one that almost makes me wonder whether I have been awake today or not, was that there lay *a used match* on the very spot, as nearly as possible, where the brooch had been—and it was broad daylight!'

Hewitt rubbed his nose and looked thoughtfully before him. 'Um—curious, certainly,' he said. 'Anything else?'

'Nothing more than you shall see for yourself. I have had the room locked and watched till you could examine it. My sister-in-law had heard of your name, and suggested that you should be called in; so, of course, I did exactly as she wanted. That she should have lost that brooch, of all things, in my house, is most unfortunate; you see, there was some small difference about the thing between my late wife and her sister when their mother died and left it. It's almost worse than the Heath's bracelet business, and altogether I'm not pleased with things, I can assure you. See what a position it is for me! Here are three ladies in the space of one year, robbed one after another in this mysterious fashion in my house, and I can't find the thief. It's horrible! People will be afraid to come near the place. And I can do nothing!'

'Ah, well—we'll see. Perhaps we had better turn back now. By the bye, were you thinking of having any alternations or additions made to your house?'

'No. What makes you ask?'

'I think you might at least consider the question of painting and decorating, Sir James—or, say, putting up another coach-house, or something. Because I should like to be (to the servants) the architect—or the builder, if you please—come to look round. You haven't told any of them about this business?'

'Not a word. Nobody knows but my relatives and Lloyd. I took every precaution myself, at once. As to your little disguise, be the architect, by all means, and do as you please. If you can only find this thief and put an end to this horrible state of affairs, you'll do me the greatest service I've ever asked for—and as to your fee, I'll gladly make it whatever is usual, and two hundred in addition.'

Martin Hewitt bowed. 'You're very generous, Sir James, and you may be sure I'll do what I can. As a professional man, of course, a good fee always stimulates my interest, although this case of yours certainly seems interesting enough by itself.'

'Most extraordinary! Don't you think so? Here are three persons, all ladies, all in my house, two even in the same room, each succes- sively robbed of a piece of jewellery, each from a dressing-table, and a used match left behind in every case. All in the most difficult—one would say impossible—circumstances for a thief, and yet there is no clue!'

'Well, we won't say that just yet, Sir James; we must see. And we must guard against any undue predisposition to consider the robberies in a lump. Here we are at the lodge gate again. Is that your gardener—the man who left the ladder by the lawn on the first occasion you spoke of?' Mr Hewitt nodded in the direction of a man who was clipping a box border.

'Yes; will you ask him anything?'

'No, no; at any rate, not now. Remember the building alterations. I think, if there is no objection, I will look first at the room that the lady—Mrs——?' Hewitt looked up inquiringly.

'My sister-in-law? Mrs Cazenove. Oh, yes, you shall come to her room at once.'

'Thank you. And I think Mrs Cazenove had better be there.'

They alighted; and a boy from the lodge led the horse and dog-cart away.

Mrs Cazenove was a thin and faded, but quick and energetic, lady of middle age. She bent her head very slightly on learning Martin Hewitt's name, and said: 'I must thank you, Mr Hewitt, for your very prompt attention. I need scarcely say that any help you can afford in tracing the thief who has my property—whoever it may be—will make me most grateful. My room is quite ready for you to examine.'

The room was on the second floor—the top floor at that part of the building. Some slight confusion of small articles of dress was observable in parts of the room.

'This, I take it,' inquired Hewitt, 'is exactly as it was at the time the brooch was missed?'

'Precisely,' Mrs Cazenove answered. 'I have used another room, and put myself to some other inconveniences, to avoid any disturbance.'

Hewitt stood before the dressing-table. 'Then this is the used match,' he observed, 'exactly where it was found?'

'Yes.'

'Where was the brooch?'

'I should say almost on the very same spot. Certainly no more than a very few inches away.'

Hewitt examined the match closely. 'It is burnt very little,' he remarked. 'It would appear to have gone out at once. Could you hear it struck?'

'I heard nothing whatever; absolutely nothing.'

'If you will step into Miss Norris's room now for a moment,' Hewitt suggested, 'we will try an experiment. Tell me if you hear matches struck, and how many. Where is the match-stand?'

The match-stand proved to be empty, but matches were found in Miss Norris's room, and the test was made. Each striking could be heard distinctly, even with one of the doors pushed to.

'Both your own door and Miss Norris's were open, I understand; the window shut and fastened inside as it is now, and nothing but the brooch was disturbed?'

'Yes, that was so.'

'Thank you, Mrs Cazenove. I don't think I need trouble you any further just at present. I think, Sir James,' Hewitt added, turning to the baronet, who was standing by the door—'I think we will see the other room and take a walk outside the house, if you please. I suppose, by the bye, that there is no getting at the matches left behind on the first and second occasions?'

'No,' Sir James answered. 'Certainly not here. The Scotland Yard man may have kept his.'

The room that Mrs Armitage had occupied presented no peculiar feature. A few feet below the window the roof of the billiard-room was visible, consisting largely of skylight. Hewitt glanced casually about the walls, ascertained that the furniture and hangings had not been materially changed since the second robbery, and expressed his desire to see the windows from the outside. Before leaving the room, however, he wished to know the names of any persons who were known to have been about the house on the occasions of all three robberies.

'Just carry your mind back, Sir James,' he said. 'Begin with yourself, for instance. Where were you at these times?'

'When Mrs Heath lost her bracelet I was in Tagley Wood all the afternoon. When Mrs Armitage was robbed, I believe I was somewhere about the place most of the time she was out. Yesterday I was down at the farm.' Sir James's face broadened. 'I don't know whether you call those suspicious movements?' he added, and laughed.

'Not at all; I only asked you so that, remembering your own movements, you might the better recall those of the rest of the household. Was anybody, to your knowledge—*anybody*, mind—in the house on all three occasions?'

'Well, you know, it's quite impossible to answer for all the servants. You'll only get that by direct questioning—I can't possibly remember things of that sort. As to the family and visitors—why, you don't suspect any of them, do you?'

'I don't suspect a soul, Sir James,' Hewitt answered, beaming genially,—'not a soul. You see, I *can't* suspect people till I know something about where they were. It's quite possible there will be independent evidence enough as it is, but you must help me if you can. The visitors, now. Was there any visitor here each time—or even on the first and last occasions only?'

'No—not one. And my own sister, perhaps you will be pleased to know, was only there at the time of the first robbery.'

'Just so. And your daughter, as I have gathered, was clearly absent from the spot each time—indeed, was in company with the party robbed. Your niece, now?'

'Why, hang it all, Mr Hewitt, I can't talk of my niece as a suspected criminal. The poor girl's under my protection, and I really can't allow——'

Hewitt raised his hand and shook his head deprecatingly.

'My dear sir, haven't I said that I don't suspect a soul? *Do* let me know how the people were distributed, as nearly as possible. Let me see. It was your niece, I think, who found that Mrs Armitage's door was locked—this door, in fact—on the day she lost her brooch?'

'Yes, it was.'

'Just so—at the time when Mrs Armitage herself had forgotten whether she locked it or not. And yesterday—was she out then?'

'No, I think not. Indeed, she goes out very little—her health is usually bad. She was indoors, too, at the time of the Heath robbery, since you ask. But come, now, I don't like this. It's ridiculous to suppose that *she* knows anything of it.'

'I don't suppose it, as I have said. I am only asking for information. That is all your resident family, I take it, and you know nothing of anybody else's movements—except, perhaps, Mr Lloyd's?'

'Lloyd? Well, you know yourself that he was out with the ladies when the first robbery took place. As to the others, I don't remember. Yesterday he was probably in his room, writing. I think that acquits *him*, eh?' Sir James looked quizzically into the broad face of the affable detective, who smiled and replied,—

'Oh, of course, nobody can be in two places at once, else what would become of the alibi as an institution? But as I have said, I am only setting my facts in order. Now, you see, we get down to the servants—unless some stranger is the party wanted. Shall we go outside now?'

Lenton Croft was a large, desultory sort of house, nowhere more than three floors high, and mostly only two. It had been added to bit by bit till it zig-zagged about its site, as Sir James Norris expressed it, 'like a game of dominoes.' Hewitt scrutinized its external features carefully as they strolled round, and stopped some little while before the windows of the two bedrooms he had just seen from the inside. Presently they approached the stables and coach-house, where a groom was washing the wheels of the dog-cart.

'Do you mind my smoking?' Hewitt asked Sir James. 'Perhaps you will take a cigar yourself—they are not so bad, I think. I will ask your man for a light.'

Sir James felt for his own match-box, but Hewitt had gone, and was lighting his cigar with a match from a box handed him by the groom. A smart little terrier was trotting about by the coach-house, and

Hewitt stooped to rub its head. Then he made some observation about the dog which enlisted the groom's interest, and was soon absorbed in a chat with the man. Sir James, waiting a little way off, tapped the stones rather impatiently with his foot, and presently moved away.

For full a quarter of an hour Hewitt chatted with the groom, and when at last he came away and overtook Sir James, that gentleman was about re-entering the house.

'I beg your pardon, Sir James,' Hewitt said, 'for leaving you in that unceremonious fashion to talk to your groom, but a dog, Sir James— a good dog—will draw me anywhere.'

'Oh,' replied Sir James shortly.

'There is one other thing,' Hewitt went on, disregarding the other's curtness, 'that I should like to know: There are two windows directly below that of the room occupied yesterday by Mrs Cazenove—one on each floor. What rooms do they light?'

'That on the ground floor is the morning-room; the other is Mr Lloyd's—my secretary. A sort of study or sitting-room.'

'Now, you will see at once, Sir James,' Hewitt pursued, with an affable determination to win the baronet back to good humour— 'you will see at once that if a ladder had been used in Mrs Heath's case, anybody looking from either of these rooms would have seen it.'

'Of course. The Scotland Yard man questioned everybody as to that, but nobody seemed to have been in either of the rooms when the thing occurred; at any rate, nobody saw anything.'

'Still, I think I should like to look out of those windows myself; it will, at least, give me an idea of what *was* in view and what was not, if anybody had been there.'

Sir James Norris led the way to the morning-room. As they reached the door, a young lady, carrying a book and walking very languidly, came out. Hewitt stepped aside to let her pass, and afterwards said, interrogatively, 'Miss Norris—your daughter, Sir James?'

'No, my niece. Do you want to ask her anything? Dora, my dear,' Sir James added, following her in the corridor, 'this is Mr Hewitt, who is investigating these wretched robberies for me. I think he would like to hear if you remember anything happening at any of the three times.'

The lady bowed slightly, and said, in a plaintive drawl, 'I, uncle? Really, I don't remember anything; nothing at all.'

'You found Mrs Armitage's door locked, I believe,' asked Hewitt, 'when you tried it on the afternoon when she lost her brooch?'

'Oh, yes; I believe it was locked. Yes, it was.'

'Had the key been left in?'

'The key? Oh, no! I think not; no.'

'Do you remember anything out of the common happening—anything whatever, no matter how trivial—on the day Mrs Heath lost her bracelet?'

'No, really I don't. I can't remember at all.'

'Nor yesterday?'

'No, nothing. I don't remember anything.'

'Thank you,' said Hewitt hastily; 'thank you. Now the morning-room, Sir James.'

In the morning-room Hewitt stayed but a few seconds, doing little more than casually glance out of the windows. In the room above he took a little longer time. It was a comfortable room, but with rather effeminate indications about its contents. Little pieces of draped silk-work hung about the furniture, and Japanese silk fans decorated the mantelpiece. Near the window was a cage containing a grey parrot, and the writing-table was decorated with two vases of flowers.

'Lloyd makes himself pretty comfortable, eh?' Sir James observed. 'But it isn't likely anybody would be here while he was out, at the time that bracelet went.'

'No,' replied Hewitt meditatively. 'No, I suppose not.'

He stared thoughtfully out of the window, and then, still deep in thought, rattled at the wires of the cage with a quill tooth-pick, and played a moment with the parrot. Then looking up at the window again, he said, 'That is Mr Lloyd, isn't it, coming back in a fly?'

'Yes, I think so. Is there anything else you would care to see here?'

'No, thank you,' Hewitt replied; 'I don't think there is.'

They went down to the smoking-room, and Sir James went away to speak to his secretary. When he returned, Hewitt said quietly, 'I think, Sir James—I *think* that I shall be able to give you your thief presently.'

'What! Have you a clue? Who do you think? I began to believe you were hopelessly stumped.'

'Well, yes. I have rather a good clue, although I can't tell you much about it just yet. But it is so good a clue that I should like to know now whether you are determined to prosecute when you have the criminal?'

'Why, bless me, of course,' Sir James replied, with surprise. 'It doesn't rest with me, you know—the property belongs to my friends. And even if *they* were disposed to let the thing slide, I shouldn't allow it I couldn't, after they had been robbed in my house.'

'Of course, of course. Then, if I can, I should like to send a message to Twyford by somebody perfectly trustworthy—not a servant. Could anybody go?'

'Well, there's Lloyd, although he's only just back from his journey. But if it's important he'll go.'

'It is important. The fact is, we must have a policeman or two here this evening, and I'd like Mr Lloyd to fetch them without telling anybody else.'

Sir James rang, and, in response to his message, Mr Lloyd appeared. While Sir James gave his secretary his instructions, Hewitt strolled to the door of the smoking-room, and intercepted the latter as he came out.

'I'm sorry to give you this trouble, Mr Lloyd,' he said; 'but I must stay here myself for a little, and somebody who can be trusted must go. Will you just bring back a police-constable with you?—or rather two—two would be better. That is all that is wanted. You won't let the servants know, will you? Of course there will be a female searcher at the Twyford police-station? Ah—of course. Well, you needn't bring her, you know. That sort of thing is done at the station.' And chatting thus confidentially, Martin Hewitt saw him off.

When Hewitt returned to the smoking-room, Sir James said suddenly, 'Why, bless my soul, Mr Hewitt, we haven't fed you! I'm awfully sorry. We came in rather late for lunch, you know, and this business has bothered me so, I clean forgot everything else. There's no dinner till seven, so you'd better let me give you something now. I'm really sorry. Come along.'

'Thank you, Sir James,' Hewitt replied; 'I won't take much. A few biscuits, perhaps, or something of that sort. And, by the bye, if you don't mind, I rather think I should like to take it alone. The fact is,

I want to go over this case thoroughly by myself. Can you put me in a room?'

'Any room you like. Where will you go? The dining-room's rather large, but there's my study, that's pretty snug, or——'

'Perhaps I can go into Mr Lloyd's room for half an hour or so—I don't think he'll mind, and it's pretty comfortable.'

'Certainly, if you'd like. I'll tell them to send you whatever they've got.'

'Thank you very much. Perhaps they'll also send me a lump of sugar and a walnut—it's—it's just a little fad of mine.'

'A—what? A lump of sugar and a walnut?' Sir James stopped for a moment, with his hand on the bell-rope. 'Oh, certainly, if you'd like it; certainly,' he added, and stared after this detective of curious tastes as he left the room.

When the vehicle, bringing back the secretary and the policemen, drew up on the drive, Martin Hewitt left the room on the first floor and proceeded downstairs. On the landing he met Sir James Norris and Mrs Cazenove, who stared with astonishment on perceiving that the detective carried in his hand the parrot-cage.

'I think our business is about brought to a head now,' Hewitt remarked, on the stairs. 'Here are the police-officers from Twyford.' The men were standing in the hall with Mr Lloyd, who, on catching sight of the cage in Hewitt's hand, paled suddenly.

'This is the person who will be charged, I think,' Hewitt pursued, addressing the officers, and indicating Lloyd with his finger.

'What, Lloyd?' gasped Sir James, aghast. 'No—not Lloyd—nonsense!'

'He doesn't seem to think it nonsense himself, does he?' Hewitt placidly observed. Lloyd had sunk on a chair, and, grey of face, was staring blindly at the man he had run against at the office door that morning. His lips moved in spasms, but there was no sound. The wilted flower fell from his button-hole to the floor, but he did not move.

'This is his accomplice,' Hewitt went on, placing the parrot and cage on the hall table, 'though I doubt whether there will be any use in charging *him*. Eh, Polly?'

The parrot put its head aside and chuckled. 'Hullo, Polly!' it quietly gurgled. 'Come along!'

Sir James Norris was hopelessly bewildered. 'Lloyd—Lloyd—' he said, under his breath, 'Lloyd—and that!'

'This was his little messenger, his useful Mercury,' Hewitt explained, tapping the cage complacently; 'in fact, the actual lifter. Hold him up.'

The last remark referred to the wretched Lloyd, who had fallen forward with something between a sob and a loud sigh. The policemen took him by the arms and propped him in his chair.

'System?' said Hewitt, with a shrug of the shoulders an hour or two after, in Sir James's study. 'I can't say I have a system. I call it nothing but common-sense and a sharp pair of eyes. Nobody using these could help taking the right road in this case. I began at the match, just as the Scotland Yard man did, but I had the advantage of taking a line through three cases. To begin with, it was plain that that match, being left there in daylight, in Mrs Cazenove's room, could not have been used to light the table-top, in the full glare of the window; therefore it had been used for some other purpose—*what* purpose I could not, at the moment, guess. Habitual thieves, you know, often have curious superstitions, and some will never take anything without leaving something behind—a pebble or a piece of coal, or something like that—in the premises they have been robbing. It seemed at first extremely likely that this was a case of that kind. The match had clearly been *brought in*—because when I asked for matches there were none in the stand—not even an empty box; and the room had not been disturbed. Also the match probably had not been struck there, nothing having been heard, although, of course, a mistake in this matter was just possible. This match then, it was fair to assume, had been lit somewhere else and blown out immediately—I remarked at the time that it was very little burnt. Plainly it could not have been treated thus for nothing, and the only possible object would have been to prevent it igniting accidentally. Following on this it became obvious that the match was used, for whatever purpose, not *as* a match, but merely as a convenient splinter of wood.

'So far so good. But on examining the match very closely I observed—as you can see for yourself—certain rather sharp indentations in the wood. They are very small, you see, and scarcely visible, except upon narrow inspection; but there they are, and their positions are regular. See—there are two on each side, each opposite the corresponding mark of the other pair. The match, in fact, would seem to have been gripped in some fairly sharp instrument, holding it at two points above, and two below—an instrument, as it may at once strike you, not unlike the beak of a bird.'

'Now, here was an idea. What living creature but a bird could possibly have entered Mrs Heath's window without a ladder—supposing no ladder to have been used—or could have got into Mrs Armitage's window without lifting the sash higher than the eight or ten inches it was already open? Plainly, nothing. Further, it is significant that only *one* article was stolen at a time, although others were about. A human being could have carried any reasonable number, but a bird could only take one at a time. But why should a bird carry a match in its beak? Certainly it must have been trained to do that for a purpose, and a little consideration made that purpose pretty clear. A noisy, chattering bird would probably betray itself at once. Therefore it must be trained to keep quiet both while going for and coming away with its plunder. What readier or more probably effectual way than by keeping its beak engaged with something to carry? Teaching it to carry without dropping would teach it also to keep quiet while carrying. The one thing would cover the other.

'I thought at once, of course, of a jackdaw or a magpie—these birds' thievish reputations made the guess natural. But the marks on the match were much too wide apart to have been made by the beak of either. I conjectured, therefore, that it must be a raven. So that when we arrived near the coach-house I seized the opportunity of a little chat with your groom on the subject of dogs and pets in general, and ascertained that there was no tame raven in the place. I also, incidentally, by getting a light from the coach-house box of matches, ascertained that the match found was of the sort generally used about the establishment—the large, thick, red-topped English match. But I further found that Mr Lloyd had a parrot which was a most intelligent pet, and had been trained into comparative quietness—for a parrot. Also, I learnt that more than once the groom had met Mr Lloyd carrying his parrot under his coat—it having, as its owner explained, learnt the trick of opening its cage-door, and escaping.

'I said nothing, of course, to you of all this, because I had as yet nothing but a train of argument and no results. I got to Lloyd's room as soon as possible. My chief object in going there was achieved when I played with the parrot, and induced it to bite a quill tooth-pick.

'When you left me in the smoking-room I compared the quill and the match very carefully, and found that the marks corresponded exactly. After this I felt very little doubt indeed. The fact of Lloyd having met the ladies walking before dark on the day of the first robbery proved nothing, because, since it was clear that the match had *not* been used to procure a light, the robbery might as easily have taken place in daylight as not—must have so taken place, in fact, if my conjectures were right. That they were right I felt no doubt. There could be no other explanation.

'When Mrs Heath left her window open and her door shut, any-body climbing upon the open sash of Lloyd's high window could have put the bird upon the sill above. The match, placed in the bird's beak for the purpose I have indicated, and struck first, in case by accident it should ignite in rubbing against something and startle the bird—this match would, of course, be dropped just where the object to be removed was taken up; as you know, in every case, the match was found almost upon the spot where the missing article had been left—scarcely a likely triple coincidence, had the match been used by a human thief. This would have been done as soon after the ladies had left as possible, and there would then have been plenty of time for Lloyd to hurry out and meet them before dark—especially plenty of time to meet them *coming back*, as they must have been, since they were carrying their ferns. The match was an article well chosen for its purpose, as being a not altogether unlikely thing to find on a dressing-table, and, if noticed, likely to lead to the wrong conclusions adopted by the official detective.

'In Mrs Armitage's case, the taking of an inferior brooch and the leaving of a more valuable ring pointed clearly either to the operator being a fool or unable to distinguish values, and certainly, from other indications, the thief seemed no fool. The door was locked, and the gasfitter, so to speak, on guard, and the window was only eight or ten inches open and propped with a brush. A human thief entering the window would have disturbed this arrangement, and would scarcely risk discovery by attempting to replace it, especially a thief in so great a hurry as to snatch the brooch up without unfastening the pin. The bird could pass through the opening as it was, and *would have* to tear the pin-cushion to pull the brooch off—probably holding the cushion down with its claw the while.

'Now, in yesterday's case we had an alteration of conditions. The window was shut and fastened, but the door was open—but only left for a few minutes, during which time no sound was heard either of coming or going. Was it not possible, then, that the thief was *already* in the room, in hiding, while Mrs Cazenove was there, and seized its first opportunity on her temporary absence? The room is full of draperies, hangings, and what-not, allowing of plenty of concealment for a bird, and a bird could leave the place noiselessly and quickly. That the whole scheme was strange mattered not at all. Robberies presenting such unaccountable features must have been effected by strange means of one sort or another. There was no improbability—consider how many hundreds of examples of infinitely higher degrees of bird-training are exhibited in the London streets every week for coppers.

'So that, on the whole, I felt pretty sure of my ground. But before taking any definite steps, I resolved to see if Polly could not be persuaded to exhibit his accomplishments to an indulgent stranger. For that purpose I contrived to send Lloyd away again and have a quiet hour alone with his bird. A piece of sugar, as everybody knows, is a good parrot bribe; but a walnut, split in half, is a better—especially if the bird be used to it; so I got you to furnish me with both. Polly was shy at first, but I generally get along very well with pets, and a little perseverance soon led to a complete private performance for my benefit. Polly would take the match, mute as wax, jump on the table, pick up the brightest thing he could see, in a great hurry, leave the match behind, and scuttle away round the room; but at first wouldn't give up the plunder to *me*. It was enough. I also took the liberty, as you know, of a general look round, and discovered that little collection of Brummagem rings and trinkets that you have just seen—used in Polly's education, no doubt. When we sent Lloyd away it struck me that he might as well be usefully employed as not, so I got him to fetch the police—deluding him a little, I fear, by talking about the servants and a female searcher. There will be no trouble about evidence—he'll confess; of that I'm sure. I know the sort of man. But I doubt if you'll get Mrs Cazenove's brooch back. You see, he has been to London today, and by this the swag is probably broken up.'

Sir James listened to Hewitt's explanation with many expressions of assent and some of surprise. When it was over he smoked a few whiffs and then said: 'But Mrs Armitage's brooch was pawned; and by a woman.'

'Exactly. I expect our friend Lloyd was rather disgusted at his small luck probably gave the brooch to some female connection in London, and she realized on it. Such persons don't always trouble to give a correct address.'

The two smoked in silence for a few minutes, and then Hewitt continued: 'I don't expect our friend has had an easy job altogether with that bird. His successes at most have only been three, and I suspect he had many failures and not a few anxious moments that we know nothing of. I should judge as much merely from what the groom told me of frequently meeting Lloyd with his parrot. But the plan was not a bad one—not at all. Even if the bird had been caught in the act, it would only have been "That mischievous parrot!" you see. And his master would only have been looking for him.'

3

FERGUS HUME

The Green-Stone God and the Stockbroker

As a rule, the average detective gets twice the credit he deserves. I am not talking of the novelist's miracle-monger, but of the flesh and blood reality who is liable to err, and who frequently proves such liability. You can take it as certain that a detective who sets down a clean run and no hitch as entirely due to his astucity, is young in years, and still younger in experience. Older men, who have been bamboozled a hundred times by the craft of criminality, recognize the influence of Chance to make or mar. There you have it! Nine times out of ten, Chance does more in clinching a case than all the dexterity and mother-wit of the man in charge. The exception must be engineered by an infallible apostle. Such a one is unknown to me—out of print.

This opinion, based rather on collective experience than on any one episode, can be substantiated by several incontrovertible facts. In this instance, one will suffice. Therefore, I take the Brixton case to illustrate Chance as a factor in human affairs. Had it not been for that Maori fetish—but such rather ends than begins the story, therefore it were wise to dismiss it for the moment. Yet that piece of green-stone hanged—a person mentioned hereafter.

When Mr and Mrs Paul Vincent set up housekeeping at Ulster Lodge they were regarded as decided acquisitions to Brixton society. She, pretty and musical; he, smart in looks, moderately well off, and an excellent tennis-player. Their progenitors, his father and her mother (both since deceased), had lived a life of undoubted middle-class respectability. The halo thereof still environed their children,

42

who were, in consequence of such inherited grace and their own individualisms, much sought after by genteel Brixtonians. Moreover, this popular couple were devoted to each other, and even after three years of marriage they posed still as lovers. This was as it should be, and by admiring friends and relations the Vincents were regarded as paragons of matrimonial perfection. Vincent was a stockbroker; therefore he passed most of his time in the City.

Judge, then, of the commotion, when pretty Mrs Vincent was discovered in the study, stabbed to the heart. So aimless a crime were scarce imaginable. She had many friends, no known enemies, yet she came to this tragic end. Closer examination revealed that the escritoire had been broken into, and Mr Vincent declared himself the poorer by two hundred pounds. Primarily, therefore, robbery was the sole object, but, by reason of Mrs Vincent's interference, the thief had been converted into a murderer.

So excellently had the assassin chosen his time, that such choice argued a close acquaintance with the domestic economy of Ulster Lodge. The husband was detained in town till midnight; the servants (cook and housemaid), on leave to attend wedding festivities, were absent till eleven o'clock. Mrs Vincent therefore was absolutely alone in the house for six hours, during which period the crime had been committed. The servants discovered the body of their unfortunate mistress, and raised the alarm at once. Later on Vincent arrived, to find his wife dead, his house in possession of the police, and the two servants in hysterics. For that night nothing could be done, but at dawn a move was made towards elucidating the mystery. At this point I come into the story.

Instructed at nine o'clock to take charge of the case, by ten I was on the spot noting details and collecting evidence. Beyond removal of the body nothing had been disturbed, and the study was in precisely the same condition as when the crime was discovered. I examined carefully the apartment, and afterwards interrogated the cook, the housemaid, and, lastly, the master of the house. The result gave me slight hope of securing the assassin.

The room (a fair-sized one, looking out on to a lawn between house and road) was furnished in cheap bachelor fashion. An old-fashioned desk placed at right angles to the window, a round table reaching nigh the sill, two arm-chairs, three of the ordinary cane-seated kind, and on the mantelpiece an arrangement of pipes, pistols, boxing-gloves, and foils. One of these latter was missing.

A single glimpse showed how terrible a struggle had taken place before the murderer had overpowered his victim. The tablecloth lay disorderly on the floor, two of the lighter chairs were overturned, and the desk, with several drawers open, was hacked about considerably. No key was in the door-lock which faced the escritoire, and the window-snick was fastened securely.

Further search resulted in the following discoveries:—

1. A hatchet used for chopping wood (found near the desk).
2. A foil with the button broken off (lying under the table).
3. A green-stone idol (edged under the fender).

The cook (defiantly courageous by reason of brandy) declared that she had left the house at four o'clock on the previous day, and had returned close on eleven. The back door (to her surprise) was open. With the housemaid she went to inform her mistress of this fact, and found the body lying midway between door and fireplace. At once she called in the police. Her master and mistress were a most attached couple, and (so far as she knew) they had no enemies.

Similar evidence was obtained from the housemaid, with the additional information that the hatchet belonged to the wood-shed. The other rooms were undisturbed.

Poor young Vincent was so broken down by the tragedy that he could hardly answer my questions with calmness. Sympathizing with his natural grief, I interrogated him as delicately as was possible, and I am bound to admit that he replied with remarkable promptitude and clearness.

'What do you know of this unhappy affair?' I asked, when we were alone in the drawing-room. He refused to stay in the study, as was surely natural under the circumstances.

'Absolutely nothing,' he replied. 'I went to the City yesterday at ten in the morning, and, as I had business to do, I wired my wife I would not return till midnight. She was full of health and spirits when I last saw her, but now——' Incapable of further speech he made a gesture of despair. Then, after a pause, he added, 'Have you any theory on the subject?'

'Judging from the wrecked condition of the desk I should say robbery——'

'Robbery?' he interrupted, changing colour. 'Yes, that was the motive. I had two hundred pounds locked up in the desk.'

'In gold or notes?'

'The latter. Four fifties. Bank of England.'

'You are sure they are missing?'

'Yes. The drawer in which they were placed is smashed to pieces.'

'Did any one know you had placed two hundred pounds therein?'

'No! Save my wife, and yet—ah!' he said, breaking off abruptly, 'that is impossible.'

'What is impossible?'

'I will tell you when I hear your theory.'

'You got that notion out of novels of the shilling sort,' I answered dryly; 'every detective doesn't theorize on the instant. I haven't any particular theory that I know of. Whosoever committed this crime must have known your wife was alone in the house, and that there was two hundred pounds locked up in that desk. Did you mention these two facts to any one?'

Vincent pulled his moustache in some embarrassment. I guessed by the action that he had been indiscreet.

'I don't wish to get an innocent person into trouble,' he said at length, 'but I did mention it—to a man called Roy.'

'For what reason?'

'It is a bit of a story. I lost two hundred to a friend at cards, and drew four fifties to pay him. He went out of town, so I locked up the money in my desk for safety. Last night Roy came to me at the club, much agitated, and asked me to loan him a hundred. Said it meant ruin else. I offered him a cheque, but he wanted cash. I then told him I had left two hundred at home, so, at the moment, I could not lay my hand on it. He asked if he could not go to Brixton for it, but I said the house was empty, and——'

'But it wasn't empty,' I interrupted.

'I believed it would be! I knew the servants were going to that wedding, and I thought my wife, instead of spending a lonely evening, would call on some friend.'

'Well, and after you told Roy that the house was empty?'

'He went away, looking awfully cut up, and swore he must have the money at any price. But it is quite impossible he could have anything to do with this.'

'I don't know. You told him where the money was, and that the house was unprotected, as you thought. What was more probable than that he should have come down with the intention of stealing the money? If so, what follows? Entering by the back door, he takes the hatchet from the wood-shed to open the desk. Your wife, hearing a noise, discovers him in the study. In a state of frenzy, he snatches a foil from the mantelpiece and kills her, then decamps with the money. There is your theory, and a mighty bad one—for Roy.'

'You don't intend to arrest him?' asked Vincent quickly.

'Not on insufficient evidence! If he committed the crime and stole the money it is certain that, sooner or later, he will change the notes. Now, if I had the numbers——'

'Here are the numbers,' said Vincent, producing his pocket-book. 'I always take the numbers of such large notes. But surely,' he added, as I copied them down—'surely you don't think Roy guilty?'

'I don't know. I should like to know his movements on that night.'

'I cannot tell you. He saw me at the Chestnut Club about seven o'clock, and left immediately afterwards. I kept my business appointment, went to the Alhambra, and then returned home.'

'Give me Roy's address, and describe his personal appearance.'

'He is a medical student, and lodges at No. —, Gower Street. Tall, fair-haired—a good-looking young fellow.'

'And his dress last night?'

'He wore evening dress, concealed by a fawn-coloured overcoat.'

I duly noted these particulars, and I was about to take my leave, when I recollected the green-stone idol. It was so strange an object to find in prosaic Brixton that I could not help thinking it must have come there by accident.

'By the way, Mr Vincent,' said I, producing the monstrosity, 'is this green-stone god your property?'

'I never saw it before,' replied he, taking it in his hand. 'Is it—ah!' he added, dropping the idol, 'there is blood on it!'

''Tis the blood of your wife, sir! If it does not belong to you, it does to the murderer. From the position in which this was found I fancy it slipped out of his breast-pocket as he stood over his victim. As you see, it is stained with blood. He must have lost his presence of mind, else he would not have left behind so damning a piece of evidence. This idol, sir, will hang the assassin of Mrs Vincent!'

'I hope so; but, unless you are sure of Roy, do not mar his life by accusing him of this crime.'

'I certainly should not arrest him without sufficient proof,' I answered promptly, and so took my departure.

Vincent showed up very well in this preliminary conversation. Much as he desired to punish the criminal, yet he was unwilling to subject Roy to possibly unfounded suspicions. Had I not forced the club episode out of him I doubt whether he would have told it. As it was, the information gave me the necessary clue. Roy alone knew that the notes were in the escritoire, and imagined (owing to the mistake of Vincent) that the house was empty. Determined to have the money at any price (his own words), he intended but robbery, till the unexpected appearance of Mrs Vincent merged the lesser in the greater crime.

My first step was to advise the Bank that four fifty-pound notes, numbered so and so, were stolen, and that the thief or his deputy would probably change them within a reasonable period. I did not say a word about the crime, and kept all special details out of the newspapers; for as the murderer would probably read up the reports, so as to shape his course by the action of the police, I judged it wiser that he should know as little as possible. Those minute press notices do more harm than good. They gratify the morbid appetite of the public, and put the criminal on his guard. Thereby the police work in the dark, but he—thanks to the posting up of special reporters—knows the doings of the law, and baffles it accordingly.

The green-stone idol worried me considerably. I wanted to know how it had got into the study of Ulster Lodge. When I knew that, I could nail my man. But there was considerable difficulty to overcome before such knowledge was available. Now a curiosity of this kind is not a common object in this country. A man who owns one must have come from New Zealand, or have obtained it from a New Zealand friend. He could not have picked it up in London. If he did, he would not carry it constantly about with him. It was therefore my idea that the murderer had received the idol from a friend on the day of the crime. That friend, to possess such an idol, must have been in communication with New Zealand. The chain of thought is somewhat complicated, but it began with curiosity about the idol, and ended in my looking up the list of steamers going to the Antipodes. Then I carried out a little design which need not be mentioned at this moment. In due time it will fit in with the hanging of Mrs Vincent's assassin. Meanwhile, I followed up the clue of the bank-notes, and left the green-stone idol to evolve its own destiny. Thus I had two strings to my bow.

The crime was committed on the twentieth of June, and on the twenty-third two fifty-pound notes, with numbers corresponding to those stolen, were paid into the Bank of England. I was astonished at the little care exercised by the criminal in concealing his crime, but still more so when I learned that the money had been banked by a very respectable solicitor. Furnished with the address, I called on this gentleman. Mr Maudsley received me politely, and he had no hesitation in telling me how the notes had come into his possession. I did not state my primary reason for the inquiry.

'I hope there is no trouble about these notes,' said he, when I explained my errand. 'I have had sufficient already.'

'Indeed, Mr Maudsley, and in what way?'

For answer he touched the bell, and when it was answered, 'Ask Mr Ford to step this way,' he said. Then, turning to me, 'I must reveal what I had hoped to keep secret, but I trust the revelation will remain with yourself.'

'That is as I may decide after hearing it. I am a detective, Mr Maudsley, and, you may be sure, I do not make these inquiries out of idle curiosity.'

Before he could reply, a slender, weak-looking young man, nervously excited, entered the room. This was Mr Ford, and he looked from me to Maudsley with some apprehension.

'This gentleman,' said his employer, not unkindly, 'comes from Scotland Yard about the money you paid me two days ago.'

'It is all right, I hope?' stammered Ford, turning red and pale and red again.

'Where did you get the money?' I asked, parrying this question.

'From my sister.'

I started when I heard this answer, and with good reason. My inquiries about Roy had revealed that he was in love with a hospital nurse whose name was Clara Ford. Without doubt she had obtained the notes from Roy, after he had stolen them from Ulster Lodge. But why the necessity of the robbery?

'Why did you get a hundred pounds from your sister?' I asked Ford.

He did not answer, but looked appealingly at Maudsley. That gentleman interposed.

'We must make a clean breast of it, Ford,' he said, with a sigh; 'if you have committed a second crime to conceal the first, I cannot help you. This time matters are not at my discretion.'

'I have committed no crime,' said Ford desperately, turning to me. 'Sir, I may as well admit that I embezzled one hundred pounds from Mr Maudsley to pay a gambling debt. He kindly and most generously consented to overlook the delinquency if I replaced the money. Not having it myself I asked my sister. She, a poor hospital nurse, had not the amount. Yet, as non-payment meant ruin to me, she asked a Mr Julian Roy to help her. He at once agreed to do so, and gave her two fifty-pound notes. She handed them to me, and I gave them to Mr Maudsley, who paid them into the bank.'

This, then, was the reason of Roy's remark. He did not refer to his own ruin, but to that of Ford. To save this unhappy man, and for love of the sister, he had committed the crime. I did not need to see Clara Ford, but at once made up my mind to arrest Roy. The case was perfectly clear, and I was fully justified in taking this course. Meanwhile I made Maudsley and his clerk promise silence, as I did not wish Roy to be put on his guard by Miss Ford, through her brother.

'Gentlemen,' I said, after a few moments' pause, 'I cannot at present explain my reasons for asking these questions, as it would take too long, and I have no time to lose. Keep silent about this interview till tomorrow, and by that time you shall know all.'

'Has Ford got into fresh trouble?' asked Maudsley anxiously.

'No, but some one else has.'

'My sister,' began Ford faintly, when I interrupted him at once.

'Your sister is all right, Mr Ford. Pray trust in my discretion; no harm shall come to her or to you, if I can help it—but, above all, be silent.'

This they readily promised, and I returned to Scotland Yard, quite satisfied that Roy would get no warning. The evidence was so clear that I could not doubt the guilt of Roy. Else how had he come in possession of the notes? Already there was sufficient proof to hang him, yet I hoped to clinch the certainty by proving his ownership of the green-stone idol. It did not belong to Vincent, or to his dead wife, yet some one must have brought it into the study. Why not Roy, who, to all appearances, had committed the crime, the more so as the image was splashed with the victim's blood? There was no difficulty in obtaining a warrant, and with this I went off to Gower Street.

Roy loudly protested his innocence. He denied all knowledge of the crime and of the idol. I expected the denial, but I was astonished at the defence he put forth. It was very ingenious, but so manifestly absurd that it did not shake my belief in his guilt. I let him talk himself out—which perhaps was wrong—but he would not be silent, and then I took him off in a cab.

'I swear I did not commit the crime,' he said passionately; 'no one was more astonished than I at the news of Mrs Vincent's death.'

'Yet you were at Ulster Lodge on the night in question?'

'I admit it,' he replied frankly; 'were I guilty I would not do so. But I was there at the request of Vincent.'

'I must remind you that all you say now will be used in evidence against you.'

'I don't care! I must defend myself. I asked Vincent for a hundred pounds, and——'

'Of course you did, to give to Miss Ford.'

'How do you know that?' he asked sharply.

'From her brother, through Maudsley. He paid the notes supplied by you into the bank. If you wanted to conceal your crime you should not have been so reckless.'

'I have committed no crime,' retorted Roy fiercely.

'I obtained the money from Vincent, at the request of Miss Ford, to save her brother from being convicted for embezzlement.'

'Vincent denies that he gave you the money!'

'Then he lies. I asked him at the Chestnut Club for one hundred pounds. He had not that much on him, but said that two hundred were in his desk at home. As it was imperative that I should have the money on the night, I asked him to let me go down for it.'

'And he refused!'

'He did not. He consented, and gave me a note to Mrs Vincent, instructing her to hand me over a hundred pounds. I went to Brixton, got the money in two fifties, and gave them to Miss Ford. When I left Ulster Lodge, between eight and nine, Mrs Vincent was in perfect health, and quite happy.'

'An ingenious defence,' said I doubtfully, 'but Vincent absolutely denies that he gave you the money.'

Roy stared hard at me to see if I were joking. Evidently the attitude of Vincent puzzled him greatly.

'That is ridiculous,' said he quietly; 'he wrote a note to his wife instructing her to hand me the money.'

'Where is that note?'

'I gave it to Mrs Vincent.'

'It cannot be found,' I answered; 'if such a note were in her possession it would now be in mine.'

'Don't you believe me?'

'How can I against the evidence of those notes and the denial of Vincent?'

'But he surely does not deny that he gave me the money?'

'He does.'

'He must be mad,' said Roy, in dismay; 'one of my best friends, and to tell so great a falsehood. Why, if——'

'You had better be silent,' I said, weary of this foolish talk; 'if what you say is true, Vincent will exonerate you from complicity in the crime. If things occurred as you say, there is no sense in his denial.'

This latter remark was made to stop the torrent of his speech. It was not my business to listen to incriminating declarations, or to ingenious defences. All that sort of thing is for judge and jury; therefore I ended the conversation as above, and marched off my prisoner. Whether the birds of the air carry news I do not know, but they must have been busy on this occasion, for next morning every newspaper in London was congratulating me on my clever capture of the supposed murderer. Some detectives would have been gratified by this public laudation—I was not. Roy's passionate protestations of innocence made me feel uneasy, and I doubted whether, after all, I had the right man under lock and key. Yet the evidence was strong against him. He admitted having been with Mrs Vincent on the fatal night, he admitted possession of two fifty-pound notes. His only defence was the letter of the stockbroker, and this was missing—if, indeed, it had ever been written.

Vincent was terribly upset by the arrest of Roy. He liked the young man and he had believed in his innocence so far as was possible. But in the face of such strong evidence, he was forced to believe him guilty: yet he blamed himself severely that he had not lent the money, and so averted the catastrophe.

'I had no idea that the matter was of such moment,' he said to me, 'else I would have gone down to Brixton myself and have given him the money. Then his frenzy would have spared my wife, and himself a death on the scaffold.'

'What do you think of his defence?'

'It is wholly untrue. I did not write a note, not did I tell him to go to Brixton. Why should I, when I fully believed no one was in the house?'

'It was a pity you did not go home, Mr Vincent, instead of to the Alhambra.'

'It was a mistake,' he assented, 'but I had no idea Roy would attempt the robbery. Besides, I was under engagement to go to the theatre with my friend Dr Monson.'

'Do you think that idol belongs to Roy?'

'I can't say, I never saw it in his possession. Why?'

'Because I firmly believe that if Roy had not the idol in his pocket on that fatal night he is innocent. Oh, you look astonished, but the man who murdered your wife owns that idol.'

The morning after this conversation a lady called at Scotland Yard, and asked to see me concerning the Brixton case. Fortunately, I was then in the neighbourhood, and, guessing who she was, I afforded her the interview she sought. When all left the room she raised her veil, and I saw before me a noble-looking woman, somewhat resembling Mr Maudsley's clerk. Yet, by some contradiction of nature, her face was the more virile of the two.

'You are Miss Ford?' I said, guessing her identity.

'I am Clara Ford,' she answered quietly. 'I have come to see you about Mr Roy.'

'I am afraid nothing can be done to save him.'

'Something must be done,' she said passionately. 'We are engaged to be married, and all a woman can do to save her lover I will do. Do you believe him to be guilty?'

'In the face of such evidence, Miss Ford——'

'I don't care what evidence is against him,' she retorted; 'he is as innocent of the crime as I am. Do you think that a man fresh from the committal of a crime would place the money won by that crime in the hands of the woman he professes to love? I tell you he is innocent.'

'Mr Vincent doesn't think so.'

'Mr Vincent!' said Miss Ford, with scornful emphasis.

'Oh, yes! I quite believe *he* would think Julian guilty.'

'Surely not if it were possible to think otherwise! He is, or rather was, a staunch friend to Mr Roy.'

'So staunch that he tried to break off the match between us. Listen to me, sir. I have told no one before, but I tell you now. Mr Vincent is a villain. He pretended to be the friend of Julian, and yet he dared to make proposals to me—dishonourable proposals, for which I could have struck him. He, a married man, a pretended friend, wished me to leave Julian and fly with him.'

'Surely you are mistaken, Miss Ford. Mr Vincent was most devoted to his wife.'

'He did not care at all for his wife,' she replied steadily. 'He was in love with me. To save Julian annoyance I did not tell him of the insults offered to me by Mr Vincent. Now that Julian is in trouble by an unfortunate mistake, Mr Vincent is delighted.'

'It is impossible. I assure you Vincent is very sorry to——'

'You do not believe me,' she said, interrupting. 'Very well, I shall give you proof of the truth. Come to my brother's rooms in Bloomsbury. I shall send for Mr Vincent, and if you are concealed you shall hear from his own lips how glad he is that my lover and his wife are removed from the path of his dishonourable passion.'

'I will come, Miss Ford, but I think you are mistaken in Vincent.'

'You shall see,' she replied coldly. Then, with a sudden change of tone, 'Is there no way of saving Julian? I am sure that he is innocent. Appearances are against him, but it was not he who committed the crime. Is there no way—no way?'

Moved by her earnest appeal, I produced the green-stone idol, and told her all I had done in connection with it. She listened eagerly, and readily grasped at the hope thus held out to her of saving Roy. When in possession of all the facts she considered in silence for some two minutes. At the end of that time she drew down her veil and prepared to take her departure.

'Come to my brother's rooms in Alfred Place, near Tottenham Court Road,' said she, holding out her hand. 'I promise you that there you shall see Mr Vincent in his true character. Good-bye till Monday at three o'clock.'

From the colour in her face and the bright light in her eye, I guessed that she had some scheme in her head for the saving of Roy. I think myself clever, but after that interview at Alfred Place I declare I am but a fool compared to this woman. She put two and two together, ferreted out unguessed-of evidence, and finally produced the most wonderful result. When she left me at this moment the green-stone idol was in her pocket. With that she hoped to prove the innocence of her lover and the guilt of another person. It was the cleverest thing I ever saw in my life.

The inquest on the body of Mrs Vincent resulted in a verdict of wilful murder against some person or persons unknown. Then she was buried, and all London waited for the trail of Roy. He was brought up charged with the crime, reserved his defence, and in due course he was committed for trial. Meantime I called on Miss Ford at the appointed time, and found her alone.

'Mr Vincent will be here shortly,' she said calmly. 'I see Julian is committed for trial.'

'And he has reserved his defence.'

'I shall defend him,' said she, with a strange look in her face; 'I am not afraid for him now. He saved my unhappy brother. I shall save him.'

'Have you discovered anything?'

'I have discovered a good deal. Hush! That is Mr Vincent,' she added, as a cab drew up to the door. 'Hide yourself behind this curtain, and do not appear until I give you the signal.'

Wondering what she was about to do, I concealed myself as directed. The next moment Vincent was in the room, and then ensued one of the strangest of scenes. She received him coldly, and motioned him to a seat. Vincent was nervous, but she might have been of stone, so little emotion did she display.

'I have sent for you, Mr Vincent,' she said, 'to ask for your help in releasing Julian.'

'How can I help you?' he answered, in amazement—'willingly would I do so, but it is out of my power.'

'I don't think it is!'

'I assure you, Clara,' he began eagerly, when she cut him short.

'Yes, call me Clara! Say that you love me! Lie, like all men, and yet refuse to do what I wish.'

'I am not going to help Julian to marry you,' declared he sullenly. 'You know that I love you—I love you dearly, I wish to marry you——'

'Is not that declaration rather soon after the death of your wife?'

'My wife is gone, poor soul, let her rest.'

'Yet you loved her?'

'I never loved her,' he said, rising to his feet. 'I love you! From the first moment I saw you I loved you. My wife is dead! Julian Roy is in prison on a charge of murdering her. With these obstacles removed there is no reason why we should not marry.'

'If I marry you,' she said slowly, 'will you help Julian to refute this charge?'

'I cannot! The evidence is too strong against him!'

'You know that he is innocent, Mr Vincent.'

'I do not! I believe that he murdered my wife.'

'You believe that he murdered your wife,' she reiterated, coming a step nearer and holding out the green-stone idol—'do you believe that he dropped this in the study when his hand struck the fatal blow?'

'I don't know!' he said, coolly glancing at the idol; 'I never saw it before.'

'Think again, Mr Vincent—think again. Who was it that went to the Alhambra at eight o'clock with Dr Monson, and met there the captain of a New Zealand steamer with whom he was acquainted?'

'It was I,' said Vincent defiantly; 'and what of that?'

'This!' she said in a loud voice. 'This captain gave you the green-stone idol at the Alhambra, and you placed it in your breast-pocket. Shortly afterwards you followed to Brixton the man whose death you had plotted. You repaired to your house, killed your unhappy wife, who received you in all innocence, took the balance of the money, hacked the desk, and then dropped by accident this idol which convicts you of the crime.'

During this speech she advanced step by step towards the wretched man, who, pale and anguished, retreated before her fury. He came right to my hiding-place, and almost fell into my arms. I had heard enough to convince me of his guilt, and the next moment I was struggling with him.

'It is a lie! a lie!' he said hoarsely, trying to escape.

'It is true!' said I, pinning him down. 'From my soul I believe you to be guilty.'

During the fight his pocket-book fell on the floor, and the papers therein were scattered. Miss Ford picked up one spotted with blood.

'The proof!' she said, holding it before us. 'The proof that Julian spoke the truth. There is the letter written by you which authorized your unhappy wife to give him one hundred pounds.'

Vincent saw that all was against him, and gave in without further struggles, like the craven he was.

'Fate is too strong for me,' he said, when I snapped the handcuffs on his wrists. 'I admit the crime. It was for love of you that I did it. I hated my wife, who was a drag on me, and I hated Roy, who loved you. In one sweep I thought to rid myself of both. His application for that money put the chance into my hand. I went to Brixton, I found that my wife had given the money as directed, and then I killed her with the foil snatched from the wall. I smashed the desk and overturned the chair, to favour the idea of the robbery, and then I left the house. Driving to a higher station than Brixton, I caught a train and was speedily back at the Alhambra. Monson never suspected my absence, thinking I was in a different corner of the house. I had thus an alibi ready. Had it not been for that letter, which I was fool enough to keep, and that infernal idol that dropped out of my pocket, I should have hanged Roy and married you. As it turns out, the idol has betrayed me. And now, sir,' he added, turning to me, 'you had better take me to gaol.'

I did so there and then. After the legal formalities were gone through Julian Roy was released, and ultimately married Miss Ford. Vincent was hanged, as he well deserved to be, for so cowardly a crime. My reward was the green-stone god, which I keep as a memento of a very curious case. Some weeks later Miss Ford told me the way in which she had laid the trap.

'When you revealed your suspicions about the idol,' she said, 'I was convinced that Vincent had something to do with the crime. You mentioned Dr Monson as having been with him at the Alhambra. He is one of the doctors at the hospital in which I am employed. I asked him about the idol, and showed it to him. He remembered it being given to Vincent by the captain of the *Kaitangata*. The curious look of the thing had impressed itself on his memory. On hearing this I went to the docks and I saw the captain. He recognized the idol, and remembered giving it to Vincent. From what you told me I guessed the way in which the plot had been carried out, so I spoke to Vincent as you heard. Most of it was guesswork, and only when I saw that letter was I absolutely sure of his guilt. It was due to the green-stone god.'

So I think, but to Chance also. But for the accident of the idol dropping out of Vincent's pocket, Roy would have been hanged for a crime of which he was innocent. Therefore do I say that in nine cases out of ten Chance does more to clinch a case than all the dexterity of the man in charge.

4

R. AUSTIN FREEMAN

The Blue Sequin

Thorndyke stood looking up and down the platform with anxiety that increased as the time drew near for the departure of the train.

'This is very unfortunate,' he said, reluctantly stepping into an empty smoking compartment as the guard executed a flourish with his green flag. 'I am afraid we have missed our friend.' He closed the door, and, as the train began to move, thrust his head out of the window.

'Now I wonder if that will be he,' he continued. 'If so, he has caught the train by the skin of his teeth, and is now in one of the rear compartments.'

The subject of Thorndyke's speculations was Mr Edward Stopford, of the firm of Stopford and Myers, of Portugal Street, solicitors, and his connection with us at present arose out of a telegram that had reached our chambers on the preceding evening. It was reply-paid, and ran thus:

Can you come here tomorrow to direct defence? Important case. All costs undertaken by us.—STOPFORD AND MYERS.

Thorndyke's reply had been in the affirmative, and early on this present morning a further telegram—evidently posted overnight—had been delivered:

Shall leave for Woldhurst by 8.25 from Charing Cross. Will call for you if possible.—EDWARD STOPFORD.

He had not called, however, and, since he was unknown personally to us both, we could not judge whether or not he had been among the passengers on the platform.

'It is most unfortunate,' Thorndyke repeated, 'for it deprives us of that preliminary consideration of the case which is so invaluable.' He filled his pipe thoughtfully, and, having made a fruitless inspection of the platform at London Bridge, took up the paper that he had bought at the bookstall, and began to turn over the leaves running his eye quickly down the columns, unmindful of the journalistic baits in paragraph or article.

'It is a great disadvantage,' he observed, while still glancing through the paper, 'to come plump into an inquiry without preparation—to be confronted with the details before one has a chance of considering the case in general terms. For instance——'

He paused, leaving the sentence unfinished, and as I looked up enquiringly I saw that he had turned over another page, and was now reading attentively.

'This looks like our case, Jervis,' he said presently, handing me the paper and indicating a paragraph at the top of the page. It was quite brief, and was headed 'Terrible Murder in Kent', the account being as follows:

'A shocking crime was discovered yesterday morning at the little town of Woldhurst, which lies on the branch line from Halbury Junction. The discovery was made by a porter who was inspecting the carriages of the train which had just come in. On opening the door of a first-class compartment, he was horrified to find the body of a fashionably dressed woman stretched upon the floor. Medical aid was immediately summoned, and on the arrival of the divisional surgeon, Dr Morton, it was ascertained that the woman had not been dead more than a few minutes.

'The state of the corpse leaves no doubt that a murder of a most brutal kind has been perpetrated, the cause of death being a penetrating wound of the head, inflicted with some pointed implement, which must have been used with terrible violence, since it has perforated the skull and entered the brain. That robbery was not the motive of the crime is made clear by the fact that an expensively fitted dressing-bag was found on the rack, and that the dead woman's jewellery, including several valuable diamond rings, was untouched. It is rumoured that an arrest has been made by the local police.'

'A gruesome affair,' I remarked, as I handed back the paper, 'but the report does not give us much information.'

'It does not,' Thorndyke agreed, 'and yet it gives us something to consider. Here is a perforating wound of the skull, inflicted with some pointed implement—that is, assuming that it is not a bullet wound. Now, what kind of implement would be capable of inflicting such an injury? How would such an implement be used in the confined space of a railway-carriage, and what sort of person would be in possession of such an implement? These are preliminary questions that are worth considering, and I commend them to you, together with the further problems of the possible motive—excluding robbery—and any circumstances other than murder which might account for the injury.'

'The choice of suitable implements is not very great,' I observed.

'It is very limited, and most of them, such as a plasterer's pick or a geological hammer, are associated with certain definite occupations. You have a notebook?'

I had, and, accepting the hint, I produced it and pursued my further reflections in silence, while my companion, with his notebook also on his knee, gazed steadily out of the window. And thus he remained, wrapped in thought, jotting down an entry now and again in his book, until the train slowed down at Halbury Junction, where we had to change on to a branch line.

As we stepped out, I noticed a well-dressed man hurrying up the platform from the rear and eagerly scanning the faces of the few passengers who had alighted. Soon he espied us, and, approaching quickly, asked, as he looked from one of us to the other:

'Dr Thorndyke?'

'Yes,' replied my colleague, adding: 'And you, I presume, are Mr Edward Stopford?'

The solicitor bowed. 'This is a dreadful affair,' he said, in an agitated manner. 'I see you have the paper. A most shocking affair. I am immensely relieved to find you here. Nearly missed the train, and feared I should miss you.'

'There appears to have been an arrest,' Thorndyke began.

'Yes—my brother. Terrible business. Let us walk up the platform; our train won't start for a quarter of an hour yet.'

We deposited our joint Gladstone and Thorndyke's travelling-case in an empty first-class compartment, and then, with the solicitor between us, strolled up to the unfrequented end of the platform.

'My brother's position,' said Mr Stopford, 'fills me with dismay—but let me give you the facts in order, and you shall judge for yourself. This poor creature who has been murdered so brutally was a Miss Edith Grant. She was formerly an artist's model, and as such was a good deal employed by my brother, who is a painter—Harold Stopford, you know, A.R.A. now——'

'I know his work very well, and charming work it is.'

'I think so, too. Well, in those days he was quite a youngster—about twenty—and he became very intimate with Miss Grant, in quite an innocent way, though not very discreet; but she was a nice respectable girl, as most English models are, and no one thought any harm. However, a good many letters passed between them, and some little presents, amongst which was a beaded chain carrying a locket, and in this he was fool enough to put his portrait and the inscription, "Edith, from Harold."

'Later on Miss Grant, who had a rather good voice, went on the stage, in the comic opera line, and, in consequence, her habits and associates changed somewhat; and, as Harold had meanwhile become engaged, he was naturally anxious to get his letters back, and especially to exchange the locket for some less compromising gift. The letters she eventually sent him, but refused absolutely to part with the locket.

'Now, for the last month Harold has been staying at Halbury, making sketching excursions into the surrounding country, and yesterday morning he took the train to Shinglehurst, the third station from here, and the one before Woldhurst.

'On the platform here he met Miss Grant, who had come down from London, and was going on to Worthing. They entered the branch train together, having a first-class compartment to themselves. It seems she was wearing his locket at the time, and he made another appeal to her to make an exchange, which she refused, as before. The discussion appears to have become rather heated and angry on both sides, for the guard and a porter at Munsden both noticed that they seemed to be quarrelling; but the upshot of the affair was that the lady snapped the chain, and tossed it together with the locket to my brother, and they parted quite amiably at Shinglehurst, where Harold got out. He was then carrying his full sketching kit, including a large holland umbrella, the lower joint of which is an ash staff fitted with a powerful steel spike for driving into the ground.

'It was about half-past ten when he got out at Shinglehurst; by eleven he had reached his pitch and got to work, and he painted steadily for three hours. Then he packed up his traps, and was just starting on his way back to the station, when he was met by the police and arrested.

'And now, observe the accumulation of circumstantial evidence against him. He was the last person seen in company with the murdered woman—for no one seems to have seen her after they left Munsden; he appeared to be quarrelling with her when she was last seen alive, he had a reason for possibly wishing for her death, he was provided with an implement—a spiked staff—capable of inflicting the injury which caused her death, and, when he was searched, there was found in his possession the locket and broken chain, apparently removed from her person with violence.

'Against all this is, of course, his known character—he is the gentlest and most amiable of men—and his subsequent conduct—imbecile to the last degree if he had been guilty; but, as a lawyer, I can't help seeing that appearances are almost hopelessly against him.'

'We won't say "hopelessly," ' replied Thorndyke, as we took our places in the carriage, 'though I expect the police are pretty cocksure. When does the inquest open?'

'Today at four. I have obtained an order from the coroner for you to examine the body and be present at the post-mortem.'

'Do you happen to know the exact position of the wound?'

'Yes; it is a little above and behind the left ear—a horrible round hole, with a ragged cut or tear running from it to the side of the forehead.'

'And how was the body lying?'

'Right along the floor, with the feet close to the off-side door.'

'Was the wound on the head the only one?'

'No; there was a long cut or bruise on the right cheek—a contused wound the police surgeon called it, which he believes to have been inflicted with a heavy and rather blunt weapon. I have not heard of any other wounds or bruises.'

'Did anyone enter the train yesterday at Shinglehurst?' Thorndyke asked.

'No one entered the train after it left Halbury.'

Thorndyke considered these statements in silence, and presently fell into a brown study, from which he roused only as the train moved out of Shinglehurst station.

'It would be about here that the murder was committed,' said Mr Stopford; 'at least, between here and Woldhurst.'

Thorndyke nodded rather abstractedly, being engaged at the moment in observing with great attention the objects that were visible from the windows.

'I notice,' he remarked presently, 'a number of chips scattered about between the rails, and some of the chair-wedges look new. Have there been any platelayers at work lately?'

'Yes,' answered Stopford, 'they are on the line now, I believe— at least, I saw a gang working near Woldhurst yesterday, and they are said to have set a rick on fire; I saw it smoking when I came down.'

'Indeed; and this middle line of rails is, I suppose, a sort of siding?'

'Yes; they shunt the goods trains and empty trucks on to it. There are the remains of the rick—still smouldering, you see.'

Thorndyke gazed absently at the blackened heap until an empty cattle-truck on the middle track hid it from view. This was succeeded by a line of goods-waggons, and these by a passenger coach, one compartment of which—a first-class—was closed up and sealed. The train now began to slow down rather suddenly, and a couple of minutes later we brought up in Woldhurst station.

It was evident that rumours of Thorndyke's advent had preceded us, for the entire staff—two porters, an inspector, and the station-master—were waiting expectantly on the platform, and the latter came forward, regardless of his dignity, to help us with our luggage.

'Do you think I could see the carriage?' Thorndyke asked the solicitor.

'Not the inside, sir,' said the station-master, on being appealed to. 'The police have sealed it up. You would have to ask the inspector.'

'Well, I can have a look at the outside, I suppose?' said Thorndyke, and to this the station-master readily agreed, and offered to accompany us.

'What other first-class passengers were there?' Thorndyke asked.

'None, sir. There was only one first-class coach, and the deceased was the only person in it. It has given us all a dreadful turn, this affair has,' he continued, as we set off up the line. 'I was on the platform when the train came in. We were watching a rick that was burning up the line, and a rare blaze it made, too; and I was just saying that we should have to move the cattle-truck that was on the mid-track, because, you see, sir, the smoke and sparks were blowing across, and I thought it would frighten the poor beasts. And Mr Felton he don't like his beasts handled roughly. He says it spoils the meat.'

'No doubt he is right,' said Thorndyke. 'But now, tell me, do you think it is possible for any person to board or leave the train on the off-side unobserved? Could a man, for instance, enter a compartment on the off-side at one station and drop off as the train was slowing down at the next, without being seen?'

'I doubt it,' replied the station-master. 'Still, I wouldn't say it is impossible.'

'Thank you. Oh, and there's another question. You have a gang of men at work on the line, I see. Now, do those men belong to the district?'

'No sir; they are strangers, every one, and pretty rough diamonds some of 'em are. But I shouldn't say there was any real harm in 'em. If you was suspecting any of 'em of being mixed up in this——'

'I am not,' interrupted Thorndyke rather shortly. 'I suspect nobody; but I wish to get all the facts of the case at the outset.'

'Naturally, sir,' replied the abashed official; and we pursued our way in silence.

'Do you remember, by the way,' said Thorndyke, as we approached the empty coach, 'whether the off-side door of the compartment was closed and locked when the body was discovered?'

'It was closed, sir, but not locked. Why, sir, did you think——?'

'Nothing, nothing. The sealed compartment is the one, of course?'

Without waiting for a reply, he commenced his survey of the coach, while I gently restrained our two companions from shadowing him, as they were disposed to do. The off-side footboard occupied his attention specially, and when he had scrutinised minutely the part opposite the fatal compartment, he walked slowly from end to end with his eyes but a few inches from its surface, as though he was searching for something.

Near what had been the rear end he stopped, and drew from his pocket a piece of paper; then, with a moistened finger-tip he picked up from the footboard some evidently minute object, which he carefully transferred to the paper, folding the latter and placing it in his pocket-book.

He next mounted the footboard, and, having peered in through the window of the sealed compartment, produced from his pocket a small insufflator or powder-blower, with which he blew a stream of impalpable smoke-like powder on to the edges of the middle window, bestowing the closest attention on the irregular dusty patches in which it settled, and even measuring one on the jamb of the window with a pocket-rule. At length he stepped down, and, having carefully looked over the near-side footboard, announced that he had finished for the present.

As we were returning down the line, we passed a working man, who seemed to be viewing the chairs and sleepers with more than casual interest.

'That, I suppose, is one of the plate-layers?' Thorndyke suggested to the station-master.

'Yes, the foreman of the gang,' was the reply.

'I'll just step back and have a word with him, if you will walk on slowly.' And my colleague turned back briskly and overtook the man, with whom he remained in conversation for some minutes.

'I think I see the police inspector on the platform,' remarked Thorndyke, as we approached the station.

'Yes, there he is,' said our guide. 'Come down to see what you are after, sir, I expect.' Which was doubtless the case, although the officer professed to be there by the merest chance.

'You would like to see the weapon, sir, I suppose?' he remarked, when he had introduced himself.

'The umbrella-spike,' Thorndyke corrected. 'Yes, if I may. We are going to the mortuary now.'

'Then you'll pass the station on the way; so, if you care to look in, I will walk up with you.'

This proposition being agreed to, we all proceeded to the police station, including the station-master, who was on the very tiptoe of curiosity.

'There you are, sir,' said the inspector, unlocking his office, and ushering us in. 'Don't say we haven't given every facility to the defence. There are all the effects of the accused, including the very weapon the deed was done with.'

'Come, come,' protested Thorndyke; 'we mustn't be premature.' He took the stout ash staff from the officer, and, having examined the formidable spike through a lens, drew from his pocket a steel calliper-gauge, with which he carefully measured the diameter of the spike, and the staff to which it was fixed. 'And now,' he said, when he had made a note of the measurements in his book, 'we will look at the colour-box and the sketch. Ha! a very orderly man, your brother, Mr Stopford. Tubes all in their places, palette-knives wiped clean, palette cleaned off and rubbed bright, brushes wiped—they ought to be washed before they stiffen—all this is very significant.' He unstrapped the sketch from the blank canvas to which it was pinned, and, standing it on a chair in a good light, stepped back to look at it.

'And you tell me that that is only three hours' work!' he exclaimed, looking at the lawyer. 'It is really a marvellous achievement.'

'My brother is a very rapid worker,' replied Stopford dejectedly.

'Yes, but this is not only amazingly rapid; it is in his very happiest vein—full of spirit and feeling. But we mustn't stay to look at it longer.' He replaced the canvas on its pins, and having glanced at the locket and some other articles that lay in a drawer, thanked the inspector for his courtesy and withdrew.

'That sketch and the colour-box appear very suggestive to me,' he remarked, as we walked up the street.

'To me also,' said Stopford gloomily, 'for they are under lock and key, like their owner, poor old fellow.'

He sighed heavily, and we walked on in silence.

The mortuary-keeper had evidently heard of our arrival, for he was waiting at the door with the key in his hand, and, on being shown the coroner's order, unlocked the door, and we entered together; but, after a momentary glance at the ghostly, shrouded figure lying upon the slate table, Stopford turned pale and retreated, saying that he would wait for us outside with the mortuary-keeper.

As soon as the door was closed and locked on the inside, Thorndyke glanced curiously round the bare, whitewashed building.

A stream of sunlight poured in through the skylight, and fell upon the silent form that lay so still under its covering-sheet, and one stray beam glanced into a corner by the door, where, on a row of pegs and a deal table, the dead woman's clothing was displayed.

'There is something unspeakably sad in these poor relics, Jervis,' said Thorndyke, as we stood before them.

'To me they are more tragic, more full of pathetic suggestion, than the corpse itself. See the smart, jaunty hat, and the costly skirts hanging there, so desolate and forlorn; the dainty *lingerie* on the table, neatly folded—by the mortuary-man's wife, I hope—the little French shoes and open-work silk stockings. How pathetically eloquent they are of harmless, womanly vanity, and the gay, careless life, snapped short in the twinkling of an eye. But we must not give way to sentiment. There is another life threatened, and it is in our keeping.'

He lifted the hat from its peg, and turned it over in his hand. It was, I think, what is called a 'picture-hat'—a huge, flat, shapeless mass of gauze and ribbon and feather, spangled over freely with dark-blue sequins. In one part of the brim was a ragged hole, and from this the glittering sequins dropped off in little showers when the hat was moved.

'This will have been worn tilted over on the left side,' said Thorndyke, 'judging by the general shape and the position of the hole.'

'Yes,' I agreed. 'Like that of the Duchess of Devonshire in Gainsborough's portrait.'

'Exactly.'

He shook a few of the sequins into the palm of his hand, and, replacing the hat on its peg, dropped the little discs into an envelope, on which he wrote, 'From the hat,' and slipped it into his pocket. Then, stepping over to the table, he drew back the sheet reverently and even tenderly from the dead woman's face, and looked down at it with grave pity. It was a comely face, white as marble, serene and peaceful in expression, with half-closed eyes, and framed with a mass of brassy, yellow hair; but its beauty was marred by a long linear wound, half cut, half bruise, running down the right cheek from the eye to the chin.

'A handsome girl,' Thorndyke commented—'a dark-haired

blonde. What a sin to have disfigured herself so with that horrible peroxide.' He smoothed the hair back from her forehead, and added: 'She seems to have applied the stuff last about ten days ago. There is about a quarter of an inch of dark hair at the roots. What do you make of that wound on the cheek?'

'It looks as if she had struck some sharp angle in falling, though, as the seats are padded in first-class carriages, I don't see what she could have struck.'

'No. And now let us look at the other wound. Will you note down the description?' He handed me his notebook, and I wrote down as he dictated: 'A clean-punched circular hole in skull, an inch behind and above margin of left ear—diameter, an inch and seven-sixteenths; starred fracture of parietal bone; membranes perforated, and brain entered deeply; ragged scalp-wound, extending forward to margin of left orbit; fragments of gauze and sequins in edges of wound. That will do for the present. Dr Morton will give us further details if we want them.'

He pocketed his callipers and rule, drew from the bruised scalp one or two loose hairs, which he placed in the envelope with the sequins, and, having looked over the body for other wounds or bruises (of which there were none), replaced the sheet, and prepared to depart.

As we walked away from the mortuary, Thorndyke was silent and deeply thoughtful, and I gathered that he was piecing together the facts that he had acquired. At length Mr Stopford, who had several times looked at him curiously, said:

'The post-mortem will take place at three, and it is now only half-past eleven. What would you like to do next?'

Thorndyke, who, in spite of his mental preoccupation, had been looking about him in his usual keen, attentive way, halted suddenly.

'Your reference to the post-mortem,' said he, 'reminds me that I forgot to put the ox-gall into my case.'

'Ox-gall!' I exclaimed, endeavouring vainly to connect this substance with the technique of the pathologist. 'What were you going to do with——'

But here I broke off, remembering my friend's dislike of any discussion of his methods before strangers.

'I suppose,' he continued, 'there would hardly be an artist's colour-man in a place of this size?'

'I should think not,' said Stopford. 'But couldn't you get the stuff from a butcher? There's a shop just across the road.'

'So there is,' agreed Thorndyke, who had already observed the shop. 'The gall ought, of course, to be prepared, but we can filter it ourselves—that is, if the butcher has any. We will try him, at any rate.'

He crossed the road towards the shop, over which the name 'Felton' appeared in gilt lettering, and, addressing himself to the proprietor, who stood at the door, introduced himself and explained his wants.

'Ox-gall?' said the butcher. 'No, sir, I haven't any just now; but I am having a beast killed this afternoon, and I can let you have some then. In fact,' he added, after a pause, 'as the matter is of importance, I can have one killed at once if you wish it.'

'That is very kind of you,' said Thorndyke, 'and it would greatly oblige me. Is the beast perfectly healthy?'

'They're in splendid condition, sir. I picked them out of the herd myself. But you shall see them—ay, and choose the one that you'd like killed.'

'You are really very good,' said Thorndyke warmly. 'I will just run into the chemist's next door, and get a suitable bottle, and then I will avail myself of your exceedingly kind offer.'

He hurried into the chemist's shop, from which he presently emerged, carrying a white paper parcel; and we then followed the butcher down a narrow lane by the side of his shop. It led to an enclosure containing a small pen, in which were confined three handsome steers, whose glossy, black coats contrasted in a very striking manner with their long, greyish-white, nearly straight horns.

'These are certainly very fine beasts, Mr Felton,' said Thorndyke, as we drew up beside the pen, 'and in excellent condition, too.'

He leaned over the pen and examined the beasts critically, especially as to their eyes and horns; then, approaching the nearest one, he raised his stick and bestowed a smart tap on the under-side of the right horn, following it by a similar tap on the left one, a proceeding that the beast viewed with stolid surprise.

'The state of the horns,' explained Thorndyke, as he moved on to the next steer, 'enables one to judge, to some extent, of the beast's health.'

'Lord bless you, sir,' laughed Mr Felton, 'they haven't got no feeling in their horns, else what good 'ud their horns be to 'em?'

Apparently he was right, for the second steer was as indifferent to a sounding rap on either horn as the first. Nevertheless, when Thorndyke approached the third steer, I unconsciously drew nearer to watch; and I noticed that, as the stick struck the horn, the beast drew back in evident alarm, and that when the blow was repeated, it became manifestly uneasy.

'He don't seem to like that,' said the butcher. 'Seems as if—— Hullo, that's queer!'

Thorndyke had just brought his stick up against the left horn, and immediately the beast had winced and started back, shaking his head and moaning. There was not, however, room for him to back out of reach, and Thorndyke, by leaning into the pen, was able to inspect the sensitive horn, which he did with the closest attention, while the butcher looked on with obvious perturbation.

'You don't think there's anything wrong with this beast, sir, I hope,' said he.

'I can't say without a further examination,' replied Thorndyke. 'It may be the horn only that is affected. If you will have it sawn off close to the head, and sent up to me at the hotel, I will look at it and tell you. And, by way of preventing any mistakes I will mark it and cover it up, to protect it from injury in the slaughter-house.'

He opened his parcel and produced from it a wide-mouthed bottle labelled 'Ox-gall', a sheet of gutta-percha tissue, a roller bandage, and a stick of sealing-wax. Handing the bottle to Mr Felton, he encased the distal half of the horn in a covering by means of the tissue and the bandage, which he fixed securely with the sealing-wax.

'I'll saw the horn off and bring it up to the hotel myself, with the ox-gall,' said Mr Felton. 'You shall have them in half an hour.'

He was as good as his word, for in half an hour Thorndyke was seated at a small table by the window of our private sitting-room in the Black Bull Hotel. The table was covered with newspaper, and on it lay the long grey horn and Thorndyke's travelling-case, now open and displaying a small microscope and its accessories. The butcher was seated solidly in an arm-chair waiting, with a half-suspicious eye on Thorndyke, for the report; and I was endeavouring by cheerful talk to keep Mr Stopford from sinking into utter despondency, though I, too, kept a furtive watch on my colleague's rather mysterious proceedings.

I saw him unwind the bandage and apply the horn to his ear, bending it slightly to and fro. I watched him, as he scanned the surface closely through a lens, and observed him as he scraped some substance from the pointed end on to a glass slide, and, having applied a drop of some reagent, began to tease out the scraping with a pair of mounted needles. Presently he placed the slide under the microscope, and, having observed it attentively for a minute or two, turned round sharply.

'Come and look at this, Jervis,' said he.

I wanted no second bidding, being on tenterhooks of curiosity, but came over and applied my eye to the instrument.

'Well, what is it?' he asked.

'A multipolar nerve corpuscle—very shrivelled, but unmistakable.'

'And this?'

He moved the slide to a fresh spot.

'Two pyramidal nerve corpuscles and some portions of fibres.'

'And what do you say the tissue is?'

'Cortical brain substance, I should say, without a doubt.'

'I entirely agree with you. And that being so,' he added, turning to Mr Stopford, 'we may say that the case for the defence is practically complete.'

'What, in Heaven's name, do you mean?' exclaimed Stopford, starting up.

'I mean that we can now prove when and where and how Miss Grant met her death. Come and sit down here, and I will explain. No, you needn't go away, Mr Felton. We shall have to subpœna you. Perhaps,' he continued, 'we had better go over the facts and see what they suggest. And first we note the position of the body, lying with the feet close to the off-side door, showing that, when she fell, the deceased was sitting, or more probably standing, close to that door. Next there is this.' He drew from his pocket a folded paper, which he opened, displaying a tiny blue disc. 'It is one of the sequins with which her hat was trimmed, and I have in this envelope several more which I took from the hat itself.

'This single sequin I picked up on the rear end of the off-side foot-board, and its presence there makes it nearly certain that at some time Miss Grant had put her head out of the window on that side.

'The next item of evidence I obtained by dusting the margins of the off-side window with a light powder, which made visible a greasy impression three and a quarter inches long on the sharp corner of the right-hand jamb (right-hand from the inside, I mean).

'And now as to the evidence furnished by the body. The wound in the skull is behind and above the left ear, is roughly circular, and measures one inch and seven-sixteenths at most, and a ragged scalp-wound runs from it towards the left eye. On the right cheek is a linear contused wound three and a quarter inches long. There are no other injuries.

'Our next facts are furnished by this.' He took up the horn and tapped it with his finger, while the solicitor and Mr Felton stared at him in speechless wonder. 'You notice it is a left horn, and you remember that it was highly sensitive. If you put your ear to it while I strain it, you will hear the grating of a fracture in the bony core. Now look at the pointed end, and you will see several deep scratches running lengthwise, and where those scratches end the diameter of the horn is, as you see by this calliper-gauge, one inch and seven-sixteenths. Covering the scratches is a dry blood-stain, and at the extreme tip is a small mass of a dried substance which Dr Jervis and I have examined with the microscope and are satisfied is brain tissue.'

'Good God!' exclaimed Stopford eagerly. 'Do you mean to say——'

'Let us finish with the facts, Mr Stopford,' Thorndyke interrupted. 'Now, if you look closely at that blood-stain, you will see a short piece of hair stuck to the horn, and through this lens you can make out the root-bulb. It is a golden hair, you notice, but near the root it is black, and our calliper-gauge shows us that the black portion is fourteen sixty-fourths of an inch long. Now, in this envelope are some hairs that I removed from the dead woman's head. They also are golden hairs, black at the roots, and when I measure the black portion I find it to be fourteen sixty-fourths of an inch long. Then, finally, there is this.'

He turned the horn over, and pointed to a small patch of dried blood. Embedded in it was a blue sequin.

Mr Stopford and the butcher both gazed at the horn in silent amazement; then the former drew a deep breath and looked up at Thorndyke.

'No doubt,' said he, 'you can explain this mystery, but for my part I am utterly bewildered, though you are filling me with hope.'

'And yet the matter is quite simple,' returned Thorndyke, 'even with these few facts before us, which are only a selection from the body of evidence in our possession. But I will state my theory, and you shall judge.' He rapidly sketched a rough plan on a sheet of paper, and continued: 'These were the conditions when the train was approaching Woldhurst: Here was the passenger-coach, here was the burning rick, and here was a cattle-truck. This steer was in that truck. Now my hypothesis is that at that time Miss Grant was standing with her head out of the off-side window, watching the burning rick. Her wide hat, worn on the left side, hid from her view the cattle-truck which she was approaching, and then this is what happened.' He sketched another plan to a larger scale. 'One of the steers—this one—had thrust its long horn out through the bars. The point of that horn struck the deceased's head, driving her face violently against the corner of the window, and then, in disengaging, ploughed its way through the scalp and suffered a fracture of its core from the violence of the wrench. This hypothesis is inherently probable, it fits all the facts, and those facts admit of no other explanation.'

The solicitor sat for a moment as though dazed, then he rose impulsively and seized Thorndyke's hands.

'I don't know what to say to you,' he exclaimed huskily, 'except that you have saved my brother's life, and for that may God reward you!'

The butcher rose from his chair with a slow grin.

'It seems to me,' said he, 'as if that ox-gall was what you might call a blind, eh, sir?'

And Thorndyke smiled an inscrutable smile.

When we returned to town on the following day we were a party of four, which included Mr Harold Stopford. The verdict of 'Death by misadventure', promptly returned by the coroner's jury, had been shortly followed by his release from custody, and he now sat with his brother and me, listening with rapt attention to Thorndyke's analysis of the case.

'So, you see,' the latter concluded, 'I had six possible theories of the cause of death worked out before I reached Halbury, and it only remained to select the one that fitted the facts. And when I had seen the cattle-truck, had picked up that sequin, had heard the description of the steers, and had seen the hat and the wounds, there was nothing left to do but the filling in of details.'

'And you never doubted my innocence?' asked Harold Stopford.

Thorndyke smiled at his quondam client.

'Not after I had seen your colour-box and your sketch,' said he, 'to say nothing of the spike.'

5

G. K. CHESTERTON

The Strange Crime of John Boulnois

Mr Calhoun Kidd was a very young gentleman with a very old face, a face dried up with its own eagerness, framed in blue-black hair and a black butterfly tie. He was the emissary in England of the colossal American daily called the *Western Sun*—also humorously described as the 'Rising Sunset'. This was in allusion to a great journalistic declaration (attributed to Mr Kidd himself) that 'he guessed the sun would rise in the west yet, if American citizens did a bit more hustling'. Those, however, who mock American journalism from the standpoint of somewhat mellower traditions forget a certain paradox which partly redeems it. For while the journalism of the States permits a pantomimic vulgarity long past anything English, it also shows a real excitement about the most earnest mental problems, of which English papers are innocent, or rather incapable. The *Sun* was full of the most solemn matters treated in the most farcical way. William James figured there as well as 'Weary Willie', and pragmatists alternated with pugilists in the long procession of its portraits.

Thus, when a very unobtrusive Oxford man named John Boulnois wrote in a very unreadable review called the *Natural Philosophy Quarterly* a series of articles on alleged weak points in Darwinian evolution, it fluttered no corner of the English papers; though Boulnois's theory (which was that of a comparatively stationary universe visited occasionally by convulsions of change) had some rather faddy fashionableness at Oxford, and got so far as to be named 'Catastrophism'. But many American papers seized on the challenge as a great event;

and the *Sun* threw the shadow of Mr Boulnois quite gigantically across its pages. By the paradox already noted, articles of valuable intelligence and enthusiasm were presented with headlines apparently written by an illiterate maniac; headlines such as 'Darwin Chews Dirt; Critic Boulnois says He Jumps the Shocks'—or 'Keep Catastrophic, says Thinker Boulnois'. And Mr Calhoun Kidd, of the *Western Sun*, was bidden to take his butterfly tie and lugubrious visage down to the little house outside Oxford where Thinker Boulnois lived in happy ignorance of such a title.

That fated philosopher had consented, in a somewhat dazed manner, to receive the interviewer, and had named the hour of nine that evening. The last of a summer sunset clung about Cumnor and the low wooded hills; the romantic Yankee was both doubtful of his road and inquisitive about his surroundings; and seeing the door of a genuine feudal old-country inn, The Champion Arms, standing open, he went in to make inquiries.

In the bar parlour he rang the bell, and had to wait some little time for a reply to it. The only other person present was a lean man with close red hair and loose, horsey-looking clothes, who was drinking very bad whisky, but smoking a very good cigar. The whisky, of course, was the choice brand of The Champion Arms; the cigar he had probably brought with him from London. Nothing could be more different than his cynical *négligé* from the dapper dryness of the young American; but something in his pencil and open notebook, and perhaps in the expression of his alert blue eye, caused Kidd to guess, correctly, that he was a brother journalist.

'Could you do me the favour,' asked Kidd, with the courtesy of his nation, 'of directing me to the Grey Cottage, where Mr Boulnois lives, as I understand?'

'It's a few yards down the road,' said the red-haired man, removing his cigar; 'I shall be passing it myself in a minute, but I'm going on to Pendragon Park to try and see the fun.'

'What is Pendragon Park?' asked Calhoun Kidd.

'Sir Claude Champion's place—haven't you come down for that, too?' asked the other pressman, looking up. 'You're a journalist, aren't you?'

'I have come to see Mr Boulnois,' said Kidd.

'I've come to see Mrs Boulnois,' replied the other. 'But I shan't catch her at home.' And he laughed rather unpleasantly.

'Are you interested in Catastrophism?' asked the wondering Yankee.

'I'm interested in catastrophes; and there are going to be some,' replied his companion gloomily. 'Mine's filthy trade, and I never pretend it isn't.'

With that he spat on the floor; yet somehow in the very act and instant one could realize that the man had been brought up as a gentleman.

The American pressman considered him with more attention. His face was pale and dissipated, with the promise of formidable passions yet to be loosed; but it was a clever and sensitive face; his clothes were coarse and careless, but he had a good seal ring on one of his long, thin fingers. His name, which came out in the course of talk, was James Dalroy; he was the son of a bankrupt Irish landlord, and attached to a pink paper which he heartily despised, called *Smart Society*, in the capacity of reporter and of something painfully like spy.

Smart Society, I regret to say, felt none of that interest in Boulnois on Darwin which was such a credit to the head and hearts of the *Western Sun*. Dalroy had come down, it seemed, to snuff up the scent of a scandal which might very well end in the Divorce Court, but which was at present hovering between Grey Cottage and Pendragon Park.

Sir Claude Champion was known to the readers of the *Western Sun* as well as Mr Boulnois. So were the Pope and the Derby Winner; but the idea of their intimate acquaintanceship would have struck Kidd as equally incongruous. He had heard of (and written about, nay, falsely pretended to know) Sir Claude Champion, as 'one of the brightest and wealthiest of England's Upper Ten'; as the great sportsman who raced yachts round the world; as the great traveller who wrote books about the Himalayas, as the politician who swept constituencies with a startling sort of Tory Democracy, and as the great dabbler in art, music, literature, and, above all, acting. Sir Claude was really rather magnificent in other than American eyes. There was something of the Renascence Prince about his omnivorous culture and restless publicity; he was not only a great amateur, but an ardent one. There was in him none of that antiquarian frivolity that we convey by the word 'dilettante'.

That faultless falcon profile with purple-black Italian eye, which had been snap-shotted so often both for *Smart Society* and the *Western Sun*, gave everyone the impression of a man eaten by ambition as by a fire, or even a disease. But though Kidd knew a great deal about Sir Claude—a great deal more, in fact, than there was to know—it would never have crossed his wildest dreams to connect so showy an aristocrat with the newly-unearthed founder of Catastrophism, or to guess that Sir Claude Champion and John Boulnois could be intimate friends. Such, according to Dalroy's account, was nevertheless the fact. The two had hunted in couples at school and college, and, though their social destinies had been very different. (Champion was a great landlord and almost a millionaire, while Boulnois was a poor scholar and, until just lately, an unknown one), they still kept in very close touch with each other. Indeed, Boulnois's cottage stood just outside the gates of Pendragon Park.

But whether the two men could be friends much longer was becoming a dark and ugly question. A year or two before, Boulnois had married a beautiful and not unsuccessful actress, to whom he was devoted in his own shy and ponderous style; and the proximity of the household to Champion's had given that flighty celebrity opportunities for behaving in a way that could not but cause painful and rather base excitement. Sir Claude had carried the arts of publicity to perfection; and he seemed to take a crazy pleasure in being equally ostentatious in an intrigue that could do him no sort of honour. Footmen from Pendragon were perpetually leaving bouquets for Mrs Boulnois; carriages and motor-cars were perpetually calling at the cottage for Mrs Boulnois; balls and masquerades perpetually filled the grounds in which the baronet paraded Mrs Boulnois, like the Queen of Love and Beauty at a tournament. That very evening, marked by Mr Kidd for the exposition of Catastrophism, had been marked by Sir Claude Champion for an open-air rendering of *Romeo and Juliet*, in which he was to play Romeo to a Juliet it was needless to name.

'I don't think it can go on without a smash,' said the young man with red hair, getting up and shaking himself. 'Old Boulnois may be squared—or he may be square. But if he's square he's thick—what you might call cubic. But I don't believe it's possible.'

'He is a man of grand intellectual powers,' said Calhoun Kidd in a deep voice.

'Yes,' answered Dalroy; 'but even a man of grand intellectual powers can't be such a blighted fool as all that. Must you be going on? I shall be following myself in a minute or two.'

But Calhoun Kidd, having finished a milk and soda, betook himself smartly up the road towards the Grey Cottage, leaving his cynical informant to his whisky and tobacco. The last of the daylight had faded; the skies were of a dark, green-grey, like slate, studded here and there with a star, but lighter on the left side of the sky, with the promise of a rising moon.

The Grey Cottage, which stood entrenched, as it were, in a square of stiff, high thorn-hedges, was so close under the pines and palisades of the Park that Kidd at first mistook it for the Park Lodge. Finding the name on the narrow wooden gate, however, and seeing by his watch that the hour of the 'Thinker's' appointment had just struck, he went in and knocked at the front door. Inside the garden hedge, he could see that the house, though unpretentious enough, was larger and more luxurious than it looked at first, and was quite a different kind of place from a porter's lodge. A dog-kennel and a beehive stood outside, like symbols of old English country-life; the moon was rising behind a plantation of prosperous pear trees; the dog that came out of the kennel was reverend-looking and reluctant to bark; and the plain, elderly manservant who opened the door was brief but dignified.

'Mr Boulnois asked me to offer his apologies, sir,' he said, 'but he has been obliged to go out suddenly.'

'But see here, I had an appointment,' said the interviewer, with a rising voice. 'Do you know where he went to?'

'To Pendragon Park, sir,' said the servant, rather sombrely, and began to close the door.

Kidd started a little.

'Did he go with Mrs——with the rest of the party?' he asked rather vaguely.

'No, sir,' said the man shortly; 'he stayed behind, and then went out alone.' And he shut the door, brutally, but with an air of duty not done.

The American, that curious compound of impudence and sensitiveness, was annoyed. He felt a strong desire to hustle them all along a bit and teach them business habits; the hoary old dog and the grizzled, heavy-faced old butler with his prehistoric shirt-front, and the drowsy old moon, and above all the scatter-brained old philosopher who couldn't keep an appointment.

'If that's the way he goes on he deserves to lose his wife's purest devotion,' said Mr Calhoun Kidd. 'But perhaps he's gone over to make a row. In that case I reckon a man from the *Western Sun* will be on the spot.'

And turning the corner by the open lodge-gates, he set off, stumping up the long avenue of black pine-woods that pointed in abrupt perspective towards the inner gardens of Pendragon Park. The trees were as black and orderly as plumes upon a hearse; there were still a few stars. He was a man with more literary than direct natural associations; the word 'Ravenswood' came into his head repeatedly. It was partly the raven colour of the pine-woods; but partly also an indescribable atmosphere almost described in Scott's great tragedy; the smell of something that died in the eighteenth century; the smell of dank gardens and broken urns, of wrongs that will never now be righted; of something that is none the less incurably sad because it is strangely unreal.

More than once, as he went up that trim, black road of tragic artifice, he stopped startled, thinking he heard steps in front of him. He could see nothing in front but the twin sombre walls of pine and the wedge of starlit sky above them. At first he thought he must have fancied it or been mocked by a mere echo of his own tramp. But as he went on he was more and more inclined to conclude, with the remains of his reason, that there really were other feet upon the road. He thought hazily of ghosts; and was surprised how swiftly he could see the image of an appropriate and local ghost, one with a face as white as Pierrot's, but patched with black. The apex of the triangle of dark-blue sky was growing brighter and bluer, but he did not realize as yet that this was because he was coming nearer to the lights of the great house and garden. He only felt that the atmosphere was growing more intense; there was in the sadness more violence and secrecy—more—he hesitated for the word, and then said it with a jerk of laughter—Catastrophism.

More pines, more pathway slid past him, and then he stood rooted as by a blast of magic. It is vain to say that he felt as if he had got into a dream; but this time he felt quite certain that he had got into a book. For we human beings are used to inappropriate things; we are accustomed to the clatter of the incongruous; it is a tune to which we can go to sleep. If one appropriate thing happens, it wakes us up like the pang of a perfect chord. Something happened such as would have happened in such a place in a forgotten tale.

Over the black pinewood came flying and flashing in the moon a naked sword—such a slender and sparkling rapier as may have fought many an unjust duel in that ancient park. It fell on the pathway far in front of him and lay there glistening like a large needle. He ran like a hare and bent to look at it. Seen at close quarters it had rather a showy look: the big red jewels in the hilt and guard were a little dubious. But there were other red drops upon the blade which were not dubious.

He looked round wildly in the direction from which the dazzling missile had come, and saw that at this point the sable façade of fir and pine was interrupted by a smaller road at right angles; which, when he turned it, brought him in full view of the long, lighted house, with a lake and fountains in front of it. Nevertheless, he did not look at this, having something more interesting to look at.

Above him, at the angle of the steep green bank of the terraced garden, was one of those small picturesque surprises common in the old landscape gardening; a kind of small round hill or dome of grass, like a giant mole-hill, ringed and crowned with three concentric fences of roses, and having a sundial in the highest point in the centre. Kidd could see the finger of the dial stand up dark against the sky like the dorsal fin of a shark, and the vain moonlight clinging to that idle clock. But he saw something else clinging to it also, for one wild moment—the figure of a man.

Though he saw it there only for a moment, though it was outlandish and incredible in costume, being clad from neck to heel in tight crimson, with glints of gold, yet he knew in one flash of moonlight who it was. That white face flung up to heaven, clean-shaven and so unnaturally young, like Byron with a Roman nose, those black curls already grizzled—he had seen the thousand public portraits of

Sir Claude Champion. The wild red figure reeled an instant against the sundial; the next it had rolled down the steep bank and lay at the American's feet, faintly moving one arm. A gaudy, unnatural gold ornament on the arm suddenly reminded Kidd of *Romeo and Juliet*; of course the tight crimson suit was part of the play. But there was a long red stain down the bank from which the man had rolled—that was no part of the play. He had been run through the body.

Mr Calhoun Kidd shouted and shouted again. Once more he seemed to hear phantasmal footsteps, and started to find another figure already near him. He knew the figure, and yet it terrified him. The dissipated youth who had called himself Dalroy had a horribly quiet way with him; if Boulnois failed to keep appointments that had been made, Dalroy had a sinister air of keeping appointments that hadn't. The moonlight discoloured everything; against Dalroy's red hair his wan face looked not so much white as pale green.

All this morbid impressionism must be Kidd's excuse for having cried out, brutally and beyond all reason: 'Did you do this, you devil?'

James Dalroy smiled his unpleasing smile; but before he could speak, the fallen figure made another movement of the arm, waving vaguely towards the place where the sword fell; then came a moan, and then it managed to speak.

'Boulnois . . . Boulnois, I say . . . Boulnois did it . . . jealous of me . . . he was jealous, he was, he was. . . .'

Kidd bent his head down to hear more, and just managed to catch the words:

'Boulnois . . . with my own sword . . . he threw it. . . .'

Again the failing hand waved towards the sword, and then fell rigid with a thud. In Kidd rose from its depth all that acrid humour that is the strange salt of the seriousness of his race.

'See here,' he said sharply and with command, 'you must fetch a doctor. This man's dead.'

'And a priest, too, I suppose,' said Dalroy in an undecipherable manner. 'All these Champions are papists.'

The American knelt down by the body, felt the heart, propped up the head and used some last efforts at restoration; but before the other journalist reappeared, followed by a doctor and a priest, he was already prepared to assert they were too late.

'Were you too late also?' asked the doctor, a solid prosperous-looking man, with conventional moustache and whiskers, but a lively eye, which darted over Kidd dubiously.

'In one sense,' drawled the representative of the *Sun*. 'I was too late to save the man, but I guess I was in time to hear something of importance. I heard the dead man denounce his assassin.'

'And who was the assassin?' asked the doctor, drawing his eyebrows together.

'Boulnois,' said Calhoun Kidd, and whistled softly.

The doctor stared at him gloomily with a reddening brow; but he did not contradict. Then the priest, a shorter figure in the background, said mildly: 'I understood that Mr Boulnois was not coming to Pendragon Park this evening.'

'There again,' said the Yankee grimly, 'I may be in a position to give the old country a fact or two. Yes, *sir*, John Boulnois was going to stay in all this evening; he fixed up a real good appointment there with me. But John Boulnois changed his mind; John Boulnois left his home abruptly and all alone, and came over to this derned Park an hour or so ago. His butler told me so. I think we hold what the all-wise police call a clue—have you sent for them?'

'Yes,' said the doctor; 'but we haven't alarmed anyone else yet.'

'Does Mrs Boulnois know?' asked James Dalroy; and again Kidd was conscious of an irrational desire to hit him on his curling mouth.

'I have not told her,' said the doctor gruffly; 'but here come the police.'

The little priest had stepped out into the main avenue, and now returned with the fallen sword, which looked ludicrously large and theatrical when attached to his dumpy figure, at once clerical and commonplace. 'Just before the police come,' he said apologetically, 'has anyone got a light?'

The Yankee journalist took an electric torch from his pocket, and the priest held it close to the middle part of the blade, which he examined with blinking care. Then, without glancing at the point or pommel, he handed the long weapon to the doctor.

'I fear I'm no use here,' he said, with a brief sigh. 'I'll say good night to you, gentlemen.' And he walked away up the dark avenue towards the house, his hands clasped behind him and his big head bent in cogitation.

The rest of the group made increased haste towards the lodge-gates, where an inspector and two constables could already be seen in consultation with the lodge-keeper. But the little priest only walked slower and slower in the dim cloister of pine, and at last stopped dead, on the steps of the house. It was his silent way of acknowledging an equally silent approach; for there came towards him a presence that might have satisfied even Calhoun Kidd's demands for a lovely and aristocratic ghost. It was a young woman in silvery satins of a Renascence design; she had golden hair in two long shining ropes, and a face so startlingly pale between them that she might have been chryselephantine—made, that is, like some old Greek statues, out of ivory and gold. But her eyes were very bright, and her voice, though low, was confident.

'Father Brown?' she said.

'Mrs Boulnois?' he replied gravely. Then he looked at her and immediately said: 'I see you know about Sir Claude.'

'How do you know I know?' she asked steadily.

He did not answer the question, but asked another: 'Have you seen your husband?'

'My husband is at home,' she said. 'He has nothing to do with this.'

Again he did not answer; and the woman drew nearer to him, with a curiously intense expression on her face.

'Shall I tell you something more?' she said, with a rather fearful smile. 'I don't think he did it, and *you* don't either.'

Father Brown returned her gaze with a long, grave stare, and then nodded, yet more gravely.

'Father Brown,' said the lady, 'I am going to tell you all I know, but I want you to do me a favour first. Will you tell me *why* you haven't jumped to the conclusion of poor John's guilt, as all the rest have done? Don't mind what you say: I—I know about the gossip and the appearances that are against him.'

Father Brown looked honestly embarrassed, and passed his hand across his forehead. 'Two very little things,' he said. 'At least, one's very trivial and the other very vague. But such as they are, they don't fit in with Mr Boulnois being the murderer.'

He turned his blank, round face up to the stars and continued absent-mindedly: 'To take the vague idea first. I attach a good deal of importance to vague ideas. All those things that "aren't evidence" are what convince me. I think a moral impossibility the biggest of all impossibilities. I know your husband only slightly, but I think this crime of his, as generally conceived, something very like a moral impossibility. Please do not think I mean that Boulnois could not be so wicked. Anybody can be wicked—as wicked as he chooses. We can direct our moral wills; but we can't generally change our instinctive tastes and ways of doing things. Boulnois might commit a murder, but not this murder. He would not snatch Romeo's sword from its romantic scabbard; or slay his foe on the sundial as on a kind of altar; or leave his body among the roses; or fling the sword away among the pines. If Boulnois killed anyone he'd do it quietly and heavily, as he'd do any other doubtful thing—take a tenth glass of port, or read a loose Greek poet. No, the romantic setting is not like Boulnois. It's more like Champion.'

'Ah!' she said, and looked at him with eyes like diamonds.

'And the trivial thing was this,' said Brown. 'There were finger-prints on that sword; finger-prints can be detected quite a time after they are made if they're on some polished surface like glass or steel. These were on a polished surface. They were half-way down the blade of the sword. Whose prints they were I have no earthly clue; but why should anybody hold a sword half-way down? It was a long sword, but length is an advantage in lunging at an enemy. At least, at most enemies. At all enemies except one.'

'Except one!' she repeated.

'There is only one enemy,' said Father Brown, 'whom it is easier to kill with a dagger than a sword.'

'I know,' said the woman. 'Oneself.'

There was a long silence, and then the priest said quietly but abruptly: 'Am I right, then? Did Sir Claude kill himself?'

'Yes,' she said, with a face like marble. 'I saw him do it.'

'He died,' said Father Brown, 'for love of you?'

An extraordinary expression flashed across her face, very different from pity, modesty, remorse, or anything her companion had expected: her voice became suddenly strong and full. 'I don't believe,' she said, 'he ever cared about me a rap. He hated my husband.'

'Why?' asked the other, and turned his round face from the sky to the lady.

'He hated my husband because . . . it is so strange I hardly know how to say it . . . because . . .'

'Yes?' said Brown patiently.

'Because my husband wouldn't hate him.'

Father Brown only nodded, and seemed still to be listening; he differed from most detectives in fact and fiction in a small point—he never pretended not to understand when he understood perfectly well.

Mrs Boulnois drew near once more with the same contained glow of certainty. 'My husband,' she said, 'is a great man. Sir Claude Champion was not a great man: he was a celebrated and successful man. My husband has never been celebrated or successful; and it is the solemn truth that he has never dreamed of being so. He no more expects to be famous for thinking than for smoking cigars. On all that side he has a sort of splendid stupidity. He has never grown up. He still liked Champion exactly as he liked him at school; he admired him as he would admire a conjuring trick done at the dinner-table. But he couldn't be got to conceive the notion of *envying* Champion. *And Champion wanted to be envied.* He went mad and killed himself for that.'

'Yes,' said Father Brown; 'I think I begin to understand.'

'Oh, don't you see?' she cried; 'the whole picture is made for that—the place is planned for it. Champion put John in a little house at his very door, like a dependant—to make him *feel* a failure. He never felt it. He thinks no more about such things than—than an absent-minded lion. Champion would burst in on John's shabbiest hours or homeliest meals with some dazzling present or announcement or expedition that made it like the visit of Haroun Alraschid, and John would accept or refuse amiably with one eye off, so to speak, like one lazy schoolboy agreeing or disagreeing with another. After five years of it John had not turned a hair; and Sir Claude Champion was a monomaniac.'

'And Haman began to tell them,' said Father Brown, 'of all the things wherein the king had honoured him; and he said: "All these things profit me nothing while I see Mordecai the Jew sitting in the gate."'

'The crisis came,' Mrs Boulnois continued, 'when I persuaded John to let me take down some of his speculations and send them to a magazine. They began to attract attention, especially in America, and one paper wanted to interview him. When Champion (who was interviewed nearly every day) heard of this late little crumb of success falling to his unconscious rival, the last link snapped that held back his devilish hatred. Then he began to lay that insane siege to my own love and honour which has been the talk of the shire. You will ask me why I allowed such atrocious attentions. I answer that I could not have declined them except by explaining to my husband, and there are some things the soul cannot do, as the body cannot fly. Nobody could have explained to my husband. Nobody could do it now. If you said to him in so many words, "Champion is stealing you wife," he would think the joke a little vulgar: that it could be anything but a joke—that notion could find no crack in his great skull to get in by. Well, John was to come and see us act this evening, but just as we were starting he said he wouldn't; he had got an interesting book and a cigar. I told this to Sir Claude, and it was his death-blow. The monomaniac suddenly saw despair. He stabbed himself, crying out like a devil that Boulnois was slaying him; he lies there in the garden dead of his own jealousy to produce jealousy; and John is sitting in the dining-room reading a book.'

There was another silence, and then the little priest said: 'There is only one weak point, Mrs Boulnois, in all your very vivid account. Your husband is not sitting in the dining-room reading a book. That American reporter told me he had been to your house, and your butler told him Mr Boulnois had gone to Pendragon Park after all.'

Her bright eyes widened to an almost electric glare; and yet it seemed rather bewilderment than confusion or fear. 'Why, what *can* you mean?' she cried. 'All the servants were out of the house, seeing the theatricals. And we don't keep a butler, thank goodness!'

Father Brown started and spun half round like an absurd teetotum. 'What, what?' he cried seeming galvanized into sudden life. 'Look here—I say—can I make you husband hear if I go to the house?'

'Oh, the servants will be back by now,' she said, wondering.

'Right, right!' rejoined the cleric energetically, and set off scuttling up the path towards the Park gates. He turned once to say: 'Better get hold of that Yankee, or "Crime of John Boulnois" will be all over the Republic in large letters.'

'You don't understand,' said Mrs Boulnois. 'He wouldn't mind. I don't think he imagines that America really is a place.'

When Father Brown reached the house with the beehive and the drowsy dog, a small and neat maid-servant showed him into the dining-room, where Boulnois sat reading by a shaded lamp, exactly as his wife described him. A decanter of port and a wineglass were at his elbow; and the instant the priest entered he noted the long ash stand out unbroken on his cigar.

'He has been here for half an hour at least,' thought Father Brown. In fact, he had the air of sitting where he had sat when his dinner was cleared away.

'Don't get up, Mr Boulnois,' said the priest in his pleasant, prosaic way. 'I shan't interrupt you a moment. I fear I break in on some of your scientific studies.'

'No,' said Boulnois; 'I was reading "The Bloody Thumb" '. He said it with neither frown nor smile, and his visitor was conscious of a certain deep and virile indifference in the man which his wife had called greatness. He laid down a gory yellow 'shocker' without even feeling its incongruity enough to comment on it humorously. John Boulnois was a big, slow-moving man with a massive head, partly grey and partly bald, and blunt, burly features. He was in shabby and very old-fashioned evening-dress, with a narrow triangular opening of shirt-front: he had assumed it that evening in his original purpose of going to see his wife act Juliet.

'I won't keep you long from "The Bloody Thumb" or any other catastrophic affairs,' said Father Brown, smiling. 'I only came to ask you about the crime you committed this evening.'

Boulnois looked at him steadily, but a red bar began to show across his broad brow; and he seemed like one discovering embarrassment for the first time.

'I know it was a strange crime,' assented Brown in a low voice. 'Stranger than murder perhaps—to you. The little sins are sometimes harder to confess than the big ones—but that's why it's so important to confess them. Your crime is committed by every fashionable hostess six times a week: and yet you find it stick to your tongue like a nameless atrocity.'

'It makes one feel,' said the philosopher slowly, 'such a damned fool.'

'I know,' assented the other, 'but one often has to choose between feeling a damned fool and being one.'

'I can't analyse myself well,' went on Boulnois; 'but sitting in that chair with that story I was as happy as a schoolboy on a half-holiday. It was security, eternity—I can't convey it . . . the cigars were within reach . . . the matches were within reach . . . the *Thumb* had four more appearances to . . . it was not only a peace, but a plenitude. Then that bell rang, and I thought for one long, mortal minute that I couldn't get out of that chair—literally, physically, muscularly couldn't. Then I did it like a man lifting the world, because I knew all the servants were out. I opened the front door, and there was a little man with his mouth open to speak and his notebook open to write in. I remembered the Yankee interviewer I had forgotten. His hair was parted in the middle, and I tell you that murder——'

'I understand,' said Father Brown. 'I've seen him.'

'I didn't commit murder,' continued the Catastrophist mildly, 'but only perjury. I said I had gone across to Pendragon Park and shut the door in his face. That is my crime, Father Brown, and I don't know what penance you would inflict for it.'

'I shan't inflict any penance,' said the clerical gentleman, collecting his heavy hat and umbrella with an air of some amusement; 'quite the contrary. I came here specially to let you off the little penance which would otherwise have followed your little offence.'

'And what,' asked Boulnois, smiling, 'is the little penance I have so luckily been let off?'

'Being hanged,' said Father Brown.

6

ERNEST BRAMAH

Who Killed Charlie Winpole?

I

Some time during November of a recent year newspaper readers who
are in the habit of being attracted by curious items of quite negligible
importance might have followed the account of the tragedy of a
St Abbots schoolboy which appeared in the Press under the headings,
'Fatal Dish of Mushrooms', 'Are Toadstools Distinguishable?' or other
similarly alluring titles.

The facts relating to the death of Charlie Winpole were simple and
straightforward and the jury sworn to the business of investigating the
cause had no hesitation in bringing in a verdict in accordance with the
medical evidence. The witnesses who had anything really material to
contribute were only two in number—Mrs Dupreen and Robert
Wilberforce Slark, M.D. A couple of hours would easily have disposed
of every detail of an inquiry that was generally admitted to have been a
pure formality, had not the contention of an interested person delayed
the inevitable conclusion by forcing the necessity of an adjournment.

Irene Dupreen testified that she was the widow of a physician
and lived at Hazlehurst, Chesset Avenue, St Abbots, with her brother.
The deceased was their nephew, an only child and an orphan,
and was aged twelve. He was a Ward of Chancery and the Court had
appointed her as guardian, with an adequate provision for the ex-
penses of his keep and education. That allowance would, of course,
cease with her nephew's death.

Coming to the particulars of the case, Mrs Dupreen explained that
for a few days the boy had been suffering from a rather severe cold.

She had not thought it necessary to call in a doctor, recognising it as a mild form of influenza. She kept him from school and restricted him to his bedroom. On the previous Wednesday, the day before his death, he was quite convalescent, with a good pulse and a normal temperature, but as the weather was cold she decided still to keep him in bed as a measure of precaution. He had a fair appetite, but did not care for the lunch they had, and so she asked him, before going out in the afternoon, if there was anything that he would especially fancy for his dinner. He had thereupon expressed a wish for some mushrooms, of which he was always very fond.

'I laughed and pulled his ear,' continued the witness, much affected at her recollection, 'and asked him if that was his idea of a suitable dish for an invalid. But I didn't think that it really mattered in the least then, so I went to several shops about them. They all said that mushrooms were over, but finally I found a few at Lackington's, the greengrocer in Park Road. I bought only half-a-pound; no one but Charlie among us cared for them and I thought that they were already very dry and rather dear.'

The connection between the mushrooms and the unfortunate boy's death seemed inevitable. When Mrs Dupreen went upstairs after dinner she found Charlie apparently asleep and breathing soundly. She quietly removed the tray and without disturbing him turned out the gas and closed the door. In the middle of the night she was suddenly and startlingly awakened by something. For a moment she remained confused, listening. Then a curious sound coming from the direction of the boy's bedroom drew her there. On opening the door she was horrified to see her nephew lying on the floor in a convulsed attitude. His eyes were open and widely dilated; one hand clutched some bed-clothes which he had dragged down with him, and the other still grasped the empty water-bottle that had been by his side. She called loudly for help and her brother and then the servant appeared. She sent the latter to a medicine cabinet for mustard leaves and told her brother to get in the nearest available doctor. She had already lifted Charlie on to the bed again. Before the doctor arrived, which was in about half-an-hour, the boy was dead.

In answer to a question the witness stated that she had not seen her nephew between the time she removed the tray and when she found him ill. The only other person who had seen him within a few hours of his death had been her brother, Philip Loudham, who had taken up Charlie's dinner. When he came down again he had made the remark: 'The youngster seems lively enough now.'

Dr Slark was the next witness. His evidence was to the effect that about three-fifteen on the Thursday morning he was hurriedly called to Hazlehurst by a gentleman whom he now knew to be Mr Philip Loudham. He understood that the case was one of convulsions and went provided for that contingency, but on his arrival he found the patient already dead. From his own examination and from what he was told he had no hesitation in diagnosing the case as one of agaric poisoning. He saw no reason to suspect any of the food except the mushrooms, and all the symptoms pointed to bhurine, the deadly principle of *Amanita Bhuroides*, or the Black Cap, as it was popularly called, from its fancied resemblance to the head-dress assumed by a judge in passing death sentence, coupled with its sinister and well-merited reputation. It was always fatal.

Continuing his evidence, Dr Slark explained that only after maturity did the Black Cap develop its distinctive appearance. Up to that stage it had many of the characteristics of *Agaricus campestris*, or common mushroom. It was true that the gills were paler than one would expect to find, and there were other slight differences of a technical kind, but all might easily be overlooked in the superficial glance of the gatherer. The whole subject of edible and noxious fungi was a difficult one and at present very imperfectly understood. He, personally, very much doubted if true mushrooms were ever responsible for the cases of poisoning which one occasionally saw attributed to them. Under scientific examination he was satisfied that all would resolve themselves into poisoning by one or other of the many noxious fungi that could easily be mistaken for the edible varieties. It was possible to prepare an artificial bed, plant it with proper spawn and be rewarded by a crop of mushroom-like growth of undoubted virulence. On the other hand, the injurious constituents of many poisonous fungi passed off in the process of cooking. There was no handy way of discriminating between the good and the bad except by the absolute identification of species. The salt test and the silver-spoon test were all nonsense and the sooner they were forgotten the better. Apparent mushrooms that were found in woods or growing in the vicinity of trees or hedges should always be regarded with the utmost suspicion.

Dr Slark's evidence concluded the case so far as the subpœnaed witnesses were concerned, but before addressing the jury the coroner announced that another person had expressed a desire to be heard. There was no reason why they should not accept any evidence that was tendered, and as the applicant's name had been mentioned in the case it was only right that he should have the opportunity of replying publicly.

Mr Lackington thereupon entered the witness-box and was sworn. He stated that he was a fruiterer and greengrocer, carrying on a business in Park Road, St Abbots. He remembered Mrs Dupreen coming to his shop two days before. The basket of mushrooms from which she was supplied consisted of a small lot of about six pounds, brought in by a farmer from a neighbouring village, with whom he had frequent dealings. All had been disposed of and in no other case had illness resulted. It was a serious matter to him as a tradesman to have his name associated with a case of this kind. That was why he had come forward. Not only with regard to mushrooms, but as a general result, people would become shy of dealing with him if it was stated that he had sold unwholesome goods.

The coroner, intervening at this point, remarked that he might as well say that he would direct the jury that, in the event of their finding the deceased to have died from the effects of the mushrooms or anything contained among them, that there was no evidence other than that the occurrence was one of pure mischance.

Mr Lackington expressed his thanks for the assurance, but said that a bad impression would still remain. He had been in business in St Abbots for twenty-seven years and during that time he had handled some tons of mushrooms without a single complaint before. He admitted, in answer to the interrogation, that he had not actually examined every mushroom in the half-pound sold to Mrs Dupreen, but he had weighed them, and he was confident that if a toadstool had been among them he would have detected it. Might it not be a cooking utensil that was the cause?

Dr Slark shook his head and was understood to say that he could not accept the suggestion.

Continuing, Mr Lackington then asked whether it was not possible that the deceased, doubtless an inquiring adventurous boy and as mischievous as most of his kind, feeling quite well again and being confined to the house, had got up in his aunt's absence and taken something that would explain this sad affair? They had heard of a medicine cabinet. What about tablets of trional or veronal or something of that sort that might perhaps look like sweets? . . . It was all very well for Dr Slark to laugh, but this matter was a serious one for the witness.

Dr Slark apologised for smiling—he had not laughed—and gravely remarked that the matter was a serious one for all concerned in the inquiry. He admitted that the reference to trional and veronal had, for the moment, caused him to forget the surroundings. He would suggest that in the circumstances perhaps the coroner would think it desirable to order a more detailed examination of the body to be made.

After some further discussion the coroner, while remarking that in most cases an analysis was quite unnecessary, decided that in view of what had transpired it would be more satisfactory to have a complete autopsy made. The inquest was accordingly adjourned.

A week later most of those who had taken part in the first inquiry assembled again in the room of the St Abbots Town Hall which did duty for the Coroner's Court. Only one witness was heard and his evidence was brief and conclusive.

Dr Herbert Ingpenny, consulting pathologist to St Martin's Hospital, stated that he had made an examination of the contents of the stomach and viscera of the deceased. He found evidence of the presence of the poison bhurine in sufficient quantity to account for the boy's death, and the symptoms, as described by Dr Slark and Mrs Dupreen, in the course of the previous hearing, were consistent with bhurine poisoning. Bhurine did not occur naturally except as a constituent of *Amanita Bhuroides*. One-fifth of a grain would be fatal to an adult; in other words a single fungus in the dish might poison three people. A child, especially if experiencing the effects of a weakening illness, would be even more susceptible. No other harmful substance was present.

Dr Ingpenny concluded by saying that he endorsed his colleague's general remarks on the subject of mushrooms and other fungi, and the jury, after a plain direction from the coroner, forthwith brought in a verdict in accordance with the medical evidence.

It was a foregone conclusion with anyone who knew the facts or had followed the evidence. Yet five days later Philip Loudham was arrested suddenly and charged with the astounding crime of having murdered his nephew.

2

It is at this point that Max Carrados makes his first appearance in the Winpole tragedy.

A few days after the arrest, being in a particularly urbane frame of mind himself, and having several hours with no demands on them that could not be fitly transferred to his subordinates, Mr Carlyle looked round for some social entertainment, and with a benevolent condescension very opportunely remembered the existence of his niece living at Groat's Heath.

'Elsie will be delighted,' he assured himself, on evolving this suggestion. 'She is rather out of the world up there, I imagine. Now if I get across by four, put in a couple of hours . . .'

Mrs Bellmark was certainly pleased, but she appeared to be still more surprised at something, and behind that lay an effervescence of excitement that even to Mr Carlyle's complacent self-esteem seemed out of proportion to the occasion. The reason could not be long withheld.

'Did you meet anyone, Uncle Louis?' was almost her first inquiry.

'Did I meet anyone?' repeated Mr Carlyle with his usual precision. 'Um, no, I cannot say that I met anyone particular. Of course——'

'I've had a visitor and he's coming back again for tea. Guess who it is? But you never will. Mr Carrados.'

'Max Carrados!' exclaimed her uncle in astonishment. 'You don't say so. Why, bless my soul, Elsie, I'd almost forgotten that you knew him. It seems years ago—what on earth is Max doing in Groat's Heath?'

'That is the extraordinary thing about it,' replied Mrs Bellmark. 'He said that he had come up here to look for mushrooms.'

'Mushrooms?'

'Yes; that was what he said. He asked me if I knew of any woods about here that he could go into and I told him of the one down Stone-cut Lane.'

'But don't you know, my dear child,' exclaimed Mr Carlyle, 'that mushrooms growing in woods or even near trees are always to be regarded with suspicion? They may look like mushrooms, but they are probably poisonous.'

'I didn't know,' admitted Mrs Bellmark; 'but if they are, I imagine Mr Carrados will know.'

'It scarcely sounds like it—going to a wood, you know. As it happens, I have been looking up the subject lately. But, in any case, you say that he is coming back here?'

'He asked me if he might call on his way home for a cup of tea, and of course I said, "of course." '

'Of course,' also said Mr Carlyle. 'Motoring, I suppose?'

'Yes, a big grey car. He had Mr Parkinson with him.'

Mr Carlyle was slightly puzzled, as he frequently was by his friend's proceedings, but it was not his custom to dwell on any topic that involved an admission of inadequacy. The subject of Carrados and his eccentric quest was therefore dismissed until the sound of a formidable motor car dominating the atmosphere of the quiet suburban road was almost immediately followed by the entrance of the blind amateur. With a knowing look towards his niece Carlyle had taken up a position at the farther end of the room, where he remained in almost breathless silence.

Carrados acknowledged the hostess's smiling greeting and then nodded familiarly in the direction of the playful guest.

'Well, Louis,' he remarked, 'we've caught each other.'

Mrs Bellmark was perceptibly startled, but rippled musically at the failure of the conspiracy.

'Extraordinary,' admitted Mr Carlyle, coming forward.

'Not so very,' was the dry reply. 'Your friendly little maid'—to Mrs Bellmark—'mentioned your visitor as she brought me in.'

'Is it a fact, Max,' demanded Mr Carlyle, 'that you have been to—er—Stonecut Wood to get mushrooms?'

'Mrs Bellmark told you?'

'Yes. And did you succeed?'

'Parkinson found something that he assured me looked just like mushrooms.'

Mr Carlyle bestowed a triumphant glance on his niece.

'I should very much like to see these so-called mushrooms. Do you know, it may be rather a good thing for you that I met you.'

'It is always a good thing for me to meet you,' replied Carrados. 'You shall see them. They are in the car. Perhaps I shall be able to take you back to town?'

'If you are going very soon. No, no, Elsie'—in response to Mrs Bellmark's protesting 'Oh!'—'I don't want to influence Max, but I really must tear myself away the moment after tea. I still have to clear up some work on a rather important case I am just completing. It is quite appropriate to the occasion, too. Do you happen to know all about the Winpole business, Max?'

'No,' admitted Carrados, without any appreciable show of interest. 'Do you, Louis?'

'Yes,' responded Mr Carlyle with crisp assurance, 'yes, I think that I may claim I do. In fact it was I who obtained the evidence that induced the authorities to take up the case against Loudham.'

'Oh, do tell us all about it,' exclaimed Elsie. 'I have only seen something in the *Indicator*.'

Mr Carlyle shook his head, hemmed and looked wise, and then gave in.

'But not a word of this outside, Elsie,' he stipulated. 'Some of the evidence won't be given until next week and it might be serious——'

'Not a syllable,' assented the lady. 'How exciting! Go on.'

'Well, you know, of course, that the coroner's jury—very rightly, according to the evidence before them—brought in a verdict of accidental death. In the circumstances it was a reflection on the business methods or the care or the knowledge or whatever one may decide of the man who sold the mushrooms, a greengrocer called Lackington. I have seen Lackington, and with a rather remarkable pertinacity in the face of the evidence he insists that he could not have made this fatal blunder—that in weighing so small a quantity as half-a-pound, at any rate, he would at once have spotted anything that wasn't quite all right.'

'But the doctor said, Uncle Louis——'

'Yes, my dear Elsie, we know what the doctor said, but, rightly or wrongly, Lackington backs his experience and practical knowledge against theoretical generalities. In ordinary circumstances nothing more would have come of it, but it happens that Lackington has for a lodger a young man on the staff of the local paper, and for a neighbour a pharmaceutical chemist. These three men talking things over more than once—Lackington restive under the damage that had been done to his reputation, the journalist stimulating and keen for a newspaper sensation, the chemist contributing his quota of practical knowledge. At the end of a few days a fabric of circumstance had been woven which might be serious or innocent according to the further development of the suggestion and the manner in which it could be met. These were the chief points of the attack:

'Mrs Dupreen's allowance for the care and maintenance of Charlie Winpole ceased with his death, as she had told the jury. What she did not mention was that the deceased boy would have come into an inheritance of some fifteen thousand pounds at age and that this fortune now fell in equal shares to the lot of his two nearest relatives—Mrs Dupreen and her brother Philip.

'Mrs Dupreen was by no means in easy circumstances. Philip Loudham was equally poor and had no assured income. He had tried several forms of business and now, at about thirty-five, was spending his time chiefly in writing poems and painting water-colours, none of which brought him in any money so far as one could learn.

'Philip Loudham, it was admitted, took up the food round which the tragedy centred.

'Philip Loudham was shown to be in debt and urgently in need of money. There was supposed to be a lady in the case—I hope I need say no more, Elsie.'

'Who is she?' asked Mrs Bellmark with poignant interest.

'We do not know yet. A married woman, it is rumoured, I regret to say. It scarcely matters—certainly not to you, Elsie. To continue:

'Mrs Dupreen got back from her shopping in the afternoon before her nephew's death at about three o'clock. In less than half-an-hour Loudham left the house and going to the station took a return ticket to Euston. He left by the 3.41 and was back in St Abbots at 5.43. That would give him barely an hour in town for whatever business he transacted. What was that business?

'The chemist next door supplied the information that although bhurine only occurs in nature in this one form, it can be isolated from the other constituents of the fungus and dealt with like any other liquid poison. But it was a very exceptional commodity, having no commercial uses and probably not half-a-dozen retail chemists in London had it on their shelves. He himself had never stocked it and never been asked for it.

'With this suggestive but by no means convincing evidence,' continued Mr Carlyle, 'the young journalist went to the editor of *The Morning Indicator*, to which he acted as St Abbots correspondent and asked him whether he cared to take up the inquiry as a "scoop". The local trio had carried it as far as they were able. The editor of the *Indicator* decided to look into it and asked me to go on with the case. This is how my connection with it arose.'

'Oh, that's how newspapers get to know things?' commented Mrs Bellmark. 'I often wondered.'

'It is one way,' assented her uncle.

'An American development,' contributed Carrados. 'It is a little overdone there.'

'It must be awful,' said the hostess. 'And the police methods! In the plays that come from the States——' The entrance of the friendly handmaiden, bringing tea, was responsible for this platitudinous wave. The conversation, in deference to Mr Carlyle's scruples, marked time until the door closed on her departure.

'My first business,' continued the inquiry agent, after making himself useful at the table, 'was naturally to discover among the chemists in London whether a sale of bhurine coincided with Philip Loudham's hasty visit. If this line failed, the very foundation of the edifice of hypothetical guilt gave way; if it succeeded ... Well, it did succeed. In a street off Caistor Square, Tottenham Court Road—Trenion Street—we found a man called Lightcraft who at once remembered making such a sale. As bhurine is a specified poison the transaction would have to be entered, and Lightcraft's book contained this unassailable piece of evidence. On Wednesday, the sixth of this month, a man signing his name as "J. D. Williams", and giving "25 Chalcott Place" as his address, purchased four drachms of bhurine. Lightcraft fixed the time as about half-past four. I went to 25 Chalcott Place and found it to be a small boarding-house. No one of the name of Williams was known there.'

If Mr Carlyle's tone of finality went for anything, Philip Loudham was as good as pinioned. Mrs Bellmark supplied the expected note of admiration.

'Just fancy!' was the form it took.

'Under the Act the purchaser must be known to the chemist?' suggested Carrados.

'Yes,' agreed Mr Carlyle; 'and there our friend Lightcraft may have let himself in for a little trouble. But, as he says—and we must admit that there is something in it—who is to define what "known to" actually means? A hundred people are known to him as regular or occasional customers and he has never heard their names; a score of names and addresses represent to him regular or occasional customers whom he has never seen. This "J. D. Williams" came in with an easy air and appeared at all events to know Lightcraft. The face seemed not unfamiliar and Lightcraft was perhaps a little too facile in assuming that he *did* know him. Well, well, Max, I can understand the circumstances. Competition is keen—especially against the private chemist—and one may give offence and lose a customer. We must all live.'

'Except Charlie Winpole,' occurred to Max Carrados, but he left the retort unspoken. 'Did you happen to come across any inquiry for bhurine at other shops?' he asked instead.

'No,' replied Carlyle, 'no, I did not. It would have been an indication then, of course, but after finding the actual place the others would have no significance. Why do you ask?'

'Oh, nothing. Only don't you think that he was rather lucky in getting it first shot if our St Abbots authority was right?'

'Yes, yes; perhaps he was. But this is of no interest to us now. The great thing is that a peculiarly sinister and deliberate murder is brought home to its perpetrator. When you consider the circumstances, upon my soul, I don't know that I have ever unmasked a more ingenious and cold-blooded ruffian.'

'Then he has confessed, uncle?'

'Confessed, my dear Elsie,' said Mr Carlyle with a tolerant smile, 'no, he has not confessed—men of that type never do. On the contrary, he asserted his outraged innocence with a considerable show of indignation. What else was he to do? Then he was asked to account for his movements between 4.15 and 5 o'clock on that afternoon. Egad, the fellow was so cocksure of the safety of his plans that he hadn't even taken the trouble to think that out. First he denied that he had been away from St Abbots at all. Then he remembered. He had run down to town in the afternoon for a few things.—What things?— Well, chiefly stationery.—Where had he bought it?—At a shop in Oxford Street; he did not know the name.—Would he be able to point it out?—He thought so.—Could he identify the attendant?—No, he could not remember him in the least.—Had he the bill?—No, he never kept small bills.—How much was the amount?—About three or four shillings.—And the return fare to Euston was three-and-eight-pence. Was it not rather an extravagant journey?—He could only say that he did so.—Three or four shillings' worth of stationery would be a moderate parcel. Did he have it sent?—No, he took it with him.— Three or four shillings' worth of stationery in his pocket?—No, it was in a parcel.—Too large to go in his pocket?—Yes.—Two independent witnesses would testify that he carried no parcel. They were townsmen of St Abbots who had travelled down in the same carriage with him. Did he still persist that he had been engaged in buying stationery? Then he declined to say anything further—about the best thing he could do.'

'And Lightcraft identifies him?'

'Um, well, not quite so positively as we might wish. You see, a fortnight has elapsed. The man who bought the poison wore a moustache—put on, of course—but Lightcraft will say that there is a resemblance and the type of the two men the same.'

'I foresee that Mr Lightcraft's accommodating memory for faces will come in for rather severe handling in cross-examination,' said Carrados, as though he rather enjoyed the prospect.

'It will balance Mr Philip Loudham's unfortunate forgetfulness for localities, Max,' rejoined Mr Carlyle, delivering the thrust with his own inimitable aplomb.

Carrados rose with smiling acquiescence to the shrewdness of the riposte.

'I will be quite generous, Mrs Bellmark,' he observed. 'I will take him away now, with the memory of that lingering in your ears—all my crushing retorts unspoken.'

'Five-thirty, egad!' exclaimed Mr Carlyle, displaying his imposing gold watch. 'We must—or, at all events, I must. You can think of them in the car, Max.'

'I do hope you won't come to blows,' murmured the lady. Then she added: 'When will the real trial come on, Uncle Louis?'

'The Sessions? Oh, early in January.'

'I must remember to look out for it.' Possibly she had some faint idea of Uncle Louis taking a leading part in the proceedings. At any rate Mr Carlyle looked pleased, but when adieux had been taken and the door was closed Mrs Bellmark was left wondering what the enigma of Max Carrados's departing smile had been.

3

It was when they were in the car that Mr Carlyle suddenly remembered the suspected mushrooms and demanded to be shown them. A very moderate collection was produced for his inspection. He turned them over sceptically.

'The gills are too pale for true mushrooms, Max,' he declared sapiently. 'Don't take any risk. Let me pitch them out of the window?'

'No.' Carrados's hand quietly arrested the threatened action. 'No; I have a use for them, Louis, but it is not culinary. You are quite right; they are rank poison. I only want to study them for . . . a case I am interested in.'

'A case! You don't mean to say that there is another mushroom poisoner going?'

'No; it is the same.'

'But—but you said——'

'That I did not know all about it? Quite true. Nor do I yet. But I know rather more than I did then.'

'Do you mean that Scotland Yard——'

'No, Louis.' Mr Carrados appeared to find something rather amusing in the situation. 'I am for the other side.'

'The other side! And you let me babble out the whole case for the prosecution! Well, really, Max!'

'But you are out of it now? The Public Prosecutor has taken it up?'

'True, true. But, for all that, I feel devilishly had.'

'Then I will give you the whole case for the defence and so we shall be quits. In fact I am relying on you to help me with it.'

'With the defence? I—after supplying the evidence that the Public Prosecutor is acting on?'

'Why not? You don't want to hang Philip Loudham—especially if he happens to be innocent—do you?'

'I don't want to hang anyone,' protested Mr Carlyle. 'At least—not as a private individual.'

'Quite so. Well, suppose you and I between ourselves find out the actual facts of the case and decide what is to be done. The more usual course is for the prosecution to exaggerate all that tells against the accused and to contradict everything in his favour; for the defence to advance fictitious evidence of innocence and to lie roundly on everything that endangers his client; while on both sides witnesses are piled up to bemuse the jury into accepting the desired version. That does not always make for impartiality or for justice. . . . Now you and I are two reasonable men, Louis——'

'I hope so,' admitted Mr Carlyle. 'I think so.'

'You can give away the case for the prosecution and I will expose the weakness of the defence, so, between us, we may arrive at the truth.'

'It strikes me as a deuced irregular proceeding. But I am curious to hear the defence all the same.'

'You are welcome to all of it that there yet is. An alibi, of course.'

'Ah!' commented Mr Carlyle with expression.

'So recently as yesterday a lady came hurriedly, and with a certain amount of secrecy, to see me. She came on the strength of the introduction afforded by a mutual acquaintanceship with Fromow, the Greek professor. When we were alone she asked me—besought me, in fact—to advise her what to do. A few hours before, Mrs Dupreen had rushed across London to her with the tale of young Loudham's arrest. Then out came the whole story. This woman—well, her name is Guestling, Louis—lives a little way down in Surrey and is married. Her husband, according to her own account—and I have certainly heard a hint about it elsewhere—leads her a studiedly outrageous existence; an admired silken-mannered gentleman in society, a tolerable pole-cat at home, one infers. About a year ago Mrs Guestling made the acquaintance of Loudham, who was staying in that neighbourhood painting his pretty unsaleable country lanes and golden sunsets. The inevitable, or, to accept the lady's protestations, half the inevitable, followed. Guestling, who adds an insatiable jealousy to his other domestic virtues, vetoed the new acquaintance and thenceforward the two met hurriedly and furtively in town. Had either of them any money they might have snatched their destinies from the hands of Fate and gone off together, but she has nothing and he has nothing and both, I suppose, are poor mortals when it comes to doing anything courageous and outright in this censorious world. So they drifted, drifting but not yet wholly wrecked.'

'A formidable incentive for a weak and desperate man to secure a fortune by hook or crook, Max,' said Carlyle drily.

'That is the motive that I wish to make you a present of. But, as you will insist on your side, it is also a motive for a weak and foolish couple to steal every brief opportunity for a secret meeting. On Wednesday, the sixth, the lady was returning home from a visit to some friends in the Midlands. She saw in the occasion an opportunity, and on the morning of the sixth a message appeared in the personal columns of the *Daily Telegraph*—their usual channel of communication—making an assignation. That much can be established by the irrefutable evidence of the newspaper. Philip Loudham kept the appointment and for half-an-hour this miserably happy pair sat holding each other's hands in a dreary deserted waiting-room of Bishop's Road Station. That half-hour was from 4.15 to 4.45. Then Loudham saw Mrs Guestling into Praed Street Station for Victoria, returned to Euston and just caught the 5.7 St Abbots.'

'Can this be corroborated—especially as regards the precise time they were together?'

'Not a word of it. They chose the waiting-room at Bishop's Road for seclusion, and apparently they got it. Not a soul even looked in while they were there.'

'Then, by Jupiter, Max,' exclaimed Mr Carlyle with some emotion, 'you have hanged your client!'

Carrados could not restrain a smile at his friend's tragic note of triumph.

'Well, let us examine the rope,' he said with his usual imperturbability.

'Here it is.' It was a trivial enough shred of evidence that the inquiry agent took from his pocket-book and put into the expectant hand; in point of fact the salmon-coloured ticket of a 'London General' omnibus.

'Royal Oak—the stage nearest Paddington—to Tottenham Court Road—the point nearest Trenion Street,' he added significantly.

'Yes,' acquiesced Carrados, taking it.

'The man who bought the bhurine dropped that ticket on the floor of the shop. He left the door open and Lightcraft followed him to close it. That is how he came to pick the ticket up, and he remembers that it was not there before. Then he threw it into a wastepaper basket underneath the counter, and that is where we found it when I called on him.'

'Mr Lightcraft's memory fascinates me, Louis,' was the blind man's unruffled comment. 'Let us drop in and have a chat with him.'

'Do you really think that there is anything more to be got in that quarter?' queried Carlyle dubiously. 'I have turned him inside out, as you may be sure.'

'True; but we approach Mr Lightcraft from different angles. You were looking for evidence to prove young Loudham guilty. I am looking for evidence to prove him innocent.'

'Very well, Max,' acquiesced his companion. 'Only don't blame me if it turns out as deuced awkward for your man as Mrs G. has done. Shall I tell you what a counsel may be expected to put to the jury as the explanation of that lady's evidence?'

'No, thanks,' said Carrados half sleepily from his corner. 'Don't trouble; I know. I told her so.'

4

Mr Lightcraft made no pretence of being glad to see his visitors. For some time he declined to open his mouth at all on the subject that had brought them there, repeating with parrot-like obstinacy to every remark on their part, 'The matter is *sub judice*. I am unable to say anything further,' until Mr Carlyle longed to box his ears and bring him to his senses. For the ears happened to be unduly prominent and at that moment glowing with sensitiveness, while the chemist was otherwise a lank and pallid man, whose transparent ivory skin and well-defined moustache gave him something of the appearance of a waxwork.

'At all events,' interposed Carrados, when his friend turned from the maddening reiteration in despair, 'you don't mind telling me a few things about bhurine—apart from this particular connection?'

'I am very busy,' and Mr Lightcraft, with his back towards the shop, did something superfluous among the bottles on a shelf.

'I imagined that the time of Mr Max Carrados, of whom even you may possibly have heard, is as valuable as yours, my good sir,' put in Mr Carlyle with scandalised dignity.

'Mr Carrados?' Lightcraft turned and regarded the blind man with interest. 'I did not know. But you must recognise the unenviable position in which I am put by this gentleman's interference.'

'It is his profession, you know,' said Carrados mildly, 'and in any case it would certainly have been someone. Why not help me to get you out of the position?'

'How is that possible?'

'If the case against Philip Loudham breaks down and he is discharged at the next hearing you would not be called upon further.'

'That would certainly be a mitigation. But why should it break down?'

'Suppose you let me try the taste of bhurine,' suggested Carrados. 'You have some left?'

'Max, Max!' cried Mr Carlyle's warning voice, 'aren't you aware that the stuff is a deadly poison? One—fifth of a grain——'

'Mr Lightcraft will know how to administer it.'

Apparently Mr Lightcraft did. He filled a graduated measure with cold water, dipped a slender glass rod into a bottle that was not kept on the shelves, and with it stirred the water. Then into another vessel of water he dropped a single drop of the dilution.

'One in a hundred and twenty-five thousand, Mr Carrados,' he said, offering him the mixture.

Carrados just touched the liquid with his lips, considered the impression and then wiped his mouth.

'Now the smell.'

The unstoppered bottle was handed to him and he took in its exhalation.

'Stewed mushrooms!' was his comment. 'What is it used for, Mr Lightcraft?'

'Nothing that I know of.'

'But your customer must have stated an application?'

The pallid chemist flushed a little at the recollection of that incident.

'Yes,' he conceded. 'There is a good deal about the whole business that is still a mystery to me. The man came in shortly after I had lit up and nodded familiarly as he said: "Good-evening, Mr Lightcraft." I naturally assumed that he was someone whom I could not quite place. "I want another half-pound of nitre," he said and I served him. Had he bought nitre before, I have since tried to recall, but I cannot. It is a common enough article and I sell it, you might say, every day. I have a poor memory for faces I am willing to admit. It has hampered me in business many a time: people expect you to remember them. We chatted about nothing in particular as I did up the packet. After he had paid and turned to go he looked back again. "By the way, do you happen to have any bhurine?" he inquired. Unfortunately I had a few ounces. "Of course you know its nature?" I cautioned him. "May I ask what you require it for?" He nodded and held up the parcel of nitre he had in his hand. "The same thing," he replied, "taxidermy." Then I supplied him with half-an-ounce.'

'As a matter of fact, is it used in taxidermy?'

'It does not seem to be. I don't stuff birds but I have made inquiry and no one knows of it. Nitre is largely used, and some of the dangerous poisons—arsenic and mercuric chloride, for instance—but not this although it might quite reasonably have been. No, it was a subterfuge.'

'Now the poison book, if you please.'

Mr Lightcraft produced it without demur and the blind man ran his finger along the indicated line.

'Yes; this is quite in form. Is it a fact, Mr Lightcraft, that not half-a-dozen chemists in London stock this particular substance? We are told that.'

'I can quite believe it. I certainly don't know of another.'

'Strangely enough, your customer of the sixth seems to have come straight here. Do you issue a price-list?'

'Only a localised one of certain photographic goods. Bhurine is not included.'

'You can suggest no reason why Mr Philip Loudham should be inspired to presume that he might be able to get this unusual drug from you? You have never corresponded with him nor come across his name or address before?'

'No. As far as I can recollect, I know nothing whatever of him.'

'Then as yet we must assume that it was pure chance. By the way, Mr Lightcraft, how does it come that *you* stock this rare poison, which has no commercial use and for which there is no demand?'

The chemist permitted himself to smile at the blunt terms of the inquiry.

'In the ordinary way I don't stock it,' he replied. 'This is a small quantity that I had over from my own use.'

'Your own use? Oh, then it has a use after all?'

'No, scarcely that. Some time ago it leaked out in a corner of the photographic world that a great revolution in colour-photography was on the point of realisation by the use of bhurine in one of the processes. I, among others, at once took it up. Unfortunately it was only another instance of a discovery that is correct in theory breaking down in practice. Nothing came of it.'

'Dear, dear me,' said Carrados softly, with sympathetic understanding in his voice; 'what a pity. You are interested in photography, Mr Lightcraft?'

'It is the hobby of my life, sir. Of course most chemists dabble in it as a part of their business, but I devote all my spare time to experimenting, Colour-photography in particular.'

'Colour-photography; yes. It has a great future. This bhurine process—I suppose it would have been of considerable financial value if it had worked?'

Mr Lightcraft laughed quietly and rubbed his hands together. For the moment he had forgotten Loudham and the annoying case and lived in his enthusiasm.

'I should rather say it would, Mr Carrados,' he replied. 'It would have been the most epoch-marking thing since Gaudin produced the first dry plate in '54. Consider it—the elaborate processes of Dyndale, Eiloff and Jupp reduced to the simplicity of a single contact print giving the entire range of chromatic variation. Financially it—it will scarcely bear thinking about in these times.'

'Was it widely taken up?' asked Carrados.

'The bhurine idea?'

'Yes. You spoke of the secret leaking out. Were many in the know?'

'Not at all. The group of initiates was only a small one and I should imagine that, on reflection, every man kept it to himself. It certainly never became public. Then when the theory was definitely exploded of course no one took any further interest in it.'

'Were all who were working on the same lines known to you, Mr Lightcraft?'

'Well, yes; more or less I suppose they would be,' said the chemist thoughtfully. 'You see, the man who stumbled on the formula was a member of the Iris—a society of those interested in this subject, of which I am the secretary—and I don't think it ever got beyond the committee.'

'How long ago was this?'

'A year—eighteen months. It led to unpleasantness and broke up the society.'

'Suppose it happened to come to your knowledge that one of the original circle was quietly pursuing his experiments on the same lines with bhurine—what should you infer from it?'

Mr Lightcraft considered. Then he regarded Carrados with a sharp, almost a startled, glance and then he fell to biting his nails in perplexed uncertainty.

'It would depend on who it was,' he replied.

'Was there by any chance one who was unknown to you by sight but whose address you were familiar with?'

'Paulden!' exclaimed Mr Lightcraft. 'Paulden by heaven! I do believe you're right. He was the ablest of the lot and he never came to the meetings—a corresponding member. Southem, the original man who struck the idea, knew Paulden and told him of it. Southem was an impractical genius who would never be able to make anything work. Paulden—yes, Paulden it was who finally persuaded Southem that there was nothing in it. He sent a report to the same effect to be read at one of the meetings. So Paulden is taking up bhurine again——'

'Where does he live?' inquired Carrados.

'Ivor House, Wilmington Lane, Enstead. As secretary I have written there a score of times.'

'It is on the Great Western—Paddington,' commented the blind man. 'Still, can you get out the addresses of the others, Mr Lightcraft?'

'Certainly, certainly. I have the book of membership. But I am convinced now that Paulden was the man. I believe that I did actually see him once some years ago, but he has grown a moustache since.'

'If you had been convinced of that a few days ago it would have saved us some awkwardness,' volunteered Mr Carlyle, with no little asperity.

'When you came before, Mr Carlyle, you were so convinced yourself of it being Mr Loudham that you wouldn't hear of me thinking of anyone else,' retorted the chemist. 'You will bear me out also that I never positively identified him as my customer. Now here is the book. Southem, Potter's Bar. Voynich, Islington. Crawford, Streatham Hill. Brown, Southampton Row. Vickers, Clapham Common. Tidey, Fulham. All those I knew quite well—associated with them week after week. Williams I didn't know so closely. He is dead. Bigwood has gone to Canada. I don't think anyone else was in the bhurine craze— as we called it afterwards.'

'But now? What would you call it now?' queried Carrados.

'Now? Well I hope that you will get me out of having to turn up at court and that sort of thing, Mr Carrados. If Paulden is going on experimenting with bhurine again on the sly I shall want all my spare time to do the same myself!'

5

A few hours later the two investigators rang the bell of a substantial detached house in Enstead, the little country town twenty miles out in Berkshire, and asked to see Mr Paulden.

'It is no good taking Lightcraft to identify the man,' Carrados had decided. 'If Paulden denied it, our friend's obliging record in that line would put him out of court.'

'I maintain an open mind on the subject,' Carlyle had replied. 'Lightcraft is admittedly a very bending reed, but there is no reason why he should not have been right before and wrong today.'

They were shown into a ceremonial reception-room to wait. Mr Carlyle diagnosed snug circumstances and the tastes of an indoors, comfort-loving man in the surroundings.

The door opened, but it was to admit a middle-aged, matronly lady with good-humour and domestic capability proclaimed by every detail of her smiling face and easy manner.

'You wished to see my husband?' she asked with friendly courtesy.

'Mr Paulden? Yes, we should like to,' replied Carlyle, with his most responsive urbanity. 'It is a matter that need not occupy more than a few minutes.'

'He is very busy just now. If it has anything to do with the election'—a local contest was at its height—'he is not interested in politics and scarcely ever votes.' Her manner was not curious, but merely reflected a business-like desire to save trouble all round.

'Very sensible too; ve-ry sensible indeed,' almost warbled Mr Carlyle with instinctive cajolery. 'After all,' he continued, mendaciously appropriating as his own an aphorism at which he had laughed heartily a few days before in the theatre, 'after all, what does an election do but change the colour of the necktie of the man who picks our pockets? No, no, Mrs Paulden, it is merely a—um—quite personal matter.'

The lady looked from one to the other with smiling amiability.

'Some little mystery,' her expression seemed to say. 'All right; I don't mind, only perhaps I could help you if I knew.'

'Mr Paulden is in his dark-room now,' was what she actually did say. 'I am afraid, I am really afraid that I shan't be able to persuade him to come out unless I can take a definite message.'

'One understands the difficulty of tempting an enthusiast from his work,' suggested Carrados, speaking for the first time. 'Would it be permissible to take us to the door of the dark-room, Mrs Paulden, and let us speak to your husband through it?'

'We can try that way,' she acquiesced readily, 'if it is really so important.'

'I think so,' he replied.

The dark-room lay across the hall. Mrs Paulden conducted them to the door, waited a moment, and then knocked quietly.

'Yes?' sang out a voice, rather irritably one might judge, from inside.

'Two gentlemen have called to see you about something, Lance——'

'I cannot see anyone when I am in here,' interrupted the voice with rising sharpness. 'You know that, Clara——'

'Yes, dear,' she said soothingly, 'but listen. They are at the door here and if you can spare the time just to come and speak you will know without much trouble if their business is as important as they think.'

'Wait a minute,' came the reply after a moment's pause, and then they heard someone approach the door from the other side.

It was a little difficult to know exactly how it happened in the obscure light of that corner of the hall. Carrados had stepped nearer to the door to speak. Possibly he trod on Mr Carlyle's toe, for there was a confused movement; certainly he put out his hand hastily to recover himself. The next moment the door of the dark-room jerked open, the light was let in and the warm odours of a mixed and vitiated atmosphere rolled out. Secure in the well-ordered discipline of his excellent household, Mr Paulden had neglected the precaution of locking himself in.

'Confound it all!' shouted the incensed experimenter in a towering rage; 'confound it all, you've spoiled the whole thing now!'

'Dear me,' apologised Carrados penitently, 'I am so sorry. I think it must have been my fault, do you know. Does it really matter?'

'Matter!' stormed Mr Paulden, recklessly flinging open the door fully now to come face to face with his disturbers—'matter letting a flood of light into a dark-room in the middle of a delicate experiment!'

'Surely it was very little,' persisted Carrados.

'Pshaw,' snarled the angry photographer, 'it was enough. You know the difference between light and dark, I suppose?'

Mr Carlyle suddenly found himself holding his breath, wondering how on earth Max had conjured that opportune challenge to the surface.

'No,' was the mild and deprecating reply—the appeal *ad misericordiam* that had never failed him yet—'no, unfortunately I don't, for I am blind. That is why I am so awkward.'

Out of the shocked silence Mrs Paulden gave a little croon of pity. The moment before she had been speechless with indignation on her husband's behalf. Paulden felt as though he had struck a suffering animal. He stammered an apology and turned away to close the unfortunate door. Then he began to walk slowly down the hall.

'You wished to see me about something?' he remarked, with matter-of-fact civility. 'Perhaps we had better go in here.' He indicated the reception-room where they had waited and followed them in. The admirable Mrs Paulden gave no indication of wishing to join the party.

Carrados came to the point at once.

'Mr Carlyle,' he said, indicating his friend, 'has recently been acting for the prosecution in a case of alleged poisoning that the Public Prosecutor has now taken up. I am interested in the defence. Both sides are thus before you, Mr Paulden.'

'How does this concern me?' asked Paulden with obvious surprise.

'You are experimenting with bhurine. The victim of this alleged crime undoubtedly lost his life by bhurine poisoning. Do you mind telling us when and where you acquired your stock of this scarce substance?'

'I have had——'

'No—a moment, Mr Paulden, before you reply,' struck in Carrados with a warning gesture. 'You must understand that nothing so grotesque as to connect you with a crime is contemplated. But a man is under arrest and the chief point against him is the half-ounce of bhurine that Lightcraft of Trenion Street sold to someone at half-past five last Wednesday fortnight. Before you commit yourself to any statement that it may possibly be difficult to recede from, you should realise that this inquiry will be pushed to the very end.'

'How do you know that I am using bhurine?'

'That,' parried Carrados, 'is a blind man's secret.'

'Oh, well. And you say that someone has been arrested through this fact?'

'Yes. Possibly you have read something of the St Abbots mushroom poisoning case?'

'I have no interest in the sensational ephemera of the Press. Very well; it was I who bought the bhurine from Lightcraft that Wednesday afternoon. I gave a false name and address, I must admit. I had a sufficient private reason for so doing.'

'This knocks what is vulgarly termed "the stuffing" out of the case for the prosecution,' observed Carlyle, who had been taking a note. 'It may also involve you in some trouble yourself, Mr Paulden.'

'I don't think that he need regard that very seriously in the circumstances,' said Carrados reassuringly.

'They must find some scapegoat, you know,' persisted Mr Carlyle. 'Loudham will raise Cain over it.'

'I don't think so. Loudham, as the prosecution will roundly tell him, has only himself to thank for not giving a satisfactory account of his movements. Loudham will be lectured, Lightcraft will be fined the minimum, and Mr Paulden will, I imagine, be virtuously told not to do it again.'

The man before them laughed bitterly.

'There will be no occasion to do it again,' he said. 'Do you know anything of the circumstances?'

'Lightcraft told us something connected with colour-photography. You distrust Mr Lightcraft, I infer?'

Mr Paulden came down to the heart-easing medium of the street.

'I've had some once, thanks,' was what he said with terse expression. 'Let me tell you. About eighteen months ago I was on the edge of a great discovery in colour-photography. It was my discovery, whatever you may have heard. Bhurine was the medium, and not being then so cautious or so suspicious as I have reason to be now, and finding it difficult—really impossible—to procure this substance casually, I sent in an order to Lightcraft to procure me a stock. Unfortunately, in a moment of enthusiasm I had hinted at the anticipated results to a man who was then my friend—a weakling called Southem. Comparing notes with Lightcraft they put two and two together and in a trice most of the secret boiled over.

'If you have ever been within an ace of a monumental discovery you will understand the torment of anxiety and self reproach that possessed me. For months the result must have trembled in the balance, but even as it evaded me so it evaded the others. And at last I was able to spread conviction that the bhurine process was a failure. I breathed again.

'You don't want to hear of the various things that conspired to baffle me. I proceeded with extreme caution and therefore slowly.

About two weeks ago I had another foretaste of success and immediately on it a veritable disaster. By some diabolical mischance I contrived to upset my stock bottle of bhurine. It rolled down, smashed to atoms on a developing dish filled with another chemical, and the precious lot was irretrievably lost. To arrest the experiments at that stage even for a day was to waste a month. In one place and one alone could I hope to replenish the stock temporarily at such short notice and to do it openly after my last experience filled me with dismay. . . . Well, you know what happened, and now, I suppose, it will all come out.'

6

A week after his arrest Philip Loudham and his sister were sitting in the drawing-room at Hazlehurst, nervous and expectant. Loudham had been discharged scarcely six hours before, with such vindication of his character as the frigid intimation that there was no evidence against him afforded. On his arrival home he had found a letter from Max Carrados—a name with which he was now familiar—awaiting him. There had been other notes and telegrams—messages of sympathy and congratulation, but the man who had brought about his liberation did not include these conventionalities. He merely stated that he purposed calling upon Mr Loudham at nine o'clock that evening and that he hoped it would be convenient for him and all other members of the household to be at home.

'He can scarcely be coming to be thanked,' speculated Loudham, breaking the silence that had fallen on them as the hour approached. 'I should have called on him myself tomorrow.'

Mrs Dupreen assented absent-mindedly. Both were dressed in black, and both at that moment had the same thought: that they were dreaming this.

'I suppose you won't go on living here, Irene?' continued the brother, speaking to make the minutes seem tolerable.

This at least had the effect of bringing Mrs Dupreen back into the present with a rush.

'Of course not,' she replied almost sharply and looking at him direct. 'Why should I, now?'

'Oh, all right,' he agreed. 'I didn't suppose you would.' Then, as the front-door bell was heard to ring: 'Thank heaven!'

'Won't you go to meet him in the hall and bring him in?' suggested Mrs Dupreen. 'He is blind, you know.'

Carrados was carrying a small leather case which he allowed Loudham to relieve him of, together with his hat and gloves. The introduction to Mrs Dupreen was made, the blind man put in touch with a chair, and then Philip Loudham began to rattle off the acknow-ledgement of gratitude of which he had been framing and rejecting openings for the last half-hour.

'I'm afraid it's no good attempting to thank you for the extraordi-nary service that you've rendered me, Mr Carrados,' he began, 'and, above all I appreciate the fact that, owing to you, it has been possible to keep Mrs Guestling's name entirely out of the case. Of course you know all about that, and my sister knows, so it isn't worth while beat-ing about the bush. Well, now that I shall have something like a decent income of my own, I shall urge Kitty—Mrs Guestling—to apply for the divorce that she is richly entitled to, and when that is all settled we shall marry at once and try to forget the experience on both sides that has led up to it. I hope,' he added tamely, 'that you don't consider us really much to blame?'

Carrados shook his head in mild deprecation.

'That is an ethical point that has lain outside the scope of my inquiry,' he replied. 'You would hardly imagine that I should disturb you at such a time merely to claim your thanks. Has it occurred to you why I should have come?'

Brother and sister exchanged looks and by their silence gave reply.

'We have still to find who poisoned Charlie Winpole.'

Loudham stared at their guest in frank bewilderment, Mrs Dupreen almost closed her eyes. When she spoke it was in a pained whisper.

'Is there anything more to be gained by pursuing that idea, Mr Car-rados?' she asked pleadingly. 'We have passed through a week of anguish, coming on a week of grief and great distress. Surely all has been done that can be done?'

'But you would have justice for your nephew if there has been foul play?'

Mrs Dupreen made a weary gesture of resignation. It was Loudham who took up the question.

'Do you really mean, Mr Carrados, that there is any doubt about the cause?'

'Will you give me my case please? Thank you.' He opened it and produced a small paper bag. 'Now a newspaper, if you will.' He opened the bag and poured out the contents. 'You remember stating at the inquest, Mrs Dupreen, that the mushrooms you bought looked rather dry? They were dry, there is no doubt, for they had been gathered four days. Here are some more under precisely the same conditions. They looked, in point of fact, like these?'

'Yes,' admitted the lady, beginning to regard Carrados with a new and curious interest.

'Dr Slark further stated that the only fungus containing the poison bhurine—the *Amanita* called the Black Cap, and also by the country folk the Devil's Scent Bottle—did not assume its forbidding appearance until maturity. He was wrong in one sense there, for experiment proves that if the Black Cap is gathered in its young and deceptive stage and kept, it assumes precisely the same appearance as it withers as if it was ripening naturally. You observe.' He opened a second bag and, shaking out the contents, displayed another little heap by the side of the first. 'Gathered four days ago,' he explained.

'Why, they are as black as ink,' commented Loudham. 'And the, phew! aroma!'

'One would hardly have got through without you seeing it, Mrs Dupreen?'

'I certainly hardly think so,' she admitted.

'With due allowance for Lackington's biased opinion I also think that his claim might be allowed. Finally, it is incredible that whoever peeled the mushrooms should have passed one of these. Who was the cook on that occasion, Mrs Dupreen?'

'My maid Hilda. She does all the cooking.'

'The one who admitted me?'

'Yes; she is the only servant I have, Mr Carrados.'

'I should like to have her in, if you don't mind.'

'Certainly, if you wish it. She is'—Mrs Dupreen felt that she must put in a favourable word before this inexorable man pronounced judgment—'she is a very good, straightforward girl.'

'So much the better.'

'I will——' Mrs Dupreen rose and began to cross the room.

'Ring for her? Thank you,' and whatever her intention had been the lady rang the bell.

'Yes, ma'am?'

A neat, modest-mannered girl, simple and nervous, with a face as full, as clear and as honest as an English apple. 'A pity,' thought Mrs Dupreen, 'that this confident, suspicious man cannot see her now.'

'Come in, Hilda. This gentleman wants to ask you something.'

'Yes, ma'am.' The round, blue eyes went appealingly to Carrados, fell upon the fungi spread out before her, and then circled the room with an instinct of escape.

'You remember the night poor Charlie died, Hilda,' said Carrados in his suavest tone, 'you cooked some mushrooms for his supper, didn't you?'

'No, sir,' came the glib reply.

' "No", Hilda!' exclaimed Mrs Dupreen in wonderment. 'You mean "yes", surely, child. Of course you cooked them. Don't you remember?'

'Yes, ma'am,' dutifully replied Hilda.

'That is all right,' said the blind man reassuringly. 'Nervous witnesses very often answer at random at first. You have nothing to be afraid of, my good girl, if you will tell the truth. I suppose you know a mushroom when you see it?'

'Yes, sir,' was the rather hesitating reply.

'There was nothing like this among them?' He held up one of the poisonous sort.

'No, sir; indeed there wasn't, sir. I should have known then.'

'You would have known *then*? You were not called at the inquest, Hilda?'

'No, sir.'

'If you had been, what would you have told them about these mushrooms that you cooked?'

'I—I don't know, sir.'

'Come, come, Hilda. What could you have told them—something

that we do not know? The truth, girl, if you want to save yourself!'
Then with a sudden, terrible directness the question cleft her trembling, guilt-stricken little brain: 'Where did you get the other mushrooms from that you put with those that your mistress brought?'

The eyes that had been mostly riveted to the floor leapt to Carrados for a single frightened glance, from Carrados to her mistress, to Philip Loudham, and to the floor again. In a moment her face changed and she was in a burst of sobbing.

'Oho, oho, oho!' she wailed. 'I didn't know; I didn't know. I meant no harm. Indeed, I didn't, ma'am.'

'Hilda! Hilda!' exclaimed Mrs Dupreen in bewilderment. 'What is it you're saying? What have you done?'

'It was his own fault. Oho, oho, oho!' Every word was punctuated by a gasp. 'He always was a little pig and making himself ill with food. You know he was, ma'am, although you were so fond of him. I'm sure I'm not to blame.'

'But *what* was it? What *have* you done?' besought her mistress.

'It was after you went out that afternoon. He put on his things and slipped down into the kitchen without the master knowing. He said what you were getting for his dinner, ma'am, and that you never got enough of them. Then he asked me not to tell about his being down, because he'd seen some white things from his bedroom window growing by the hedge at the bottom of the garden and he was going to get them. He brought in four or five and said they were mushrooms all right and would I cook them with the others and not say anything because you'd only say too many weren't good for him if you knew. And I didn't know any difference. Indeed I'm telling you the truth, ma'am.'

'Oh, Hilda, Hilda!' was torn reproachfully from Mrs Dupreen. 'You know what we've gone through. Why didn't you tell us this before?'

'I was afraid. I was afraid of what they'd do. And no one ever guessed until I thought I was safe. Indeed I meant no harm to anyone, but I was afraid that they'd punish me instead.'

Carrados had risen and was picking up his things.

'Yes,' he said, half musing to himself, 'I knew it must exist: the one explanation that accounts for everything and cannot be assailed. We have reached the bed-rock of truth at last.'

7

EDGAR WALLACE

The Poetical Policeman

I

The day Mr Reeder arrived at the Public Prosecutor's office was indeed a day of fate for Mr Lambton Green, Branch Manager of the London Scottish and Midland Bank.

That branch of the bank which Mr Green controlled was situate at the corner of Pell Street and Firling Avenue on the 'country side' of Ealing. It is a fairly large building and, unlike most suburban branch offices, the whole of the premises were devoted to banking business, for the bank carried very heavy deposits, the Lunar Traction Company, with three thousand people on its pay-roll, the Associated Novelties Corporation, with its enormous turnover, and the Laraphone Company being only three of the L.S.M.'s customers.

On Wednesday afternoons, in preparation for the pay days of these corporations, large sums in currency were brought from the head office and deposited in the steel and concrete strong-room, which was immediately beneath Mr Green's private office, but admission to which was gained through a steel door in the general office. This door was observable from the street, and to assist observation there was a shaded lamp fixed to the wall immediately above, which threw a powerful beam of light upon the door. Further security was ensured by the employment of a night watchman, Arthur Malling, an army pensioner.

The bank lay on a restricted police beat which had been so arranged that the constable on patrol passed the bank every forty minutes. It was his practice to look through the window and exchange signals

120

with the night watchman, his orders being to wait until Malling appeared.

On the night of October 17th Police-Constable Burnett stopped as usual before the wide peep-hole and glanced into the bank. The first thing he noticed was that the lamp above the strong-room door had been extinguished. The night watchman was not visible, and, his suspicions aroused, the officer did not wait for the man to put in an appearance as he would ordinarily have done, but passed the window to the door, which, to his alarm, he found ajar. Pushing it open, he entered the bank, calling Malling by name. There was no answer.

Permeating the air was a faint, sweet scent which he could not locate. The general offices were empty and, entering the manager's room in which a light burnt, he saw a figure stretched upon the ground. It was the night watchman. His wrists were handcuffed, two straps had been tightly buckled about his knees and ankles.

The explanation for the strange and sickly aroma was now clear. Above the head of the prostrate man was suspended, by a wire hooked to the picture-rail, an old tin can, the bottom of which was perforated so that there fell an incessant trickle of some volatile liquid upon the thick cotton pad which covered Malling's face.

Burnett, who had been wounded in the war, had instantly recognised the smell of chloroform and, dragging the unconscious man into the outer office, snatched the pad from his face and, leaving him only long enough to telephone to the police station, sought vainly to bring him to consciousness.

The police reserves arrived within a few minutes, and with them the divisional surgeon who, fortunately, had been at the station when the alarm came through. Every effort to restore the unfortunate man to life proved unavailing.

'He was probably dead when he was found,' was the police doctor's verdict. 'What those scratches are on his right palm is a mystery.'

He pulled open the clenched fist and showed half a dozen little scratches. They were recent, for there was a smear of blood on the palm.

Burnett was sent at once to arouse Mr Green, the manager, who lived in Firling Avenue, at the corner of which the bank stood; a street of semi-detached villas of a pattern familiar enough to the Londoner.

As the officer walked through the little front garden to the door he saw a light through the panels, and he had hardly knocked before the door was opened and Mr Lambton Green appeared, fully dressed and, to the officer's discerning eye, in a state of considerable agitation. Constable Burnett saw on a hall chair a big bag, a travelling rug and an umbrella.

The little manager listened, pale as death, whilst Burnett told him of his discovery.

'The bank robbed? Impossible!' he almost shrieked. 'My God! this is awful!'

He was so near the point of collapse that Burnett had to assist him into the street.

'I—I was going away on a holiday,' he said incoherently, as he walked up the dark thoroughfare towards the bank premises.

'The fact is—I was leaving the bank. I left a note—explaining to the directors.'

Into a circle of suspicious men the manager tottered. He unlocked the drawer of his desk, looked and crumbled up.

'They're not here!' he said wildly. 'I left them here—my keys—with the note!'

And then he swooned. When the dazed man recovered he found himself in a police cell and, later in the day, he drooped before a police magistrate, supported by two constables and listened, like a man in a dream, to a charge of causing the death of Arthur Malling, and further, of converting to his own use the sum of £100,000.

It was on the morning of the first remand that Mr John G. Reeder, with some reluctance for he was suspicious of all Government departments, transferred himself from his own office on Lower Regent Street to a somewhat gloomy bureau on the top floor of the building which housed the Public Prosecutor. In making this change he advanced only one stipulation: that he should be connected by private telephone wire with his old bureau.

He did not demand this—he never demanded anything. He asked, nervously and apologetically. There was a certain wistful helplessness about John G. Reeder that made people feel sorry for him, that caused even the Public Prosecutor a few uneasy moments of doubt as to whether he had been quite wise in substituting this weak-appearing man of middle age for Inspector Holford—bluff, capable and heavily mysterious.

Mr Reeder was something over fifty, a long-faced gentleman with sandy-grey hair and a slither of side whiskers that mercifully distracted attention from his large outstanding ears. He wore half-way down his nose a pair of steel-rimmed pince-nez, through which nobody had ever seen him look—they were invariably removed when he was reading. A high and flat-crowned bowler hat matched and yet did not match a frock-coat tightly buttoned across his sparse chest. His boots were square-toed, his cravat—of the broad, chest-protector pattern—was ready-made and buckled into place behind a Gladstonian collar. The neatest appendage to Mr Reeder was an umbrella rolled so tightly that it might be mistaken for a frivolous walking cane. Rain or shine, he carried this article hooked to his arm, and within living memory it had never been unfurled.

Inspector Holford (promoted now to the responsibilities of Superintendent) met him in the office to hand over his duties, and a more tangible quantity in the shape of old furniture and fixings.

'Glad to know you, Mr Reeder. I haven't had the pleasure of meeting you before, but I've heard a lot about you. You've been doing Bank of England work, haven't you?'

Mr Reeder whispered that he had had that honour, and sighed as though he regretted the drastic sweep of fate that had torn him from the obscurity of his labours. Mr Holford's scrutiny was full of misgivings.

'Well,' he said awkwardly, 'this job is different, though I'm told that you are one of the best informed men in London, and if that is the case this will be easy work. Still, we've never had an outsider—I mean, so to speak, a private detective—in this office before, and naturally the Yard is a bit——'

'I quite understand,' murmured Mr Reeder, hanging up his immaculate umbrella. 'It is very natural. Mr Boland expected the appointment. His wife is annoyed—very properly. But she has no reason to be. She is an ambitious woman. She has a third interest in a West End dancing club that might be raided one of these days.'

Holford was staggered. Here was news that was little more than a whispered rumour at Scotland Yard.

'How the devil do you know that?' he blurted.

Mr Reeder's smile was one of self-depreciation.

'One picks up odd scraps of information,' he said apologetically. 'I—I see wrong in everything. That is my curious perversion—I have a criminal mind!'

Holford drew a long breath.

'Well—there is nothing much doing. That Ealing case is pretty clear. Green is an ex-convict, who got a job at the bank during the war and worked up to manager. He has done seven years for conversion.'

'Embezzlement and conversion,' murmured Mr Reeder. 'I—er—I'm afraid I was the principal witness against him: bank crimes were rather—er—a hobby of mine. Yes, he got into difficulties with money-lenders. Very foolish—extremely foolish. And he doesn't admit his error.' Mr Reeder sighed heavily. 'Poor fellow! With his life at stake one may forgive and indeed condone his pitiful prevarications.'

The inspector stared at the new man in amazement.

'I don't know that there is much "poor fellow" about him. He has cached £100,000 and told the weakest yarn that I've ever read—you'll find copies of the police reports here, if you'd like to read them. The scratches on Malling's hand are curious—they've found several on the other hand. They are not deep enough to suggest a struggle. As to the yarn that Green tells——'

Mr J. G. Reeder nodded sadly.

'It was not an ingenious story,' he said, almost with regret. 'If I remember rightly, his story was something like this: he had been recognised by a man who served in Dartmoor with him, and this fellow wrote a blackmailing letter telling him to pay or clear out. Sooner than return to a life of crime, Green wrote out all the facts to his directors, put the letter in the drawer of his desk with his keys, and left a note for his head cashier on the desk itself, intending to leave London and try to make a fresh start where he was unknown.'

'There were no letters in or on the desk, and no keys,' said the inspector decisively. 'The only true part of the yarn was that he had done time.'

'Imprisonment,' suggested Mr Reeder plaintively. He had a horror of slang. 'Yes, that was true.'

Left alone in his office, he spent a very considerable time at his private telephone, communing with the young person who was still a young person, although the passage of time had dealt unkindly with her. For the rest of the morning he was reading the depositions which his predecessor had put on the desk.

It was late in the afternoon when the Public Prosecutor strolled into his room and glanced at the big pile of manuscript through which his subordinate was wading.

'What are you reading—the Green business?' he asked, with a note of satisfaction in his voice. 'I'm glad that is interesting you—though it seems a fairly straightforward case. I have had a letter from the president of the man's bank, who for some reason seems to think Green was telling the truth.'

Mr Reeder looked up with that pained expression of his which he invariably wore when he was puzzled.

'Here is the evidence of Policeman Burnett,' he said. 'Perhaps you can enlighten me, sir. Policeman Burnett stated in his evidence—let me read it:

'"Some time before I reached the bank premises I saw a man standing at the corner of the street, immediately outside the bank. I saw him distinctly in the light of a passing mail van. I did not attach any importance to his presence, and I did not see him again. It was possible for this man to have gone round the block and come to 120, Firling Avenue without being seen by me. Immediately after I saw him, my foot struck against a piece of iron on the sidewalk. I put my lamp on the object and found it was an old horse-shoe; I had seen children playing with this particular shoe earlier in the evening. When I looked again towards the corner, the man had disappeared. He would have seen the light of my lamp. I saw no other person, and so far as I can remember, there was no light showing in Green's house when I passed it."'

Mr Reeder looked up.

'Well?' said the Prosecutor. 'There's nothing remarkable about that. It was probably Green who dodged round the block and came in at the back of the constable.'

Mr Reeder scratched his chin.

'Yes,' he said thoughtfully, 'ye-es.' He shifted uncomfortably in his chair. 'Would it be considered indecorous if I made a few inquiries, independent of the police?' he asked nervously. 'I should not like them to think that a mere dilettante was interfering with their lawful functions.'

'By all means,' said the Prosecutor heartily. 'Go down and see the officer in charge of the case: I'll give you a note to him—it is by no means unusual for my officer to conduct a separate investigation, though I am afraid you will discover very little. The ground has been well covered by Scotland Yard.'

'It would be permissible to see the man?' hesitated Reeder.

'Green? Why, of course! I will send you up the necessary order.'

The light was fading from a grey, blustering sky, and rain was falling fitfully, when Mr Reeder, with his furled umbrella hooked to his arm, his coat collar turned up, stepped through the dark gateway of Brixton Prison and was led to the cell where a distracted man sat, his head upon his hands, his pale eyes gazing into vacancy.

'It's true; it's true! Every word.' Green almost sobbed the words.

A pallid man, inclined to be bald, with a limp yellow moustache, going grey. Reeder, with his extraordinary memory for faces, recognised him the moment he saw him, though it was some time before the recognition was mutual.

'Yes, Mr Reeder, I remember you now. You were the gentleman who caught me before. But I've been as straight as a die. I've never taken a farthing that didn't belong to me. What my poor girl will think——'

'Are you married?' asked Mr Reeder sympathetically.

'No, but I was going to be—rather late in life. She's nearly thirty years younger than me, and the best girl that ever——'

Reeder listened to the rhapsody that followed, the melancholy deepening in his face.

'She hasn't been into the court, thank God, but she knows the truth. A friend of mine told me that she has been absolutely knocked out.'

'Poor soul!' Mr Reeder shook his head.

'It happened on her birthday, too,' the man went on bitterly.

'Did she know you were going away?'

'Yes, I told her the night before. I'm not going to bring her into the case. If we'd been properly engaged it would be different; but she's married and is divorcing her husband, but the decree hasn't been made absolute yet. That's why I never went about with her or saw much of her. And of course, nobody knew about our engagement, although we lived in the same street.'

'Firling Avenue?' asked Reeder, and the bank manager nodded despondently.

'She was married when she was seventeen to a brute. It was pretty galling for me, having to keep quiet about it—I mean, for nobody to know about our engagement. All sorts of rotten people were making up to her, and I had just to grind my teeth and say nothing. Impossible people! Why, that fool Burnett, who arrested me, he was sweet on her; used to write her poetry—you wouldn't think it possible in a policeman, would you?'

The outrageous incongruity of a poetical policeman did not seem to shock the detective.

'There is poetry in every soul, Mr Green,' he said gently, 'and a policeman is a man.'

Though he dismissed the eccentricity of the constable so lightly, the poetical policeman filled his mind all the way home to his house in the Brockley Road, and occupied his thoughts for the rest of his waking time.

It was a quarter to eight o'clock in the morning, and the world seemed entirely populated by milkmen and whistling newspaper boys, when Mr J. G. Reeder came into Firling Avenue.

He stopped only for a second outside the bank, which had long since ceased to be an object of local awe and fearfulness, and pursued his way down the broad avenue. On either side of the thoroughfare ran a row of pretty villas—pretty although they bore a strong family resemblance to one another; each house with its little forecourt, sometimes laid out simply as a grass plot, sometimes decorated with flower-beds. Green's house was the eighteenth in the road on the right-hand side. Here he had lived with a cook-housekeeper, and apparently gardening was not his hobby, for the forecourt was covered with grass that had been allowed to grow at its will.

Before the twenty-sixth house in the road Mr Reeder paused and gazed with mild interest at the blue blinds which covered every window. Evidently Miss Magda Grayne was a lover of flowers, for geraniums filled the window-boxes and were set at intervals along the tiny border under the bow window. In the centre of the grass plot was a circular flower-bed with one flowerless rose tree, the leaves of which were drooping and brown.

As he raised his eyes to the upper window, the blind went up slowly, and he was dimly conscious that there was a figure behind the white lace curtains. Mr Reeder walked hurriedly away, as one caught in an immodest act, and resumed his peregrinations until he came to the big nursery gardener's which formed the corner lot at the far end of the road.

Here he stood for some time in contemplation, his arm resting on the iron railings, his eyes staring blankly at the vista of greenhouses. He remained in this attitude so long that one of the nurserymen, not unnaturally thinking that a stranger was seeking a way into the gardens, came over with the laborious gait of the man who wrings his living from the soil, and asked if he was wanting anybody.

'Several people,' sighed Mr Reeder; 'several people!'

Leaving the resentful man to puzzle out his impertinence, he slowly retraced his steps. At No. 412 he stopped again, opened the little iron gate and passed up the path to the front door. A small girl answered his knock and ushered him into the parlour.

The room was not well furnished; it was scarcely furnished at all. A strip of almost new linoleum covered the passage; the furniture of the parlour itself was made up of wicker chairs, a square of art carpet and a table. He heard the sound of feet above his head, feet on bare boards, and then presently the door opened and a girl came in.

She was pretty in a heavy way, but on her face he saw the marks of sorrow. It was pale and haggard; the eyes looked as though she had been recently weeping.

'Miss Magda Grayne?' he asked, rising as she came in.

She nodded.

'Are you from the police?' she asked quickly.

'Not exactly the police,' he corrected carefully. 'I hold an—er—an appointment in the office of the Public Prosecutor, which is analogous to, but distinct from, a position in the Metropolitan Police Force.'

She frowned, and then:

'I wondered if anybody would come to see me,' she said. 'Mr Green sent you?'

'Mr Green told me of your existence: he did not send me.'

There came to her face in that second a look which almost startled him. Only for a fleeting space of time, the expression had dawned and passed almost before the untrained eye could detect its passage.

'I was expecting somebody to come,' she said. Then: 'What made him do it?' she asked.

'You think he is guilty?'

'The police think so.' She drew a long sigh. 'I wish to God I had never seen—this place!'

He did not answer; his eyes were roving round the apartment. On a bamboo table was an old vase which had been clumsily filled with golden chrysanthemums, of a peculiarly beautiful variety. Not all, for amidst them flowered a large Michaelmas daisy that had the forlorn appearance of a parvenu that had strayed by mistake into noble company.

'You're fond of flowers?' he murmured.

She looked at the vase indifferently.

'Yes, I like flowers,' she said. 'The girl put them in there.' Then: 'Do you think they will hang him?'

The brutality of the question, put without hesitation, pained Reeder.

'It is a very serious charge,' he said. And then: 'Have you a photograph of Mr Green?'

She frowned.

'Yes; do you want it?'

He nodded.

She had hardly left the room before he was at the bamboo table and had lifted out the flowers. As he had seen through the glass, they were roughly tied with a piece of string. He examined the ends, and here again his first observation had been correct: none of these flowers had been cut; they had been plucked bodily from their stalks. Beneath the string was the paper which had been first wrapped about the stalks. It was a page torn from a notebook; he could see the red lines, but the pencilled writing was indecipherable.

As her foot sounded on the stairs, he replaced the flowers in the vase, and when she came in he was looking through the window into the street.

'Thank you,' he said, as he took the photograph from her.

It bore an affectionate inscription on the back.

'You're married, he tells me, madam?'

'Yes, I am married, and practically divorced,' she said shortly.

'Have you been living here long?'

'About three months,' she answered. 'It was his wish that I should live here.'

He looked at the photograph again.

'Do you know Constable Burnett?'

He saw a dull flush come to her face and die away again.

'Yes, I know the sloppy fool!' she said viciously. And then, realising that she had been surprised into an expression which was not altogether ladylike, she went on, in a softer tone: 'Mr Burnett is rather sentimental, and I don't like sentimental people, especially—well, you understand, Mr——'

'Reeder,' murmured that gentleman.

'You understand, Mr Reeder, that when a girl is engaged and in my position, those kind of attentions are not very welcome.'

Reeder was looking at her keenly. Of her sorrow and distress there could be no doubt. On the subject of the human emotions, and the ravages they make upon the human countenance, Mr Reeder was almost as great an authority as Mantegazza.

'On your birthday,' he said. 'How very sad! You were born on the seventeenth of October. You are English, of course?'

'Yes, I'm English,' she said shortly. 'I was born in Walworth—in Wallington. I once lived in Walworth.'

'How old are you?'

'Twenty-three,' she answered.

Mr Reeder took off his glasses and polished them on a large silk handkerchief.

'The whole thing is inexpressibly sad,' he said. 'I am glad to have had the opportunity of speaking with you, young lady. I sympathise with you very deeply.'

And in this unsatisfactory way he took his departure.

She closed the door on him, saw him stop in the middle of the path and pick up something from a border bed, and wondered, frowning, why this middle-aged man had picked up the horseshoe she had thrown through the window the night before. Into Mr Reeder's tail pocket went this piece of rusted steel and then he continued his thoughtful way to the nursery gardens, for he had a few questions to ask.

The men of Section 10 were parading for duty when Mr Reeder came timidly into the charge room and produced his credentials to the inspector in charge.

'Oh, yes, Mr Reeder,' said that officer affably. 'We have had a note from the P.P.'s office, and I think I had the pleasure of working with you on that big slush[1] case a few years ago. Now what can I do for you? . . . Burnett? Yes, he's here.'

He called the man's name and a young and good-looking officer stepped from the ranks.

'He's the man who discovered the murder—he's marked for promotion,' said the inspector. 'Burnett, this gentleman is from the Public Prosecutor's office and he wants a little talk with you. Better use my office, Mr Reeder.'

The young policeman saluted and followed the shuffling figure into the privacy of the inspector's office. He was a confident young man: already his name and portrait had appeared in the newspapers, the hint of promotion had become almost an accomplished fact, and before his eyes was the prospect of a supreme achievement.

'They tell me that you are something of a poet, officer,' said Mr Reeder.

Burnett blushed.

'Why, yes, sir. I write a bit,' he confessed.

'Love poems, yes?' asked the other gently. 'One finds time in the night—er—for such fancies. And there is no inspiration like—er—love, officer.'

Burnett's face was crimson.

'I've done a bit of writing in the night, sir,' he said, 'though I've never neglected my duty.'

'Naturally,' murmured Mr Reeder. 'You have a poetical mind. It was a poetical thought to pluck flowers in the middle of the night——'

'The nurseryman told me I could take any flowers I wanted,' Burnett interrupted hastily. 'I did nothing wrong.'

Reeder inclined his head in agreement.

---

[1] Slush: forged Bank of England notes.

'That I know. You picked the flowers in the dark—by the way, you inadvertently included a Michaelmas daisy with your chrysanthemums—tied up your little poem to them and left them on the doorstep with—er—a horseshoe. I wondered what had become of that horseshoe.'

'I threw them up on to her—to the lady's window-sill,' corrected the uncomfortable young man. 'As a matter of fact, the idea didn't occur to me until I had passed the house——'

Mr Reeder's face was thrust forward.

'This is what I want to confirm,' he said softly. 'The idea of leaving the flowers did not occur to you until you had passed her house? The horseshoe suggested the thought? Then you went back, picked the flowers, tied them up with the little poem you had already written, and tossed them up to her window—we need not mention the lady's name.'

Constable Burnett's face was a study.

'I don't know how you guessed that, but it is a fact. If I've done anything wrong——'

'It is never wrong to be in love,' said Mr J. G. Reeder soberly. 'Love is a very beautiful experience—I have frequently read about it.'

Miss Magda Grayne had dressed to go out for the afternoon and was putting on her hat, when she saw the queer man who had called so early that morning, walking up the tessellated path. Behind him she recognised a detective engaged in the case. The servant was out; nobody could be admitted except by herself. She walked quickly behind the dressing-table into the bay of the window and glanced up and down the road. Yes, there was a taxicab which usually accompanies such visitations, and, standing by the driver, another man, obviously a 'busy'.

She pulled up the overlay of her bed, took out the flat pad of banknotes that she found, and thrust them into her handbag, then, stepping on tiptoe, she went out to the landing, into the unfurnished back room, and, opening the window, dropped to the flat roof of the kitchen. In another minute she was in the garden and through the back gate. A narrow passage divided the two lines of villas that backed on one another. She was in High Street and had boarded a car before Mr Reeder grew tired of knocking. To the best of his knowledge Mr Reeder never saw her again.

2

At the Public Prosecutor's request, he called at his chief's house after dinner and told his surprising story.

'Green, who had the unusual experience of being promoted to his position over the heads of his seniors, for special services he rendered during the war, was undoubtedly an ex-convict, and he spoke the truth when he said that he had received a letter from a man who had served a period of imprisonment with him. The name of his blackmailer is, or rather was, Arthur George Crater, whose other name was Malling!'

'Not the night watchman?' said the Public Prosecutor, in amazement. Mr Reeder nodded.

'Yes, sir, it was Arthur Malling. His daughter, Miss Magda Crater, was, as she very truly said, born at Walworth on the 17th of October, 1900. She said Wallington after, but Walworth first. One observes that when people adopt false family names, they seldom change their given names, and the "Magda" was easy to identify.

'Evidently Malling had planned this robbery of the bank very carefully. He had brought his daughter, in a false name, to Ealing, and had managed to get her introduced to Mr Green. Magda's job was to worm her way into Green's confidence and learn all that she could. Possibly it was part of her duty to secure casts of the keys. Whether Malling recognised in the manager an old prison acquaintance, or whether he obtained the facts from the girl, we shall never know. But when the information came to him, he saw, in all probability, an opportunity of robbing the bank and of throwing suspicion upon the manager.

'The girl's role was that of a woman who was to be divorced, and I must confess this puzzled me until I realised that in no circumstances would Malling wish his daughter's name to be associated with the bank manager.

'The night of the seventeenth was chosen for the raid. Malling's plan to get rid of the manager had succeeded. He saw the letter on the table in Green's private office, read it, secured the keys—although he had in all probability a duplicate set—and at a favourable moment cleared as much portable money from the bank vaults as he could carry, hurried them round to the house in Firling Avenue, where they were buried in the central bed of the front garden, under a rose bush—

I rather imagined there was something interfering with the nutrition of that unfortunate bush the first time I saw it. I can only hope that the tree is not altogether dead, and I have given instructions that it shall be replanted and well fertilised.'

'Yes, yes,' said the Prosecutor, who was not at all interested in horticulture.

'In planting the tree, as he did in some haste, Malling scratched his hand. Roses have thorns—I went to Ealing to find the rose bush that had scratched his hand. Hurrying back to the bank, he waited, knowing that Constable Burnett was due at a certain time. He had prepared the can of chloroform, the handcuffs and straps were waiting for him, and he stood at the corner of the street until he saw the flash of Burnett's lamp; then, running into the bank and leaving the door ajar, he strapped himself, fastened the handcuffs and lay down, expecting that the policeman would arrive, find the open door and rescue him before much harm was done.

'But Constable Burnett had had some pleasant exchanges with the daughter. Doubtless she had received instructions from her father to be as pleasant to him as possible. Burnett was a poetical young man, knew it was her birthday, and as he walked along the street his foot struck an old horseshoe and the idea occurred to him that he should return, attach the horseshoe to some flowers, which the nurseryman had given him permission to pick, and leave his little bouquet, so to speak, at his lady's feet—a poetical idea, and one worthy of the finest traditions of the Metropolitan Police Force. This he did, but it took some time; and all the while this young man was philandering— Arthur Crater was dying!

'In a few seconds after lying down he must have passed from consciousness . . . the chloroform still dripped, and when the policeman eventually reached the bank, ten minutes after he was due, the man was dead!'

The Public Prosecutor sat back in his padded chair and frowned at his new subordinate.

'How on earth did you piece together all this?' he asked in wonder.

Mr Reeder shook his head sadly.

'I have that perversion,' he said. 'It is a terrible misfortune, but it is true. I see evil in everything . . . in dying rose bushes, in horseshoes— in poetry even. I have the mind of a criminal. It is deplorable!'

8

DOROTHY L. SAYERS

The Man with No Face

'And what would *you* say, sir,' said the stout man, 'to this here business of the bloke what's been found down on the beach at East Felpham?'

The rush of travellers after the Bank Holiday had caused an overflow of third-class passengers into the firsts, and the stout man was anxious to seem at ease in his surroundings. The youngish gentleman whom he addressed had obviously paid full fare for a seclusion which he was fated to forgo. He took the matter amiably enough, however, and replied in a courteous tone:

'I'm afraid I haven't read more than the headlines. Murdered, I suppose, wasn't he?'

'It's murder, right enough,' said the stout man, with relish. 'Cut about he was, something shocking.'

'More like as if a wild beast had done it,' chimed in the thin, elderly man opposite. 'No face at all he hadn't got, by what my paper says. It'll be one of these maniacs, I shouldn't be surprised, what goes about killing children.'

'I wish you wouldn't talk about such things,' said his wife, with a shudder. 'I lays awake at nights thinking what might 'appen to Lizzie's girls, till my head feels regular in a fever, and I has such a sinking in my inside I has to get up and eat biscuits. They didn't ought to put such dreadful things in the papers.'

'It's better they should, ma'am,' said the stout man, 'then we're warned, so to speak, and can take our measures accordingly. Now, from what I can make out, this unfortunate gentleman had gone bathing all by himself in a lonely spot. Now, quite apart from cramps, as is a thing that might 'appen to the best of us, that's a very foolish thing to do.'

135

'Just what I'm always telling my husband,' said the young wife. The young husband frowned and fidgeted. 'Well, dear, it really isn't safe, and you with your heart not strong—' Her hand sought his under the newspaper. He drew away, self-consciously, saying: 'That'll do, Kitty.'

'The way I look at it is this,' pursued the stout man. 'Here we've been and had a war, what has left 'undreds o' men in what you might call a state of unstable ekilibrium. They've seen all their friends blown up or shot to pieces. They've been through five years of 'orrors and bloodshed, and it's given 'em what you might call a twist in the mind towards 'orrors. They may seem to forget it and go along as peaceable as anybody to all outward appearance, but it's all artificial, if you get my meaning. Then, one day something 'appens to upset them—they 'as words with the wife, or the weather's extra hot, as it is today—and something goes pop inside their brains and makes raving monsters of them. It's all in the books. I do a good bit of reading myself of an evening, being a bachelor without encumbrances.'

'That's all very true,' said a prim little man, looking up from his magazine, 'very true indeed—too true. But do you think it applies in the present case? I've studied the literature of crime a good deal—I may say I make it my hobby—and it's my opinion there's more in this than meets the eye. If you will compare this murder with some of the most mysterious crimes of late years—crimes which, mind you, have never been solved, and, in my opinion, never will be—what do you find?' He paused and looked round. 'You will find many features in common with this case. But especially you will find that the face—and the face only, mark you—has been disfigured, as though to prevent recognition. As though to blot out the victim's personality from the world. And you will find that, in spite of the most thorough investigation, the criminal is never discovered. Now what does all that point to? To organization. Organization. To an immensely powerful influence at work behind the scenes. In this very magazine that I'm reading now—' he tapped the page impressively—'there's an account—not a faked-up story, but an account extracted from the annals of the police—of the organization of one of these secret societies, which mark down men against whom they bear a grudge, and destroy them. And, when they do this, they disfigure their faces with the mark of the Secret Society, and they cover up the track of the assassin so completely—having money and resources at their disposal—that nobody is ever able to get at them.'

'I've read of such things, of course,' admitted the stout man, 'but I thought as they mostly belonged to the medeevial days. They had a thing like that in Italy once. What did they call it now? A Gomorrah, was it? Are there any Gomorrahs nowadays?'

'You spoke a true word, sir, when you said Italy,' replied the prim man. 'The Italian mind is made for intrigue. There's the Fascisti. That's come to the surface now, of course, but it started by being a secret society. And, if you were to look below the surface, you would be amazed at the way in which that country is honeycombed with hidden organizations of all sorts. Don't you agree with me, sir?' he added, addressing the first-class passenger.

'Ah!' said the stout man, 'no doubt this gentleman has been in Italy and knows all about it. Should you say this murder was the work of a Gomorrah, sir?'

'I hope not, I'm sure,' said the first-class passenger. 'I mean, it rather destroys the interest, don't you think? I like a nice, quiet, domestic murder myself, with the millionaire found dead in the library. The minute I open a detective story and find a Camorra in it, my interest seems to dry up and turn to dust and ashes—a sort of Sodom and Camorra, as you might say.'

'I agree with you there,' said the young husband, 'from what you might call the artistic standpoint. But in this particular case I think there may be something to be said for this gentleman's point of view.'

'Well,' admitted the first-class passenger, 'not having read the details——'

'The details are clear enough,' said the prim man. 'This poor creature was found lying dead on the beach at East Felpham early this morning, with his face cut about in the most dreadful manner. He had nothing on him but his bathing-dress——'

'Stop a minute. Who was he, to begin with?'

'They haven't identified him yet. His clothes had been taken——'

'That looks more like robbery, doesn't it?' suggested Kitty.

'If it was just robbery,' retorted the prim man, 'why should his face have been cut up in that way? No—the clothes were taken away, as I said, to prevent identification. That's what these societies always try to do.'

'Was he stabbed?' demanded the first-class passenger.

'No,' said the stout man. 'He wasn't. He was strangled.'

'Not a characteristically Italian method of killing,' observed the first-class passenger.

'No more it is,' said the stout man. The prim man seemed a little disconcerted.

'And if he went down there to bathe,' said the thin, elderly man, 'how did he get there? Surely somebody must have missed him before now, if he was staying at Felpham. It's a busy spot for visitors in the holiday season.'

'No,' said the stout man, 'not East Felpham. You're thinking of West Felpham, where the yacht-club is. East Felpham is one of the loneliest spots on the coast. There's no house near except a little pub all by itself at the end of a long road, and after that you have to go through three fields to get to the sea. There's no real road, only a cart-track, but you can take a car through. I've been there.'

'He came in a car,' said the prim man. 'They found the track of the wheels. But it had been driven away again.'

'It looks as though the two men had come there together,' suggested Kitty.

'I think they did,' said the prim man. 'The victim was probably gagged and bound and taken along in the car to the place, and then he was taken out and strangled and——'

'But why should they have troubled to put on his bathing-dress?' said the first-class passenger.

'Because,' said the prim man, 'as I said, they didn't want to leave any clothes to reveal his identity.'

'Quite; but why not leave him naked? A bathing-dress seems to indicate an almost excessive regard for decorum, under the circumstances.'

'Yes, yes,' said the stout man impatiently, 'but you 'aven't read the paper carefully. The two men couldn't have come there in company, and for why? There was only one set of footprints found, and they belonged to the murdered man.'

He looked round triumphantly.

'Only one set of footprints, eh?' said the first-class passenger quickly. 'This looks interesting. Are you sure?'

'It says so in the paper. A single set of footprints, it says, made by bare feet, which by a careful comparison 'ave been shown to be those of the murdered man, lead from the position occupied by the car to the place where the body was found. What do you make of that?'

'Why,' said the first-class passenger, 'that tells one quite a lot, don't you know. It gives one a sort of a bird's-eye view of the place, and it tells one the time of the murder, besides castin' quite a good bit of light on the character and circumstances of the murderer—or murderers.'

'How do you make that out, sir?' demanded the elderly man.

'Well, to begin with—though I've never been near the place, there is obviously a sandy beach from which one can bathe.'

'That's right,' said the stout man.

'There is also, I fancy, in the neighbourhood, a spur of rock running out into the sea, quite possibly with a handy diving-pool. It must run out pretty far; at any rate, one can bathe there before it is high water on the beach.'

'I don't know how you know that, sir, but it's a fact. There's rocks and a bathing-pool, exactly as you describe, about a hundred yards farther along. Many's the time I've had a dip off the end of them.'

'And the rocks run right back inland, where they are covered with short grass.'

'That's right.'

'The murder took place shortly before high-tide, I fancy, and the body lay just about at high-tide mark.'

'Why so?'

'Well, you say there were footsteps leading right up to the body. That means that the water hadn't been up beyond the body. But there were no other marks. Therefore the murderer's footprints must have been washed away by the tide. The only explanation is that the two men were standing together just below the tide-mark. The murderer came up out of the sea. He attacked the other man—maybe he forced him back a little on his own tracks—and there he killed him. Then the water came up and washed out any marks the murderer may have left. One can imagine him squatting there, wondering if the sea was going to come up high enough.'

'Ow!' said Kitty, 'you make me creep all over.'

'Now, as to these marks on the face,' pursued the first-class passenger. 'The murderer, according to the idea I get of the thing, was already in the sea when the victim came along. You see the idea?'

'I get you,' said the stout man. 'You think as he went in off them rocks what we was speaking of, and came up through the water, and that's why there weren't no footprints.'

'Exactly. And since the water is deep round those rocks, as you say, he was presumably in a bathing-dress too.'

'Looks like it.'

'Quite so. Well, now—what was the face-slashing done with? People don't usually take knives out with them when they go for a morning dip.'

'That's a puzzle,' said the stout man.

'Not altogether. Let's say, either the murderer had a knife with him or he had not. If he had——'

'If he had,' put in the prim man eagerly, 'he must have laid wait for the deceased on purpose. And, to my mind, that bears out my idea of a deep and cunning plot.'

'Yes. But, if he was waiting there with the knife, why didn't he stab the man and have done with it? Why strangle him, when he had a perfectly good weapon there to hand? No—I think he came unprovided, and, when he saw his enemy there, he made for him with his hands in the characteristic British way.'

'But the slashing?'

'Well, I think that when he had got his man down, dead before him, he was filled with a pretty grim sort of fury and wanted to do more damage. He caught up something that was lying near him on the sand—it might be a bit of old iron, or even one of those sharp shells you sometimes see about, or a bit of glass—and he went for him with that in a desperate rage of jealousy or hatred.'

'Dreadful, dreadful!' said the elderly woman.

'Of course, one can only guess in the dark, not having seen the wounds. It's quite possible that the murderer dropped his knife in the struggle, and had to do the actual killing with his hands, picking the knife up afterwards. If the wounds were clean knife-wounds, that is probably what happened, and the murder was premeditated. But if they were rough, jagged gashes, made by an impromptu weapon, then I should say it was a chance encounter, and that the murderer was either mad or——'

'Or?'

'Or had suddenly come upon somebody whom he hated very much.'

'What do you think happened afterwards?'

'That's pretty clear. The murderer, having waited, as I said, to see that all his footprints were cleaned up by the tide, waded or swam back to the rock where he had left his clothes, taking the weapon with him. The sea would wash away any blood from his bathing-dress or body. He then climbed out upon the rocks, walked, with bare feet, so as to leave no tracks on any seaweed or anything, to the short grass of the shore, dressed, went along to the murdered man's car, and drove it away.'

'Why did he do that?'

'Yes, why? He may have wanted to get somewhere in a hurry. Or he may have been afraid that if the murdered man were identified too soon it would cast suspicion on him. Or it may have been a mixture of motives. The point is, where did he come from? How did he come to be bathing at that remote spot, early in the morning? He didn't get there by car, or there would be a second car to be accounted for. He may have been camping near the spot; but it would have taken him a long time to strike camp and pack all his belongings into the car, and he might have been seen. I am rather inclined to think he had bicycled there, and that he hoisted the bicycle into the back of the car, and took it away with him.'

'But, in that case, why take the car?'

'Because he had been down at East Felpham longer than he expected, and he was afraid of being late. Either he had to get back to breakfast at some house, where his absence would be noticed, or else he lived some distance off, and had only just time enough for the journey home. I think, though, he had to be back to breakfast.'

'Why?'

'Because, if it was merely a question of making up time on the road, all he had to do was to put himself and his bicycle on the train for part of the way. No; I fancy he was staying in a smallish hotel somewhere. Not a large hotel, because there nobody would notice whether he came in or not. And not, I think, in lodgings, or somebody would have mentioned before now that they had had a lodger who went bathing at East Felpham. Either he lives in the neighbourhood, in which case he should be easy to trace, or was staying with friends who have an interest in concealing his movements. Or else—which I think is more likely—he was in a smallish hotel, where he would be missed from the breakfast-table, but where his favourite bathing-place was not a matter of common knowledge.'

'That seems feasible,' said the stout man.

'In any case,' went on the first-class passenger, 'he must have been staying within easy bicycling distance of East Felpham, so it shouldn't be too hard to trace him. And then there is the car.'

'Yes. Where is the car, on your theory?' demanded the prim man, who obviously still had hankerings after the Camorra theory.

'In a garage, waiting to be called for,' said the first-class passenger promptly.

'Where?' persisted the prim man.

'Oh, somewhere on the other side of wherever it was the murderer was staying. If you have a particular reason for not wanting it to be known that you were in a certain place at a specified time, it's not a bad idea to come back from the opposite direction. I rather think I should look for the car at West Felpham, and the hotel in the nearest town on the main road beyond where the two roads to East and West Felpham join. When you've found the car, you've found the name of the victim, naturally. As for the murderer, you will have to look for an active man, a good swimmer, and ardent cyclist— probably not very well off, since he cannot afford to have a car—who has been taking a holiday in the neighbourhood of the Felphams, and who has a good reason for disliking the victim, whoever he may be.'

'Well, I never,' said the elderly woman admiringly. 'How beautiful you do put it all together. Like Sherlock Holmes, I do declare.'

'It's a very pretty theory,' said the prim man, 'but, all the same, you'll find it's a secret society. Mark my words. Dear me! We're just running in. Only twenty minutes late. I call that very good for holiday time. Will you excuse me? My bag is just under your feet.'

There was an eighth person in the compartment, who had

remained throughout the conversation apparently buried in a newspaper. As the passengers decanted themselves upon the platform, this man touched the first-class passenger upon the arm.

'Excuse me, sir,' he said. 'That was a very interesting suggestion of yours. My name is Winterbottom, and I am investigating this case. Do you mind giving me your name? I might wish to communicate with you later on.'

'Certainly,' said the first-class passenger. 'Always delighted to have a finger in any pie, don't you know. Here is my card. Look me up any time you like.'

Detective-Inspector Winterbottom took the card, and read the name:

LORD PETER WIMSEY
110A Piccadilly.

*

The *Evening Views* vendor outside Piccadilly Tube Station arranged his placard with some care. It looked very well, he thought.

MAN WITH
NO FACE
IDENTIFIED

It was, in his opinion, considerably more striking than that displayed by a rival organ, which announced, unimaginatively:

BEACH MURDER
VICTIM
IDENTIFIED

A youngish gentleman in a grey suit who emerged at that moment from the Criterion Bar appeared to think so too, for he exchanged a copper for the *Evening Views*, and at once plunged into its perusal with such concentrated interest that he bumped into a hurried man outside the station, and had to apologize.

The *Evening Views*, grateful to murderer and victim alike for providing so useful a sensation in the dead days after the Bank Holiday, had torn Messrs Negretti & Zambra's rocketing thermometrical statistics from the 'banner' position which they had occupied in the lunch edition, and substituted:

FACELESS VICTIM of BEACH OUTRAGE IDENTIFIED

MURDER OF PROMINENT
PUBLICITY ARTIST

POLICE CLUES

The body of a middle-aged man who was discovered, attired only in a bathing costume, and with his face horribly disfigured by some jagged instrument, on the beach at East Felpham last Monday morning, has been identified as that of Mr Coreggio Plant, studio manager of Messrs Crichton, Ltd., the well-known publicity experts of Holborn.

Mr Plant, who was forty-five years of age and a bachelor, was spending his annual holiday in making a motoring tour along the West Coast. He had no companion with him, and had left no address for the forwarding of letters, so that, without the smart work of Detective-Inspector Winterbottom of the Westshire Police, his disappearance might not in the ordinary way have been noticed until he became due to return to his place of business in three weeks' time. The murderer had no doubt counted on this, and had removed the motor-car, containing the belongings of his victim, in the hope of covering up all traces of this dastardly outrage so as to gain time for escape.

A rigorous search for the missing car, however, eventuated in its discovery in a garage at West Felpham, where it had been left for decarbonization and repairs to the magneto. Mr Spiller, the garage proprietor, himself saw the man who left the car, and has furnished a description of him to the police. He is said to be a small, dark man of foreign appearance. The police hold a clue to his identity, and an arrest is confidently expected in the near future.

Mr Plant was for fifteen years in the employment of Messrs Crichton, being appointed Studio Manager in the latter years of the war. He was greatly liked by all his colleagues, and his skill in the lay-out and designing of advertisements did much to justify the truth of Messrs Crichton's well-known slogan: 'Crichton's for Admirable Advertising'.

The funeral of the victim will take place tomorrow at Golders Green Cemetery.

(Pictures on Back Page.)

Lord Peter Wimsey turned to the back page. The portrait of the victim did not detain him long; it was one of those characterless studio photographs which establish nothing except that the sitter has a tolerable set of features. He noted that Mr Plant had been thin rather than fat, commercial in appearance rather than artistic, and that the photographer had chosen to show him serious rather than smiling. A picture of East Felpham beach, marked with a cross where the body was found, seemed to arouse in him rather more than a casual interest. He studied it intently for some time, making little surprised noises. There was no obvious reason why he should have been surprised, for the photograph bore out in every detail the deductions he had made in the train. There was the curved line of sand, with a long spur of rock stretching out behind it into deep water, and running back till it mingled with the short, dry turf. Nevertheless, he looked at it for several minutes with close attention before folding the newspaper and hailing a taxi; and when he was in the taxi he unfolded the paper and looked at it again.

*

'Your lordship having been kind enough,' said Inspector Winterbottom, emptying his glass rather too rapidly for true connoisseurship, 'to suggest I should look you up in Town, I made so bold to give you a call in passing. Thank you, I won't say no. Well, as you've seen in the papers by now, we found that car, all right.'

Wimsey expressed his gratification at this result.

'And very much obliged I was to your lordship for the hint,' went on the Inspector generously, 'not but what I wouldn't say but I should have come to the same conclusion myself, given a little more time. And, what's more, we're on the track of the man.'

'I see he's supposed to be foreign-looking. Don't say he's going to turn out to be a Camorrist, after all!'

'No, my lord.' The Inspector winked. 'Our friend in the corner had got his magazine stories a bit on the brain, if you ask me. And *you* were a bit out, too, my lord, with your bicyclist idea.'

'Was I? That's a blow.'

'Well, my lord, these here theories *sound* all right, but half the time they're too fine-spun altogether. Go for the facts—that's our motto in the Force—facts and motive, and you won't go far wrong.'

'Oh, you've discovered the motive, then?'

The Inspector winked again.

'There's not many motives for doing a man in,' said he. 'Women or

145

money—or women *and* money—it mostly comes down to one or the other. This fellow Plant went in for being a bit of a lad, you see. He kept a little cottage down Felpham way, with a nice little skirt to furnish it and keep the love-nest warm for him—see?'

'Oh! I thought he was doing a motor tour.'

'Motor tour your foot!' said the Inspector, with more energy than politeness. 'That's what the old (epithet) told 'em at the office. Handy reason, don't you see, for leaving no address behind him. No, no. There was a lady in it all right. I've seen her. A very taking piece, too, if you like 'em skinny, which I don't. I prefer 'em better upholstered, myself.'

'That chair is really more comfortable with a cushion,' put in Wimsey, with anxious solicitude. 'Allow me.'

'Thanks, my lord, thanks. I'm doing very well. It seems that this woman—by the way, we're speaking in confidence, you understand. I don't want this to go further till I've got my man under lock and key.'

Wimsey promised discretion.

'That's all right, my lord, that's all right. I know I can rely on you. Well, the long and the short is, this young woman had another fancy man—a sort of an Italiano, whom she'd chucked for Plant, and this same dago got wind of the business, and came down to East Felpham on the Sunday night looking for her. He's one of these professional partners in a Palais de Dance up Cricklewood way, and that's where the girl comes from, too. I suppose she thought Plant was a cut above him. Anyway, down he comes, and busts in upon them Sunday night when they were having a bit of supper—and that's when the row started.'

'Didn't you know about this cottage and the goings-on there?'

'Well, you know, there's such a lot of these weekenders nowadays. We can't keep tabs on all of them, so long as they behave themselves and don't make a disturbance. The woman's been there—so they tell me—since last June, with him coming down Saturday to Monday; but it's a lonely spot, and the constable didn't take much notice. He came in the evenings, so there wasn't anybody much to recognize him, except the old girl who did the slops and things, and she's half-blind. And of course, when they found him, he hadn't any face to recognize. It'd be thought he'd just gone off in the ordinary way. I dare say the dago fellow reckoned on that. As I was saying, there was a big row, and the dago was kicked out. He must have lain in wait for Plant down by the bathing-place, and done him in.'

'By strangling?'

'Well, he *was* strangled.'

'Was his face cut up with a knife, then?'

'Well, no—I don't think it was a knife. More like a broken bottle, I should say, if you ask me. There's plenty of them come in with the tide.'

'But then we're brought back to our old problem. If this Italian was lying in wait to murder Plant, why didn't he take a weapon with him, instead of trusting to the chance of his hands and a broken bottle?'

The Inspector shook his head.

'Flighty,' he said. 'All these foreigners are flighty. No headpiece. But there's our man, and there's our motive, plain as a pikestaff. You don't want more.'

'And where is the Italian fellow now?'

'Run away. That's pretty good proof of guilt in itself. But we'll have him before long. That's what I've come to Town about. He can't get out of the country. I've had an all-stations call sent out to stop him. The dance-hall people were able to supply us with a photo and a good description. I'm expecting a report in now any minute. In fact, I'd best be getting along. Thank you very much for your hospitality, my lord.'

'The pleasure is mine,' said Wimsey, ringing the bell to have the visitor shown out. 'I have enjoyed our little chat immensely.'

*

Sauntering into the Falstaff at twelve o'clock the following morning, Wimsey, as he had expected, found Salcombe Hardy supporting his rather plump contours against the bar. The reporter greeted his arrival with a heartiness amounting almost to enthusiasm, and called for two large Scotches immediately. When the usual skirmish as to who should pay had been honourably settled by the prompt disposal of the drinks and the standing of two more, Wimsey pulled from his pocket the copy of last night's *Evening Views*.

'I wish you'd ask the people over at your place to get hold of a decent print of this for me,' he said, indicating the picture of East Felpham beach.

Salcombe Hardy gazed limpid inquiry at him from eyes like drowned violets.

'See here, you old sleuth,' he said, 'does this mean you've got a theory about the thing? I'm wanting a story badly. Must keep up the excitement, you know. The police don't seem to have got any further since last night.'

'No; I'm interested in this from another point of view altogether. I did have a theory—of sorts—but it seems it's all wrong. Bally old Homer nodding, I suppose. But I'd like a copy of the thing.'

'I'll get Warren to get you one when we come back. I'm just taking him down with me to Crichton's. We're going to have a look at a picture. I say, I wish you'd come, too. Tell me what to say about the damned thing.'

'Good God! I don't know anything about commercial art.'

''Tisn't commercial art. It's supposed to be a portrait of this blighter Plant. Done by one of the chaps in his studio or something. Kid who told me about it says it's clever. I don't know. Don't suppose she knows, either. You go in for being artistic, don't you?'

'I wish you wouldn't use such filthy expressions, Sally. Artistic! Who is this girl?'

'Typist in the copy department.'

'Oh, Sally!'

'Nothing of that sort. I've never met her. Name's Gladys Twitterton. I'm sure that's beastly enough to put anybody off. Rang us up last night and told us there was a bloke there who'd done old Plant in oils, and was it any use to us? Drummer thought it might be worth looking into. Make a change from that everlasting syndicated photograph.'

'I see. If you haven't got an exclusive story, an exclusive picture's better than nothing. The girl seems to have her wits about her. Friend of the artist's?'

'No—said he'd probably be frightfully annoyed at her having told me. But I can wangle that. Only I wish you'd come and have a look at it. Tell me whether I ought to say it's an unknown masterpiece or merely a striking likeness.'

'How the devil can I say if it's a striking likeness of a bloke I've never seen?'

'I'll say it's that, in any case. But I want to know if it's well painted.'

'Curse it, Sally, what's it matter whether it is or not? I've got other things to do. Who's the artist, by the way? Anybody one's ever heard of?'

'Dunno. I've got the name here somewhere.' Sally rooted in his hip-pocket, and produced a mass of dirty correspondence, its angles blunted by constant attrition. 'Some comic name like Buggle or Snag-tooth—wait a bit—here it is. Crowder. Thomas Crowder. I knew it was something out of the way.'

'Singularly like Buggle or Snagtooth. All right, Sally. I'll make a martyr of myself. Lead me to it.'

'We'll have another quick one. Here's Warren. This is Lord Peter Wimsey. This is on me.'

'On me,' corrected the photographer, a jaded young man with a disillusioned manner. 'Three large White Labels, please. Well, here's all the best. Are you fit, Sally? Because we'd better make tracks. I've got to be up at Golders Green by two for the funeral.'

Mr Crowder of Crichton's appeared to have had the news broken to him already by Miss Twitterton, for he received the embassy in a spirit of gloomy acquiescence.

'The directors won't like it,' he said, 'but they've had to put up with such a lot that I suppose one irregularity more or less won't give 'em apoplexy.' He had a small, anxious, yellow face like a monkey. Wimsey put him down as being in the late thirties. He noticed his fine, capable hands, one of which was disfigured by a strip of sticking-plaster.

'Damaged yourself?' said Wimsey pleasantly, as they made their way upstairs to the studio. 'Mustn't make a practice of that, what? An artist's hands are his livelihood—except, of course for Armless Wonders, and people of that kind! Awkward job, painting with your toes.'

'Oh, it's nothing much,' said Crowder, 'but it's best to keep the paint out of surface scratches. There's such a thing as lead-poisoning. Well, here's this dud portrait, such as it is. I don't mind telling you that it didn't please the sitter. In fact, he wouldn't have it at any price.'

'Not flattering enough?' asked Hardy.

'As you say.' The painter pulled out a four by three canvas from its hiding-place behind a stack of poster cartoons, and heaved it up on to the easel.

'Oh!' said Hardy, a little surprised. Not that there was any reason for surprise as far as the painting itself was concerned. It was a straightforward handling enough; the skill and originality of the

149

brushwork being of the kind that interests the painter without shocking the ignorant.

'Oh!' said Hardy. 'Was he really like that?'

He moved closer to the canvas, peering into it as he might have peered into the face of the living man, hoping to get something out of him. Under this microscopic scrutiny, the portrait, as is the way of portraits, dislimned, and became no more than a conglomeration of painted spots and streaks. He made the discovery that, to the painter's eye, the human face is full of green and purple patches.

He moved back again, and altered the form of his question:

'So that's what he was like, was he?'

He pulled out the photograph of Plant from his pocket, and compared it with the portrait. The portrait seemed to sneer at his surprise.

'Of course, they touch these things up at these fashionable photographers,' he said. 'Anyway, that's not my business. This thing will make a jolly good eye-catcher, don't you think so, Wimsey? Wonder if they'd give us a two-column spread on the front page? Well, Warren, you'd better get down to it.'

The photographer, bleakly unmoved by artistic or journalistic considerations, took silent charge of the canvas, mentally resolving it into a question of pan-chromatic plates and coloured screens. Crowder gave him a hand in shifting the easel into a better light. Two or three people from other departments, passing through the studio on their lawful occasions, stopped, and lingered in the neighbourhood of the disturbance, as though it were a street accident. A melancholy, grey-haired man, temporary head of the studio, *vice* Coreggio Plant, deceased, took Crowder aside, with a muttered apology, to give him some instructions about adapting a whole quad to an eleven-inch treble. Hardy turned to Lord Peter.

'It's damned ugly,' he said. 'Is it good?'

'Brilliant,' said Wimsey. 'You can go all out. Say what you like about it.'

'Oh, splendid! Could we discover one of our neglected British masters?'

'Yes; why not? You'll probably make the man the fashion, and ruin him as an artist, but that's his pigeon.'

'But, I say—do you think it's a good likeness? He's made him look a most sinister sort of fellow. After all, Plant thought it was so bad he wouldn't have it.'

'The more fool he. Ever heard of the portrait of a certain statesman that was so revealing of his inner emptiness that he hurriedly bought it up and hid it to prevent people like you from getting hold of it?'

Crowder came back.

'I say,' said Wimsey, 'whom does that picture belong to? You? Or the heirs of the deceased, or what?'

'I suppose it's back on my hands,' said the painter. 'Plant—well, he more or less commissioned it, you see, but——'

'How more or less?'

'Well, he kept on hinting, don't you know, that he would like me to do him, and, as he was my boss, I thought I'd better. No price actually mentioned. When he saw it, he didn't like it, and told me to alter it.'

'But you didn't.'

'Oh—well, I put it aside, and said I'd see what I could do with it. I thought he'd perhaps forget about it.'

'I see. Then presumably it's yours to dispose of.'

'I should think so. Why?'

'You have a very individual technique, haven't you?' pursued Wimsey. 'Do you exhibit much?'

'Here and there. I've never had a show in London.'

'I fancy I once saw a couple of small seascapes of yours somewhere. Manchester, was it? Or Liverpool? I wasn't sure of your name, but I recognized the technique immediately.'

'I dare say. I did send a few things to Manchester about two years ago.'

'Yes—I felt sure I couldn't be mistaken. I want to buy the portrait. Here's my card, by the way. I'm not a journalist; I collect things.'

Crowder looked from the card to Wimsey, and from Wimsey to the card a little reluctantly.

'If you want to exhibit it, of course,' said Lord Peter, 'I should be delighted to leave it with you as long as you liked.'

'Oh, it's not that,' said Crowder. 'The fact is, I'm not altogether keen on the thing. I should like to—that is to say, it's not really finished.'

'My dear man, it's a bally masterpiece.'

'Oh, the painting's all right. But it's not altogether satisfactory as a likeness.'

'What the devil does the likeness matter? I don't know what the late Plant looked like, and I don't care. As I look at the thing it's a damn' fine bit of brushwork, and if you tinker about with it you'll spoil it. You know that as well as I do. What's biting you? It isn't the price, is it? You know I shan't boggle about that. I can afford my modest pleasures, even in these thin and piping times. You don't want me to have it? Come, now—what's the real reason?'

'There's no reason at all why you shouldn't have it if you really want it, I suppose,' said the painter, still a little sullenly. 'If it's really the painting that interests you.'

'What do you suppose it is? The notoriety? I can have all I want of *that* commodity, you know, for the asking—or even without asking. Well, anyhow, think it over, and when you've decided, send me a line and name your price.'

Crowder nodded without speaking, and the photographer having by this time finished his job, the party took their leave.

As they left the building, they became involved in the stream of Crichton's staff going out to lunch. A girl, who seemed to have been loitering in a semi-intentional way in the lower hall, caught them as the lift descended.

'Are you the *Evening Views* people? Did you get your picture all right?'

'Miss Twitterton?' said Hardy interrogatively. 'Yes, rather—thank you so much for giving us the tip. You'll see it on the front page this evening.'

'Oh, that's splendid! I'm frightfully thrilled. It has made an excitement here—all this business. Do they know anything yet about who murdered Mr Plant? Or am I being horribly indiscreet?'

'We're expecting news of an arrest any minute now,' said Hardy. 'As a matter of fact, I shall have to buzz back to the office as fast as I can to sit with one ear glued to the telephone. You will excuse me, won't you? And, look here—will you let me come round another day, when things aren't so busy, and take you out to lunch?'

'Of course. I should love to.' Miss Twitterton giggled. 'I do so want to hear about all the murder cases.'

'Then here's the man to tell you about them, Miss Twitterton,' said

Hardy, with mischief in his eye. 'Allow me to introduce Lord Peter Wimsey.'

Miss Twitterton offered her hand in an ecstasy of excitement which almost robbed her of speech.

'How do you do?' said Wimsey. 'As this blighter is in such a hurry to get back to his gossip-shop, what do you say to having a spot of lunch with me?'

'Well, really—' began Miss Twitterton.

'He's all right,' said Hardy; 'he won't lure you into any gilded dens of infamy. If you look at him you will see he has a kind, innocent face.'

'I'm sure I never thought of such a thing,' said Miss Twitterton. 'But, you know—really—I've only got my old things on. It's no good wearing anything decent in this dusty old place.'

'Oh, nonsense!' said Wimsey. 'You couldn't possibly look nicer. It isn't the frock that matters—it's the person who wears it. *That's* all right, then. See you later, Sally! Taxi! Where shall we go? What time do you have to be back, by the way?'

'Two o'clock,' said Miss Twitterton regretfully.

'Then we'll make the Savoy do,' said Wimsey; 'it's reasonably handy.'

Miss Twitterton hopped into the waiting taxi with a little squeak of agitation.

'Did you see Mr Crichton?' she said. 'He went by just as we were talking. However, I dare say he doesn't really know me by sight. I hope not—or he'll think I'm getting too grand to need a salary.' She rooted in her handbag. 'I'm sure my face is getting all shiny with excitement. What a silly taxi. It hasn't got a mirror—and I've bust mine.'

Wimsey solemnly produced a small looking-glass from his pocket.

'How wonderfully competent of you!' exclaimed Miss Twitterton. 'I'm afraid, Lord Peter, you are used to taking girls about.'

'Moderately so,' said Wimsey. He did not think it necessary to mention that the last time he had used that mirror it had been to examine the back teeth of a murdered man.

*

'Of course,' said Miss Twitterton, 'they had to say he was popular with his colleagues. Haven't you noticed that murdered people are always well dressed and popular?'

'They have to be,' said Wimsey. 'It makes it more mysterious and pathetic. Just as girls who disappear are always bright and home-loving, and have no men friends.'

'Silly, isn't it?' said Miss Twitterton, with her mouth full of roast duck and green peas. 'I should think everybody was only too glad to get rid of Plant—nasty, rude creature. So mean, too, always taking credit for other people's work. All those poor things in the studio, with all the spirit squashed out of them. I always say, Lord Peter, you can tell if a head of a department's fitted for his job by noticing the atmosphere of the place as you go into it. Take the copy-room, now. We're all as cheerful and friendly as you like, though I must say the language that goes on there is something awful, but these writing fellows are like that, and they don't mean anything by it. But then, Mr Ormerod is a real gentleman—that's our copy-chief, you know—and he makes them all take an interest in the work, for all they grumble about the cheese-bills and the department store bilge they have to turn out. But it's quite different in the studio. A sort of dead-and-alive feeling about it, if you understand what I mean. We girls notice things like that more than some of the high-up people think. Of course, I'm very sensitive to these feelings—almost psychic, I've been told.'

Lord Peter said there was nobody like a woman for sizing up character at a glance. Women, he thought, were remarkably intuitive.

'That's a fact,' said Miss Twitterton. 'I've often said, if I could have a few frank words with Mr Crichton, I could tell him a thing or two. There are wheels within wheels beneath the surface of a place like this that these brass-hats have no idea of.'

Lord Peter said he felt sure of it.

'The way Mr Plant treated people he thought were beneath him,' went on Miss Twitterton, 'I'm sure it was enough to make your blood boil. I'm sure, if Mr Ormerod sent me with a message to him, I was glad to get out of the room again. Humiliating, it was, the way he'd speak to you. I don't care if he's dead or not; being dead doesn't make a person's past behaviour any better, Lord Peter. It wasn't so much the rude things he said. There's Mr Birkett, for example; *he's* rude enough, but nobody minds him. He's just like a big, blundering puppy—rather a lamb, really. It was Mr Plant's nasty sneering way we all hated so. And he was always running people down.'

'How about this portrait?' asked Wimsey. 'Was it like him at all?'

'It was a lot too like him,' said Miss Twitterton emphatically. 'That's why he hated it so. He didn't like Crowder, either. But, of course, he knew he could paint, and he made him do it because he thought he'd be getting a valuable thing cheap. And Crowder couldn't very well refuse or Plant would have got him sacked.'

'I shouldn't have thought that would have mattered much to a man of Crowder's ability.'

'Poor Mr Crowder! I don't think he's ever had much luck. Good artists don't always seem able to sell their pictures. And I know he wanted to get married—otherwise he'd never have taken up this commercial work. He's told me a good bit about himself. I don't know why—but I'm one of the people men seem to tell things to.'

Lord Peter filled Miss Twitterton's glass.

'Oh, please! No, really! Not a drop more! I'm talking a lot too much as it is. I don't know what Mr Ormerod will say when I go in to take his letters. I shall be writing down all kinds of funny things. Ooh! I really must be getting back. Just look at the time!'

'It's not really late. Have a black coffee—just as a corrective.' Wimsey smiled. 'You haven't been talking at all too much. I've enjoyed your picture of office life enormously. You have a very vivid way of putting things, you know. I see now why Mr Plant was not altogether a popular character.'

'Not in the office, anyway—whatever he may have been elsewhere,' said Miss Twitterton darkly.

'Oh?'

'Oh, he was a one!' said Miss Twitterton. 'He certainly was a one. Some friends of mine met him one evening up in the West End, and they came back with some nice stories. It was quite a joke in the office—old Plant and his rosebuds, you know. Mr Cowley—he's *the* Cowley, you know, who rides in the motor-cycle races—he always said he knew what to think of Mr Plant and his motor tours. That time Mr Plant pretended he'd gone touring in Wales, Mr Cowley was asking him about the roads, and he didn't know a thing about them. Because Mr Cowley really had been touring there, and he knew quite well Mr Plant hadn't been where he said he had; and, as a matter of fact, Mr Cowley knew he'd been staying the whole time in a hotel at Aberystwyth, in very attractive company.'

Miss Twitterton finished her coffee, and slapped the cup down defiantly.

'And now I really *must* run away, or I shall be most dreadfully late. And thank you ever so much.'

*

'Hullo!' said Inspector Winterbottom, 'you've bought that portrait, then?'

'Yes,' said Wimsey. 'It's a fine bit of work.' He gazed thoughtfully at the canvas. 'Sit down, Inspector; I want to tell you a story.'

'And I want to tell *you* a story,' replied the Inspector.

'Let's have yours first,' said Wimsey, with an air of flattering eagerness.

'No, no, my lord. You take precedence. Go ahead.'

He snuggled down with a chuckle into his arm-chair.

'Well,' said Wimsey. 'Mine's a sort of a fairy-story. And, mind you, I haven't verified it.'

'Go ahead, my lord, go ahead.'

'Once upon a time—' said Wimsey sighing.

'That's the good old-fashioned way to begin a fairy-story,' said Inspector Winterbottom.

'Once upon a time,' repeated Wimsey, 'there was a painter. He was a good painter, but the bad fairy of Financial Success had not been asked to his christening—what?'

'That's often the way with painters,' agreed the Inspector.

'So he had to take up a job as a commercial artist, because nobody would buy his pictures and, like so many people in fairy-tales, he wanted to marry a goose-girl.'

'There's many people want to do the same,' said the Inspector.

'The head of his department,' went on Wimsey, 'was a man with a mean, sneering soul. He wasn't even really good at his job, but he had been pushed into authority during the war, when better men went to the Front. Mind you, I'm rather sorry for the man. He suffered from an inferiority complex'—the Inspector snorted—'and he thought the only way to keep his end up was to keep other people's end down. So he became a little tin tyrant and a bully. He took all the credit for the work of the men under his charge, and he sneered and harassed them till they got inferiority complexes even worse than his own.'

'I've known that sort,' said the Inspector, 'and the marvel to me is how they get away with it.'

'Just so,' said Wimsey. 'Well, I dare say this man would have gone on getting away with it all right if he hadn't thought of getting this painter to paint his portrait.'

'Damn silly thing to do,' said the Inspector. 'It was only making the painter fellow conceited with himself.'

'True. But, you see, this tin tyrant person had a fascinating female in tow, and he wanted the portrait for the lady. He thought that, by making the painter do it, he would get a good portrait at starvation price. But unhappily he'd forgotten that, however much an artist will put up with in the ordinary way, he is bound to be sincere with his art. That's the one thing a genuine artist won't muck about with.'

'I dare say,' said the Inspector. 'I don't know much about artists.'

'Well, you can take it from me. So the painter painted the portrait as he saw it, and he put the man's whole creeping, sneering, paltry soul on the canvas for everybody to see.'

Inspector Winterbottom stared at the portrait, and the portrait sneered back at him.

'It's not what you'd call a flattering picture, certainly,' he admitted.

'Now, when a painter paints a portrait of anybody,' went on Wimsey, 'that person's face is never the same to him again. It's like—what shall I say? Well, it's like the way a gunner, say, looks at a landscape where he happens to be posted. He doesn't see it as a landscape. He doesn't see it as a thing of magic beauty, full of sweeping lines and lovely colour. He sees it as so much cover, so many landmarks to aim by, so many gun-emplacements. And when the war is over and he goes back to it, he will still see it as cover and landmarks and gun-emplacements. It isn't a landscape any more. It's a war map.'

'I know that,' said Inspector Winterbottom. 'I was a gunner myself.'

'A painter gets just the same feeling of deadly familiarity with every line of a face he's once painted,' pursued Wimsey. 'And, if it's a face he hates, he hates it with a new and more irritable hatred. It's like a defective barrel-organ, everlastingly grinding out the same old maddening tune, and making the same damned awful wrong note every time the barrel goes round.'

'Lord, how you can talk!' ejaculated the Inspector.

'That was the way the painter felt about this man's hateful face. All day and every day he had to see it. He couldn't get away because he was tied to his job, you see.'

'He ought to have cut loose,' said the Inspector. 'It's no good going on like that, trying to work with uncongenial people.'

'Well, anyway, he said to himself, he could escape for a bit during his holidays. There was a beautiful little quiet spot he knew on the West Coast where nobody ever came. He'd been there before and painted it. Oh, by the way, that reminds me—I've got another picture to show you.'

He went to a bureau and extracted a small panel in oils from a drawer.

'I saw that two years ago at a show in Manchester, and I happened to remember the name of the dealer who bought it.'

Inspector Winterbottom gaped at the panel.

'But that's East Felpham!' he exclaimed.

'Yes. It's only signed T.C., but the technique is rather unmistakable, don't you think?'

The Inspector knew little about technique, but initials he understood. He looked from the portrait to the panel, and back at Lord Peter.

'The painter——'

'Crowder?'

'If it's all the same to you, I'd rather go on calling him the painter. He packed up his traps on his push-bike carrier, and took his tormented nerves down to this beloved and secret spot for a quiet week-end. He stayed at a quiet little hotel in the neighbourhood, and each morning he cycled off to this lovely little beach to bathe. He never told anybody at the hotel where he went, because it was *his* place, and he didn't want other people to find it out.'

Inspector Winterbottom set the panel down on the table, and helped himself to whisky.

'One morning—it happened to be the Monday morning'—Wimsey's voice became slower and more reluctant—'he went down as usual. The tide was not yet fully in, but he ran out over the rocks to where he knew there was a deep bathing pool. He plunged in and swam about, and let the small noise of his jangling troubles be swallowed up in the innumerable laughter of the sea.'

'Eh?'

'χυμάτων ανήριθμον γέλασμα—quotation from the classics. Some people say it means the dimpled surface of the waves in the sunlight—but how could Prometheus, bound upon his rock, have seen it? Surely it was the chuckle of the incoming tide among the stones that came up to his ears on the lonely peak where the vulture fretted at his heart. I remember arguing about it with old Philpotts in class, and getting rapped over the knuckles for contradicting him. I didn't know at the time that he was engaged in producing a translation on his own account, or doubtless I should have contradicted him more rudely, and been told to take my trousers down. Dear old Philpotts!'

'I don't know anything about that,' said the Inspector.

'I beg your pardon. Shocking way I have of wandering. The painter—well, he swam round the end of the rocks, for the tide was nearly in by that time; and, as he came up from the sea he saw a man standing on the beach—that beloved beach, remember, which he thought was his own sacred haven of peace. He came wading towards it, cursing the Bank Holiday rabble who must needs swarm about everywhere with their cigarette-packets and their kodaks and their gramophones—and then he saw that it was a face he knew. He knew every hated line in it, on that clear, sunny morning. And, early as it was, the heat was coming up over the sea like a haze.'

'It was a hot weekend,' said the Inspector.

'And then the man hailed him, in his smug, mincing voice. 'Hullo!' he said, 'you here? How did you find my little bathing-place?' And that was too much for the painter. He felt as if his last sanctuary had been invaded. He leapt at the lean throat—it's rather a stringy one, you may notice, with a prominent Adam's apple—an irritating throat. The water chuckled round their feet as they swayed to and fro. He felt his thumbs sink into the flesh he had painted. He saw, and laughed to see, the hateful familiarity of the features change and swell into an unrecognizable purple. He watched the sunken eyes bulge out, and the thin mouth distort itself as the blackened tongue thrust through it—I am not unnerving you, I hope?'

The Inspector laughed.

'Not a bit. It's wonderful, the way you describe things. You ought
to write a book.'

> 'I sing but as the throstle sings,
> Amid the branches dwelling,'

replied his lordship negligently, and went on without further
comment.

'The painter throttled him. He flung him back on the sand. He
looked at him, and his heart crowed within him. He stretched out his
hand, and found a broken bottle, with a good jagged edge. He went to
work with a will, stamping and tearing away every trace of the face he
knew and loathed. He blotted it out, and destroyed it utterly.

'He sat beside the thing he had made. He began to be frightened.
They had staggered back beyond the edge of the water, and there
were the marks of his feet on the sand. He had blood on his face and
on his bathing-suit, and he had cut his hand with the bottle. But the
blessed sea was still coming in. He watched it pass over the blood-
stains and the footprints, and wipe the story of his madness away. He
remembered that this man had gone from his place, leaving no
address behind him. He went back, step by step, into the water, and as
it came up to his breast, he saw the red stains smoke away like a faint
mist in the brown-blueness of the tide. He went—wading and swim-
ming and plunging his face and arms deep in the water, looking back
from time to time to see what he had left behind him. I think that
when he got back to the point and drew himself out, clean and cool,
upon the rocks, he remembered that he ought to have taken the body
back with him, and let the tide carry it away, but it was too late. He was
clean, and he could not bear to go back for the thing. Besides, he was
late, and they would wonder at the hotel if he was not back in time for
breakfast. He ran lightly over the bare rocks and the grass that showed
no footprint. He dressed himself, taking care to leave no trace of his
presence. He took the car, which would have told a story. He put his
bicycle in the back seat, under the rugs, and he went—but you know
as well as I do where he went.'

Lord Peter got up with an impatient movement, and went over to
the picture, rubbing his thumb meditatively over the texture of the
painting.

'You may say, if he hated the face so much, why didn't he destroy the picture? He couldn't. It was the best thing he'd ever done. He took a hundred guineas for it. It was cheap at a hundred guineas. But then—I think he was afraid to refuse me. My name is rather well known. It was a sort of blackmail, I suppose. But I wanted that picture.'

Inspector Winterbottom laughed again.

'Did you take any steps, my lord, to find out if Crowder has really been staying at East Felpham?'

'No.' Wimsey swung round abruptly. 'I have taken no steps at all. That's your business. I have told you the story, and, on my soul, I'd rather have stood by and said nothing.'

'You needn't worry.' The Inspector laughed for the third time. 'It's a good story, my lord, and you told it well. But you're right when you say it's a fairy-story. We've found this Italian fellow—Francesco, he called himself, and he's the man, all right.'

'How do you know? Has he confessed?'

'Practically. He's dead. Killed himself. He left a letter to the woman, begging for forgiveness, and saying that when he saw her with Plant he felt murder come into his heart. "I have revenged myself," he says, "on him who dared to love you." I suppose he got the wind up when he saw we were after him—I wish these newspapers wouldn't be always putting these criminals on their guard—so he did away with himself to cheat the gallows. I may say it's been a disappointment to me.'

'It must have been,' said Wimsey. 'Very unsatisfactory, of course. But I'm glad my story turned out to be only a fairy-tale, after all. You're not going?'

'Got to get back to my duty,' said the Inspector, heaving himself to his feet. 'Very pleased to have met you, my lord. And I mean what I say—you ought to take to literature.'

Wimsey remained after he had gone, still looking at the portrait.

' "What is Truth?" said jesting Pilate. No wonder, since it is so completely unbelievable. . . . I could prove it . . . if I liked . . . but the man had a villainous face, and there are few good painters in the world.'

9

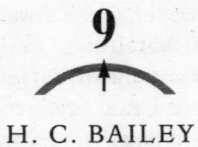

H. C. BAILEY

The Yellow Slugs

The big car closed up behind a florid funeral procession which held the middle of the road. On either side was a noisy congestion of lorries. Mr Fortune sighed and closed his eyes.

When he looked out again he was passing the first carriage of another funeral, and saw beneath the driver's seat the white coffin of a baby. For the road served the popular cemetery of Blaney.

Two slow miles of dingy tall houses and cheap shops slid by, with vistas of meaner streets opening on either side. The car gathered speed across Blaney Common, an expanse of yellow turf and bare sand, turbid pond and scrubwood, and stopped at the brown pile of an old poor law hospital.

Entering its carbolic odour, Mr Fortune was met by Superintendent Bell. 'Here I am,' he moaned. 'Why am I?'

'Well, she's still alive, sir,' said Bell. 'They both are.'

Mr Fortune was taken to a ward in which, secluded by a screen, a little girl lay asleep.

Her face had a babyish fatness, but in its pallor looked bloated and unhealthy. Though the close July air was oppressive and she was covered with heavy bed-clothes, her skin showed no sign of heat and she slept still as death.

Reggie sat down beside her. His hands moved gently within the bed. . . . He listened . . . he looked . . .

A nurse followed him to the door. 'How old, do you think?' he murmured.

'That was puzzling me, sir. She's big enough for seven or eight, but all flabby. And when she came to, she was talking almost baby talk. I suppose she may be only about five.'

Reggie nodded. 'Quite good, yes. All right. Carry on.'

From the ward he passed to a small room where a nurse and a doctor stood together watching the one bed.

A boy lay in it, restless and making noises—inarticulate words mixed with moaning and whimpering.

The doctor lifted his eyebrows at Reggie. 'Get that?' he whispered. 'Still talking about hell. He came absolutely unstuck. I had to risk a shot of morphia. I——' He broke off in apprehension as Reggie's round face hardened to a cold severity. But Reggie nodded and moved to the bed. . . .

The boy tossed into stertorous sleep, one thin arm flung up above a tousled head. His sunken cheeks were flushed, and drips of sweat stood on the upper lip and the brow. Not a bad brow—not an uncomely face but for its look of hungry misery—not the face of a child—a face which had been the prey of emotions and thwarted desires. . . .

Reggie's careful hands worked over him . . . bits of the frail body were laid bare. . . . Reggie stood up, and still his face was set in ruthless, passionless determination.

Outside the door the doctor spoke nervously. 'I hope you don't——'

'Morphia's all right,' Reggie interrupted. 'What do you make of him?'

'Well, Mr Fortune, I wish you'd seen him at first.' The doctor was uncomfortable beneath the cold insistence of a questioning stare. 'He was right out of hand—a sort of hysterical fury. I should say he's quite abnormal. Neurotic lad, badly nourished—you can't tell what they won't do, that type.'

'I can't. No. What age do you give him?'

'Now you've got me. To hear him raving, you'd think he was grown up, such a flow of language. Bible phrases and preaching. I'd say he was a twelve-year-old, but he might only be eight or ten. His development is all out of balance. He's unhealthy right through.'

'Yes, that is so,' Reggie murmured. 'However. You ought to save him.'

'Poor little devil,' said the doctor.

In a bare, grim waiting-room Reggie sat down with Superintendent Bell, and Bell looked anxiety. 'Well, sir?'

'Possible. Probable,' Reggie told him. 'On the evidence.'

'Ah. Cruel, isn't it? I hate these child cases.'

'Any more evidence?' Reggie drawled.

Bell stared at his hard calm gloomily. 'I have. Plenty.'

The story began with a small boy on the bank of one of the ponds on Blaney Common. That was some time ago. That was the first time anybody in authority had been aware of the existence of Eddie Hill. One of the keepers of the common made the discovery. The pond was that one which children used for the sailing of toy boats. Eddie Hill had no boat, but he loitered round all the morning, watching the boats of other children. There was little wind, and one boat lay becalmed in the middle of the pond when the children had to go home to dinner.

An hour later the keeper saw Eddie Hill wade into the pond and run away. When the children came back from dinner there was no boat to be seen. Its small owner made weeping complaint to the keeper, who promised to keep his eyes open, and some days later found Eddie Hill and his little sister Bessie lurking among the gorse of the common with the stolen boat.

It was taken from them and their sin reported to their mother, who promised vengeance.

Their mother kept a little general shop. She had been there a dozen years—ever since she married her first husband. She was well liked and looked up to; a religious woman, regular chapel-goer and all that. Her second husband, Brightman, was the same sort—hard-working, respectable man; been at the chapel longer than she had.

The day-school teachers had nothing against Eddie or the little girl. Eddie was rather more than usually bright, but dreamy and careless; the girl a bit stodgy. Both of 'em rather less naughty than most.

'Know a lot, don't you?' Reggie murmured. 'Got all this today?'

'No, this was all on record,' Bell said. 'Worked out for another business.'

'Oh. Small boy and small girl already old offenders. Go on.'

The other business was at the chapel Sunday school. Eddie Hill, as the most regular of its pupils, was allowed the privilege of tidying up at the end of the afternoon. On a Sunday in the spring the superintendent came in unexpectedly upon the process and found Eddie holding the money-box in which had been collected the contributions of the school to the chapel missionary society.

Eddie had no need nor right to handle the money-box. Moreover, on the bench beside him were pennies and a sixpence. Such wealth could not be his own. Only the teachers ever put in silver. Moreover, he confessed that he had extracted the money by rattling the box upside down, and his small sister wept for the sin.

The superintendent took him to the police-station and charged him with theft.

'Virtuous man,' Reggie murmured.

'It does seem a bit harsh,' Bell said. 'But they'd had suspicions about the money-box before. They'd been watching for something like this. Well, the boy's mother came and tried to beg him off, but of course the case had to go on. The boy came up in the Juvenile Court—you know the way, Mr Fortune; no sort of criminal atmosphere, magistrate talking like a father. He let the kid off with a lecture.'

'Oh, yes. What did he say? Bringin' down mother's grey hairs in sorrow to the grave—wicked boy—goin' to the bad in this world and the next—anything about hell?'

'I couldn't tell you.' Bell was shocked. 'I heard he gave the boy a rare old talking to. I don't wonder. Pretty bad, wasn't it, the Sunday-school money-box? What makes you bring hell into it?'

'I didn't. The boy did. He was raving about hell today. Part of the evidence. I was only tracin' the origin.'

'Ah. I don't like these children's cases,' Bell said gloomily. 'They don't seem really human sometimes. You get a twisted kind of child and he'll talk the most frightful stuff—and do it too. We can only go by acts, can we?'

'Yes. That's the way I'm goin'. Get on.'

The sharp impatience of the tone made Bell look at him with some reproach. 'All right, sir. The next thing is this morning's business. I gave you the outline of that on the phone. I've got the full details now. This is what it comes to. Eddie and his little sister were seen on the common; the keepers have got to keeping an eye on him. He wandered about with her—he has a casual, drifting sort of way, like some of these queer kids do have—and they came to the big pond. That's not a children's place at all; it's too deep; only dog bathing and fishing. There was nobody near; it was pretty early. Eddie and Bessie went along the bank, and a labourer who was scything thistles says the little girl was crying, and Eddie seemed to be scolding her, and then he fair chucked her in and went in with her. That's what it looked like to the keeper who was watchin' 'em. Him and the other chap, they nipped down and chucked the lifebuoy; got it right near, but Eddie didn't take hold of it; he was clutching the girl and sinking and coming up again. So the keeper went in to 'em and had trouble getting 'em out. The little girl was unconscious, and Eddie sort of fought him.' Bell stopped and gave a look of inquiry, but Reggie said nothing, and his face showed neither opinion nor feeling. 'Well, you know how it is with these rescues from the water,' Bell went on. 'People often seem to be fighting to drown themselves and it don't mean anything except fright. And about the boy throwing the girl in—that might have been just a bit of a row or play—it's happened often—not meant vicious at all; and then he'd panic, likely enough.' Again Bell looked an anxious question at the cold, passionless face. 'I mean to say, I wouldn't have bothered you with it, Mr Fortune, but for the way the boy carried on when they got him out. There he was with his little sister unconscious, and the keeper doing artificial respiration, and he called out: 'Don't do it. Bessie's dead. She must be dead.' And the keeper asked him: 'Do you want her dead, you little devil?' And he said: 'Yes, I do. I had to.' Then the labourer chap came back with help and they got hold of Eddie; he was raving, flinging himself about and screaming if she lived she'd only get like him and go to hell, so she must be dead. While they brought him along here he was sort of preaching to 'em bits of the Bible, and mad stuff about the wicked being sent to hell and tortures for 'em.'

'Curious and interestin',' Reggie drawled. 'Any particular torture?'

'I don't know. The whole thing pretty well gave these chaps the horrors. They didn't get all the boy's talk. I don't wonder. There was something about worms not dying, they told me. That almost turned 'em up. Well—there you are, Mr Fortune. What do you make of it?'

'I should say it happened,' Reggie said. 'All of it. As stated.'

'You feel sure he could have thrown that fat little girl in? He seemed to me such a weed.'

'Yes. Quite a sound point. I took that point. Development of both children unhealthy. Girl wrongly nourished. Boy inadequately nourished. Boy's physique frail. However. He could have done it. Lots of nervous energy. Triumph of mind over matter.'

Bell drew in his breath. 'You take it cool.'

'Only way to take it,' Reggie murmured, and Bell shifted uncomfortably. He has remarked since that he had seen Mr Fortune look like that once or twice before—sort of inhuman, heartless, and inquisitive; but there it seemed all wrong, it didn't seem his way at all.

Reggie settled himself in his chair and spoke—so Bell has reported, and this is the only criticism which annoys Mr Fortune—like a lecturer. 'Several possibilities to be considered. The boy may be merely a precocious rascal. Having committed some iniquity which the little girl knew about, he tried to drown her to stop her giving him away. Common type of crime, committed by children as well as their elders.'

'I know it is,' Bell admitted. 'But what could he have done that was worth murdering his sister?'

'I haven't the slightest idea. However. He did steal. Proved twice by independent evidence. Don't blame if you don't want. 'There, but for the grace of God, go I.' I agree. Quite rational to admit that consideration. We shall certainly want it. But he knew he was a thief; he knew it got him into trouble—that's fundamental.'

'All right,' said Bell gloomily. 'We have to take it like that.'

'Yes. No help. Attempt to murder sister may be connected with consciousness of sin. I should say it was. However. Other possibilities. He's a poor little mess of nerves; he's unsound, physically, mentally, spiritually. He may not have meant to murder her at all; may have got in a passion and not known what he was doing.'

'Ah. That's more likely.' Bell was relieved.

'You think so? Then why did he tell everybody he did mean to murder her?'

'Well, he was off his head, as you were saying. That's the best explanation of the whole thing. It's really the only explanation. Look at your first idea: he wanted to kill her so she couldn't tell about some crime he'd done. You get just the same question, why did he say he meant murder? He must know killing is worse than stealing. However you take the thing, you work back to his being off his head.'

Reggie's eyelids drooped. 'I was brought here to say he's mad. Yes. I gather that. You're a merciful man, Bell. Sorry not to satisfy your gentle nature. I could swear he's mentally abnormal. If that would do any good. I couldn't say he's mad. I don't know. I can find you mental experts who would give evidence either way.'

'I know which a jury would believe,' Bell grunted.

'Yes. So do I. Merciful people, juries. Like you. Not my job. I'm lookin' for the truth. One more possibility. The boy's motive was just what he said it was—to kill his little sister so she shouldn't get wicked and go to hell. That fits the other facts. He'd got into the way of stealing; it had been rubbed into him that he was doomed to hell. So, if he found her goin' the same way, he might think it best she should die while she was still clean.'

'Well, if that isn't mad!' Bell exclaimed.

'Abnormal, yes. Mad—I wonder,' Reggie murmured.

'But it's sheer crazy, sir. If he believed he was so wicked, the thing for him to do was to pull up and go straight, and see that she did too.'

'Yes. That's common sense, isn't it?' A small, contemptuous smile lingered a moment on Reggie's stern face. 'What's the use of common sense here? If he was like this—sure he was going to hell; sure she was bein' driven there too—kind of virtuous for him to kill her to save her. Kind of rational. Desperately rational. Ever know any children, Bell? Some of 'em do believe what they're taught. Some of 'em take it seriously. Abnormal, as you say. Eddie Hill is abnormal.' He turned and looked full at Bell, his blue eyes dark in the failing light. 'Aged twelve or so—too bad to live—or too good. Pleasant case.'

Bell moved uneasily. 'These things do make you feel queer,' he grunted. 'What it all comes to, though—we mean much the same— the boy ought to be in a home. That can be worked.'

'A home!' Reggie's voice went up, and he laughed. 'Yes. Official home for mentally defective. Yes. We can do that. I dare say we shall.' He stood up and walked to the window and looked out at the dusk. 'These children had a home of their own. And a mother. What's she doing about 'em?'

'She's been here, half off her head, poor thing,' said Bell. 'She wouldn't believe the boy meant any harm. She told me he couldn't, he was so fond of his sister. She said it must have been accident.'

'Quite natural and motherly. Yes. But not adequate. Because it wasn't accident, whatever it was. We'd better go and see mother.'

'If you like,' Bell grunted reluctantly.

'I don't like,' Reggie mumbled. 'I don't like anything. I'm not here to do what I like.' And they went.

People were drifting home from the common. The mean streets of Blaney had already grown quiet in the sultry gloom.

Shutters were up at the little shop which was the home of Eddie Hill, and still bore in faded paint his father's name. No light, showed in the windows above. Bell rapped on the door, and they waited in vain. He moved to a house door close beside the shop. 'Try this. This may be theirs too,' he said, and knocked and rang.

After a minute it was opened by a woman who said nothing, but stared at them. From somewhere inside came the sound of a man's voice, talking fervently.

The light of the street lamp showed her of full figure, in neat black, and a face which was still pretty but distressed.

'You remember me, Mrs Brightman,' said Bell. 'I'm Superintendent Bell.'

'I know.' She was breathless. 'What's the matter? Are they—is Eddie—what's happened?'

'They're doing all right. I just want a little talk with you.'

'Oh, they're all right. Praise God!' She turned; she called out: 'Matthew, Matthew dear, they're all right.'

The man's voice went on talking with the same fervour, but not in answer.

'I'll come in, please,' said Bell.

'Yes, do. Thank you kindly. Mr Brightman would like to see you. We were just asking mercy.'

She led the way along a passage, shining clean, to a room behind the shop. There a man was on his knees praying, and most of the prayer was texts: 'And we shall sing of mercy in the morning. Amen. Amen.' He made an end.

He stood up before them, tall and gaunt, a bearded man with

melancholy eyes. He turned to his wife. 'What is it, my dear? What do the gentlemen want?'

'It's about the children, Matthew.' His wife came and took his arm. 'It's the police superintendent, I told you. He was so kind.'

The man sucked in his breath. 'Ay, ay. Please sit down. They must sit down, Florrie.' There was a fluster of setting chairs. 'This is kind, sir. What can you tell us tonight?'

'Doin' well. Both of 'em,' Reggie said.

'There's our answer, Florrie,' the man said, and smiled and his sombre eyes glowed. 'There's our prayers answered.'

'Yes. I think they're going to live,' said Reggie. 'But that's not the only thing that matters. We have to ask how it was they were nearly drowned.'

'It was an accident. It must have been,' the woman cried. 'I'm sure Eddie wouldn't—he never would, would he, Matthew?'

'I won't believe it,' Brightman answered quickly.

'Quite natural you should feel like that,' Reggie nodded. 'However. We have to deal with the facts.'

'You must do what you think right, sir, as it is shown you.' Brightman bent his head.

'Yes, I will. Yes. Been rather a naughty boy, hasn't he?'

Brightman looked at his wife's miserable face and turned to them again. 'The police know,' he said. 'He has been a thief—twice he has been a thief—but little things. There is mercy, surely there is mercy for repentance. If his life is spared, he should not be lost; we must believe that.'

'I do,' Reggie murmured. 'Any special reason why he should have been a thief?'

Brightman shook his head. 'He's always had a good home, I'm sure,' the woman moaned. She looked round her room, which was ugly and shabby, but all in the cleanest order.

'What can I say?' Brightman shook his head. 'We've always done our best for him. There's no telling how temptation comes, sir, and it's strong and the little ones are weak.'

'That is so. Yes. How much pocket-money did they have?'

'Eddie has had his twopence a week since he was ten,' Brightman answered proudly. 'And Bessie has her penny.'

'I see. And was there anything happened this morning which upset Bessie or Eddie?'

'Nothing at all, sir. Nothing that I know.' Brightman turned to his wife. 'They went off quite happy, didn't they?'

'Yes, of course they did,' she said eagerly. 'They always loved to have a day on the common. They took their lunch, and they went running as happy as happy—and then this,' she sobbed.

'My dearie.' Brightman patted her.

'Well, well.' Reggie stood up. 'Oh. By the way. Has Eddie —or Bessie—ever stolen anything at home here—money or what not?'

Brightman started and stared at him. 'That's not fair, sir. That's not a right thing to ask. There isn't stealing between little ones and their mother and father.'

'No. As you say. No,' Reggie murmured. 'Good night. You'll hear how they go on. Good night.'

'Thank you, sir. We shall be anxious to hear. Good night, sir,' said Brightman, and Mrs Brightman showed them out with tearful gratitude. As the door was opened, Brightman called: 'Florrie! Don't bolt it. Mrs Wiven hasn't come back.'

'I know. I know,' she answered, and bade them good night and shut the door.

A few paces away, Reggie stopped and looked back at the shuttered shop and the dark windows. 'Well, well. What does the professional mind make of all that?'

'Just what you'd expect, wasn't it?' Bell grunted.

'Yes. Absolutely. Poor struggling shopkeepers, earnestly religious, keeping the old house like a new pin. All in accordance with the evidence.' He sniffed the night air. 'Dank old house.'

'General shop smell. All sorts of things mixed up.'

'As you say. There were. And there would be. Nothing you couldn't have guessed before we went. Except that Mrs Wiven is expected— whoever Mrs Wiven is.'

'I don't know. Sounds like a lodger.'

'Yes, that is so. Which would make another resident in the home of Eddie and Bessie. However. She's not come back yet. So we can go home. The end of a beastly day. And tomorrow's another one. I'll be

171

out to see the children in the morning. Oh, my Lord! Those children.' His hand gripped Bell's arm. . . .

By eight o'clock in the morning he was at the bedside of Bessie Hill—an achievement of stupendous but useless energy, for she did not wake till half-past.

Then he took charge. A responsible position, which he interpreted as administering to her cups of warm milk and bread and butter. She consumed them eagerly; she took his service as a matter of course.

'Good girl.' Reggie wiped her mouth. 'Feelin' better?'

She sighed and snuggled down, and gazed at him with large eyes. 'Umm. Who are you?'

'They call me Mr Fortune. Is it nice here?'

'Umm. Comfy.' The big eyes were puzzled and wondering. 'Where is it?'

'Blaney Hospital. People brought you here after you were in the pond. Do you remember?'

She shook her head. 'Is Eddie here?'

'Oh, yes. Eddie's asleep. He's all right. Were you cross with Eddie?'

Tears came into the brown eyes. 'Eddie was cross wiv me,' the child whimpered. 'I wasn't. I wasn't. Eddie said must go into ve water. I didn't want. But Eddie was so cross. Love Eddie.'

'Yes. Little girl.' Reggie stroked her hair. 'Eddie shouldn't have been cross. Just a little girl. But Eddie isn't often cross, is he?'

'No. Love Eddie. Eddie's dear.'

'Why was he cross yesterday?'

The brown eyes opened wider. 'I was naughty. It was Mrs Wiven. Old Mrs Wiven. I did go up to her room. I didn't fink she was there. Sometimes is sweeties. But she was vere. She scolded me. She said I was little fief. We was all fiefs. And Eddie took me away and oh, he was so cross; he said I would be wicked and must not be. But I aren't. I aren't. Eddie was all funny and angry, and said not to be like him and go to hell, and then he did take me into pond wiv him. I didn't want! I didn't want!'

'No. Of course not. No. Poor little girl. Eddie didn't understand. But it's all right now.'

'Is Eddie still cross wiv me?' she whimpered.

'Oh, no. No. Eddie won't be cross any more. Nobody's cross, little girl.' Reggie bent over her. 'Everybody's going to be kind now. You only have to be quiet and happy. That's all.'

'Oooh.' She gazed up at him. 'Tell Eddie I'm sorry.'

'Yes. I'll tell him.' Reggie kissed her hand and turned away.

The nurse met him at the door. 'Did she wake in the night?' he whispered.

'Yes, sir, asking for Eddie. She's a darling, isn't she?' She makes me cry, talking like that of him.'

'That won't do any harm,' Reggie said, and his face hardened. 'But you mustn't talk about him.'

He went to the room where Eddie lay. The doctor was there, and turned from the bedside to confer with him. 'Not too bad. We've put in a long sleep. Quite quiet since we waked. Very thirsty. Taken milk with a dash of coffee nicely. But we're rather flat.'

Reggie sat down by the bed. The boy lay very still. His thin face was white. Only his eyes moved to look at Reggie, so little open, their pupils so small that they seemed all greenish-grey. He gave no sign of recognition, or feeling, or intelligence. Reggie put a hand under the clothes and found him cold and damp, and felt for his pulse.

'Well, young man, does anything hurt you now?'

'I'm tired. I'm awful tired,' the boy said.

'Yes. I know. But that's going away.'

'No, it isn't; it's worse. I didn't ought to have waked up.' The faint voice was drearily peevish. 'I didn't want to. It's no good. I thought I was dead. And it was good being dead.'

'Was it?' Reggie said sharply.

'The boy gave a quivering cry. 'Yes, it was!' His face was distorted with fear and wonder. 'I thought it would be so dreadful and it was all quiet and nice, and then I wasn't dead, I was alive and everything's awful again. I've got to go on still.'

'What's awful in going on?' said Reggie. 'Bessie wants you. Bessie sent you her love. She's gettin' well quick.'

'Bessie? Bessie's here in bed like I am?' The unnatural greenish eyes stared.

'Of course she is. Only much happier than you are.'

The boy began to sob.

'Why do you cry about that?' Reggie said. 'She's got to be happy.

Boys and girls have to be happy. That's what they're for. You didn't
want Bessie to die.'

'I did. You know I did,' the boy sobbed.

'I know you jumped in the pond with her. That was silly. But you'd
got rather excited, hadn't you? What was it all about?'

'They'll tell you,' the boy muttered.

'Who will?'

'The keepers, the p'lice, the m-magistrate, everybody. I'm wicked.
I'm a thief. I can't help it. And I didn't want Bessie to be wicked too.'

'Of course you didn't. And she isn't. What ever made you think she
was?'

'But she was.' The boy's voice was shrill. 'She went to Mrs Wiven's
room. She was looking for pennies. I know she was. She'd seen me.
And Mrs Wiven said we were all thieves. So I had to.'

'Oh, no, you hadn't. And you didn't. You see? Things don't happen
like that.'

'Yes, they do. There's hell. Where their worms don't die.'

The doctor made a muttered exclamation.

Reggie's hand held firm at the boy's as he moved and writhed.
'There's God too,' he murmured. 'God's kind. Bessie's not going to
be wicked. You don't have to be wicked. That's what's come of it
all. Somebody's holding you up now.' His hand pressed. 'Feel?' The
boy's lips parted; he looked up in awe. 'Yes. Like that. You'll see me
again and again. Now good-bye. Think about me. I'm thinking
about you.' . . . He stayed a while longer before he said another
'Good-bye.'

Outside, in the corridor, the doctor spoke: 'I say, Mr Fortune, you
got him then. That was the stuff. I thought you were driving hard
before. Sorry I spoke.'

'I was.' Reggie frowned. His round face was again of a ruthless
severity. ' "Difficult matter to play with souls," ' he mumbled. 'We've
got to.' He looked under drooping eyelids. 'Know the name of the
keeper who saw the attempted drowning? Fawkes? Thanks.'

He left the hospital and walked across the common.

The turf was parched and yellow, worn away on either side of paths
loosened by the summer drought. Reggie descried the brown coat of
a keeper, made for him, and was directed to where Fawkes would be.

Fawkes was a slow-speaking, slow-thinking old soldier, but he knew his own mind.

There was no doubt in it that Eddie had tried to kill Bessie, no indignation, no surprise. Chewing his words, he gave judgment. He had known Eddie's sort, lots of 'em. 'Igh strung, wanting the earth, kicking up behind and before 'cause they couldn't get it. He didn't mind 'em. Rather 'ave 'em than young 'uns like sheep. But you 'ad to dress 'em down proper. They was devils else. Young Eddie would 'ave to be for it.

That business of the boat? Yes, Eddie pinched that all right. Smart kid; you'd got to 'and him that. And yet not so smart. Silly, lying up with it on the common; just the way to get nabbed. Ought to 'ave took it 'ome and sailed it over at Wymond Park. Never been spotted then. But 'im and 'is sister, they made a reg'lar den up in the gorse. Always knew where to look for 'em. Silly. Why, they was up there yesterday, loafing round, before 'e did 'is drowning act.

'Take you there? I can, if you like.'

Reggie did like. They went up the brown slopes of the common to a tangle of gorse and bramble over small sand-hills.

'There you are.' The keeper pointed his stick to a patch of loose sand in a hollow. 'That's young Eddie's funk-'ole. That's where we spotted 'em with the blinking boat.'

Reggie came to the place. The sand had been scooped up by small hands into a low wall round a space which was decked out with pebbles, yellow petals of gorse, and white petals of bramble.

'Ain't that just like 'em!' The keeper was angrily triumphant. 'They know they didn't ought to pick the flowers. As well as you and me they do, and they go and do it.'

Reggie did not answer. He surveyed the pretence of a garden and looked beyond. 'Oh, my Lord!' he muttered. On the ground lay a woman's bag.

''Allo, 'allo.' The keeper snorted. 'They've been pinching something else.'

Reggie took out his handkerchief, put his hand in it, and thus picked up the bag. He looked about him; he wandered to and fro, going delicately, examining the confusion of small footmarks, further and further away.

'Been all round, ain't they?' the keeper greeted him on his return.

'That is so. Yes.' Reggie mumbled and looked at him with searching eyes. 'Had any notice of a bag lost or stolen?'

'Not as I've 'eard. Better ask the 'ead keeper. 'E'll be up at the top wood about now.'

The wood was a thicket of birch and crab-apple and thorn. As they came near, they saw on its verge the head keeper and two other men who were not in the brown coats of authority. One of these was Super-intendent Bell. He came down the slope in a hurry.

'I tried to catch you at the hospital, Mr Fortune,' he said. 'But I suppose you've heard about Mrs Wiven?'

'Oh. The Mrs. Wiven who hadn't come back,' Reggie said slowly. 'No. I haven't heard anything.'

'I thought you must have, by your being out here on the common. Well, she didn't come back at all. This morning Brightman turned up at the station very fussy and rattled to ask if they had any news of his lodger, Mrs Wiven. She never came in last night, and he thought she must have had an accident or something. She'd been lodging with them for years. Old lady, fixed in her habits. Never went anywhere, that he knew of, except to chapel and for a cup o' tea with some of her chapel friends, and none of them had seen her. These fine summer days she'd take her food out and sit on the common here all day long. She went off yesterday morning with sandwiches and a vacuum flask of tea and her knitting. Often she wouldn't come home till it was getting dark. They didn't think much of her being late; sometimes she went in and had a bit o' supper with a friend. She had her key, and they left the door unbolted, like we heard, and went to bed, being worn out with the worry of the kids. But when Mrs Brightman took up her cup of tea this morning and found she wasn't in her room, Brightman came running round to the station. Queer business, eh?'

'Yes. Nasty business. Further you go the nastier.'

Bell looked at him curiously and walked him away from the keeper. 'You feel it that way? So do I. Could you tell me what you were look-ing for out here—as you didn't know she was missing?'

'Oh, yes. I came to verify the reports of Eddie's performances.'

'Ah! Have you found any error?'

'No. I should say everything happened as stated.'

'The boy's going to get well, isn't he?'

'It could be. If he gets the chance.'

'Poor little beggar,' Bell grunted. 'What do you really think about him, Mr Fortune?'

'Clever child, ambitious child, imaginative child. What children ought to be—twisted askew.'

'Kind of perverted, you mean.'

'That is so. Yes. However. Question now is, not what I think of the chances of Eddie's soul, but what's been happening. Evidence inadequate, curious, and nasty. I went up to the private lair of Eddie and Bessie. Same where he was caught with the stolen boat. I found this.' He showed Bell the woman's bag.

'My oath!' Bell muttered, and took it from him gingerly. 'You wrapped it up! Thinkin' there might be fingerprints.'

'Yes. Probably are. They might even be useful.'

'And you went looking for this—not knowing the woman was missing?'

'Wasn't lookin' for it,' Reggie snapped. 'I was lookin' for anything there might be. Found a little pretence of a garden they'd played at—and this.'

'Ah, but you heard last night about Mrs Wiven, and this morning you go up where Eddie hides what he's stolen. Don't that mean you made sure there was something fishy? You see when we're blind, Mr Fortune.'

'Oh, no. I don't see. I knew more than you did. Little Bessie told me this morning she was in Mrs Wiven's room yesterday, privily and by stealth, and Mrs Wiven caught her and called her a thief, and said they were all thieves. I should think little Bessie may have meant to be a thief. Which would agree with Eddie's effort to drown her so she should die good and honest. But I don't see my way.'

'All crazy, isn't it?' Bell grunted.

'Yes. The effort of Eddie is an incalculable factor. However. You'd better look at the bag.'

Bell opened it with cautious fingers. A smell of peppermint came out. Within was a paper bag of peppermint lozenges, two unclean handkerchiefs marked E.W., an empty envelope addressed to Mrs Wiven, a bottle of soda-mint tablets, and some keys.

'Evidence that it is the bag of the missing Mrs Wiven strong,' Reggie murmured. He peered into it. 'But no money. Not a penny.' He looked up at Bell with that cold, ruthless curiosity which Bell always talks about in discussing the case. 'Stealin' is the recurrin' motive. You notice that?'

'I do.' Bell stared at him. 'You take it cool, Mr Fortune. I've got to own it makes me feel queer.'

'No use feelin' feelings,' Reggie drawled. 'We have to go on. We want the truth, whatever it is.'

'Well, all right, I know,' Bell said gloomily. 'They're searching the common for her. That's why I came out here. They knew her. She did sit about here in summer.' He went back to the head keeper and conferred again. . . .

Reggie purveyed himself a deck-chair, and therein sat extended and lit a pipe and closed his eyes. . . .

'Mr Fortune!' Bell stood over him. His lips emitted a stream of smoke. No other part of him moved. 'They've found her. I suppose you expected that.'

'Yes. Obvious possibility. Probable possibility.' It has been remarked that Mr Fortune has a singular capacity for becoming erect from a supine position. A professor of animal morphology once delivered a lecture upon him—after a hospital dinner—as the highest type of the invertebrates. He stood up from the deck-chair in one undulating motion. 'Well, well. Where is the new fact?' he moaned.

Bell took him into the wood. No grass grew in it. Where the sandy soil was not bare, dead leaves made a carpet. Under the crab-apple trees, between the thorn-brakes, were nooks obviously much used by pairs of lovers. By one of these, not far from the whale-back edge of rising ground which was the wood's end, some men stood together.

On the grey sand there lay a woman's body. She was small; she was dressed in a coat and skirt of dark grey cloth and a black and white blouse. The hat on her grey hair was pulled to one side, giving her a look of absurd frivolity in ghastly contrast to the distortion of her pallid face. Her lips were closely compressed and almost white. The dead eyes stared up at the trees with dilated pupils.

Reggie walked round the body, going delicately, rather like a dog in doubt how to deal with another dog.

Beside the body was a raffia bag which held some knitting, a vacuum flask, and an opened packet of sandwiches.

Reggie's discursive eyes looked at them and looked again at the dead face, but not for long. He was more interested in the woman's skirt. He bent over that, examined it from side to side, and turned away and went on prowling further and further away, and as he went he scraped at the dry sand here and there.

When he came back to the body, his lips were curved in a grim, mirthless smile. He looked at Bell. 'Photographer,' he mumbled.

'Sent a man to phone, sir,' Bell grunted.

Reggie continued to look at him. 'Have you? Why have you?'

'Just routine.' Bell was startled.

'Oh. Only that. Well, well.' Reggie knelt down by the body. His hands went to the woman's mouth. . . . He took something from his pocket and forced the mouth open and looked in. . . . He closed the mouth again, and sat down on his heels and contemplated the dead woman with dreamy curiosity. . . . He opened her blouse. Upon the underclothes was a dark stain. He bent over that and smelt it; he drew the clothes from her chest.

'No wound, is there?' Bell muttered.

'Oh, no. No.' Reggie put back the clothes and stood up and went to the flask and the sandwiches. He pulled the bread of an unfinished sandwich apart, looked at it, and put it down. He took the flask and shook it. It was not full. He poured some of the contents into its cup.

'Tea, eh?' said Bell. 'Strong tea.'

'Yes. It would be,' Reggie murmured. He tasted it and spat, and poured what was in the cup back into the flask and corked it again and gave it to Bell.

'There you are. Cause of death, poisoning by oxalic acid or binoxalate of potassium—probably the latter—commonly called salts of lemon. And we shall find some in that awful tea. We shall also find it in the body. Tongue and mouth, white, contracted, eroded. Time of death, probably round about twenty-four hours ago. No certainty.'

'My oath! It's too near certainty for my liking,' Bell muttered.

'Is it?' Reggie's eyelids drooped. 'Wasn't thinkin' about what you'd like. Other interestin' facts converge.'

'They do!' Bell glowered at him. 'One of the commonest kinds of poisoning, isn't it?'

'Oh, yes. Salts of lemon very popular.'

'Anybody can get it.'

'As you say. Removes stains, cleans brass and what not. Also quickly fatal, with luck. Unfortunate chemical properties.'

'This boy Eddie could have got some easy.'

'That is so. Yes. Lethal dose for a penny or two anywhere.'

'Well, then—look at it!'

'I have,' Reggie murmured. 'Weird case. Ghastly case.'

'Gives me the horrors,' said Bell. 'The old lady comes out here to spend the day as usual, and somebody's put a spot of poison in her drop o' tea and she dies; and her bag's stolen, and found without a farthing where the boy Eddie hides his loot. And, about the time the old lady's dying, Eddie tries to drown his sister. What are you going to make of that? What can you make of it? It was a poison any kid could get hold of. One of 'em must have poisoned her to steal her little bit o' money. But the girl's not much more than a baby. It must have been Eddie that did it—and that goes with the rest of his doings. He's got the habit of stealing. But his little sister saw something of it, knew too much, so he put up this drowning to stop her tongue—and then, when she was saved, made up this tale about killing her to keep her honest. Devilish, isn't it? And when you find a child playing the devil—my oath! But it is devilish clever—his tale would put the stealing and all the rest on the baby. And we can't prove anything else. She's too little to be able to get it clear, and he's made himself out driven wild by her goings on. If a child's really wicked, he beats you.'

'Yes, that is so,' Reggie drawled. 'Rather excited, aren't you? Emotions are not useful in investigation. Prejudice the mind into exaggeratin' facts and ignorin' other facts. Both fallacies exhibited in your argument. You mustn't ignore what Bessie did say—that she went into Mrs Wiven's room yesterday morning and Mrs Wiven caught her. I shouldn't wonder if you found Bessie's fingerprints on that bag.'

'My Lord!' Bell stared at him. 'It's the nastiest case I ever had. When it comes to babies in murder——'

'Not nice, no. Discoverin' the possibilities of corruption of the soul. However. We haven't finished yet. Other interestin' facts have been ignored by Superintendent Bell. Hallo!' Several men were approaching briskly. 'Is this your photographer and other experts?'

'That's right. Photographer and fingerprint men.'

'Very swift and efficient.' Reggie went to meet them. 'Where did you spring from?'

'By car, sir.' The photographer was surprised. 'On the road up there. We had the location by phone.'

'Splendid. Now then. Give your attention to the lady's skirt. Look.' He indicated a shining streak across the dark stuff. 'Bring that out.'

'Can do, sir,' the photographer said, and fell to work.

Reggie turned to Bell. 'Then they'll go over the whole of her for fingerprints, what? And the sandwich paper. And the flask. Not forgettin' the bag. That's all. I've finished here. She can be taken to the mortuary for me.'

'Very good,' Bell said, and turned away to give the orders, but, having given them, stood still to stare at the thin glistening streak on the skirt.

Reggie came quietly to his elbow. 'You do notice that? Well, well.' Bell looked at him with a puzzled frown and was met for the first time in this case by a small, satisfied smile which further bewildered him. He bent again to pore over the streak. 'It's all right.' Reggie's voice was soothing. 'That's on the record now. Come on.' Linking arms, he drew Bell away from the photographers and the fingerprint men. 'Well? What does the higher intelligence make of the line on the skirt?'

'I don't know. I can't make out why you think so much of it.'

'My dear chap! Oh, my dear chap!' Reggie moaned. 'Crucial fact. Decisive fact.' He led Bell on out of the wood and across the common, and at a respectful distance Bell's two personal satellites followed.

'Decisive, eh?' Bell frowned. 'It was just a smear of something to me. You mean salts of lemon would leave a shiny stain?'

'Oh, no. No. Wouldn't shine at all.'

'Had she been sick on her skirt?'

'Not there. No. Smear wasn't human material.'

'Well, I thought it wasn't. What are you thinking of?'

'I did think of what Eddie said—where their worm dieth not.'

'My God!' Bell muttered. 'Worms?' He gave a shudder. 'I don't get you at all, sir. It sounds mad.'

'No. Connection is sort of desperate rational. I told you Eddie was like that. However. Speakin' scientifically, not a worm, but a slug. That streak was a slug's trail.'

'Oh. I see.' Bell was much relieved. 'Now you say so, it did look like that. The sort o' slime a slug leaves behind. It does dry shiny, of course.'

'You have noticed that?' Reggie admired him. 'Splendid!'

Bell was not pleased. 'I have seen slugs before,' he grunted. 'But what is there to make a fuss about? I grant you, it's nasty to think of a slug crawling over the woman as she lay there dead. That don't mean anything, though. Just what you'd expect, with the body being all night in the wood. Slugs come out when it gets dark.'

'My dear chap! Oh, my dear chap!' Reggie moaned. 'You mustn't talk like that. Shakes confidence in the police force. Distressin' mixture of inadequate observation and fallacious reasonin'.'

'Thank you. I don't know what's wrong with it.' Bell was irritated.

'Oh, my Bell! You shock me. Think again. Your general principle's all right. Slugs do come out at night. Slugs like the dark. That's a general truth which has its particular application. But you fail to observe the conditions. The body was in a wood with no herbage on the ground: and the ground was a light dry sand. These are not conditions which attract the slug. I should have been much surprised if I'd found any slugs there, or their tracks. But I looked for 'em—which you didn't, Bell. I'm always careful. And there wasn't a trace. No. I can't let you off. A slug had crawled over her skirt, leavin' his slime from side to side. And yet his slime didn't go beyond her skirt on to the ground anywhere. How do you suppose he managed that? Miracle—by a slug. I don't believe in miracles if I can help it. I object to your simple faith in the miraculous gasteropod. It's lazy.'

'You go beyond me,' said Bell uneasily. 'You grasp the whole thing while I'm only getting bits. What do you make of it all?'

'Oh, my Bell!' Reggie reproached him. 'Quite clear. When the slug walked over her, she wasn't lying where she was found.'

'Is that all?' Bell grunted. 'I dare say. She might have had her dose, and felt queer and lay down, and then moved on to die where we found her. Nothing queer in that, is there?'

'Yes. Several things very queer. It could be. Oxalic poisoning might lay her out and still let her drag herself somewhere else to die. Not likely she'd take care to bring her flask and her sandwiches with her. Still less likely she'd lie long enough for a slug to walk over her and then recover enough to move somewhere else—and choose to move into the wood, where she wouldn't be seen. Why should she? She'd try for help if she could try for anything. And, finally, most unlikely she'd find any place here with slugs about. Look at it; it's all arid and sandy and burnt up by the summer. No. Quite unconvincin' explanation. The useful slug got on to her somewhere else. The slug is decisive.'

'Then you mean to say she was poisoned some other place, and brought here dead?' Bell frowned. 'It's all very well. You make it sound reasonable. But would you like to try this slug argument on a jury? They'd never stand for it, if you ask me. It's all too clever.'

'You think so?' Reggie murmured. 'Well, well. Then it does give variety to the case. We haven't been very clever so far. However. Study to improve. There is further evidence. She'd been sick. Common symptom of oxalic poisoning. But she'd been sick on her underclothes and not on her outside clothes. That's very difficult. Think about it. Even juries can be made to think sometimes. Even coroners, which is very hard. Even judges. I've done it in my time, simple as I am. I might do it again. Yes, I might. With the aid of the active and intelligent police force. Come on.'

'What do you want to do?'

'Oh, my Bell! I want to call on Mr and Mrs Brightman. We need their collaboration. We can't get on without it.'

'All right. I don't mind trying 'em,' Bell agreed gloomily. 'We've got to find out all about the old woman somehow. We don't really know anything yet.'

'I wouldn't say that. No,' Reggie mumbled. 'However. One moment.'

They had come to the edge of the common by the hospital, where his car waited. He went across to it and spoke to his chauffeur.

'Just calmin' Sam,' he apologized on his return. 'He gets peevish when forgotten. Come on.'

They arrived again at the little general shop. Its unshuttered window now enticed the public with a meagre array of canned goods and cartons which had been there some time. The door was shut but not fastened. Opening it rang a bell. They went in, and found the shop empty, and for a minute or two stood in a mixture of smells through which soap was dominant.

Mrs Brightman came from the room behind, wiping red arms and hands on her apron. Her plump face, which was tired and sweating, quivered alarm at the sight of them. 'Oh, it's you!' she cried. 'What is it? Is there anything?'

'Your children are doing well,' said Reggie. 'Thought I'd better let you know that.'

She stared at him, and tears came into her eyes. 'Praise God!' she gasped. 'Thank you, sir, you're very kind.'

'No. You don't have to thank me. I'm just doin' my job.'

But again she thanked him, and went on nervously: 'Have you heard anything of Mrs Wiven?'

'I want to have a little talk about her. Is Mr Brightman in?'

'No, he isn't, not just now. Have you got any news of her, sir?'

'Yes. There is some news. Sorry Mr Brightman's out. Where's he gone?'

'Down to the yard, sir.'

'Out at the back here?'

'No. No. Down at his own yard.'

'Oh. He has a business of his own?'

'Yes, sir, a little business. Furniture dealing it is. Second-hand furniture.'

'I see. Well, well. We could get one of the neighbours to run down and fetch him, what?' Reggie turned to Bell.

'That's the way,' Bell nodded. 'What's the address, ma'am?'

She swallowed. 'It's just round the corner. Smith's Buildings. Anybody would tell you. But he might be out on a job, you know; I couldn't say.'

Bell strode out, and the messenger he sent was one of his satellites.

'Well, while we're waitin', we might come into your nice little room,' Reggie suggested. 'There's one or two things you can tell me.'

'Yes, sir, I'm sure, anything as I can, I'll be glad. Will you come through, please?' She lifted the flap of the counter for him, she opened the curtained glass door of the room behind. It was still in exact order, but she had to apologize for it. 'I'm sorry we're all in a mess. I'm behindhand with my cleaning, having this dreadful trouble with the children and being so worried I can't get on. I don't half know what I'm doing, and then poor Mrs Wiven being lost——' She stopped, breathless. 'What is it about Mrs Wiven, sir? What have you heard?'

'Not good news,' Reggie said. 'Nobody will see Mrs Wiven alive again.'

The full face grew pale beneath its sweat, the eyes stood out. 'She's dead! Oh, the poor soul! But how do you know? How was it?'

'She's been found dead on the common.'

Mrs Brightman stared at him: her mouth came open and shook: she flung her apron over her head and bent and was convulsed with hysterical sobbing.

'Fond of her, were you?' Reggie sympathized.

A muffled voice informed him that she was a dear old lady—and so good to everybody.

'Was she? Yes. But I wanted to ask you about the children. What time did they go out yesterday?' Still sobbing under her apron, Mrs Brightman seemed not to hear. 'Yesterday morning,' Reggie insisted. 'You must remember. What time was it when Eddie and Bessie went out?'

After a moment the apron was pulled down from a swollen, tearful face. 'What time?' she repeated looking at her lap and wiping her eyes. 'I don't know exactly, sir. Just after breakfast. Might be somewheres about nine o'clock.'

'Yes, it might be,' Reggie murmured. 'They were pulled out of the pond about then.'

'I suppose so,' she whimpered. 'What's it got to do with Mrs Wiven?'

'You don't see any connection?'

She stared at him. 'How could there be?'

The shop-door bell rang, and she started up to answer it. She found Bell in the shop. 'Oh, have you found Mr Brightman?' she cried.

'No, not yet. Where's Mr Fortune?'

Reggie called to him, 'Come on, Bell,' and she brought him into the back room and stood looking from one to the other. 'So Mr Brightman wasn't in his yard?'

'No, sir. Nobody there. At least, they couldn't make anybody hear.'

'Well, well,' Reggie murmured.

'But I told you he might have gone off on a job. He often has to go to price some stuff or make an offer or something.'

'You did say so. Yes,' Reggie murmured. 'However. I was asking about the children. Before they went out yesterday—Bessie got into trouble with Mrs Wiven, didn't she?'

The woman looked down and plucked at her apron.

'You didn't tell us that last night,' Reggie said.

'I didn't want to. I didn't see as it mattered. And I didn't want to say anything against Bessie. She's my baby.' Her eyes were streaming. 'Don't you see?'

'Bessie told me,' said Reggie.

'Bessie confessed! Oh, it's all too dreadful. The baby! I don't know why this was to come on us. I brought 'em up to be good, I have. And she was such a darling baby. But it's God's will.'

'Yes. What did happen?' said Reggie.

'Mrs Wiven was always hard on the children. She never had a child herself, poor thing. Bessie got into her room, and Mrs Wiven caught her and said she was prying and stealing like Eddie. I don't know what Bessie was doing there. Children will do such, whatever you do. And there was Bessie crying and Eddie all wild. He does get so out of himself. I packed 'em off, and I told Mrs Wiven it wasn't nothing to be so cross about, and she got quite nice again. She was always a dear with me and Brightman. A good woman at heart, sir, she was.'

'And when did Mrs Wiven go out?' said Reggie.

'It must have been soon after. She liked her days on the common in summer, she did.'

'Oh, yes. That's clear.' Reggie stood up and looked out at the yard, where some washing was hung out to dry. 'What was Mrs Wiven wearing yesterday?'

'Let me see——' Mrs Brightman was surprised by the turn in the conversation. 'I don't rightly remember—she had on her dark coat and skirt. She always liked to be nicely dressed when she went out.' Under the frown of this mental effort swollen eyes blinked at him. 'But you said she'd been found. You know what she had on.'

'Yes. When she was on the common. Before she got there—what was she wearing?'

Mrs Brightman's mouth opened and shut.

'I mean, when she caught Bessie in her room. What was she wearing then?'

'The same—she wouldn't have her coat on—I don't know as I remember—but the same—she knew she was going out—she'd dress for it—she wouldn't ever dress twice in a morning.'

'Wouldn't she? She didn't have that overall on?' Reggie pointed to a dark garment hanging on the line in the yard which stretched from house to shed.

'No, she didn't, I'm sure. That was in the dirty clothes.'

'But you had to wash it today. Well, well. Now we want to have a look at Mrs Wiven's room.'

'If you like. Of course, nothing's been done. It's all untidy.' She led the way upstairs, lamenting that the house was all anyhow, she'd been so put about.

But Mrs Wiven's room was primly neat and as clean as the shining passage and stairs. The paint had been worn thin by much washing, the paper was so faded that its rosebud pattern merged into a uniform pinkish grey. An old fur rug by the bedside, a square of threadbare carpet under the rickety round table in the middle of the room, were the only coverings of the scoured floor. The table had one cane chair beside it, and there was a small basket chair by the empty grate—nothing else in the room but the iron bedstead and a combination of chest of drawers, dressing-table, and washstand, with its mirror all brown spots.

Mrs Brightman passed round the room, pulling this and pushing that. 'I haven't even dusted,' she lamented.

'Is this her own furniture?' Reggie asked.

'No, sir, she hadn't anything. We had to furnish it for her.'

'Quite poor, was she?'

'I don't really know how she managed. And, of course, we didn't ever press her; you couldn't. She had her savings, I suppose. She'd been in good service, by what she used to say.'

'No relations?'

'No, sir. She was left quite alone. That was really why she came to us, she was that lonely. She'd say to me she did so want a home, till we took her. When she was feeling down, she used to cry and tell me she didn't know what would become of her. Of course, we wouldn't ever have let her want, poor dear. But it's my belief her bit of money was running out.'

Reggie gazed about the room. On the walls were many cards with texts.

'Mr Brightman put up the good words for her,' Mrs Brightman explained, and gazed at one of the texts and cried.

' "In My Father's house are many mansions." ' Reggie read it out slowly, and again looked round the bare little room.

Mrs Brightman sobbed. 'Ah, she's gone there now. She's happy.'

Bell was moving from one to other of the cupboards beside the grate. Nothing was in them but clothes. He went on to the dressing-table. 'She don't seem to have any papers. Only this.' He lifted a cash-box, and money rattled in it.

'I couldn't say, I'm sure,' Mrs Brightman whimpered.

Reggie stood by the table. 'Did she have her meals up here?' he asked.

Mrs Brightman thought about that. 'Mostly she didn't. She liked to sit down with us. She used to say it was more homely.'

Reggie fingered the table-cloth, pulled it off, and looked at the cracked veneer beneath. He stooped, felt the strip of old carpet under the table, drew it back. On the boards beneath was a patch of damp.

Mrs Brightman came nearer. 'Well there!' she said. 'That comes of my not doing out the room. She must have had a accident with her slops and never told me. She always would do things for herself.'

Reggie did not answer. He wandered round the room, stopped by the window a moment, and turned to the door.

'I'm taking this cash-box, ma'am,' said Bell.

'If you think right——' Mrs Brightman drew back.

'It's not for me to say—I don't mind, myself.' She looked from one to the other. 'Will that be all, then?'

'Nothing more here.' Reggie opened the door.

As they went downstairs, the shop bell rang again, and she hurried on to answer it. The two men returned to the room behind the shop.

'Poor old woman,' Bell grunted. 'You can see what sort of life she was having—that mingy room and her money running out—I wouldn't wonder if she committed suicide.'

'Wouldn't be wonderful. No,' Reggie murmured. 'Shut up.'

From the shop came a man's voice, lazy and genial. 'Good afternoon, mum. I want a bit o' salts o' lemon. About two penn'orth would do me. 'Ow do you sell it?'

There was a mutter from Mrs Brightman. 'We don't keep it.'

'What? They told me I'd be sure to get it 'ere. Run out of it, 'ave you? Ain't that too bad!'

'We never did keep it,' Mrs Brightman said. 'Whoever told you we did?'

'All right, all right. Keep your hair on, missis. Where can I get it?'

'How should I know? I don't rightly know what it is.'

'Don't you? Sorry I spoke. Used for cleaning, you know.'

Bell glowered at Reggie, for the humorous cockney voice was the voice of his chauffeur. But the cold severity of Reggie's round face gave no sign.

'We don't use it, nor we don't keep it, nor any chemist's stuff,' Mrs Brightman was answering.

'Oh, good day!' The bell rang again as the shop door closed.

Mrs Brightman came back. 'Running in and out of the shop all day with silly people,' she panted. She looked from one to the other, questioning, afraid.

'I was wonderin',' Reggie murmured. 'Did Mrs Wiven have her meals with you yesterday—or in her room?'

'Down here.' The swollen eyes looked at him and looked away. 'She did usual, I told you. She liked to.'

'And which was the last meal she ever had?'

Mrs Brightman suppressed a cry. 'You do say things! Breakfast was the last she had here. She took out a bit o' lunch and tea.'

'Yes. When was that put ready?'

'I had it done first thing, knowing she meant to get out—and she always liked to start early. It was there on the sideboard waiting at breakfast.'

'Then it was ready before the children went out? Before she had her quarrel with Bessie?'

Mrs Brightman swallowed. 'So it was.'

'Oh. Thank you. Rather strong, the tea in her flask,' Reggie mumbled.

'She always had it fairly strong. Couldn't be too strong for her. I'm just the same myself.'

'Convenient,' Reggie said. 'Now you'll take me down into the cellar, Mrs Brightman.'

'What?' She drew back so hastily that she was brought up by the wall. 'The cellar?' Her eyes seemed to stand out more than ever, so they stared at him, the whites of them more widely bloodshot. With an unsteady hand she thrust back the hair from her sweating brow. 'The cellar? Why ever do you want to go there? There's nothing in the cellar.'

'You think not?' Reggie smiled. 'Come down and see.'

She gave a moaning cry; she stumbled away to the door at the back, and opened it, and stood holding by the door-post, looking out to the paved yard.

From the shed in it appeared Brightman's bearded face. 'Were you looking for me, dearie?' he asked, and brought his lank shape into sight, brushing it as it came.

She made a gesture to him; she went to meet him and muttered: 'Matthew! They're asking me to take 'em down to the cellar.'

'Well, to be sure!' Brightman gave Reggie and Bell a glance of melancholy, pitying surprise. 'I don't see any reason in that.' He held her up, he stroked her and gently remonstrated. 'But there's no reason they shouldn't go to the cellar if they want to, Florrie. We ain't to stand in the way of anything as the police think right. We ain't got anything to hide, have we? Come along, dearie.'

An inarticulate quavering sound came from her.

'That's all right, my dearie, that's all right,' Brightman soothed her.

'Is it?' Bell growled. 'So you've been here all the time, Mr Brightman. While she sent us to look for you down at your own place. Why didn't you show up before?'

'I've only just come in, sir,' Brightman said quietly. 'I came in by the back. I was just putting things to rights in the wash-house. The wife's been so pushed. I didn't know you gentlemen were here. You're searching all the premises, are you? I'm agreeable. I'm sure it's in order, if you say so. But I don't know what you're looking for.'

'Mrs Brightman will show us,' said Reggie, and grasped her arm.

'Don't, don't,' she wailed.

'You mustn't be foolish, dearie,' said Brightman. 'You know there's nothing in the cellar. Show the gentlemen if they want. It's all right. I'll go with you.'

'Got a torch, Bell?' said Reggie.

'I have.' Bell went back into the room. 'And here's a lamp, too.' He lit it.

Reggie drew the shaking woman through the room into the passage. 'That's the door to your cellar. Open it. Come on.'

Bell held the lamp overhead behind them. Reggie led her stumbling down the stairs, and Brightman followed close.

A musty, dank smell came about them. The lamp-light showed a large cellar of brick walls and an earth floor. There was in it a small heap of coal, some sacks and packing-cases and barrels, but most of the dim space was empty. The light glistened on damp.

'Clay soil,' Reggie murmured, and smiled at Brightman. 'Yes. That was indicated.'

'I don't understand you, sir,' said Brightman.

'No. You don't. Torch, Bell.' He took it and flashed its beam about the cellar. 'Oh, yes.' He turned to Bell. With a finger he indicated the shining tracks of slugs. 'You see?'

'I do,' Bell muttered.

Mrs Brightman gave a choked, hysterical laugh.

Reggie moved to and fro. He stooped. He took out his pocket-book and from it a piece of paper, and with that scraped something from a barrel side, something from the clay floor, and sighed satisfaction.

Standing up, he moved the ray of the torch from place to place, held it steady at last to make a circle of light on the ground beneath the steps. 'There,' he said, and Mrs Brightman screamed. 'Yes. I know. That's where you put her. Look, Bell.' His finger pointed to a slug's trail which came into the circle of light, stopped, and went on again at another part of the circle. 'It didn't jump. They don't.'

He swung round upon Mrs Brightman. He held out to her the piece of paper cupped in his hand. On it lay two yellow slugs.

She flung herself back, crying loathing and fear.

'Really, gentlemen, really now,' Brightman stammered. 'This isn't right. This isn't proper. You've no call to frighten a poor woman so. Come away now, Florrie, dearie.' He pulled at her.

'Where are you going?' Reggie murmured. She did not go. Her

eyes were set on the two yellow slugs. ' "Where their worm dieth not",' Reggie said slowly.

She broke out in screams of hysterical laughter; she tore herself from Brightman, and reeled and fell down writhing and yelling.

'So that is that, Mr Brightman.' Reggie turned to him.

'You're a wicked soul!' Brightman whined. 'My poor dearie!' He fell on his knees by her; he began to pray forgiveness for her sins.

'My oath!' Bell muttered, and ran up the steps shouting to his men. . . .

Some time afterwards the detective left to keep the little shop ushered Reggie out.

On the other side of the street, aloof from the gaping, gossiping crowd, superior and placid, his chauffeur smoked a cigarette. It was thrown away; the chauffeur followed him, fell into step beside him. 'Did I manage all right, sir?' The chauffeur invited praise.

'You did. Very neat. Very effective. As you know. Side, Sam, side. We are good at destruction. Efficient incinerators. Humble function. Other justification for existence, doubtful. However. Study to improve. What we want now is a toyshop.'

'Sir?' Sam was puzzled.

'I said a toyshop,' Reggie complained. 'A good toyshop. Quick.' . . .

The light of the sunlight was shining into the little room at the hospital where Eddie Hill lay. Upon his bed stood part of a bridge built of strips of metal bolted together, a bridge of grand design. He and Reggie were working on the central span.

There was a tap at the door, a murmur from Reggie, and the nurse brought in Bell. He stood looking at Reggie with reproachful surprise. 'So that's what you're doing,' he protested.

'Yes. Something useful at last.' Reggie sighed. 'Well, well. We'll have to call this a day, young man. You've done enough. Mustn't get yourself tired.'

'I'm not tired,' the boy protested eagerly. 'I'm not really.'

'No. Of course not. Ever so much better. But there's another day tomorrow. And you have a big job. Must keep fit to go on with it.'

'All right.' The boy lay back, looked at his bridge, looked wistfully at Reggie. 'I can keep this here, can I, sir?'

'Rather. On the table by the bed. So it'll be there when you wake. Nice, making things, isn't it? Yes. You're going to make a lot now.

Good-bye. Jolly, tomorrow, what? Good-bye.' He went out with Bell. 'Now what's the matter with you?' he complained.

'Well, I had to have a word with you, sir. This isn't going to be so easy. I thought I'd get you at the mortuary doing the post-mortem.'

'Minor matter. Simple matter. Only the dead buryin' their dead. The boy was urgent. Matter of savin' life there.'

'I'm not saying you're not right,' said Bell wearily. 'But it is a tangle of a case. The divisional surgeon reports Mrs Brightman's mad. Clean off her head.'

'Yes. I agree. What about it?'

'Seemed to me you pretty well drove her to it. Those slugs—oh, my Lord!'

'Got you, did it? It rather got me. I'd heard Eddie talk of "the worm that dieth not". I should say he'd seen that cellar. Dreamed of it. However. I didn't drive the woman mad. She'd been mad some time. Not medically mad. Not legally mad. But morally. That was the work of our Mr Brightman. I only clarified the situation. He almost sent the boy the same way. That's been stopped. That isn't going to happen now. That's the main issue. And we win on it. Not too bad. But rather a grim day. Virtue has gone out of me. My dear chap!' He took Bell's arm affectionately. 'You're tucked up too.'

'I don't mind owning I've had enough,' said Bell. 'This sort of thing tells me I'm not as young as I was. And it's all a tangle yet.'

'My dear chap! Oh, my dear chap!' Reggie murmured. 'Empty, aren't we? Come on. Come home with me.'

While Sam drove them back, he declined to talk. He stretched in the corner of the car and closed his eyes, and bade Bell do the same. While they ate a devilled sole and an entrecôte Elise, he discussed the qualities of Elise, his cook, and of the Romanée which they drank, and argued bitterly (though he shared it) that the cheese offered in deference to Bell's taste, a bland Stilton, was an insult to the raspberries, the dish of which he emptied.

But when they were established in big chairs in his library, with brandy for Bell and seltzer for himself, and both pipes were lit, 'Did you say a tangle?' he murmured. 'Oh, no. Not now. The rest is only routine for your young men and the lawyers. It'll work out quite easy. You can see it all. When Mrs Brightman was left a widow with her little shop, the pious Brightman pounced on her and mastered her. The little shop was only a little living. Brightman wanted more. Children were kept very short—they might fade out, they might go to the bad—either way the devout Brightman would be relieved of their keep; and meanwhile it was pleasant making 'em believe they were wicked. Old Mrs Wiven was brought in as a lodger—not out of charity, as the wretched Mrs Brightman was trained to say; she must have had a bit of money. Your young men will be able to trace that. And they'll find Brightman got it out of her and used it to set up his second-hand furniture business. Heard of that sort of thing before, what?'

'I should say I have,' Bell grunted. 'My Lord, how often! The widow that falls for a pious brute—the old woman lodger with a bit of money.'

'Oh, yes. Dreary old game. And then the abnormal variations began. Pious bullyin' and starvin' didn't turn the boy into a criminal idiot. He has a mind. He has an imagination, poor child. Mrs Wiven didn't give herself up to Brightman like his miserable wife. She had a temper. So the old game went wrong. Mrs Wiven took to fussin' about her money. As indicated by Bessie. Mrs Wiven was going to be very awkward. Your young men will have to look about and get evidence she'd been grumbling. Quite easy. Lots of gossip will be goin'. Some of it true. Most of it useful at the trial. Givin' the atmosphere.'

Bell frowned. 'Fighting with the gloves off, aren't you?'

'Oh, no. No. Quite fair. We have to fight the case without the children. I'm not going to have Eddie put in the witness-box, to be tortured about his mad mother helpin' murder. That might break him up for ever. And he's been tortured enough. The brute Brightman isn't going to hurt him any more. The children won't be givin' evidence. I'll get half the College of Physicians to certify they're not fit, if they're asked for. But that's not goin' to leave Mr Brightman any way out. Now then. Things bein' thus, Brightman had his motive to murder Mrs Wiven. If he didn't stop her mouth she'd have him in jail. Being a clever fellow, he saw that Eddie's record of stealin' would be very useful. By the way—notice that queer little incident, Bessie bein' caught pilferin' by Mrs Wiven yesterday morning? Brightman may have fixed that up for another black mark against the children. I wonder. But it didn't go right. He must have had a jolt when Mrs Wiven called out

they were all thieves. Kind of compellin' immediate action. His plan
would have been all ready, of course—salts of lemon in her favourite
strong tea; a man don't think of an efficient way of poisonin' all of a
sudden. And then the incalculable Eddie intervened. Reaction of Mrs
Wiven's explosion on him, a sort of divine command to save his sister
from hell by seeing she died innocent. When Brightman had the news
of that effort at drowning, he took it as a godsend. Hear him thanking
heaven? Boy who was wicked enough to kill a little sister was wicked
enough for anything. Mr Brightman read his title clear to mansions in
the skies. And Mrs Wiven was promptly given her cup o' tea. She was
sick in her room, sick on her overall and on her underclothes. Evidence for all that conclusive. Remember the damp floor. I should say
Mrs Brightman had another swab at that today. She has a craze about
cleaning. We saw that. Feels she never can get clean, poor wretch.
Well. Mrs Wiven died. Oxalic poisoning generally kills quick. I hope it
did. They hid the body in the cellar. Plan was clever. Take the body out
in the quiet of the night and dump it on the common with a flask of
poisoned tea—put her bag in Eddie's den. All clear for the intelligent
police. Devil of a boy poisoned the old lady to steal her money, and
was drownin' his little sister so she shouldn't tell on him. That's what
you thought, wasn't it? Yes. Well-made plan. It stood up against us last
night.'

'You did think there was something queer,' Bell said.

'I did,' Reggie sighed. 'Physical smell. Damp musty smell. Probably
the cellar. And the Brightmans didn't smell nice spiritually. However.
Lack of confidence in myself. And I have no imagination. I ought to
have waited and watched. My error. My grave error. Well. It was a
clever plan. But Brightman was rather bustled. That may account for
his errors. Fatal errors. Omission to remove the soiled underclothes
when the messed-up overall was taken off. Failure to allow for the
habits of Limax flavus.'

'What's that?' said Bell.

'Official name of yellow slug—cellar slug. The final, damning evidence. I never found any reason for the existence of slugs before.
However. To round it off—when you look into Mr Brightman's furniture business, you'll find that he has a van, or the use of one. You must
prove it was used last night. That's all. Quite simple now. But a wearin''

case.' He gazed at Bell with large, solemn eyes. 'His wife! He'd schooled her thorough. Ever hear anything more miserably appealing than her on her dear babies and poor old Mrs Wiven? Not often? No. Took a lot of breakin' down.

'Ah. You were fierce,' Bell muttered.

'Oh, no. No.' Reggie sighed. 'I was bein' merciful. She couldn't be saved. My job was to save the children. And she—if that brute hadn't twisted her, she'd have done anything to save 'em too. She'd been a decent soul once. No. She won't be giving evidence against me.'

'Why, how should she?' Bell gaped.

'I was thinkin' of the day of judgment,' Reggie murmured. 'Well, well. Post-mortem in the morning. Simple straight job. Then I'll be at the hospital if you want me. Have to finish Eddie's bridge. And then we're going to build a ship. He's keen on ships.'

10

E. C. BENTLEY

The Unknown Peer

When Philip Trent went down to Lackington, with the mission of throwing some light upon the affair of Lord Southrop's disappearance, it was without much hope of adding anything to the simple facts already known to the police and made public in the newspapers. Those facts were plain enough, pointing to but one sad conclusion.

In the early morning of Friday, September 23rd, a small touring car was found abandoned by the shore at Merwin Cove, some three miles along the coast from the flourishing Devonian resort of Brademouth. It had been driven off the road over turf to the edge of the pebble beach.

Examined by the police, it was found to contain a heavy overcoat, a folding stool, and a case of sketching materials with a sketching-block on the back seat; a copy of Anatole France's *Mannequin d'Osier*, two pipes, some chocolate, a flask of brandy, and a pair of binoculars in the shelves before the driving-seat; and in the pockets a number of maps and the motoring papers of Lord Southrop, of Hingham Blewitt, near Wymondham, in Norfolk. Inquiries in the neighbourhood led to the discovery that a similar car and its driver were missing from the Crown Inn at Lackington, a small place a few miles inland; and later the car was definitely recognized.

In the hotel register, however, the owner had signed his name as L. G. Coxe; and it was in that name that a room had been booked by telephone early in the day. A letter too, addressed to Coxe, had been delivered at the 'Crown', and had been opened by him on his arrival about 6.30. A large suit-case had been taken up to his room where it still lay, and the mysterious Coxe had deposited an envelope containing £35 in bank-notes in the hotel safe. He had dined in the coffee-room, smoked in the lounge for a time, then gone out again in his car, saying nothing of his destination. No more had been seen or heard of him.

Some needed light had been cast on the affair when Lord Southrop was looked up in *Who's Who*—for no one in the local force had ever heard of such a peer. It appeared that his family name was Coxe, and that he had been christened Lancelot Graham; that he was the ninth baron, was thirty-three years old, and had succeeded to the title at the age of twenty-six; that he had been educated at Harrow and Trinity, Cambridge; that he was unmarried, and that his heir was a first cousin, Lambert Reeves Coxe. No public record of any kind, nor even any 'recreation', was noted in this unusually brief biography, which, indeed, bore the marks of having been compiled in the office, without any assistance from its subject.

Trent, however, had heard something more than this about Lord Southrop. Sir James Molloy, the owner of the *Record*, who had sent Trent to Lackington, had met everybody, including even the missing peer, who was quite unknown in society. Society, according to Molloy, was heartily detested and despised by Lord Southrop. His interests were exclusively literary and artistic, apart from his taste in the matter of wine, which he understood better than most men. He greatly preferred Continental to English ways of life, and spent much of his time abroad. He had a very large income, for most of which he seemed to have no use. He had good health and a kindly disposition; but he had a passion for keeping himself to himself, and had indulged it with remarkable success. One of his favourite amusements was wandering about the country alone in his car, halting here and there to make a sketch, and staying always at out-of-the-way inns under the name he had used at Lackington.

Lord Southrop had been, however, sufficiently like other men to fall in love, and Molloy had heard that his engagement to Adela Tindal was on the point of being announced at the time of his disappearance. His choice had come as a surprise to his friends; for though Miss Tindal took art and letters as seriously as himself, she was, as an authoress, not at all averse to publicity. She enjoyed being talked about, Molloy declared; and talked about she had certainly been—

especially in connection with Lucius Kelly, the playwright. Their relationship had not been disguised; but a time came when Kelly's quarrelsome temper was no longer to be endured, and she refused to see any more of him.

All this was quite well known to Lord Southrop, for he and Kelly had been friends from boyhood; and the knowledge was a signal proof of the force of his infatuation. On all accounts, in Molloy's judgment, the match would have been a complete disaster; and Trent, as he thought the matter over in the coffee-room of the 'Crown', was disposed to agree with him.

*

Shortly before his arrival that day, a new fact for his first dispatch to the *Record* had turned up. A tweed cap had been found washed up by the waves on the beach between Brademouth and Merwin Cove, and the people at the 'Crown' were sure that it was Lord Southrop's. He had worn a suit of unusually rough, very light-grey homespun tweed, the sort of tweed that, as the head waiter at the 'Crown' vividly put it, you could smell half a mile away; and his cap had been noted because it was made of the same stuff as the suit. After a day and a half in salt water it had still an aroma of Highland sheep. Apart from this and its colour, or absence of colour, there was nothing by which it could be identified; not even a maker's name; but there was no reasonable doubt about its being Lord Southrop's, and it seemed to settle the question, if question there were, of what had happened to him. It was, Trent reflected, just like an eccentric intellectual—with money—to have his caps made for him, and from the same material as his clothes.

It was these garments, together with the very large horn-rimmed spectacles which Lord Southrop affected, which had made most impression on the head waiter. Otherwise, he told Trent, there was nothing unusual about the poor gentleman, except that he seemed a bit absent-minded-like. He had brought a letter to the table with him—the waiter supposed it would be the one that came to the hotel for him—and it had seemed to worry him. He had read and re-read it, all through his dinner what there was of it; he didn't have only some soup and a bit of fish. Yes, sir; consommé and a nice fillet of sole, like there is this evening. There was roast fowl, but he wouldn't have that, nor nothing else. Would Trent be ordering his own dinner now?

'Yes, I want to—but the fish is just what I won't have,' Trent decided, looking at the menu. 'I will take the rest of the hotel dinner.' An idea occurred to him. 'Do you remember what Lord Southrop had to drink? I might profit by his example.'

The waiter produced a fly-blown wine list. 'I can tell you that, sir. He had a bottle of this claret here, Château Margaux 1922.'

'You're quite sure? And did he like it?'

'Well, he didn't leave much,' the waiter answered. Possibly, Trent thought, he took a personal interest in unfinished wine. 'Were you thinking of trying some of it yourself, sir? It's our best claret.'

'I don't think I will have your best claret,' Trent said, thoughtfully scanning the list. 'There's a Beychevelle 1924 here, costing eighteen pence less, which is good enough for me. I'll have that.' The waiter hurried away, leaving Trent to his reflections in the deserted coffee-room.

Trent had learned from the police that the numbers of the notes left in the charge of the hotel had been communicated by telephone to Lord Southrop's bank in Norwich, the reply being that these notes had been issued to him in person ten days before. Trent had also been allowed to inspect the objects, including the maps, found in the abandoned car. Lackington he found marked in pencil with a cross; and working backwards across the country he found similar crosses at the small towns of Hawbridge, Wringham and Candley. The police, acting on these indications, had already established that 'L. G. Coxe' had passed the Thursday, Wednesday, and Tuesday nights respectively at inns in these places; and they had learned already of his having started from Hingham Blewitt on the Monday.

Trent, finding no more to be done at Lackington, decided to follow this designated trail in his own car. On the morning after his talk with the waiter at the 'Crown' he set out for Hawbridge. The distances in Lord Southrop's progress, as marked, were not great by the most direct roads; but it could be guessed that he had been straying about to this and that point of interest—not, Trent imagined, to sketch, for there had been no sketches found among his belongings. Hawbridge was reached in time for lunch; and at the Three Bells Inn Trent again found matter for thought in a conversation—much like that which he had already enjoyed at the Crown Inn—with the head waiter. So it was again at the 'Green Man' in Wringham that evening. The next day, however, when Trent dined at the 'Running Stag' in Candley, the remembered record of Lord Southrop's potations took a different turn. What Trent was told convinced him that he was on the right track.

*

The butler and housekeeper at Hingham Blewitt, when Trent spoke with them the following day, were dismally confident that Lord Southrop would never be seen again. The butler had already given to the police investigator from Devon what little information he could. He admitted that none of it lent the smallest support to the idea that Lord Southrop had been contemplating suicide; that he had, in fact, been unusually cheerful, if anything, on the day of his departure. But what, the butler asked, could a person think? Especially, the housekeeper observed, after the cap was found. Lord Southrop was, of course, eccentric in his views; and you never knew—here the housekeeper, with a despondent head-shake, paused, leaving unspoken the suggestion that a man who did not think or behave like other people might go mad at any moment.

Lord Southrop, they told Trent, never left any address when he went on one of these motoring tours. What he used to say was, he never knew where he was going till he got there. But this time he did have one object in mind, though what it was or where it was the butler did not know; and the police officer, when he was informed, did not seem to make any more of it. What had happened was that, a few days before Lord Southrop started out, he had been rung up by someone on the 'phone in his study; and as the door of the room was open, the butler, in passing through the hall, had happened to catch a few words of what he said.

He had told this person he was going next Tuesday to visit the old moor; and that if the weather was right he was going to make a sketch. He had said: 'You remember the church and chapel'—the butler heard that distinctly; and he had said that it must be over twenty years. 'What must be over twenty years?' Trent wanted to know. Impossible to tell: Lord Southrop had said just that.

The butler had heard nothing further. He thought the old moor might perhaps be Dartmoor or Exmoor, seeing where it was that

Lord Southrop had disappeared. Trent thought otherwise, but he did not discuss the point. 'There's one thing you can perhaps tell me,' he said. 'Lord Southrop was at Harrow and Cambridge, I believe. Do you know if he went to a preparatory school before Harrow?'

'I can tell you that, sir,' the housekeeper said. 'I have been with the family since I was a girl. It was Marsham House he went to, near Sharnsley in Derbyshire. The school was founded by his lordship's grandfather's tutor, and all the Coxe boys have gone there for two generations. It stands very high as a school, sir; the best families send their sons there.'

'Yes, I've heard of it,' Trent said. 'Should you say, Mrs Pillow, that Lord Southrop was happy as a schoolboy—popular, I mean, and fond of games, and so forth?'

Mrs Pillow shook her head decisively. 'He always hated school, sir; and as for games, he had to play them, of course, but he couldn't abide them. And he didn't get on with the other boys—he used to say he wouldn't be a sheep, just like all the other something sheep—he learned bad language at school if he didn't learn anything else. But at Cambridge—that was very different. He came alive there for the first time—so he used to say.'

In Norwich, that same afternoon, Trent furnished himself with a one-inch Ordnance Survey map of a certain section of Derbyshire. He spent the evening at his hotel with this and a small-scale map of England, on which he marked the line of small towns which he had already visited; and he drew up, not for publication, a brief and clear report of his investigation so far.

The next morning's run was long. He had lunch at Sharnsley, where he made a last and very gratifying addition to his string of coffee-room interviews. Marsham House, he learned, stood well outside Sharnsley on the verge of the Town Moor; which, as the map had already told him, stretched its many miles away to the south and west. He learned, too, what and where were 'the Church and Chapel', and was thankful that his inquiring mind had not taken those simple terms at their face value.

An hour later he halted his car at a spot on the deserted road that crossed the moor; a spot whence, looking up the purple slope, he could see its bareness broken by a huge rock, and another less huge, whose summits pierced the skyline. They looked, Trent told himself, not more unlike what they were called than rocks with names usually do. Away to the right of them was a small clump of trees, the only ones in sight, to which a rough cart-track led from the road; and from that point, he thought an artist might well consider that the Church and Chapel and their background made the best effect. He left his car and took the path through the heather.

Arrived at the clump, which stood well above the road, he looked over a desolate scene. If anyone had met Lord Southrop there, they would have had the world to themselves. Not a house or hut was in sight, and no live thing but the birds. He looked about for traces of any human visitor; and he had just decided that nothing of the sort could reasonably be expected, after the lapse of a week, when something white, lodged in the root of a fir tree, caught his eye.

It was a small piece of torn paper, pencilled on one side with lines and shading, the look of which he knew well. A rapid search discovered another piece near by among the heather. It was all that the wind had left undispersed of an artist's work, but for Trent, as he scanned the remnants closely, it was enough.

His eyes turned now over a wider range; for this, though to him it spelt certainty, was not what he had been looking for. Slowly following the track over the moor, he came at length to the reason for its existence—a small quarry, to all appearance long abandoned. A roughly circular pond of muddy water, some fifty yards across, filled the lower part of it; and about the margin was a confusion of stony fragments, broken and rusted implements, bits of rotting wood and smashed earthenware—a typical scene of industrial litter. With his arm bare to the shoulder Trent could feel no bottom to the pond. If it held any secret, that opaque yellow water kept it well.

There was no soil to take a footprint near the pond. For some time he raked among the debris in which the track ended, finding nothing. Then, as he turned over a broken fire-bucket, something flashed in the sunlight. It was a small, flat fragment of glass, about as large as a farthing, with one smooth and two fractured edges. Trent examined it thoughtfully. It had no place in his theory; it might mean nothing. On the other hand . . . he stowed it carefully in his note-case along with the remnants of paper.

Two hours later, at the police headquarters in Derby, he was laying his report and maps, with the objects found on the moor, before Superintendent Allison, a sharp-faced, energetic officer to whom Trent's name was well known.

*

It was well known also to Mr Gurney Bradshaw, head of the firm of Bradshaw & Co., legal advisers to Lord Southrop and to his father before him. He had, at Trent's telephoned request, given him an appointment at three o'clock; and he appeared at that hour on the day after his researches in Derbyshire. Mr Bradshaw, a courteous but authoritative old gentleman, wore a dubious expression as they shook hands.

'I cannot guess,' he said, 'what it is that you wish to put before me. It seems to me a case in which we should get the Court to presume death with the minimum of difficulty; and I wish I thought otherwise, for I had known Lord Southrop all his life, and I was much attached to him. Now I must tell you that I have asked a third party to join us here—Mr Lambert Coxe, who perhaps you know is the heir to the title and to a very large estate. He wrote me yesterday that he had just returned from France, and wanted to know what the position was; and I thought he had better hear what you have to say, so I asked him for the same time as yourself.'

'I know of him as a racing man,' Trent said, 'I had no idea he was what you say until I saw it in the papers.'

The buzzer on the desk-telephone sounded, and Bradshaw put it to his ear. 'Show him in,' he said.

Lambert Coxe was a tall, spare, hard-looking man with a tanned, clean-shaven face and a cordless monocle screwed into his left eye. As they were introduced he looked at the other with a keen and curious scrutiny.

'And now,' Bradshaw said, 'let us hear your statement, Mr Trent.'

Trent put his folded hands on the table. 'I will begin by making a suggestion which may strike you gentlemen as an absurd one. It's this. The man who drove that car to Lackington, and afterwards down to the seashore, was not Lord Southrop.'

Both men stared at him blankly; then Bradshaw, composing his features, said impassively: 'I shall be interested to hear your reasons for thinking so. You have not a name for making absurd suggestions, Mr Trent, but I may call this an astonishing one.'

'I should damned well think so,' observed Coxe.

'I got the idea originally,' Trent said, 'from the wine which this man chose to drink with his dinner at the Crown Inn before the disappearance. Do you think that absurd?'

'There is nothing absurd about wine,' Mr Bradshaw replied with gravity. 'I take it very seriously myself. Twice a day, as a rule,' he added.

'Lord Southrop, I am told, also took it seriously. He had the reputation of a first-rate connoisseur. Now this man I'm speaking of had little appetite that evening, it seems. The dinner they offered him consisted mainly of soup, fillet of sole, and roast fowl.'

'I am sure it did,' Bradshaw said grimly. 'It's what you get nine times out of ten in English hotels. Well?'

'This man took only the soup and the fish. And with it he had a bottle of claret.'

The solicitor's composure deserted him abruptly.

'Claret!' he exclaimed.

'Yes, claret, and a curious claret, too. You see, mine host of the 'Crown' kept a perfectly good Beychevelle 1924—I had some myself. But he had also a Château Margaux 1922; and I suppose because it was an older wine he thought it ought to be dearer, so he marked it in his list eighteen pence more than the other. That was the wine which was chosen by our traveller that evening. What do you think of it? With a fish dinner he had claret, and he chose a wine of a notoriously bad year when he could have had a wine of 1924 for less money.'

While Coxe looked his bewilderment, Mr Bradshaw got up and began to pace the room slowly. 'I will admit so much,' he said. 'I cannot conceive of Lord Southrop doing such a thing if he was in his right mind.'

'If you still think it was he, and that he was out of his senses,' Trent rejoined, 'there was a method in his madness. Because the night before, at Hawbridge, he chose one of those wines bearing the name of a château which doesn't exist, and is merely a label that sounds well; and the night before that, at Wringham, he had two whiskies and soda just before dinner, and another inferior claret at an excessive price on top of them. I have been to both the inns and got these facts. But when I worked back to Candley, the first place where Lord Southrop stayed after leaving home, it was another story. I found he had picked out about the best thing on the list, a Rhine wine, which hardly anybody ever asked for. The man who ordered that, I think, was really Lord Southrop.'

Bradshaw pursed up his mouth. 'You are suggesting that some one in Lord Southrop's car was impersonating him at the other three places, and that, knowing his standing as a connoisseur, this man did his ignorant best to act up to it. Very well; but Lord Southrop signed the register in his usual way at those places. He received and read a letter addressed to him at Lackington. The motor tour as a whole was just such a haphazard tour as he had often made before. The description given of him at Lackington was exact—the clothes, the glasses, the abstracted manner. The cap that was washed up was certainly his. No, no, Mr Trent. We are bound to assume that it was Lord Southrop; and the presumption is that he drove down to the sea and drowned himself. The alternative is that he was staging a sham suicide, so as to be able to disappear, and there is no sense in that.'

'Just so,' observed Lambert Coxe. 'What you say about the wine may be all right as far as it goes, Mr Trent, but I agree with Mr Bradshaw. Southrop committed suicide; and if he was insane enough to do that, he was insane enough to go wrong about his drinks.'

Trent shook his head. 'There are other things to be accounted for. I'm coming to them. And the clothes and the cap and the rest are all part of my argument. This man was wearing Lord Southrop's tweed suit just because it was so easily identifiable. He knew all about Lord Southrop and his ways. He had letters from Lord Southrop in his possession, and had learned to imitate his writing. It was he who wrote and posted that letter addressed to L. G. Coxe; and he made a pretence of being worried by it. He knew that Lord Southrop's notes could be traced; so he left them at the bureau to clinch the thing. And, of course, he did not drown himself. He only threw the cap into the sea. What he may have done is to change out of those conspicuous clothes, put them in a bag which he had in the car, and which contained another suit in which he proceeded to dress himself. He may then have walked, with his bag, the few miles into Brademouth, and travelled to London by the 12.15—quite a popular train, in which you can get a comfortable sleeping-berth.'

'So he may,' Bradshaw agreed with some acidity, while Lambert Coxe laughed shortly. 'But what I am interested in is facts, Mr Trent.'

'Well here are some. A few days before Lord Southrop set out from his place in Norfolk, some one rang him up in his library. The door was ajar, and the butler heard a little of what he said to the caller. He said he was going on the following Tuesday to visit a place he called the old moor, as if it was a place as well known to the other as to himself. He said: "You remember the Church and the Chapel," and that it must be over twenty years; and that he was going to make a sketch.'

Coxe's face darkened. 'If Southrop was alive,' he sneered, 'I am sure he would appreciate your attention to his private affairs. What are we supposed to gather from all this keyhole business?'

'I think we can gather,' Trent said gently, 'that some person, ringing Lord Southrop up about another matter, was told incidentally where Lord Southrop expected to be on that Tuesday—the day, you remember, when he suddenly developed a taste for bad wine in the evening. Possibly the information gave this person an idea, and he had a few days to think it over. Also we can gather that Lord Southrop was talking to some one who shared his recollection of a moor which they had known over twenty years ago—that's to say, when he was at the prep. school age, as he was thirty three this year. And then I found that he had been at a school called Marsham House, on the edge of Sharnsley Town Moor in Derbyshire. So I went off there to explore, and I discovered that the Church and Chapel were a couple of great rocks on the top of the moor, about two miles from the school. If you were there with your cousin, Mr Coxe, you may remember them.'

Coxe was drumming on the table with his fingers. 'Of course I do,' he said aggressively. 'So do hundreds of others who were at Marsham House. What about it?'

Bradshaw, who was now fixing him with an attentive eye, held up a hand. 'Come, come, Mr Coxe,' he said; 'don't let us lose our tempers. Mr Trent is helping to clear up what begins to look like an even worse business than I thought. Let us hear him out peaceably, if you please.'

'I am in the sketching business myself,' Trent continued, 'so I looked about for what might seem the best view-point for Lord

Southrop's purpose. When I went to the spot, I found two pieces of torn-up paper, the remains of a pencil sketch; and that paper is of precisely the same quality as the paper of Lord Southrop's sketching-block, which I was able to examine at Lackington. The sketch was torn from the block and destroyed, I think, because it was evidence of his having been to Sharnsley. That part of the moor is a wild, desolate place. If some one went to meet Lord Southrop there, as I believe, he could hardly have had more favourable circumstances for what he meant to do. I think it was he who appeared in the car at Wringham that evening; and I think it was on Sharnsley Moor, not at Lackington, that Lord Southrop—disappeared.'

Bradshaw half-rose from his chair. 'Are you not well, Mr Coxe?' he asked.

'Perfectly well, thanks,' Coxe answered. He drew a deep breath, then turned to Trent. 'And so that's all you have to tell us. I can't say that——'

'Oh no, not nearly all,' Trent interrupted him. 'But let me tell you now what I believe it was that really happened. If the man who left the moor in Lord Southrop's car was not Lord Southrop, I wanted an explantation of the masquerade that ended at Lackington. What would explain it was the idea that the man who drove the car down to Devonshire had murdered him, and then staged a sham suicide for him three hundred miles away. That would have been an ingenious plan. It would have depended on every one making the natural assumption that the man in the car was Lord Southrop. And how was any one to imagine that he wasn't?

'Lord Southrop was the very reverse of a public character. He lived quite out of the world; he had never been in the news; very few people knew what he looked like. He depended on all this for maintaining his privacy in the way he did when touring in his car—staying always at small places where there was no chance of his being recognized, and pretending not to be a peer. The murderer knew all about that, and it was the essence of his plan. The people at the inns would note what was conspicuous about the traveller; all that they could say about his face would be more vague, and would fit Lord Southrop well enough, so long as there was no striking difference in looks between the two men. Those big horn-rims are a disguise in themselves.'

Bradshaw rubbed his hands slowly together. 'I suppose it could happen so,' he said. 'What do you think, Mr Coxe?'

'It's just a lot of ridiculous guesswork,' Coxe said impatiently. 'I've heard enough of it, for one.' He rose from his chair.

'No, no, don't go, Mr Coxe,' Trent advised him. 'I have some more of what you prefer—facts, you know. They are important, and you ought to hear them. Thinking as I did, I looked about for any places where a body could be concealed. In that bare and featureless expanse I could find only one: an old abandoned quarry in the hill-side, with a great pond of muddy water at the bottom of it. And by the edge of it I picked up a small piece of broken glass.

'Yesterday evening this piece of glass was shown by a police officer and myself to an optician in Derby. He stated that it was a fragment of a monocle—what they call a spherical lens—so that he could tell us all about it from one small bit. Its formula was not a common one—minus 5; so that it had been worn by a man very short-sighted in one eye. The police think that as very few people wear monocles, and hardly any of them would wear one of that power, an official inquiry should establish the names of those who had been supplied with such a glass in recent years. You see,' Trent went on, 'this man had dropped and broken his glass on the stones while busy about something at the edge of the pond. Being a tidy man, he picked up all the pieces that he could see; but he missed this one.'

Lambert Coxe put a hand to his throat. 'It's infernally stuffy in here,' he muttered. 'I'll open a window, if you don't mind.' Again he got to his feet, but the lawyer's movement was quicker. 'I'll see to that,' he said, and stayed by the window when he had opened it.

Trent drew a folded paper from his pocket. 'This is a telegram I received just before lunch from Superintendent Allison of the Derbyshire police. I have told him all I am telling you.' He unfolded the paper with deliberation. 'He says that the pond was dragged this morning, and they recovered the body of a man who had been shot in the head from behind. It was stripped to the underclothing and secured by a chain to a pedal bicycle.

'That, you see, clears up the question how the murderer got to the remote spot where Lord Southrop was. He couldn't go there in a car, because he would have had to leave it there. He used a cycle, because there was to be a very practical use for the machine afterwards. The police believe they can trace the seller of the cycle, because it is in perfectly new condition, and he may give them a line on the buyer.'

Bradshaw, his hands thrust into his pockets, stared at Coxe's ghastly face as he inquired: 'Has the body been identified?'

'The superintendent says the inquest will be the day after tomorrow. He knows whose body I believe it is, so he will already be sending down to Hingham Blewitt about evidence of identity. He says my own evidence will probably not be required until a later stage of the inquest, after a charge has been——'

A sobbing sound came from Lambert Coxe. He sprang to his feet, pressing his hands to his temples, then crashed unconscious to the floor.

While Trent loosened his collar, the lawyer splashed water from the bottle on his table upon the upturned face. The eyelids began to flicker. 'He'll do,' Bradshaw said coolly. 'My congratulations, Mr Trent. This man is not a client of mine, so I may say that I don't think he will enjoy the title for long—or the money, which was what really mattered, I have reason to believe. He's dropped his monocle again, you see. I happen to know, by the way, that he has been half-blind of that eye since it was injured by a cricket ball at Marsham.'

11

MICHAEL INNES

Lesson in Anatomy

Already the anatomy theatre was crowded with students, tier upon tier of faces pallid beneath the clear shadowless light cast by the one elaborate lamp, large as a giant cart-wheel, near the ceiling. The place gleamed with an aggressive cleanliness; the smell of Formalin pervaded it; its centre was a faintly sinister vacancy—the spot to which would presently be wheeled the focal object of the occasion.

At Nessfield University Professor Finlay's final lecture was one of the events of the year. He was always an excellent teacher. For three terms he discoursed lucidly from his dais or tirelessly prowled his dissecting rooms, encouraging young men and women who had hitherto dismembered only dogfish and frogs to address themselves with resolution to human legs, arms and torsos. The Department of Anatomy was large; these objects lay about in a dispersed profusion; Finlay moved among them now with gravity and now with a whimsical charm which did a good deal to humanize his macabre environment. It was only once a year that he yielded to his taste for the dramatic.

The result was the final lecture. And the final lecture was among the few academic activities of Nessfield sufficiently abounding in human appeal to be regularly featured in the local Press. Perhaps the account had become a little stereotyped with the years, and always there was virtually the same photograph showing the popular professor (as Finlay was dubbed for the occasion) surrounded by wreaths, crosses, and other floral tributes. Innumerable citizens of Nessfield who had never been inside the doors of their local university looked forward to this annual report, and laid it down with the comfortable conviction that all was well with the pursuit of learning in the district. Their professors were still professors—eccentric, erudite, and amiable. Their students were still as students should be, giving much of their thought to the perpetration of elaborate, tasteless, and sometimes slightly dangerous practical jokes.

For the lecture was at once a festival, a rag, and a genuine display of virtuosity. It took place in this large anatomy theatre. Instead of disjointed limbs and isolated organs there was a whole new cadaver for the occasion. And upon this privileged corpse Finlay rapidly demonstrated certain historical developments of his science to an audience in part attentive and in part concerned with lowering skeletons from the rafters, releasing various improbable living creatures—lemurs and echidnas and opossums—to roam the benches, or contriving what quainter japes they could think up. On one famous occasion the corpse itself had been got at, and at the first touch of the professor's scalpel had awakened to an inferno of noise presently accounted for by the discovery that its inside consisted chiefly of alarm clocks. Nor were these diversions and surprises all one-sided, since Finlay himself, entering into the spirit of the occasion, had more than once been known to forestall his students with some extravagance of his own. It was true that this had happened more rarely of recent years, and by some it was suspected that this complacent scholar had grown a little out of taste with the role in which he had been cast. But the affair remained entirely good-humoured; tradition restrained the excesses into which it might have fallen; it was, in its own queer way, an approved social occasion. High University authorities sometimes took distinguished visitors along—those, that is to say, who felt they had a stomach for *post-mortem* curiosity. There was quite a number of strangers on the present occasion.

The popular professor had entered through the glass-panelled double doors which gave directly upon the dissecting table. Finlay was florid and very fat; his white gown was spotlessly laundered; a high cap of the same material would have given him the appearance of a generously self-dieted chef. He advanced to the low rail that separated him from the first tier of spectators and started to make some preliminary remarks. What these actually were, or how they were designed to conclude, he had probably forgotten years ago, for this was the point at which the first interruption traditionally occurred. And, sure enough, no sooner had Finlay opened his mouth than three young men near the back of the theatre stood up and delivered themselves of a fanfare of trumpets. Finlay appeared altogether surprised—he possessed, as has been stated, a dramatic sense—and this was the signal for the greater part of those present to rise in their seats and sing 'For he's a Jolly Good Fellow'. In older forms of the last-lecture ritual this had been reserved for the close, but now it was delivered three or four times in the course of the proceedings. Flowers—single blooms, for the present—began to float through the air and fall about the feet of the professor. The strangers, distinguished and otherwise, smiled at each other benevolently, thereby indicating their pleased acquiescence in these time-honoured academic junketings. A bell began to toll.

'*Never ask for whom the bell tolls,*' said a deep voice from somewhere near the professor's left hand. And the whole student body responded in a deep chant: '*It tolls for THEE.*'

And now there was a more urgent bell—one that clattered up and down some adjacent corridor to the accompaniment of tramping feet and the sound as of a passing tumbrel. '*Bring out your dead,*' cried the deep voice. And the chant was taken up all round the theatre. '*Bring out your dead,*' everybody shouted with gusto. '*Bring out your DEAD!*'

This was the signal for the entrance of Albert, Professor Finlay's dissecting-room attendant. Albert was perhaps the only person in Nessfield who uncompromisingly disapproved of the last lecture and all that went with it—this perhaps because, as an ex-policeman, he felt bound to hold all disorder in discountenance. The severely aloof expression on the face of Albert as he wheeled in the cadaver was one of the highlights of the affair—nor on this occasion did it by any means fail of its effect. Indeed, Albert appeared to be more than commonly upset. A severe frown lay across his ample and unintelligent countenance. He held his six foot three sternly erect; behind his vast leather apron his bosom discernibly heaved with manly emotion. Albert wheeled in the body—distinguishable as a wisp of ill-nourished humanity beneath the tarpaulin that covered it—and Finlay raised his right hand as if to bespeak attention. The result was a sudden squawk and the flap of heavy wings near the ceiling. Somebody had released a vulture. The ominous bird blundered twice round the theatre and then settled composedly on a rafter. It craned its scrawny neck and fixed a beady eye on the body.

Professor Finlay benevolently smiled; at the same time he produced a handkerchief and rapidly mopped his forehead. To several people, old-stagers, it came that the eminent anatomist was uneasy this year. The vulture was a little bit steep, after all.

There was a great deal of noise. One group of students was doggedly and pointlessly singing a sea chanty; others were perpetrating or preparing to perpetrate sundry jokes of a varying degree of effectiveness. Albert, standing immobile beside the cadaver, let his eyes roam resentfully over the scene. Then Finlay raised not one hand, but two—only for a moment, but there was instant silence. He took a step backwards amid the flowers which lay around him; carefully removed a couple of forget-me-nots from his hair; gave a quick nod to Albert; and began to explain—in earnest this time—what he was proposing to do.

Albert stepped to the body and pulled back the tarpaulin.

'And ever,' said a voice from the audience, 'at my back I hear the rattle of dry bones and chuckle spread from ear to ear.'

It was an apt enough sally. The cadaver seemed to be mostly bones already—the bones of an elderly, withered man—and its most prominent feature was a ghastly *rictus* or fixed grin which exposed two long rows of gleamingly white and utterly incongruous-seeming teeth. From somewhere high up in the theatre there was a little sigh followed by a slumping sound. A robust and football-playing youth had fainted. Quite a number of people, as if moved by a mysterious or chameleon-like sympathy, were rapidly approximating the complexion of the grisly object displayed before them. But there was nothing unexpected in all this. Finlay, knowing that custom allowed him perhaps another five minutes of sober attention at this point, continued his remarks. The cadaver before the class was exactly as it would be had it come before a similar class four hundred years ago. The present anatomy lesson was essentially a piece of historical reconstruction. His hearers would recall that in one of Rembrandt's paintings depicting such a subject. . . .

For perhaps a couple of minutes the practised talk flowed on. The audience was quite silent. Finlay for a moment paused to recall a date. In the resulting complete hush there was a sharp click, rather like the lifting of a latch. A girl screamed. Every eye in the theatre was on the cadaver. For its lower jaw had sagged abruptly open and the teeth, which were plainly dentures, had half extruded themselves from the gaping mouth, rather as if pushed outwards by some spasm within.

Such things do happen. There is a celebrated story of just such startling behaviour on the part of the body of the philosopher Schopenhauer. And Finlay, perceiving that his audience was markedly upset, perhaps debated endeavouring to rally them with just this learned and curious anecdote. But, even as he paused, the cadaver had acted again. Abruptly the jaws closed like a powerful vice, the lips and cheeks sagged; it was to be concluded that this wretched remnant of humanity had swallowed its last meal.

For a moment something like panic hovered over the anatomy theatre. Another footballer fainted; a girl laughed hysterically; two men in the back row, having all the appearance of case-hardened physicians, looked at each other in consternation and bolted from the building. Finlay, with a puzzled look on his face, again glanced backwards at the cadaver. Then he nodded abruptly to Albert, who replaced the tarpaulin. Presumably, after this queer upset, he judged it best to interpose a little more composing historical talk before getting down to business.

He was saying something about the anatomical sketches of Leonardo da Vinci. Again he glanced back at the cadaver. Suddenly the lights went out. The anatomy theatre was in darkness.

For some moments nobody thought of an accident. Finlay often had recourse to an epidiascope or lantern, and the trend of his talk led people to suppose that something of the sort was in train now. Presently, however, it became plain that there was a hitch—and at this the audience broke into every kind of vociferation. They were like children in a cinema when something has gone wrong with the projection. Above the uproar the vulture could be heard overhead, vastly agitated. Matches were struck, but cast no certain illumination. Various objects were being pitched about the theatre. There was a strong scent of lilies.

Albert's voice made itself heard, cursing medical students, cursing the University of Nessfield, cursing Professor Finlay's final lecture. From the progress of this commination it was possible to infer that he was groping his way towards the switches. There was a click, and once more the white and shadowless light flooded the theatre.

Everything was as it had been—save in two particulars. Most of the wreaths and crosses which had been designed for the end of the lecture had proved missiles too tempting to ignore in that interval of darkness; they had been lobbed into the centre of the theatre and lay there about the floor, except for two which had actually landed on the shrouded cadaver.

And Finlay had disappeared.

The audience was bewildered and a little apprehensive. Had the failure of the lighting really been an accident? Or was the popular professor obligingly coming forward with one of his increasingly rare and prized pranks? The audience sat tight, awaiting developments. Albert, returning from the switchboard, impatiently kicked a wreath of lilies from his path. The audience, resenting this display of nervous irritation, catcalled and booed. In this diversion perhaps a further half-minute passed. Then a voice from one of the higher benches called out boisterously: 'The corpse has caught the dropsy!'

'It's a-swelling,' cried another voice—that of a devotee of Dickens—'It's a-swelling wisibly before my eyes.'

And something had certainly happened to the meagre body beneath its covering; it was as if during the darkness it had been inflated by a gigantic pump.

With a final curse Albert sprang forward and pulled back the tarpaulin. What lay beneath was the body of Professor Finlay, quite dead. The original cadaver was gone.

The vulture swooped hopefully from its rafter.

'Publicity?' said Detective-Inspector John Appleby. 'I'm afraid you can scarcely expect anything else. Or perhaps it would be better to say notoriety. Nothing remotely like it has happened in England for years.'

Sir David Evans, Nessfield's very Welsh Vice-Chancellor, passed a hand dejectedly through his flowing white hair and softly groaned. 'A scandal!' he said. 'A scandal—look you, Mr Appleby—that peggars description. There must be infestigations. There must be arrests. Already there are reporters from the pig papers. This morning I have been photographed.' Sir David paused and glanced across the room at the handsome portrait of himself which hung above the fireplace. 'This morning,' he repeated, momentarily comforted, 'I have been photographed, look you, five or six times.'

Appleby smiled. 'The last case I remember as at all approaching it was the shooting of Viscount Auldearn, the Lord Chancellor, during a private performance of *Hamlet* at the Duke of Horton's seat, Scamnum Court.'

For a second Sir David looked almost cheerful. It was plain that he gained considerable solace from this august comparison. But then he shook his head. 'In the anatomy theatre!' he said. 'And on the one day of the year when there is these unseemly pehaviours. And a pody vanishes. And there is futures—fultures, Mr Appleby!'

'One vulture.' Dr Holroyd, Nessfield's Professor of Human Physiology, spoke as if this comparative paucity of birds of prey represented one of the bright spots of the affair. 'Only one vulture, and apparently abstracted by a group of students from the Zoo. The Director rang up as soon as he saw the first report. He might be described as an angry man.'

Appleby brought out a notebook. 'What we are looking for,' he said, 'is angry men. Perhaps you know of someone whose feelings of anger towards the late Professor Finlay at times approached the murderous?'

Sir David Evans looked at Dr Holroyd and Dr Holroyd looked at Sir David Evans. And it appeared to Appleby that the demeanour of each was embarrassed. 'Of course,' he added, 'I don't mean mere passing irritations between colleagues.'

'There is frictions,' said Sir David carefully. 'Always in a university there is frictions. And frictions produce heat. There was pad frictions between Finlay and Dr Holroyd here. There was personalities, I am sorry to say. For years there has been most fexatious personalities.' Sir David, who at all times preserved an appearance of the most massive benevolence, glanced at his colleague with an eye in which there was a nasty glint. 'Dr Holroyd is Dean of the Faculty of Medicine, look you. It is why I have asked him to meet you now. And last week at a meeting there was a most disgraceful scene. It was a meeting about lavatories. It was a meeting of the Committee for Lavatories.'

'Dear me!' said Appleby. Universities, he was thinking, must have changed considerably since his day.

'Were there to be more lavatories in the Physiology Puilding? Finlay said he would rather put in a path.'

'A path? said Appleby, perplexed.

'A path, with hot and cold laid on, and an efficient shower. Finlay said that in his opinion Dr Holroyd here padly needed a path.'

'I see. And did Dr Holroyd retaliate?'

'I am sorry to say that he did, Mr Appleby. He said that if he had his way in the matter Finlay's own path would be a Formalin one. Which is what they keep the cadavers in, Mr Appleby.'

Dr Holroyd shifted uneasily on his chair. 'It was unfortunate,' he admitted. 'I must freely admit the unfortunate nature of the dispute.'

'It was unacademic,' said Sir David severely. 'There is no other words for it, Dr Holroyd. It was unacademic.'

'I am afraid it was. And most deplorably public. Whereas your own quarrel with Finlay, Sir David, had been a discreetly unobtrusive matter.' Dr Holroyd smiled with sudden frank malice. 'And over private, not University, affairs. In fact, over a woman. Or was it several women? Accounts vary.'

'These,' said Appleby rather hastily, 'are matters which it may be unnecessary to take up.' Detectives are commonly supposed to expend all their energy in dragging information out of people; actually, much of it goes in preventing irrelevant and embarrassing disclosures. 'May I ask, Sir David, your own whereabouts at the time of the fatality?'

'I was in this room, Mr Appleby, reading Plato. Even Vice-Chancellors are entitled to read Plato at times, and I had given orders not to be disturbed.'

'I see. And I take it that nobody interrupted you, and that you might have left the room for a time without being observed?'

Sir David gloomily nodded.

'And you, Dr Holroyd?'

'I went to poor Finlay's final lecture and sat near the back. But the whole stupid affair disgusted me and I came away—only a few minutes, it seems, before the lights went out. I composed myself by taking a quiet walk along the canal. It was quite deserted.'

'I see. And now about the manner of Finlay's death. I understand that you have inspected the body and realize that he was killed by the thrust of a fine dagger from behind? The deed was accomplished in what must have been almost complete darkness. Would you say that it required—or at least that it suggests—something like the professional knowledge of another anatomist or medical man?'

Holroyd was pale. 'It certainly didn't strike me as the blind thrust of an amateur made in a panic. But perhaps there is a species of particularly desperate criminal who is skilled in such things.'

'Possibly so.' Appleby glanced from Holroyd to Sir David. 'But is either of you aware of Finlay's having any connections or interests which might bring upon him the violence of such people? No? Then I think we must be very sceptical about anything of the sort. To kill a man in extremely risky circumstances simply for the pleasure of laying the body on his own dissecting table before his own students is something quite outside my experience of professional crime. It is much more like some eccentric act of private vengeance. And one conceived by a mind theatrical in the highest degree.'

Once more Sir David Evans looked at Dr Holroyd and Dr Holroyd looked at Sir David Evans. 'Finlay himself,' said Sir David, 'had something theatrical about him. Otherwise, look you, he would not have let himself pecome the central figure in this pig yearly joke.' He paused. 'Now, Dr Holroyd here is not theatrical. He is pad-tempered. He is morose. He is underpred. But theatrical he is not.'

'And no more is Sir David.' Holroyd seemed positively touched by the character sketch of himself just offered. 'He is a bit of a humbug, of course—all philosophers are. And he is not a good man, since it is impossible for a Vice-Chancellor to be that. Perhaps he is even something of a *poseur*. If compelled to characterize him freely'—and Holroyd got comfortably to his feet—'I should describe him as Goethe described Milton's *Paradise Lost*.' Holroyd moved towards the door, and as he did so paused to view Sir David's portrait. 'Fair outside, but rotten inwardly,' he quoted thoughtfully. 'But of positive theatrical instinct I would be inclined to say that Sir David is tolerably free. Good afternoon.'

There was a moment's silence. Sir David Evans' fixed expression of benevolence had never wavered. 'Pad passions,' he said. 'Look you, Mr Appleby, there is pad passions in that man.'

Albert was pottering gloomily among his cadaver-racks. His massive frame gave a jump as Appleby entered; it was clear that he was not in full possession of that placid repose which expolicemen should enjoy.

Appleby looked round with brisk interest. 'Nice place you have here,' he said. 'Everything convenient and nicely thought out.'

The first expression on Albert's face had been strongly disapproving. But at this he perceptibly relaxed. 'Ball-bearing,' he said huskily. 'Handles them like lambs.' He pushed back a steel shutter and proudly drew out a rack and its contents. 'Nicely developed gal,' he said appreciatively. 'Capital pelvis for child-bearing she was going to have. Now, if you'll just step over here I can show you one or two uncommonly interesting lower limbs.'

'Thank you—another time.' Appleby, though not unaccustomed to such places, had no aspirations towards connoisseurship. 'I want your own story of what happened this morning.'

'Yes, sir.' From old professional habit Albert straightened up and stood at attention. 'As you'll know, there's always been this bad be'aviour at the final lecture, so there was nothing out of the way in that. But then the lights went out, and they started throwing things, and something 'it me 'ard on the shins.'

'Hard?' said Appleby. 'I doubt if that could have been anything thrown from the theatre.'

'No more do I.' Albert was emphatic. 'It was someone came in through the doors the moment the lights went out and got me down with a regular Rugby tackle. Fair winded I was, and lost my bearings as well.'

'So it was some little time before you managed to get to the switch, which is just outside the swing doors. And in that time Professor Finlay was killed and substituted for the cadaver, and the cadaver was got clean away. Would you say that was a one-man job?'

'No, sir, I would not. Though—mind you—that body 'ad only to be carried across a corridor and out into the courtyard. Anyone can 'ave a car waiting there, so the rest would be easy enough.'

Appleby nodded. 'The killing of Finlay, and the laying him out like

that, may have been a sheer piece of macabre drama, possibly conceived and executed by a lunatic—or even by an apparently sane man
with some specific obsession regarding corpses. But can you see any
reason why such a person should actually carry off the original
corpse? It meant saddling himself with an uncommonly awkward
piece of evidence.'

'You can't ever tell what madmen will do. And as for corpses, there
are more people than you would reckon what 'as uncommon queer
interests in them at times.' And Albert shook his head. 'I seen things,'
he added darkly.

'No doubt you have. But have you seen anything just lately? Was
there anything that might be considered as leading up to this shocking
affair?'

Albert hesitated. 'Well, sir, in this line wot I come down to since
they retired me it's not always possible to up'old the law. In fact, it's
sometimes necessary to circumvent it, like. For, as the late professor
was given to remarking, science must be served.' Albert paused and
tapped his cadaver-racks. 'Served with these 'ere. And of late we've
been uncommon short. And there's no doubt that now and then him
and me was stretching a point.'

'Good heavens!' Appleby was genuinely alarmed. 'This affair is bad
enough already. You don't mean to say that it's going to lead to some
further scandal about body-snatching?'

'Nothing like that, sir.' But as he said this Albert looked doubtful.
'Nothing *quite* like that. They comes from institutions, you know. And
nowadays they 'as to be got to sign papers. It's a matter of tact. Sometimes relatives comes along afterwards and says there been too much
tact by a long way. It's not always easy to know just how much tact
you can turn on. There's no denying but we've 'ad one or two
awkwardnesses this year. And it's my belief as 'ow this sad affair is just
another awkwardness—but more violent like than the others by a
long way.'

'It was violent, all right.' Appleby had turned and led the way into
the deserted theatre. Flowers still strewed it. There was a mingled
smell of lilies and Formalin. Overhead, the single great lamp was like
a vast all-seeing eye. But that morning the eye had blinked. And what
deed of darkness had followed?

'The professor was killed and laid out like that, sir, as an act of revenge by some barmy and outraged relations. And the cadaver was carried off by that same relation as what you might call an act of piety.'

'Well, it's an idea.' Appleby was strolling about, measuring distances with his eye. 'But what about this particular body upon which Finlay was going to demonstrate? *Had* it outraged and pious relations?'

'It only come in yesterday. Quite unprepared it was to be, you see— the same as hanatomists 'ad them in the sixteenth century. Very interesting the late professor was on all that, I'm bound to say. And why all them young varmints of students should take this partikler occasion to fool around——'

'Quite so. It was all in extremely bad taste, I agree. And I don't doubt that the Coroner will say so. And an Assize Judge too, if we have any luck. But you were going to tell me about this particular corpse.'

'I was saying it only come in yesterday. And it was after that that somebody tried to break into the cadaver-racks. Last night, they did— and not a doubt of it. Quite professional, too. If this whole part of the building, sir, weren't well-nigh like a strong room they'd have done it, without a doubt. And when the late professor 'eard of it 'e was as worried as I was. Awkwardness we've 'ad. But body-snatching in reverse, as you might say, was a new one on both of us.'

'So you think that the outraged and pious relation had an earlier shot, in the programme for which murder was not included? I think it's about time we hunted him up.'

Albert looked sorely perplexed. 'And so it would be—if we knew where to find him. But it almost seems as if there never was a cadaver with less in the way of relations than this one wot 'as caused all the trouble. A fair ideal cadaver it seemed to be. You don't think, now'— Albert was frankly inconsequent—'that it might 'ave been an accident? You don't think it might 'ave been one of them young varmint's jokes gone a bit wrong?'

'I do not.'

'But listen, sir.' Albert was suddenly urgent. 'Suppose there was a plan like this. The lights was to be put out and a great horrid dagger thrust into the cadaver. That would be quite like one of their jokes, believe me. For on would go the lights again and folk would get a pretty nasty shock. But now suppose—just suppose, sir—that when the lights were put out for that there purpose there came into the professor's head the notion of a joke of his own. He would change places with the cadaver———'

'But the man wasn't mad!' Appleby was staring at the late Professor Finlay's assistant in astonishment. 'Anything so grotesque———'

'He done queer things before now.' Albert was suddenly stubborn. 'It would come on him sometimes to do something crazier than all them young fools could cudgel their silly brains after. And then the joke would come first and decency second. I know, sir, I seen some queer things at final lectures before this. And that would mean that the varmint thinking to stick the dagger in the cadaver would stick it in the late professor instead.'

'I see.' Appleby was looking at Albert with serious admiration; the fellow didn't look very bright—nevertheless, his days in the Force should have been spent in the Detective Branch. 'It's a better theory than we've had yet, I'm bound to say. But it leaves out two things: the disappearance of the original body, and the fact that Finlay was stabbed from behind. For if he did substitute himself for the body it would have been in the same position—a supine position, and not a prone one. So I don't think your notion will do. And, anyway, we must have all the information about the cadaver that we can get.'

'It isn't much.' Albert bore the discountenance of his hypothesis well. 'We don't know much more about 'im than this—that 'e was a seafaring man.'

The cadaver, it appeared, had at least possessed a name: James Cass. He had also possessed a nationality, for his seaman's papers declared him to be a citizen of the United States, and his next-of-kin was a certain Martha Cass, with an indecipherable address in Seattle, Washington. For some years he had been sailing pretty constantly in freighters between England and America. Anybody less likely to bring down upon the Anatomy Department of Nessfield University the vengeance of outraged and pious relations it would have been difficult to conceive. And the story of Cass's death and relegation to the service of science was an equally bare one. He had come off his ship and was making his way to an unknown lodging when he had been knocked down by a tram and taken to the casualty ward of Nessfield Infirmary.

There he had been visited by the watchful Albert, who had surreptitiously presented him with a flask of gin, receiving in exchange Cass's signature to a document bequeathing his remains for the purposes of medical science. Cass had then died and his body had been delivered at the Anatomy School.

And, after that, somebody had ruthlessly killed Professor Finlay and then carried James Cass's body away again. Stripped of the bewildering nonsense of the final lecture, thought Appleby, the terms of the problem were fairly simple. And yet that nonsense, too, was relevant. For it had surely been counted upon in the plans of the murder.

For a few minutes Appleby worked with a stop watch. Then he turned once more to Albert. 'At the moment,' he said, 'Cass himself appears to be something of a dead end. So now, let us take the lecture—or the small part of it that Finlay had got through before the lights went out. You were a witness of it—and a trained police witness, which is an uncommonly fortunate thing. I want you to give me every detail you can—down to the least squawk or flutter by that damned vulture.'

Albert was gratified, and did as he was bid. Appleby listened, absorbed. Only once a flicker passed over his features. But when Albert was finished he had some questions to ask.

'There was the audience,' he said, '—if audience is the right name for it. Apparently all sorts of people were accustomed to turn up?'

'All manner of unlikely and unsuitable folk.' Albert looked disgusted. 'Though most of them would be medical, one way or another. As you can imagine, sir, a demonstration of a sixteenth-century dissecting technique isn't every layman's fancy.'

'It certainly wouldn't be mine.'

'I couldn't put a name to a good many of them. But there was Dr Holroyd, whom you'll have met, sir; he's our Professor of Human Physiology. Went away early, he did; and looking mighty disgusted, too. Then there was Dr Wesselmann, the Lecturer in Prosthetics—an alien, he is, and not been in Nessfield many years. He brought a friend I have never had sight of before. And out they went too.'

'Well, that's very interesting. And can you recall anyone else?'

'I don't know that I can, sir. Except, of course, our Vice-Chancellor, Sir David Evans.'

Appleby jumped. 'Evans! But he swore to me that——'

Albert smiled indulgently. 'Bless you, that's his regular way. Did you ever know a Welshman who could let a day pass without a bit of 'armless deceit like?'

'There may be something in that.'

' 'E don't think it dignified, as you might say, to attend the final lecture openly. But more often than not he's up there at the far doorway, peering in at the fun. Well, this time 'e 'ad more than 'e bargained for.'

'No doubt he had. And the same prescription might be good for some of the rest of us.' Appleby paused and glanced quickly round the empty theatre. 'Just step to a telephone, will you, and ask Dr Holroyd to come over here.'

Albert did as he was asked, and presently the physiologist came nervously in. 'Is another interview really necessary?' he demanded. 'I have a most important——'

'We shall hope not to detain you long.' Appleby's voice was dry rather than reassuring. 'It is merely that I want you to assist me in a reconstruction of the crime.'

Holroyd flushed. 'And may I ask by what right you ask me to take part in such a foolery?'

Appleby suddenly smiled. 'None, sir—none at all. I merely wanted a trained mind—and one with a pronounced instinct to get at the truth of a problem when it arises. I was sure you would be glad to help.'

'Perhaps I am. Anyway, go ahead.'

'Then I should be obliged if you would be the murderer. Perhaps I should say the first murderer, for it seems likely enough that there were at least two—accomplices. You have no objection to so disagreeable a part?'

Holroyd shrugged his shoulders. 'Naturally, I have none whatever. But I fear I must be coached in it and given my cues. For I assure you it is a role entirely foreign to me. And I have no theatrical flair, as Sir David pointed out.'

Once more Appleby brought out his stop watch. 'Albert,' he said briskly, 'shall be the cadaver and I shall be Finlay standing in front of it. Your business is to enter by the back, switch off the light, step into the theatre and there affect to stab me. I shall fall to the floor. You must then dislodge Albert, hoist me into his place and cover me with the tarpaulin. Then you must get hold of Albert by the legs or shoulders and haul him from the theatre.'

'And all this in the dark? It seems a bit of a programme.'

Appleby nodded. 'I agree with you. But we shall at least discover if it is at all possible of accomplishment by one man in the time available. So are you ready?'

'One moment, sir.' Albert, about to assume the passive part of the late James Cass, sat up abruptly. 'You seemed to have missed me out. Me as I was, that is to say.'

'Quite true.' Appleby looked at him thoughtfully. 'We are short of a stand-in for you as you were this morning. But I shall stop off being Finlay's body and turn on the lights again myself. So go ahead.'

Albert lay down and drew the tarpaulin over his head. Holroyd slipped out. Appleby advanced as if to address an audience. 'Now,' he said.

And Appleby talked. Being thorough, he made such anatomical observations as his ignorance allowed. Once he glanced round at the corpse, and out of the corner of his eye glimpsed Holroyd beyond the glass-panelled door, his hand already going up to flick at the switch. A moment later the theatre was in darkness, and seconds after that Appleby felt a sharp tap beneath the shoulder blade. He pitched to the floor, pressing his stop watch as he did so. Various heaving sounds followed as Holroyd got the portly Albert off the table; then Appleby felt himself seized in surprisingly strong arms and hoisted up in Albert's place. Next came a shuffle and a scrape as Holroyd, panting heavily now, dragged the inert Albert from the theatre. Appleby waited for a couple of seconds, threw back the tarpaulin and lowered himself to the floor. Then he groped his way through the door, flicked on the light and looked at his watch. 'And the audience,' he said, 'is now sitting back and waiting—until presently somebody points out that the cadaver is the wrong size. Thank you very much. The reconstruction has been more instructive than I hoped.' He turned to Holroyd. 'I am still inclined to think that it has the appearance of being the work of two men. And yet you managed it pretty well on schedule when single-handed. Never a fumble and just the right lift. You might almost have been practising it.'

Holroyd frowned. 'Yachting,' he said briefly, '—and particularly at night. It makes one handy.'

And Albert looked with sudden suspicion at Nessfield's Professor of Human Physiology. 'Yachting?' he asked. 'Now, would that have put you in the way of acquaintance with many seafaring men?'

Of James Cass, that luckless waif who would be a seafarer no longer, Appleby learned little more that afternoon. The cargo vessel from which he had disembarked was already at sea again, and a couple of days must elapse before any line could be tapped there. But one elderly seaman who had recently made several voyages with him a little research did produce, and from this witness two facts emerged. There was nothing out of the way about Cass—except that he was a man distinctly on the simple side. Cass had been suggestible, Appleby gathered; so much so as to have been slightly a butt among his fellows. And Appleby asked a question: had the dead man appeared to have any regular engagement or preoccupation when he came into port? The answer to this was definitive. Within a couple of hours, Appleby felt, the file dealing with this queer mystery of the anatomy theatre would be virtually closed for good.

Another fifteen minutes found him mounting the staircase of one of Nessfield's most superior blocks of professional chambers. But the building, if imposing, was gloomy as well, and when Appleby was overtaken and jostled by a hurrying form it was a second before he recognized that he was again in the presence of Dr Holroyd.

'Just a moment.' Appleby laid a hand on the other's arm. 'May I ask if this coincidence extends to our both aiming at the third floor?'

Holroyd was startled, but made no reply. They mounted the final flight side by side and in silence. Appleby rang a bell before a door with a handsome brass plate. After a perceptible delay the door was opened by a decidedly flurried nurse, who showed the two men into a sombre waiting room. 'I don't think,' she said, 'that you have an appointment? And as an emergency has just arisen I am afraid there is no chance of seeing Dr——'

She stopped at an exclamation from Appleby. Hunched in a corner of the waiting-room was a figure whose face was almost entirely swathed in a voluminous silk muffler. But there was no mistaking that flowing silver hair. 'Sir David!' exclaimed Appleby. 'This is really a most remarkable rendezvous.'

Sir David Evans groaned. 'My chaw,' he said. 'It is one pig ache, look you.'

Holroyd laughed nervously. 'Shakespeare was demonstrably right. There was never yet philosopher could bear the toothache patiently—nor Vice-Chancellor either.'

But Appleby paid no attention; he was listening keenly to something else. From beyond a door on the right came sound of hurried, heavy movement. Appleby strode across the room and turned the handle. He flung back the door and found himself looking into the dentist's surgery. 'Dr Wesselmann?' he said.

The answer was an angry shout from a bullet-headed man in a white coat. 'How dare you intrude in this way!' he cried. 'My colleague and myself are confronted with a serious emergency. Be so good as to withdraw at once.'

Appleby stood his ground and surveyed the room; Holroyd stepped close behind him. The dentist's chair was empty, but on a surgical couch nearby lay a patient covered with a light rug. Over this figure another white-coated man was bending, and appeared to be holding an oxygen mask over its face.

And Nessfield's Lecturer in Prosthetics seemed to find further explanations necessary. 'A patient,' he said rapidly, 'with an unsuspected idiosyncrasy to intravenous barbiturates. Oxygen has to be administered and the position is critical. So be so good——'

Appleby leaped forward and sent the white-coated holder of the oxygen mask spinning; he flung back the rug. There could be no doubt that what was revealed was James Cass's body. And since lying on Professor Finlay's dissecting table it had sustained a great gash in the throat. It had never been very pleasant to look at. It was ghastly enough now.

Wesselmann's hand darted to his pocket; Holroyd leaped on him with his yachtsman litheness and the alien dentist went down heavily on the floor. The second man showed no fight as he was handcuffed. Appleby looked curiously at Holroyd. 'So you saw,' he asked, 'how the land lay?'

'In my purely amateur fashion, I suppose I did. And I think I finished on schedule once again.'

Appleby laughed. 'Your intervention saved me from something decidedly nasty at the hands of Nessfield's authority on false teeth. By the way, would you look round for the teeth in question? And then we can have in Sir David—seeing he is so conveniently in attendance—and say an explanatory word.'

'I got the hang of it,' said Appleby, 'when we did a very rough-and-ready reconstruction of the crime. For when, while playing Finlay's part, I glanced round at the cadaver, I found myself catching a glimpse of Dr Holroyd here when he was obligingly playing First Murderer and turning off the lights. There was a glass panel in the door, and through this he was perfectly visible. I saw at once why Finlay had been killed. It was merely because he had seen, *and recognized*, somebody who was about to plunge the theatre in darkness for some nefarious, but not necessarily murderous, end. What did this person want? There could be only one answer: the body of James Cass. Already he had tried to get it in the night, but the housebreaking involved had proved too difficult.'

The benevolent features of Sir David Evans were shadowed by perplexity. 'But why, Mr Appleby, should this man want such a pody?'

'I shall come to that in a moment. But first keep simply to this: that the body had to be stolen even at great hazard; that when glimpsed and recognized by Finlay the potential thief was sufficiently ruthless to silence him with a dagger secreted for such an emergency—and was also sufficiently quick witted to exploit this extemporaneous murder to his own advantage. If he had simply bolted with Cass's body and left that of Finlay the hunt would of course have been up the moment somebody turned the lights on. By rapidly substituting one body for the other—Finlay's for that of Cass—on the dissecting table, he contrived the appearance first of some more or less natural momentary absence of Finlay from the theatre, and, secondly, the suggestion of some possible joke which kept the audience wary and quiet for some seconds longer. All this gave additional time for his getaway. And—yet again—the sheerly grotesque consequence of the substitution had great potential value as a disguise. By suggesting some maniacal act of private vengeance it masked the purely practical—and the professionally criminal—nature of the crime.

'And now, what did we know of Cass? We knew that he was a seaman; that he travelled more or less regularly between England and
America; that he was knocked down and presently died shortly after
landing; and that he was a simple-minded fellow, easily open to per-
suasion. And we also knew this: that he had a set of rather incongru-
ously magnificent false teeth; that in the anatomy theatre these first
protruded themselves and then by some muscular spasm appeared to
lodge themselves in the throat, the jaw closing like a vice. And we also
knew that, hard upon this, a certain Dr Wesselmann, an alien comparatively little known in Nessfield and actually a specialist in false
teeth, hurried from the theatre accompanied by a companion. When
I also learned from a seaman who had sailed with Cass that he was
often concerned about his teeth and would hurry off to a dentist as
soon as he reached shore, I saw that the case was virtually complete.'

'And would be wholly so when you recovered Cass's body and got
hold of these.' Holroyd came forward as he spoke, carrying two den-
tal plates on an enamel tray. 'Sir David, what would you say about
Cass's teeth?'

Nessfield's Vice-Chancellor had removed the muffler from about
his jaw; the excitement of the hunt had for the moment banished the
pain which had driven him to Wesselmann's rooms. He inspected the
dentures carefully—and then spoke the inevitable words. 'They are
pig,' he said decisively.

'Exactly so. And now, look.' Holroyd gave a deft twist to a molar;
the denture which he was holding fell apart; in the hollow of each
gleaming tooth there could be discerned a minute oil-silk package.

'What they contain,' said Appleby, 'is probably papers covered with
a microscopic writing. I had thought perhaps of uncut diamonds. But
now I am pretty sure that what we have run to earth is espionage.
What one might call the Unwitting Intermediary represents one
of the first principles of that perpetually fantastic game at its higher
levels. Have a messenger who has no notion that he *is* a messenger
and you at once supply yourself with the sort of insulating device
between cell and cell that gives spies a comforting feeling of security.
Cass has been such a device. And it was one perfectly easy to operate.
He had merely to be persuaded that his false teeth were always likely
to give him trouble, and that he must regularly consult (at an obli-

gingly low fee) this dentist at one end and that dentist at the other—and the thing was practically foolproof. Only Wesselmann and his friends failed to reckon on sudden death, and much less on Cass's signing away his body—dentures and all—to an anatomy school.' Appleby paused. 'And now, gentlemen, that concludes the affair. So what shall we call it?'

Holroyd smiled. 'Call it the Cass Case. You couldn't get anything more compendious than that.'

But Sir David Evans shook his beautiful silver locks. 'No!' he said authoritatively. 'It shall be called *Lesson in Anatomy*. The investigation has been most interesting, Mr Appleby. And now let us go. For the photographers, look you, are waiting.'

12

JULIAN SYMONS

The Flaw

I

'Drink your coffee.'

Celia sat feet up on the sofa reading a fashion magazine, the coffee cup on the table beside her. 'What's that?'

'I said drink your coffee. You know you like it to be piping hot.'

She contemplated the coffee, stirred it with a spoon, then put the spoon back in the saucer. 'I'm not sure it's hot enough now.'

'I poured it only a couple of minutes ago.'

'Yes, but still. I don't know that I feel like coffee tonight. But I do want a brandy.' She swung her legs off the sofa and went across to the drinks tray. 'A celebratory brandy. Can I pour one for you?'

'What are we celebrating?'

'Me, Giles, not you. I'm celebrating. But you want me to drink my coffee, don't you? All right.' She went swiftly back, lifted the coffee cup, drank the contents in two gulps and made a face. 'Not very hot. Now may I have my brandy?'

'Of course. Let me pour it for you.'

'Oh no, I'll do it myself. After all, you poured the coffee.' She smiled sweetly.

'What do you mean?'

'Just that we've both had coffee. And you poured it. But I gave it to you on the tray, remember?'

Sir Giles got up, put a hand to his throat. 'What are you trying to say?'

'Only that if I turned the tray round you'll have got my cup and I shall have got yours. But it wouldn't matter. Or would it?'

He made for the door and turned the handle, but it did not open. 'It's locked. What have you done with the key?'

'I can't imagine.' As he lumbered towards her, swaying a little, she easily evaded him. 'You think I'm a fool, Giles, don't you? I'm not, that's your mistake. So this is a celebration.'

'Celia.' His hand was at his throat again. He choked, collapsed on to the carpet and lay still.

Celia looked at him thoughtfully, finished her brandy, prodded him with her foot and said, 'Now, what to do about the body?'

The curtain came down. The first act of *Villain* was over.

2

'I enjoyed it enormously,' Duncan George said. 'Is it all right if I smoke?'

'Of course.' Oliver Glass was busy at the dressing table, removing the makeup that had turned him into Sir Giles. In the glass he saw Dunc packing his pipe and lighting it. Good old Dunc, he thought, reliable dull old Dunc, his reactions are always predictable. 'Pour yourself a drink.'

'Not coffee, I hope.'

Oliver's laugh was perfunctory.

'I thought the play was really clever. All those twists and turns in the plot. And you enjoy being the chief actor as well as the writer, don't you, it gives you an extra kick?'

'My dear fellow, you're a psychologist as well as a crime writer yourself, you should know. But after all, who can interpret one's own writing better than oneself? The play . . . well, between these four walls it's a collection of tricks. The supreme trick is to make the audience accept it, to deceive them not once or twice but half-a-dozen times, to make them leave the theatre gasping at the cleverness of it all. And if that's to be done, Sir Giles has to be played on just the right note, so that we're never certain whether he's fooling everybody else or being fooled himself, never quite sure whether he's the villain or the hero. And who knows that better than the author? So if he happens to be an actor too, he must be perfect for the part.'

'Excellent special pleading. I'll tell you one thing, though. When the curtain comes down at the end of the first act, nobody really believes you're dead. Oliver Glass is the star, and if you're dead they've been cheated. So they're just waiting for you to come out of that cupboard.'

'But think of the tension that's building while they wait. Ready, Dunc.'

He clapped the other on the shoulder, and they walked out into the London night. Oliver Glass was a slim, elegant man in his fifties, successful both as actor and dramatist, so successful that he could afford to laugh at the critic who said that he had perfected the art of overacting, and the other critic who remarked that after seeing an Oliver Glass play he was always reminded of the line that said life is mostly froth and bubble. Whether Oliver did laugh was another matter, for he disliked any adverse view of his abilities. He had a flat in the heart of the West End, a small house in Sussex, and a beautiful wife named Elizabeth who was fifteen years his junior.

Duncan George looked insignificant by his side. He was short and square, a practising psychiatrist who also wrote crime stories, and he had known Oliver for some years. He was typified for Oliver by the abbreviation of his first name, *Dunc*. He was exactly the kind of person Oliver could imagine dunking a doughnut into a cup of coffee, or doing something equally vulgar. With all that, however, Dunc was a good fellow, and Oliver tolerated him as a companion.

They made their way through the West End to a street off Leicester Square where the Criminologists' Club met once a quarter, to eat a late supper followed by a talk on a subject of criminal interest. The members were all writers about real or fictitious crime, and on this evening Oliver Glass was to speak to them on 'The Romance of Crime', with Duncan George as his chairman. When he rose and looked around, with that gracious look in which there was just a touch of contempt, the buzz of conversation ceased.

'Gentlemen,' he began, 'Criminologists . . . fellow crime writers . . . perhaps fellow criminals. I have come tonight to plead for romance in the world of crime, for the locked-room murder, the impossible theft, the crime committed by the invisible man. I have come to plead that you should bring wit and style and complexity to your writings about crime, that you should remember Stevenson's view that life is a bazaar of dangerous and smiling chances, and the remark of Thomas Griffith Wainewright when he confessed to poisoning his pretty sister-in-law: "It was a terrible thing to do, but she had thick ankles." I beseech you not to forget those thick ankles as a motive, and to abandon the dreary books some of you write concerned with examining the psychology of two equally dull people to decide which destroyed the other, or to looking at bits of intestines under a microscope to determine whether a tedious husband killed his boring wife. Your sights should be set instead on the Perfect Crime. . . .'

Oliver Glass spoke, as always, without notes, fluently and with style, admiring the fluency and stylishness as the words issued from his mouth. Afterwards he was challenged by some members, Duncan George among them, about that conjectural Perfect Crime. Wasn't it out of date? Not at all, Oliver said, Sir Giles in *Villain* attempted it.

'Yes, but as you remarked yourself, *Villain*'s a mass of clever tricks,' Dunc said. 'Sir Giles wants to kill Celia as a kind of trick, just to prove that he can get away with it. Or at least, we think he does. Then you play all sorts of variations on the idea: is the poison really a sleeping draught? does she know about it? that kind of thing. Splendid to watch, but nobody would actually try it. In every perfect murder, so called, there is actually a flaw.' There was a chorus of agreement, by which Oliver found himself a little irritated.

'How do you know that? The Perfect Crime is one in which the criminal never puts himself within reach of the law. Perhaps, even, no crime is known to have taken place, although that is a little short of perfection. But how do we know, gentlemen, what variations on the Perfect Crime any of us may be planning, may even have carried out? "The desires of the heart are as crooked as corkscrews", as the poet says, and I'm sure Dunc can bear that out from his psychiatric experience.'

'Any of us is capable of violence under certain circumstances, if that's what you mean. But to set out to commit a Perfect Crime without a motive is the mark of a psychopath.'

'I didn't say without motive. A good motive for one man may be trivial to another.'

'Tell us when you're going to commit the Perfect Crime, and we'll see if we can solve it,' somebody said. There was a murmur of laughter.

235

Upon this note he left, and strolled home to Everley Court, passing the drunks on the pavements, the blacks and yellows and all conditions of foreigners, who jostled each other or stood gaping outside the sex cinemas. He made a slight detour to pass by the theatre, and saw with a customary glow of pleasure the poster: *Oliver Glass in Villain. The Mystery Play by Oliver Glass*. Was he really planning the Perfect Crime? There can be no doubt, he said to himself, that the idea is in your mind. And the elements are there, Elizabeth and deliciously unpredictable Evelyn, and above all the indispensable Eustace. But is it more than a whim? Do I really dislike Elizabeth enough? The answer to that, of course, was that it was not a question of hatred but of playing a game, the game of Oliver Glass versus Society, even Oliver Glass versus the World.

And so home. And to Elizabeth.

A nod to Tyler, the night porter at the block of flats. Up in the lift to the third floor. Key in the door.

From the entrance hall the apartment stretched left and right. To the left Elizabeth's bedroom and bathroom. Almost directly in front of him the living room, further to the right dining room and kitchen, at the extreme right Oliver's bedroom and bathroom. He went into the living room, switched on the light. On the mantelpiece there was a note in Elizabeth's scrawl: *O. Please come to see me if back before 2 a.m. E.*

For two years now they had communicated largely by means of such notes. It had begun—how had it begun?—because she was so infuriatingly talkative when he wanted to concentrate. 'I am an artist,' he had said. 'The artist needs isolation, if the fruits of genius are to ripen on the bough of inspiration.' The time had been when Elizabeth listened open-eyed to such words, but those days had gone. For a long while now she had made comments suggesting that his qualities as actor and writer fell short of genius, or had pointed out that last night he had happily stayed late at a party. She did not understand the artistic temperament. Her nagging criticism had become, quite simply, a bore.

There was, he admitted as he turned the note in his fingers, something else. There were the girls needed by the artist as part of his inspiration, the human clay turned by him into something better. Elizabeth had never understood about them, and in particularly had failed to understand when she had returned to find one of them with him on the living room carpet. She had spoken of divorce, but he knew the words to be idle. Elizabeth had extravagant tastes, and divorce would hardly allow her to indulge them. So the notes developed. They lived separate lives, with occasional evenings when she acted as hostess, or came in and chatted amiably enough to friends. For the most part the arrangement suited him rather well, although just at present his absorption with Evelyn was such. . . .

He went in to see Elizabeth.

She was sitting on a small sofa, reading. Although he valued youth above all things, he conceded, as he looked appraisingly at her, that she was still attractive. Her figure was slim (no children, he could not have endured the messy noisy things), legs elegant, dainty feet. She had kept her figure, as—he confirmed, looking at himself in the glass—he had kept his. How curious that he no longer found her desirable.

'Oliver.' He turned. 'Stop looking at yourself.'

'Was I doing that?'

'You know you were. Stop acting.'

'But I am an actor.'

'Acting off stage, I mean. You don't know anybody exists outside yourself.'

'There is a respectable philosophical theory maintaining that very proposition. I have invented you, you have invented me. A charming idea.'

'A very silly idea. Oliver, why don't you divorce me?'

'Have you given me cause?'

'You know how easily it can be arranged.'

He answered with a weary, a world-weary sigh. She exclaimed angrily and he gave her a look of pure dislike, so that she exclaimed again.

'You *do* dislike me, don't you? A touch of genuine feeling. So why not?' She went over to her dressing table, sat down, took out a pot of cream.

He placed a hand on his heart. 'I was—'

'I know. You were born a Catholic. But when did you last go to church?'

'Very well. Say simply that I don't care to divorce you. It would be too vulgar.'

'You've got a new girl. I can always tell.'

'Is there anything more tedious than feminine intuition?'

'Let me tell you something. This time I shall have you followed. And *I* shall divorce *you*. What do you think of that?'

'Very little.' And indeed, who would pay her charge account at Harrods, provide the jewellery she loved? Above all, where would she get the money she gambled away at casinos and race meetings? She had made similar threats before, and he knew them to be empty ones.

'You want me as a kind of butterfly you've stuck with a pin, nothing more.'

She was at work with the cream. She used one cream on her face, another on her neck, a third on her legs. Then she covered her face with a black mask, which was supposed to increase the effectiveness of the cream. She often kept this face cream on all night.

There had been a time when he found it exciting to make love to a woman whose face was not visible, but in her case that time had gone long ago. What was she saying now?

'Nothing gets through to you, does it? You have a sort of armour of conceit. But you have the right name, do you know that? *Glass*—if one could see through you there would be nothing, absolutely nothing there. Oliver Glass, *you don't exist.*'

Very well, he thought, very well, I am an invisible man. I accept the challenge. Elizabeth, you have signed your death warrant.

3

The idea, then, was settled. Plans had to be made. But they were still unsettled, moving around in what he knew to be his marvellously ingenious mind, when he went to visit Evelyn after lunch on the following day. Evelyn was in her early twenties, young enough—oh yes, he acknowledged it—to be his daughter, young enough also to be pleased by the company of a famous actor. But beyond that, Evelyn fascinated him by her unpredictability. She was a photographer's model much in demand, and he did not doubt that she had other lovers. There were times when she said that she was too busy to see him, or simply that she wanted to be alone, and he accepted these refusals as part of the excitement of the chase. There was a perversity about Evelyn, an abandonment to the whim of the moment, that reached out to something in his own nature. He felt sometimes that there was no suggestion so outrageous that she would refuse to consider it. She had once opened the door of her flat naked, and asked him to strip and accompany her down to the street.

Her flat was off Baker Street, and when he rang the bell there was no reply. At the third ring he felt annoyance. He had telephoned in advance, as always, and she had said she would be there. He pushed the door in a tentative way, and it swung open. In the hall he called her name. There was no reply.

The flat was not large. He went into the living room, which was untidy as usual, glanced into the small kitchen, then went into the bedroom with its unmade bed. What had happened to her, where was she? He entered the bathroom, and recoiled from what he saw.

Evelyn lay face down, half in and half out of the bath. One arm hung over the side of the bath, the other trailed in the water. Her head rested on the side of the bath as though her neck was broken.

He went across to her, touched the arm outside the bath. It was warm. He bent down to feel the pulse. As he did so the arm moved, the body turned, and Evelyn was laughing at him.

'You frightened me. You bitch.' But he was excited, not angry.

'The author of *Villain* should be used to tricks.' She got out, handed him a towel. 'Dry me.'

Their lovemaking afterwards had the frantic, paroxysmic quality that he had found in few women. It was as though he were bringing her back from the dead. A thought struck him. 'Have you done that with anybody else?'

'Does it matter?'

'Perhaps not. I should still like to know.'

'Nobody else.'

'It was as though you were another person.'

'Good. I'd like to be a different person every time.'

He was following his own train of thought. 'My wife puts on a black mask after creaming her face at night. That should be exciting, but it isn't.'

Evelyn was insatiably curious about the details of sex, and he had told her a good deal about Elizabeth.

'I'm good for you,' she said now. 'You get a kick each time, don't you?'

'Yes. And you?'

She considered this. She had a similar figure to Elizabeth's but her features were very different, the nose snub instead of aquiline, the eyes blue and wide apart. 'In a way. Being who you are gives me a kick.'

'Is that all?'

'What do you mean?'

'Don't you like me?'

'It's wet to ask things like that. I never thought you were wet.' She looked at him directly with her large, slightly vacant blue eyes. 'If you want to know, I get a kick out of you because you're acting all the time. It's the acting you like, not the act. And then I get a kick out of you being an old man.'

He was so angry that he slapped her face. She said calmly, 'Yes, I like that too.'

By the time that night's performance was over his plan was made.

4

In the next two weeks Tyler, the night porter at Everley Court, was approached three times by a tall, bulky man wearing horn-rimmed spectacles. The man asked for Mrs Glass, and seemed upset to learn on every occasion that she was out. Once he handed a note to Tyler and then took it back, saying that it wouldn't do to leave a letter lying around. Twice he left messages, to say that Charles had called and wanted to talk to Mrs Glass. On his third visit the man smelled of drink, and his manner was belligerent. 'You tell her I must talk to her,' he said in an accent that Tyler could not place, except that the man definitely came from somewhere up north.

'Yes, sir. And the name is—'

'Charles. She'll know.'

Tyler coughed. 'Begging your pardon, sir, but wouldn't it be better to telephone?'

The man glared at him. 'Do you think I haven't tried? You tell her to get in touch. If she doesn't I won't answer for the consequences.'

'Charles?' Elizabeth said when Tyler rather hesitantly told her this. 'I know two or three people named Charles, but this doesn't seem to fit any of them. What sort of age?'

'Perhaps about forty, Miss Glass. Smartly dressed. A gentleman. Comes from the north, maybe Scotland, if that's any help.'

'No doubt it should be, but it isn't.'

'He seemed—' Tyler hesitated. 'Very concerned.'

On the following day Oliver left a note for her. *E. Man rang while you were out, wouldn't leave message. O.* She questioned him about the call.

'He wouldn't say what he wanted. Just rang off when I said you weren't here.'

'It must be the same man.' She explained about him. 'Tyler said he had a northern accent, probably Scottish.'

'What Scots do you know named Charles?'

'Charlie Rothsey, but I haven't seen him for years. I wish he'd ring when I'm here.'

A couple of evenings later the wish was granted, although she did not speak to the man. Oliver had asked her to give a little supper party after the show for three members of the cast, and because two of them were women Duncan was invited to even up the numbers. Elizabeth was serving the cold salmon when the telephone rang in the living room. Oliver went to answer it. He came back almost at once, looking thoughtful. When Elizabeth said it had been a quick call, he looked sharply at her. 'It was your friend Charles. He rang off. Just announced himself, then rang off when he heard my voice.'

'Who's Charles?' one of the women asked. 'He sounds interesting.'

'You'd better ask Elizabeth.'

She told the story of the man who had called, and it caused general amusement. Only Oliver remained serious. When the guests were going he asked Duncan to stay behind.

'I just wanted your opinion, Dunc. This man has called three times and now he's telephoning. What sort of man would do this kind of thing, and what can we do about it?'

'What sort of man? Hard to say.' Duncan took out his pipe, filled and lit it with maddening deliberation. 'Could be a practical joker, harmless enough. Or it could be somebody . . . well, not so harmless. But I don't see that you can do much about it. Obscene and threatening phone calls are ten a penny, as the police will tell you. Of course if he does show up again Elizabeth could see him, but I'd recommend having somebody else here.'

This was, Oliver considered, adequate preparation of the ground. It had been established that Elizabeth was being pursued by a character named Charles. There was no doubt about Charles's existence. He obviously existed independently of Oliver Glass, since Tyler had seen him and Oliver himself had spoken to him on the telephone. If Elizabeth was killed, the mysterious Charles would be the first suspect.

Charles had been created as somebody separate from Oliver by that simplicity which is the essence of all fine art. Oliver, like Sir Giles in *Villain*, was a master of disguise. He had in particular the ability possessed by the great Vidocq, of varying his height by twelve inches or more. Charles had been devised from a variety of props like cheek pads, body cushions and false eyebrows, plus the indispensable platform heels. He would make one more appearance, and then vanish from the scene. He would never have to meet anybody who knew Oliver well, something which he slightly regretted. And Charles on the telephone had been an actor whom Oliver had asked to ring during the evening. Oliver had merely said he couldn't talk now but would call him tomorrow, and then put down the receiver.

In the next few days he noticed with amusement tinged with annoyance that Elizabeth had fulfilled her threat of putting a private enquiry agent on his track. He spotted the man hailing a taxi just after he had got one himself, and then getting out a few yards behind him when he stopped outside Evelyn's flat. Later he pointed out the man to Evelyn, standing in a doorway opposite. She giggled, and suggested that they should ask him up.

'I believe you would,' he said admiringly. 'Is there anything you wouldn't do?'

'If I felt like it, nothing.' She was high on some drug or other. 'What about you?'

'A lot of things.'

'*Careful* old Oliver.'

What would she say if she knew what he was planning? He was tempted to say something but resisted, although so far as he could tell nothing would shock her. She suddenly threw up the window, leaned out and gave a piercing whistle. When the man looked up, she beckoned. He turned his head and then began to walk away. Oliver was angry, but what was the use of saying anything? It was her recklessness that fascinated him.

His annoyance was reflected in a note left for Elizabeth. *E. This kind of spying is degrading. O.* He found a reply that night when he came back from the theatre. *O. Your conduct is degrading. Your present fancy is public property. E.*

5

That Oliver Glass had charm was acknowledged even by those not susceptible to it. In the days after the call from Charles he exerted this charm upon Elizabeth. She went out a good deal in the afternoons, where or with whom he really didn't care, and this gave him the chance to leave little notes. One of them ran: *E. You simply MUST be waiting here for me after the theatre. I have a small surprise for you. O.*, and another: *E. Would supper at Wheeler's amuse you this evening? Remembrance of things past . . . O.* On the first occasion he gave her a pretty ruby ring set with pearls, and the reference in the second note was to the fact that they had often eaten at Wheeler's in the early months after marriage. On these evenings he set out to dazzle and amuse her as he had done in the past, and she responded. Perhaps the response was unwilling, but that no doubt was because of Evelyn. He noticed, however, that the man following him was no longer to be seen, and at their Wheeler's supper mentioned this to her.

'I know who she is. I know you've always been like that. Perhaps I have to accept it.' Her eyes flashed. 'Although if I want to get divorce evidence it won't be difficult.'

'An artist needs more than one woman,' Oliver said. 'But you must not think that I can do without you. I need you. You are a fixed point in a shifting world.'

'What nonsense I do talk,' he said to himself indulgently. The truth was that contact with her nowadays was distasteful to him. By the side of Evelyn she was insipid. A great actor, however, can play any part, and this one would not be maintained for long.

Only one faintly disconcerting thing happened in this, as he thought of it, second honeymoon period. He came back to the flat unexpectedly early one afternoon, and heard Elizabeth's voice on the telephone. She replaced the receiver as he entered the room. Her face was flushed. When he asked who she had been speaking to, she said, 'Charles'.

'Charles?' For a moment he could not think who she was talking about. Then he stared at her. Nobody knew better than he that she could not have been speaking to Charles, but of course he could not say that.

'What did he say?'

'Beastly things. I put down the receiver.'

Why was she lying? How absurd, how deliciously absurd, if she had a lover. Or was it possible that somebody at the supper party was playing a practical joke? He brushed aside such conjectures because they did not matter now. Nothing could interfere with the enactment of the supreme drama of his life.

6

Celia's intention in *Villain* was to explain Sir Giles's absence by saying that he had gone away on a trip, something he did from time to time. Hence the remark about disposition of the body at the end of Act One. Just after the beginning of the second act the body was revealed by Celia to her lover shoved into a cupboard, a shape hidden in a sack. A few minutes later the cupboard was opened again, and the shape was seen by the audience, although not by Celia, to move slightly. Then, after twenty-five minutes of the second act, there was a brief blackout on stage. When the lights went up Sir Giles emerged from the cupboard, not dead but drugged.

To be enclosed within a sack for that length of time is no pleasure, and in any ordinary theatrical company the body in the sack would have been that of the understudy, with the leading man changing over only a couple of minutes before he was due to emerge from the cupboard. But Oliver believed in what he called the theatre of the actual.

In another play he had insisted that the voice of an actress shut up for some time in a trunk must be real and not a recording, so that the actress herself had to be in the trunk. In *Villain* he maintained that the experience of being actually in the sack was emotionally valuable, so that he always stayed in it for the whole length of time it was in the cupboard.

The body in the sack was to provide Oliver with an unbreakable alibi. The interval after Act One lasted fifteen minutes, so that he had nearly forty minutes free. Everley Court was seven minutes' walk from the theatre, and he did not expect to need much more than twenty minutes all told. The body in the sack would be seen to twitch by hundreds of people, and who could be in it but Oliver?

In fact Useful Eustace would be the sack's occupant. Eustace was a dummy used by stage magicians who wanted to achieve very much the effect at which Oliver aimed, of persuading an audience that there was a human being inside a container. He was made of plastic, and inflated to the size of a small man. You then switched on a mechanism which made Eustace kick out arms and legs in a galvanic manner. A battery-operated timer in his back could be set to operate at intervals ranging from thirty seconds to five minutes. When deflated, Eustace folded up neatly, into a size no larger than a plastic macintosh.

Eustace was the perfect accomplice. Useful Eustace indeed. Oliver had tried him out half a dozen times inside a sack of similar size, and he looked most convincing.

On the afternoon of The Day he rested. Elizabeth was out, but said that she would be back before seven. His carefully worded note was left on her mantelpiece. *E. I want you at the flat ALL this evening. A truly sensational surprise for you. All the evening, mind, not just after the show. O.* Her curiosity would not, he felt sure, be able to resist such a note.

During Act One he admired, with the detachment of the artist, his own performance. He was cynical, ironic, dramatic—in a word, superb. When it was over he went unobtrusively to his dressing room. He had no fear of visitors, for he was known to detest any interruption during the interval.

And now came what in advance he felt to be the only ticklish part of the operation. The cupboard with the sack in it opened on to the back of the stage. The danger of carrying out an inflated Eustace from dressing room to stage was too great—he must be inflated on site, as it were, and it was possible, although unlikely, that a wandering stage hand might see him at work. The Perfect Crime does not depend upon chance or upon the taking of risks, and if the worst happened, if he was seen obviously inflating a dummy, the project must be abandoned for the present time. But fortune favours the creative artist, or did so on this occasion. Inflation of Eustace by pump took only a few moments as he knelt by the cupboard, and nobody came near. The timer had been set for movement every thirty seconds. He put Eustace into the sack, waited to see him twitch, closed the cupboard's false back, and strolled away.

He left the theatre by an unobtrusive exit used by those who wanted to avoid the autograph hunters outside the stage door, and walked along head down until he reached the nearest Underground station, one of the few in London equipped with lockers and lavatories. Unhurriedly he took Charles's clothes and shoes from the locker, went into a lavatory, changed, put his acting clothes back in the locker. Spectacles and revolver were in his jacket pocket. He had bought the revolver years ago, when he had been playing a part in which he was supposed to be an expert shot. By practice in a shooting range he had in fact become a quite reasonable one.

As he left the station he looked at his watch. Six minutes. Very good.

Charles put on a pair of grey gloves from another jacket pocket. Three minutes brought him to Everley Court. He walked straight across to the lift, something he could not do without being observed by Tyler. The man came over, and in Charles's husky voice, with its distinctive accent, he said: 'Going up to Mrs Glass. Expecting me.'

'I'll ring, sir. It's Mr Charles, isn't it?'

'No need. I said, she's expecting me.'

Perfectly, admirably calm. But in the lift he felt, quite suddenly, that he would be unable to do it. To allow Elizabeth to divorce him and then to marry or live with Evelyn until they tired of each other, wouldn't that after all be the sensible, obvious thing? But to be *sensible*, to be *obvious*. Were such things worthy of Oliver Glass? Wasn't the whole point that by this death, which in a practical sense was needless, he would show the character of a great artist and a great actor, a truly superior man?

The lift stopped. He got out. The door confronted him. Put key in lock, turn. Enter.

The flat was in darkness, no light in the hall. No sound. 'Elizabeth', he called, in a voice that did not seem his own. He had difficulty in not turning and leaving the flat.

He opened the door of the living room. This also was in darkness. Was Elizabeth not there after all, had she ignored his note or failed to return? He felt a wave of relief at the thought, but still there was the bedroom. He must look in the bedroom.

The door was open, a glimmer of light showed within. He did not remember taking the revolver from his pocket, but it was in his gloved hand.

He took two steps into the room. Her dimmed bedside light was switched on. She lay on the bed naked, the black mask over her face. He called out something and she sat up, stretched out arms to him. His reaction was one of disgust and horror. He was not conscious of squeezing the trigger, but the revolver in his hand spoke three times.

She did not call out but gave a kind of gasp. A patch of darkness showed between her breasts. She sank back on the bed.

With the action taken, certainty returned to him. Everything he did now was efficient, exact. He got into the lift, took it down to the basement and walked out through the garage down there, meeting nobody. Tyler would be able to say when Mr Charles had arrived, but not when he left.

Back to the Underground lavatory, clothes changed, Charles's clothing and revolver returned to locker for later disposal, locker key put in handkerchief pocket of jacket. Return to the theatre, head down to avoid recognition. A quick glance at his watch as he opened the back door and moved silently up the stairs. Nearly thirty minutes had passed.

He knelt at the back of the cupboard and listened to a few lines of dialogue. The moment at which the body was due to give its twitch had gone, and Eustace proved his lasting twitching capacity by giving another shudder, of course not seen by the audience because the cupboard door was closed. Eustace had served his purpose. Oliver withdrew him from the sack and switched him off. With slight pressure to get out the air he was quickly reduced and folded into a bundle. Oliver slipped the bundle inside his trousers, and secured it with a safety pin. The slight bulge might have been apparent on close examination, but who would carry out such an examination upon stage?

Beautiful, he thought, as he wriggled into the sack for the few minutes before he had to appear on stage. Oliver Glass, I congratulate you in the name of Thomas de Quincey and Thomas Griffith Wainewright. You have committed the Perfect Crime.

7

The euphoria lasted through the curtain calls and his customary few casual words with the audience, in which he congratulated them on being able to appreciate an intelligent mystery. It lasted—oh, how he was savouring the only real achievement of his life—while he leisurely removed Sir Giles's makeup, said goodnight, and left the theatre still with Eustace pinned to him. He made one further visit to the Underground, as a result of which Eustace joined Charles's clothes in the locker. The key back in the handkerchief pocket.

As he was walking back to Everley Court, however, he realized with a shock that something had been forgotten. The note! The note which said positively that he would be at the flat during the interval, a note which if the police saw it would certainly lead to uncomfortable questions, perhaps even to a search, and discovery of the locker key. The note was somewhere in the flat, perhaps in Elizabeth's bag. It must be destroyed before he rang the police.

He nodded to Tyler, took the lift up. Key in door again. The door open. Then he stopped.

Light gleamed under the living room door.

Impossible, he thought, impossible. I know that I did not switch on the light when I opened that door. But then who could be inside the room? He took two steps forward, turned the handle, and when the door was open sprang back with a cry.

'Why, Oliver. What's the matter?' Elizabeth said. She sat on the sofa. Duncan stood beside her.

He pulled at his collar, feeling as though he was about to choke, then tried to ask a question but could not utter words.

'Come and see,' Duncan said. He approached and took Oliver by the arm. Oliver shook his head, resisted, but in the end let himself be led to the bedroom. The body still lay there, the patch of red between the breasts.

'You even told her about Elizabeth's bedtime habits,' Dunc said. 'She must have thought you'd have some fun.' He lifted the black mask. Evelyn looked up at him.

Back in the living room he poured himself brandy and said to Elizabeth, 'You knew?'

'Of course. *Would supper at Wheeler's amuse you this evening?* Do you think I didn't know you were acting as you always are, making some crazy plan. Though I could never have believed—it was Dunc who guessed how crazy it was.'

He looked from one of them to the other. 'You're lovers?' Duncan nodded. 'My dreary wife and my dull old friend Dunc—a perfect pair.'

Duncan took out his pipe, looked at it, put it back in his pocket. 'Liz had kept me in touch with what was going on, naturally. It seemed that you must be going to do something or other tonight. So Liz spent the evening with me.'

'Why was Evelyn here?' His mind moved frantically from one point to another to see where he had gone wrong.

'We knew about her from having you watched, and all that nonsense about Charles made me think that Elizabeth must be in some sort of danger. So it seemed a good idea to send your note to Evelyn, so that she could be here to greet you. We put the flat key in the envelope.'

'The initials were the same.'

'Just so,' Dunc said placidly.

'You planned for me to kill her.'

'I wouldn't say that. Of course, if you happened to mistake her for Liz—but we couldn't guess that she'd put on Liz's mask. We just wanted to warn you that playing games is dangerous.'

'You can't prove anything.'

'Oh, I think so,' Dunc said sagely. 'I don't know how you managed to get away from the theatre, some sort of dummy in the sack I suppose? No doubt the police will soon find out. But the important thing is that note. It's in Evelyn's handbag. Shows you arranged to meet her here. Jealous of some younger lover, I suppose.'

'But I *wasn't* jealous, I didn't arrange—' He stopped.

'Can't very well say it was for Liz, can you? Not when Evelyn turned up.' The door bell rang. 'Oh, I forgot to say we called the police when we found the body. Our duty, you know.' He looked at Oliver and said reflectively, 'You remember I said there was always a flaw in the Perfect Crime? Perhaps I was wrong. I suppose you might say the Perfect Crime is one you benefit from but don't commit yourself, so that nobody can say you're responsible. Do you see what I mean?' Oliver saw what he meant. 'And now it's time to let in the police.'

BIOGRAPHICAL NOTES

1

'The Adventure of the Stockbroker's Clerk' by A[rthur] Conan Doyle (1859–1930). From *The Memoirs of Sherlock Holmes* (Newnes, 1893); first published in the *Strand Magazine* (Mar. 1893). Educated at Stonyhurst and Edinburgh, Conan Doyle became a doctor and practised at Southsea from 1882 to 1890. Sherlock Holmes made his first appearance in *A Study in Scarlet* in 1887. The last collection of Holmes stories, *The Case-Book of Sherlock Holmes*, was published in 1927.

2

'The Lenton Croft Robberies' by Arthur Morrison (1863–1945). From *Martin Hewitt Investigator* (Ward, Lock & Bowden, 1894); first published in the *Strand Magazine* (Mar. 1894). Morrison achieved popularity for his 'realist' stories about life in the East End of London, first published in *Macmillan's Magazine* and later collected as *Tales of Mean Streets* (1894). His most famous novel, *A Child of the Jago*, was published in 1896. He was a noted collector of oriental art and wrote an authoritative monograph, *The Painters of Japan*, in 1911. His other detective stories can be found in *The Dorrington Deed-Box* (1897).

3

'The Green-Stone God and the Stockbroker' by Fergus[on] Hume (1859–1932). From *The Dwarf's Chamber, and Other Stories* (Ward, Lock & Bowden, 1896). Though born in England, Hume spent his childhood in New Zealand and was called to the bar there in 1885. After moving to Melbourne he wrote *The Mystery of a Hansom Cab*, which was published in Australia to little notice. But when it appeared in Britain in 1887 it was sensationally popular, though Hume, who had disposed of the copyright for £50, received nothing. The book went on to become one of the biggest bestsellers of the century.

4

'The Blue Sequin' by R[ichard] Austin Freeman (1862–1943). From *John Thorndyke's Cases* (Chatto & Windus, 1909); first published in *Pearson's Magazine* (Christmas Number, 1908). Freeman was apprenticed to an apothecary before studying medicine at the Middlesex Hospital. He qualified as a doctor in 1887 and for several years worked as a surgeon in West Africa. The short stories he wrote as 'Clifford Ashdown' (in collaboration with J. J. Pitcairn) were collected as *The Adventures of Romney Pringle* in 1902. He is now remembered by crime fiction enthusiasts as the creator of Dr Thorndyke, who made his first appearance in *The Red Thumb Mark* in 1907. Freeman's other contribution to the genre was the 'inverted' detective story, in which the denouement is presented to the reader at the start of the story.

5

'The Strange Crime of John Boulnois' by G[ilbert] K[eith] Chesterton (1874–1936). From *The Wisdom of Father Brown* (Cassell, 1914). Chesterton was educated at St Paul's School and went on to study art at the Slade School. He made his name in journalism (which he called 'the easiest of all professions') and published his first novel, *The Napoleon of Notting Hill*, in 1904. His highly original detective, the Catholic priest Father Brown, first appeared in *The Innocence of Father Brown* (1911). Tinged with fantasy and underpinned by a strongly moral and philosophical outlook, the Father Brown stories have a unique position in the history of detective fiction.

6

'Who Killed Charlie Winpole?' by Ernest Bramah [Smith] (1868–1942). From *The Eyes of Max Carrados* (Grant Richards, 1923). Smith began his working life as a farmer before becoming a journalist. He made a name through his Kai Lung Chinese stories, beginning with *The Wallet of Kai Lung* in 1900, but is now best known for his stories about the blind detective Max Carrados in volumes such as *Max Carrados* (1914) and *The Eyes of Max Carrados* (1923).

7

'The Poetical Policeman' by [Richard Horatio] Edgar Wallace (1875–1932). From *The Mind of Mr J. G. Reeder* (Hodder & Stoughton, 1925). Wallace was a prodigiously prolific author, with over a hundred thrillers to his name. He was the illegitimate son of an actor and actress and was brought up by a Billingsgate fish-porter and his wife. After becoming a reporter he made his name with his first novel, *The Four Just Men* (1905). Amongst his other well-known works was *Sanders of the River* (1911), set in West Africa and later made into an equally celebrated film. His eccentric detective J. G. Reeder made his first appearance in *Room 13* (1924).

8

'The Man with No Face' by Dorothy L[eigh] Sayers (1893–1957). From *Lord Peter Wimsey Views the Body* (Gollancz, 1928). Sayers was the daughter of a clergyman and after marrying in 1926 worked in an advertising agency, which formed the background of her novel *Murder Must Advertise* (1933). Her detective, Lord Peter Wimsey, appears in eleven novels, beginning with *Whose Body?* (1923), and a number of short stories. Sayers was also an influential anthologist, compiling two collections of tales of 'detection, mystery and horror', and in her later years devoted herself to a translation of Dante's *Divina Commedia*.

9

'The Yellow Slugs' by H[enry] C[hristopher] Bailey (1878–1961). From *Mr Fortune Objects* (Gollancz, 1935). Bailey was educated at the City of London School and Corpus Christi College, Oxford. He began his career as a journalist with the *Daily Telegraph*, though his first novel, *My Lady of Orange*, was published while he was still an undergraduate. Known first as a historical novelist, Bailey turned to crime fiction with *Call Mr Fortune* in 1920. Other Reggie Fortune stories and novels followed, including *Mr Fortune's Practice* (1924), *Mr Fortune Objects* (1935), and *The Bishop's Crime* (1940).

10

'The Unknown Peer' by E[dmund] C[lerihew] Bentley (1875–1956). From *Trent Intervenes* (T. Nelson, 1938). Bentley was educated at Merton College, Oxford, and was called to the bar in 1902, though he abandoned the law for journalism. Famous for inventing the Clerihew—a light verse epigram—he made a lasting contribution to detective fiction in *Trent's Last Case* (1913). Though he intended to satirize the detective story genre, Bentley did the job too well, and the novel, ironically, is generally regarded as a classic in its own right.

11

'Lesson in Anatomy' by 'Michael Innes' (John Innes Mackintosh Stewart, 1906–94). From *The Queen's Awards, 1946* (Little, Brown & Co., 1946; Gollancz, 1948). J. I. M. Stewart, novelist and critic, was born in Edinburgh and educated at Oriel College, Oxford. In 1949 he became a Student (i.e. a fellow) of Christ Church, Oxford, where he remained for over twenty years. Under the pseudonym 'Michael Innes' he wrote a successful series of novels and stories featuring Inspector John Appleby, including *Death at the President's Lodgings* (1936), *Hamlet, Revenge!* (1937), and *Appleby on Ararat* (1941). Amongst the works published under his own name are *Eight Modern Writers* (1963), a volume in the Oxford History of English Literature, and a quintet of novels about Oxford under the collective title *A Staircase in Surrey*.

12

'The Flaw' by Julian [Gustave] Symons (1912–95). From *John Creasey's Crime Collection 1986* (Gollancz, 1986); first published in *Ellery Queen's Mystery Magazine*. Born in London, Julian Symons grew up in Battersea and began his literary career as editor of a small poetry magazine, *Twentieth Century Verse*. A novelist, poet, critic, and biographer, Symons wrote a classic study of crime fiction, *Bloody Murder* (first published in 1972), and a string of detective stories and novels such as *The Immaterial Murder Case* (1945) and *The Blackheath Poisonings* (1978).

ACKNOWLEDGEMENTS

The editor and publisher gratefully acknowledge permission to use the following copyright material:

H. C. Bailey, 'The Yellow Slugs' from *Mr Fortune Objects* (Gollancz, 1935). Copyright © H. C. Bailey.

E. C. Bentley, 'The Unknown Peer' from *Trent Intervenes* (1913), reprinted by permission of Curtis Brown Ltd., London, on behalf of the Estate of E. C. Bentley. Copyright the Estate of E. C. Bentley.

Ernest Bramah, 'Who Killed Charlie Winpole?' from *The Eyes of Max Carrados* (Grant Richards, 1923), reprinted by permission of A. P. Watt Ltd. on behalf of the estate of the late Mr W. P. Watt.

G. K. Chesterton, 'The Strange Crime of John Boulnois' from *The Wisdom of Father Brown* (Cassell, 1914), reprinted by permission of A. P. Watt Ltd. on behalf of The Royal Literary Fund.

Arthur Conan Doyle, 'The Adventure of the Stockbroker's Clerk' from *The Memoirs of Sherlock Holmes* (Newnes, 1893). Copyright © 1996 The Sir Arthur Conan Doyle Copyright Holders. Reprinted by kind permission of Jonathan Clowes Ltd., London, on behalf of Andrea Plunket, Administrator of the Sir Arthur Conan Doyle Copyrights.

Richard Austin Freeman, 'The Blue Sequin' from *John Thorndyke's Cases* (Chatto & Windus, 1909), reprinted by permission of A. P. Watt Ltd. on behalf of the estate of Winifred Lydia Bryant.

Michael Innis (J. I. M. Stewart), 'Lesson in Anatomy' from *The Queen's Awards, 1946* (Little Brown & Co. 1946, Gollancz, 1948), reprinted by permission of A. P. Watt Ltd. on behalf of Michael Stewart.

Arthur Morrison, 'The Lenton Croft Robberies' from *Martin Hewitt, Investigator* (Ward, Lock & Bowden, 1894), reprinted by permission of A. P. Watt Ltd. on behalf of Special Trustees of Westminster and Roehampton Hospitals and NSPCC.

Dorothy L. Sayers, 'The Man with No Face' from *Lord Peter Views the Body* (Hodder & Stoughton, 1928), reprinted by permission of David Higham Associates.

Julian Symons, 'The Flaw' from *John Creasey's Crime Collection, 1986* (Gollancz, 1986), reprinted by permission of Curtis Brown Ltd., London on behalf of Julian Symons. Copyright Julian Symons 1986.

Edgar Wallace, 'The Poetical Policeman' from *The Mind of Mr J. G. Reeder* (Hodder & Stoughton, 1925), reprinted by permission of A. P. Watt Ltd. on behalf of the executors of the estate of Penelope Halcrow.

OXFORD

MORE OXFORD PAPERBACKS

This book is just one of nearly 1000 Oxford Paperbacks currently in print. If you would like details of other Oxford Paperbacks, including titles in the World's Classics, Oxford Reference, Oxford Books, OPUS, Past Masters, Oxford Authors, and Oxford Shakespeare series, please write to:

UK and Europe: Oxford Paperbacks Publicity Manager, Arts and Reference Publicity Department, Oxford University Press, Walton Street, Oxford OX2 6DP.

Customers in UK and Europe will find Oxford Paperbacks available in all good bookshops. But in case of difficulty please send orders to the Cash-with-Order Department, Oxford University Press Distribution Services, Saxon Way West, Corby, Northants NN18 9ES. Tel: 01536 741519; Fax: 01536 746337. Please send a cheque for the total cost of the books, plus £1.75 postage and packing for orders under £20; £2.75 for orders over £20. Customers outside the UK should add 10% of the cost of the books for postage and packing.

USA: Oxford Paperbacks Marketing Manager, Oxford University Press, Inc., 200 Madison Avenue, New York, N.Y. 10016.

Canada: Trade Department, Oxford University Press, 70 Wynford Drive, Don Mills, Ontario M3C 1J9.

Australia: Trade Marketing Manager, Oxford University Press, G.P.O. Box 2784Y, Melbourne 3001, Victoria.

South Africa: Oxford University Press, P.O. Box 1141, Cape Town 8000.

A Very Short Introduction

CLASSICS

Mary Beard and John Henderson

This *Very Short Introduction* to Classics links a haunting temple on a lonely mountainside to the glory of ancient Greece and the grandeur of Rome, and to Classics within modern culture—from Jefferson and Byron to Asterix and Ben-Hur.

'This little book should be in the hands of every student, and every tourist to the lands of the ancient world . . . a splendid piece of work'
Peter Wiseman
Author of *Talking to Virgil*

'an eminently readable and useful guide to many of the modern debates enlivening the field . . . the most up-to-date and accessible introduction available'
Edith Hall
Author of *Inventing the Barbarian*

'lively and up-to-date . . . it shows classics as a living enterprise, not a warehouse of relics'
New Statesman and Society

'nobody could fail to be informed and entertained—the accent of the book is provocative and stimulating'
Times Literary Supplement

POLITICS

Kenneth Minogue

Since politics is both complex and controversial it is easy to miss the wood for the trees. In this Very Short Introduction Kenneth Minogue has brought the many dimensions of politics into a single focus: he discusses both the everyday grind of democracy and the attraction of grand ideals such as freedom and justice.

'Kenneth Minogue is a very lively stylist who does not distort difficult ideas.'
Maurice Cranston

'a dazzling but unpretentious display of great scholarship and humane reflection'
Professor Neil O'Sullivan, University of Hull

'Minogue is an admirable choice for showing us the nuts and bolts of the subject.'
Nicholas Lezard, *Guardian*

'This is a fascinating book which sketches, in a very short space, one view of the nature of politics . . . the reader is challenged, provoked and stimulated by Minogue's trenchant views.'
Talking Politics

ARCHAEOLOGY

Paul Bahn

'Archaeology starts, really, at the point when the first recognizable 'artefacts' appear—on current evidence, that was in East Africa about 2.5 million years ago—and stretches right up to the present day. What you threw in the garbage yesterday, no matter how useless, disgusting, or potentially embarrassing, has now become part of the recent archaeological record.'

This Very Short Introduction reflects the enduring popularity of archaeology—a subject which appeals as a pastime, career, and academic discipline, encompasses the whole globe, and surveys 2.5 million years. From deserts to jungles, from deep caves to mountain-tops, from pebble tools to satellite photographs, from excavation to abstract theory, archaeology interacts with nearly every other discipline in its attempts to reconstruct the past.

'very lively indeed and remarkably perceptive . . . a quite brilliant and level-headed look at the curious world of archaeology'
Professor Barry Cunliffe,
University of Oxford

BUDDHISM

Damien Keown

'Karma can be either good or bad. Buddhists speak of good karma as "merit", and much effort is expended in acquiring it. Some picture it as a kind of spiritual capital—like money in a bank account—whereby credit is built up as the deposit on a heavenly rebirth.'

This Very Short Introduction introduces the reader both to the teachings of the Buddha and to the integration of Buddhism into daily life. What are the distinctive features of Buddhism? Who was the Buddha, and what are his teachings? How has Buddhist thought developed over the centuries, and how can contemporary dilemmas be faced from a Buddhist perspective?

'Damien Keown's book is a readable and wonderfully lucid introduction to one of mankind's most beautiful, profound, and compelling systems of wisdom. The rise of the East makes understanding and learning from Buddhism, a living doctrine, more urgent than ever before. Keown's impressive powers of explanation help us to come to terms with a vital contemporary reality.'
Bryan Appleyard

A Very Short Introduction

JUDAISM

Norman Solomon

'Norman Solomon has achieved the near impossible with his enlightened very short introduction to Judaism. Since it is well known that Judaism is almost impossible to summarize, and that there are as many different opinions about Jewish matters as there are Jews, this is a small masterpiece in its success in representing various shades of Jewish opinion, often mutually contradictory. Solomon also manages to keep the reader engaged, never patronizes, assumes little knowledge but a keen mind, and takes us through Jewish life and history with such gusto that one feels enlivened, rather than exhausted, at the end.'
Rabbi Julia Neuberger

'This book will serve a very useful purpose indeed. I'll use it myself to discuss, to teach, agree with, and disagree with, in the Jewish manner!'
Rabbi Lionel Blue

'A magnificent achievement. Dr Solomon's treatment, fresh, very readable, witty and stimulating, will delight everyone interested in religion in the modern world.'
Dr Louis Jacobs, University of Lancaster